NUMBE

INSIDIO

INSECTS

overwhelming. And the
darkness is immortal."
—Carl Sagan

CONTINUED ON NEXT PAGE

Black Infinity: Insidious Insects (Issue #6, Summer 2020) is published by Rocket Science Books, an imprint of Dead Letter Press. *Black Infinity* #6 is copyright © Tom English and Dead Letter Press, PO Box 134, New Kent, VA 23124-0134. All rights reserved, including the right to reproduce this book, or portions thereof, in any form including but not limited to electronic and print media, without written permission from the publisher.

Black Infinity is published semi-annually by Rocket Science Books, an imprint of Dead Letter Press.

www.DeadLetterPress.com   www.BlackInfinityMagazine.com   ISBN-13: 978-1732434462

COVER ILLUSTRATION BY ALLEN KOSZOWSKI
INTERIOR ILLUSTRATIONS: ALLEN KOSZOWSKI, DAN ADKINS,
DICK FRANCIS, PAUL HARDY, LEO MOREY, RUDOLPH PALAIS and H.R. SMITH

EDITOR AND PUBLISHER: TOM ENGLISH
COLUMNISTS: MATT COWAN; TODD TREICHEL
PRODUCTION STAFF: HAL-9000, ROBBY R. & ROBOT B-9

INSECTS GIVE ME THE CREEPS. WELL, NOT *ALL* INSECTS. I LOVE THE COLORFUL ONES, THE *CUTE* BUGS: BUTTERFLIES, MOTHS, DRAGONFLIES, grasshoppers, ladybugs, honeybees, and even those big beetles with iridescent bodies; and I'm generally tolerant of ants—in small numbers—because I know how beneficial these industrious little guys are, like many, but definitely not all, insects. To be sure, some of these multi-legged creatures can be extremely destructive or, at the very least, extremely aggravating. Talk to a homeowner dealing with a termite infestation, or the manager of a restaurant that's been over-run by cockroaches. Or just ask any dog how it feels about fleas. (Of course, if you get a reply, insects may be the least of your problems.)

On a more frightening note, as I write this, parts of East Africa and South Asia are battling swarms of locusts numbering in the billions. These ravenous winged insects have decimated hundreds of thousands of acres of croplands, and placed millions of people at risk of starvation. Meanwhile, recent sightings in North America of a notorious Asian hornet have made headlines and alarmed more than a few people here in the U.S. Commonly known as the "murder hornet," the insect is approximately two inches in length with a quarter-inch stinger, and is capable of injecting a potent neurotoxin which can prove lethal. Multiple stings have killed dozens in China.

Entomologists, however, doubt the murder hornet poses any significant threat here. Indeed, most of us will never face a bad-bug invasion with such devastating consequences. We may never have a close encounter with a killer bee, or a poisonous spider, or even a disease-carrying tick. Instead, many of us will find dealing with insects of a more common variety sufficiently challenging: we may be pestered by mosquitos at a family cookout, annoyed by a few uninvited ants at a picnic in the park, or aggravated by those tiny fruit flies that seemingly appear out of nowhere when we're trying to enjoy a slice of ripe melon. Perhaps we'll find ample reason for anxiety when we discover that silverfish have been slowly consuming those vintage paperbacks lovingly boxed up and stored in the garage; or completely freak out when suddenly faced by that rather large, fast-moving house spider lurking in the corner of the shower.

By the way, I draw the line at spiders. I can not—*will not*—abide them. There's just something about arachnids that makes my skin crawl. And apparently, I'm not alone in my feelings: spiders have infested the work of writers for over a hundred years, in books and magazines, and later, in comics and movies. In fact, spiders, more than any other insects, seem to be the bad bugs of choice, popping up in just about everything from Mark Twain's controversial 1884 novel *The Adventures of Huckleberry Finn* to an episode of the mid-1960s TV comedy *Gilligan's Island* ("The Pigeon").

Spiders frequently creep into mystery and adventure flicks—Sherlock Holmes, James Bond, Indiana Jones, and Frodo Baggins have all had hair-raising encounters with arachnids[1]—and feature in numerous sci-fi B-movies, such as *Cat-Women of the Moon* (1953), *Tarantula* ('55; with an uncredited appearance by Clint Eastwood as a Jet Squadron Leader), *World Without End* ('56), *The Incredible Shrinking Man* ('57), *The Spider* ('58; originally *Earth vs the Spider*), *Missile to the Moon* ('58; a remake of *Cat-Women*); *The Angry Red Planet* ('59), *Have Rocket—Will Travel* ('59; yes, even The Three Stooges had a run-in with a giant spider), and ... the list continues. Matt Cowan discusses a few of these films, along with other insect-themed movies, in this issue's Threat Watch.

Tarantulas don't bug Indiana Jones. Harrison Ford in *Raiders of the Lost Ark* (Paramount Pictures)

Rod Taylor and Hugh Marlowe wrestle a mutant spider in *World Without End*. (Warner Archive)

ALTHOUGH I SUSPECT there are numerous, brief appearances of various insects in the gothic novels of the 18th century, the oldest insect-themed weird fiction I could track down is Jeremias Gotthelf's 1842 novel *The Black Spider*, translated from the German *Die Schwarze Spinne*, in which a deal with the devil unleashes a deadly, demonic spider. In 1921 the tale was adapted as a silent film, probably the first in the long line of bad-bug movies.

Other works of fantastic fiction featuring insects followed Gotthelf's novel, including Edgar Allan Poe's short 1846 tale "The Sphinx," basically an inspired description of the monstrous appearance of a common moth caught in a web "which some spider has wrought along the window-sash."

The frequently reprinted writing team of Émile Erckmann and Alexandre Chatrian penned two insect-related tales: "La Reine des Abeilles," published in France in 1862, with the English translation, "The Queen of the Bees," appearing in the 1876 collection *The Man-Wolf and Other Tales*; and "L'Araignée-Crabe," published in 1860, with an English translation first appearing in an 1893 issue of *Romance Magazine*, as "The Crab Spider." The latter tale was reprinted as "The Spider of Guyana" in the January 1899 issue of *The Strand Magazine*. Lovecraft praised the story,[2] under another of its translation titles, "The Waters of Death," writing that it is "full of engulfing darkness and mystery ... embodying the familiar overgrown-spider theme so frequently employed

---

[1] Respectively, *Sherlock Holmes and the Spider Woman* (1943); *Dr. No* (1962); *Raiders of the Lost Ark* (1981); and *The Lord of the Rings: The Return of the King* (2003).

[2] H. P. Lovecraft, "Supernatural Horror in Literature," *The Recluse,* 1927, p. 23.

by weird fictionists." The story is reprinted in this issue with the original illustrations from its appearance in *The Strand*.

Post-nuclear war scorpions, from *Damnation Alley* (1977, 20th Century Fox)

Around the turn of the 20th century, H. G. Wells gave readers four, now-classic fantastic tales of insect horrors: "The Moth" (1895); "The Valley of Spiders" (1903); "The Empire of the Ants" (1905) and the novel *The Food of the Gods* (serialized in 1904). All but "The Moth" have been adapted for film.

Over the next several years M. R. James, E. F. Benson, Algernon Blackwood, Hanns Heinz Ewers, Edward Heron-Allen and a few other writers all published bug-related stories. James' "The Ash Tree" (1904) is arguably the creepiest of these tales, and is included in this issue.

Finally, with the proliferation of pulp magazines during the early 1900s, the creative floodgates for publishable fiction opened wide—and insects are definitely serviceable plot devices; writers began dropping bugs into just about every genre imaginable, including science fiction, mystery, crime, and adventure stories. And science fiction on the big screen followed suit, beginning in the early 1950s, with movies featuring nearly every type bug imaginable—most of them supersized: *Them!* (big ants; 1954); *Tarantula* ('55) and all the other, aforementioned spider flicks; *The Deadly Mantis* ('57); *The Monster that Challenged the World* (giant caterpillar-like mollusks; '57); *The Beginning of the End* (giant grasshoppers; '57); *The Monster from Green Hell* (giant wasps; '57); *The Black Scorpion* (Also from 1957. Notice how these celluloid insects are starting to swarm.); *The Fly* (1958); *The Strange World of Planet X* (aka *Cosmic Monsters*, featuring various insects; also 1958); *Return of the Fly*, *Attack of the Giant Leeches*, and *The Wasp Woman* (all in 1959).

Since the 1950s cinematic invasion of bad bugs, dozens of similar movies have flown, crawled or squirmed into theaters, with not a single type of insect neglected. Killer bees, ticks, wasps, locusts, mosquitoes, worms, roaches, centipedes and slugs—not to mention *alien* insects—have all joined ants, flies and spiders—especially spiders—as bankable film subjects. From *Mothra* (1961) to *Damnation Alley* (1977) to *Honey, I Shrunk the Kids* ('89), from *Mimic* and *Starship Troopers* (both in 1997) to Stephen King's *The Mist* (2007), bad-bug flicks are good business.

Although far fewer in their television appearances, various insects eventually

Return of the Fly (1959, 20th Century Fox)
ALLEN K. '07

crawled across the small screen too. There are none to be found in the earliest fantasy and horror anthologies, probably due to tight budgets and limited special effects. Or perhaps network executives simply felt insects were too scary for family viewing. But after the bad bugs finally did arrive on TV sets the evening of December 30, 1963, thousands of pleasantly terrified kids started checking the sheets each night before going to bed. The bad bugs here are intelligent insects with grotesque human-like faces and really bad attitudes. In "The Zanti Misfits," a Season-One episode of *The Outer Limits* ('63–'65), an alien civilization exiles the worst elements of its society to planet Earth. And wouldn't you know it, the minute these marauding insects get off the prison ship they overrun a secret U.S. Military operation in the desert.

A few weeks later, TOL presented another bug-themed episode, "ZZZZZ" (1964), in which a queen bee—in an attempt to advance her species—takes on human form in order to seduce and mate with an entomologist. (Trust me, the proceedings are far more eerie than my one-sentence synopsis reveals.) Author and screenwriter Gary Gerani takes a loving look at the classic series that brought these and other imaginative nightmares into our homes, in this issue's special feature, "The Outer Limits: A Remembrance."

Other examples of insect terrors on the tube include "The Monster's Web" (1966), a second-season episode of creator/producer Irwin Allen's *Voyage to the Bottom of the Sea*, in which a mission to reach a disabled sub and its dangerous cargo of experimental fuel is jeopardized when the Seaview encounters a giant underwater spider. As silly as this concept sounds, and despite some rather bad acting by the spider—which had appeared five weeks earlier in Allen's *Lost in Space* episode "The Keeper: Part II"—the story plays out surprisingly well.

Two tales of insect horror spring to mind when considering Rod Serling's *Night Gallery*: "A Fear of Spiders" (based on a 1967 story by Elizabeth Walter) and "The Caterpillar" (based

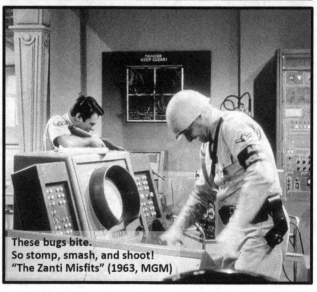

These bugs bite.
So stomp, smash, and shoot!
"The Zanti Misfits" (1963, MGM)

on the 1931 story "Boomerang" by Oscar Cook). Both were adapted by Serling for the second season and broadcast in 1971 and '72, respectively. "The Caterpillar" is of special interest; Cook's terrifying idea of an insect (an earwig) crawling into a man's ear and then painfully burrowing through his brain (after first laying eggs there) was shared in smoke-filled bars and on school playgrounds until it achieved urban-legend status. In Serling's version, Laurence Harvey plays Stephen Macy, an evil fellow with amorous designs on the wife of a Borneo plantation owner. Macy plots to get rid of the husband by paying another evil fellow to put an earwig on the man's pillow—but the plan backfires with horrible consequences. (Moral of the story? Let me "put the bug in your ear": it doesn't pay to be an evil fellow. Interestingly, the idea of sending a harmful insect crawling into a person's ear resurfaces in a frightful scene in *Star Trek: The Wrath of Khan,* the inspiration for which is most probably this memorable *Night Gallery* episode.)

In "Death's Head," a segment of *Circle of Fear* (1973), a long-neglected wife uses poison to get rid of her husband, who had become consumed by his bug-collecting hobby. Later, the guilt-ridden woman is plagued by spiders, wasps, flies and other insects—while being haunted by a sinister death's-head moth, which may be carrying the dead man's spirit. Janet Leigh, fondly remembered for her horrifying shower scene in

the original *Psycho* (1960), plays the terrified wife to the hilt.

Insects also feature in several made-for-television movies, including *Killer Bees* (1974), *The Savage Bees* ('76), *Tarantulas: The Deadly Cargo* ('77); *Ants!* (aka *It Happened at Lakewood Manor;* '77); *Curse of the Black Widow* ('77), directed by Dan Curtis, creator of the original, 1960s *Dark Shadows* TV series); and *Terror Out of the Sky* (a poor, 1978 sequel to *The Savage Bees*). The best of these movies is without a doubt Dan Curtis' creepy *Curse of the Black Widow*.

Jumping to the next decade, arguably the best Season-One episode of *Star Trek: The Next*

Apparently, Picard and Riker like their bugs well toasted; Sir Patrick Stewart and Jonathan Frakes in "Conspiracy." (*ST: TNG*, CBS Paramount Television). Left: With his hands restrained, Chekov fearfully awaits an aural invasion by the Ceti eel that was lovingly dropped into his helmet; Walter Koenig in *The Wrath of Khan* (Paramount Pictures). Above: Just your friendly neighborhood earwig.

Generation features an alien race of intelligent, scorpion-like insects. In "Conspiracy" (1988), these mind-controlling, parasitic creatures attempt an intergalactic takeover by invading the bodies of some of Star Fleet Command's highest-ranking officers. With phasers blasting, Captain Picard and First Officer Riker *raid* the clandestine operations of these bad bugs.

Before moving on I'll cover one last, excellent appearance of insects on TV: "Sandkings," the premiere episode of the 1995 revival of *The Outer Limits.* Based on the 1979 novelette by George R. R. Martin (*Game of Thrones*), this feature-length segment features Beau Bridges as an emotionally unbalanced scientist who smuggles Martian sand containing alien insects from a government research facility. These insects soon grow and begin to show uncanny intelligence and a worshipful devotion to the scientist who nurtured them—until the man makes a fatal mistake. Although "Sandkings" doesn't really do justice to Martin's novelette, it's probably the scariest episode of the entire run of the rebooted series, evoking the same sense of wonder mixed with skin-crawling fear that characterized "The Zanti Misfits" and other episodes of the original show.

As to the stories in this issue, I've chosen a mix of recent and older tales featuring a wide variety of insects, real or imagined, natural or supernatural, earthly or alien. Several of the older stories are considered classics of dark fantasy and horror. A few have historical significance, and at least one is iconic. I frequently hear that reading such tales of terror can provide a much-needed form of catharsis from the true horrors in life, but editing the creepy bug stories in this issue only led to me scratching at my scalp and occasionally buttoning up my shirt collar ... imagining some uninvited six- or eight-legged creature attempting to crawl down the back of my neck. And

since I'm a nice fellow who likes to share, I'm hoping you'll be similarly creeped out by the

Clockwise from top left: *Them!* (1954, Warner Archive); *The Monster that Challenged the World* ('57, MGM); *The Astounding She-Monster* ('57, AIP); *Return of the Fly* ('59, 20th Century Fox); *The Atomic Submarine* ('59, Allied Artists)

stories that follow.

So grab a can of bug spray, find a comfy chair, and try not to squirm too much while reading these tales of insidious insects.

Tom English
New Kent, VA

MEETING OF THE MINDS

BY ROBERT SHECKLEY

THE QUEDAK LAY ON A SMALL HILLTOP AND WATCHED A SLENDER JET OF LIGHT DESCEND THROUGH THE SKY. The feather-tailed jet was golden, and brighter than the sun. Poised above it was a glistening metallic object, fabricated rather than natural, hauntingly familiar. The Quedak tried to think what it was.

He couldn't remember. His memories had atrophied with his functions, leaving only scattered fragments of images. He searched among them now, leafing through his brief scraps of ruined cities, dying populations, a blue-water-filled canal, two moons, a spaceship....

That was it. The descending object was a *spaceship*. There had been many of them during the great days of the Quedak.

Those great days were over, buried forever beneath the powdery sands. Only the Quedak remained. He had life and he had a mission to perform. The driving urgency of his mission remained, even after memory and function had failed.

As the Quedak watched, the spaceship dipped lower. It wobbled and sidejets kicked out to straighten it. With a gentle explosion of dust, the spaceship settled tail first on the arid plain.

And the Quedak, driven by the imperative Quedak mission, dragged itself painfully down from the little hilltop. Every movement was an agony. If he were a selfish creature, the Quedak would have died. But he was not selfish. Quedaks owed a duty to the universe; and that spaceship, after all the blank years, was a link to other worlds, to planets where the Quedak could live again and give his services to the native fauna.

He crawled, a centimeter at a time, and wondered whether he had the strength to reach the alien spaceship before it left this dusty, dead planet.

CAPTAIN JENSEN of the spaceship *Southern Cross* was bored sick with Mars. He and his men had been here for ten days. They had found no important archeological specimens, no tantalizing hints of ancient cities such as the *Polaris* expedition had discovered at the South Pole. Here there was nothing but sand, a few weary shrubs, and a rolling hill or two. Their biggest find so far had been three pottery shards.

Jensen readjusted his oxygen booster. Over the rise of a hill he saw his two men returning.

"Anything interesting?" he asked.

"Just this," said engineer Vayne, holding up an inch of corroded blade without a handle.

"Better than nothing," Jensen said. "How about you, Wilks?"

The navigator shrugged his shoulders. "Just photographs of the landscape."

"OK," Jensen said. "Dump everything into the sterilizer and let's get going."

Wilks looked mournful. "Captain, one quick sweep to the north might turn up something really—"

"Not a chance," Jensen said. "Fuel, food, water, everything was calculated for a ten-day stay. That's three days longer than *Polaris* had. We're taking off this evening."

The men nodded. They had no reason to complain. As the second to land on Mars, they were sure of a small but respectable footnote in the history books. They put their equipment through the sterilizer vent, sealed it, and climbed the ladder to the lock. Once they were inside, Vayne closed and dogged the hatch, and started to open the inside pressure door.

"Hold it!" Jensen called out.

"What's the matter?"

"I thought I saw something on your boot," Jensen said. "Something like a big bug."

Vayne quickly ran his hands down the sides of his boots. The two men circled him, examining his clothing.

"Shut that inner door," the captain said. "Wilks, did you see anything?"

"Not a thing," the navigator said. "Are you sure, Cap? We haven't found anything that looks like animal or insect life here. Only a few plants."

"I could have sworn I saw something," Jensen said. "Maybe I was wrong.... Anyhow, we'll fumigate our clothes before we enter the ship proper. No sense taking any chance of bringing back some kind of Martian bug."

The men removed their clothing and boots and stuffed them into the chute. They searched the bare steel room carefully.

"Nothing here," Jensen said at last. "OK, let's go inside."

Once inside the ship, they sealed off the lock and fumigated it. The Quedak, who had crept inside earlier through the partially opened pressure door, listened to the distant hiss of gas. After a while he heard the jets begin to fire.

The Quedak retreated to the dark rear of the ship. He found a metal shelf and attached himself to the underside of it near the wall. After a while he felt the ship tremble.

THE QUEDAK CLUNG to the shelf during the long, slow flight through space. He had forgotten what spaceships were like, but now memory revived briefly. He felt blazing heat and freezing cold. Adjusting to the temperature changes drained his small store of vitality, and the Quedak began to wonder if he was going to die.

He *refused* to die. Not while there was still a possibility of accomplishing the Quedak mission.

In time he felt the harsh pull of gravity, and felt the main jets firing again. The ship was coming down to its planet.

AFTER A ROUTINE LANDING, Captain Jensen and his men were taken to Medic Checkpoint, where they were thumped, probed and tested for any sign of disease.

Their spaceship was lowered to a flatcar and taken past rows of moonships and ICBMs to Decontamination Stage One. Here the sealed outer hull was washed down with powerful cleansing sprays. By evening, the ship was taken to Decontamination Stage Two.

A team of two inspectors equipped with bulky tanks and hoses undogged the hatch and entered, shutting the hatch behind them.

They began at the bow, methodically spraying as they moved toward the rear. Everything seemed in order; no animals or plants, no trace of mold such as the first Luna expedition had brought back.

"Do you really think this is necessary?" the assistant inspector asked. He had already requested a transfer to Flight Control.

"Sure it is," the senior inspector said. "Can't tell what these ships might bring in."

"I suppose so," the assistant said. "Still, a Martian whoosis wouldn't even be able to live on Earth. Would it?"

"How should I know?" the senior inspector said. "I'm no botanist. Maybe they don't know, either."

"Seems like a waste of—hey!"

"What is it?" the senior inspector asked.

"I thought I saw something," the assistant said. "Looked a little like a palmetto bug. Over by that shelf."

The senior inspector adjusted his respirator more snugly over his face and motioned to his assistant to do the same. He advanced slowly toward the shelf, unfastening a second nozzle from the pressure tank on his back. He turned it on, and a cloud of greenish gas sprayed out.

"There," the senior inspector said. "That should take care of your bug." He knelt down and looked under the shelf. "Nothing here."

"It was probably a shadow," the assistant said.

Together they sprayed the entire interior of the ship, paying particular attention to the small box of Martian artifacts. They left the gas-filled ship and dogged the hatch again.

"Now what?" the assistant asked.

"Now we leave the ship sealed for three days," the senior inspector said. "Then we inspect again. You find me the animal that'll live through that."

THE QUEDAK, who had been clinging to the underside of the assistant's shoe between the heel and the sole, released his hold. He watched the shadowy biped figures move away, talking in their deep, rumbling, indecipherable voices. He felt tired and unutterably lonely.

But buoying him up was the thought of the Quedak mission. Only that was important. The first part of the mission was accomplished. He had landed safely on an inhabited planet. Now he needed food and drink. Then he had to have rest, a great deal of rest to restore his dormant faculties. After that he would be ready to give this world what it so obviously needed—the co-operation possible only through the Quedak mind.

He crept slowly down the shadowy yard, past the deserted hulls of spaceships. He came to a wire fence and sensed the high-voltage electricity running through it. Gauging his distance carefully, the Quedak jumped safely through one of the openings in the mesh.

This was a very different section. From here the Quedak could smell water and food. He moved hastily forward, then stopped.

He sensed the presence of a man. And something else. Something much more menacing.

"WHO'S THERE?" the watchman called out. He waited, his revolver in one hand, his flashlight in the other. Thieves had broken into the yards last week; they had stolen three cases of computer parts bound for Rio. Tonight he was ready for them.

He walked forward, an old, keen-eyed man holding his revolver in a rock-steady fist. The beam of his flashlight probed among the cargoes. The yellow light flickered along a great pile of precision machine tools for South Africa, past a water-extraction plant for Jordan and a pile of mixed goods for Rabaul.

"You better come out," the watchman shouted. His flashlight probed at sacks of rice for Shanghai and power saws for Burma. Then the beam of light stopped abruptly.

"I'll be damned," the watchman said. Then he laughed. A huge and red-eyed rat was glaring into the beam of his flashlight. It had something in its jaws, something that looked like an unusually large cockroach.

"Good eating," the watchman said. He holstered his revolver and continued his patrol.

A LARGE BLACK ANIMAL had seized the Quedak, and he felt heavy jaws close over his back. He tried to fight; but, blinded by a sudden beam of yellow light, he was betrayed by total and enervating confusion.

The yellow light went off. The black beast bit down hard on the Quedak's armored back. The Quedak mustered his remaining strength, and, uncoiling his long, scorpion-jointed tail, lashed out.

He missed, but the black beast released him hastily. They circled each other, the Quedak hoisting his tail for a second blow, the beast unwilling to turn loose this prey.

The Quedak waited for his chance. Elation filled him. This pugnacious animal could be the first, the first on this planet to experience the Quedak mission. From this humble creature a start could be made....

The beast sprang and its white teeth clicked together viciously. The Quedak moved out of the way and its barb-headed tail flashed out, fastening itself in the beast's back. The Quedak held on grimly while the beast leaped and squirmed. Setting his feet, the Quedak concentrated on the all-important task of pumping a tiny white crystal down the length of his tail and under the beast's skin.

But this most important of the Quedak faculties was still dormant. Unable to accomplish anything, the Quedak released his barbs, and, taking careful aim, accurately drove his sting home between the black beast's eyes. The blow, as the Quedak had known, was lethal.

The Quedak took nourishment from the body of its dead foe; regretfully, for by inclination the Quedak was herbivorous. When he had finished, the Quedak knew that he was in desperate need of a long period of rest. Only after that could the full Quedak powers be regained.

He crawled up and down the piles of goods in the yard, looking for a place to hide. Carefully he examined several bales. At last he reached a stack of heavy boxes. One of the boxes had a crack just large enough to admit him.

The Quedak crawled inside, down the shiny, oil-slick surface of a machine, to the far end of the box. There he went into the dreamless, defenseless sleep of the Quedak, serenely trusting in what the future would bring.

PART TWO

I

THE BIG GAFF-HEADED SCHOONER was pointed directly at the reef-enclosed island, moving toward it with the solidity of an express train. The sails billowed under powerful gusts of the northwest breeze, and the rusty Allison-Chambers diesel rumbled beneath a teak grating. The skipper and mate stood on the bridge deck and watched the reef approach.

"Anything yet?" the skipper asked. He was a stocky, balding man with a perpetual frown on his face. He had been sailing his schooner among the uncharted shoals and reefs of the Southwest Pacific for twenty-five years. He frowned because his old ship was not insurable. His deck cargo, however, *was* insured. Some of it had come all the way from Ogdensville, that transshipment center in the desert where spaceships landed.

"Not a thing," the mate said. He was watching the dazzling white wall of coral, looking for the gleam of blue that would reveal the narrow pass to the inner lagoon. This was his first trip to the Solomon Islands. A former television repairman in Sydney before he got the wanderlust, the mate wondered if the skipper had gone crazy and planned a spectacular suicide against the reef.

"Still nothing!" he shouted. "Shoals ahead!"

"I'll take it," the skipper said to the helmsman. He gripped the wheel and watched the unbroken face of the reef.

"Nothing," the mate said. "Skipper, we'd better come about."

"Not if we're going to get through the pass," the skipper said. He was beginning to get worried. But he had promised to deliver goods to the American treasure-hunters on this island, and the skipper's word was his bond. He had picked up the cargo in Rabaul and made his usual stops at the settlements on New Georgia and Malaita. When he finished here, he could look forward to a thousand-mile run to New Caledonia.

"There it is!" the mate shouted.

A thin slit of blue had appeared in the coral wall. They were less than thirty yards from it now, and the old schooner was making close to eight knots.

As the ship entered the pass, the skipper threw the wheel hard over. The schooner spun on its keel. Coral flashed by on either side, close enough to touch. There was a metallic shriek as an upper main-mast spreader snagged and came free. Then they were in the pass, bucking a six-knot current.

The mate pushed the diesel to full throttle,

then sprang back to help the skipper wrestle with the wheel. Under sail and power the schooner forged through the pass, scraped by an outcropping to port, and came onto the placid surface of the lagoon.

The skipper mopped his forehead with a large blue bandanna. "Very snug work," he said.

"*Snug!*" the mate cried. He turned away, and the skipper smiled a brief smile.

They slid past a small ketch riding at anchor. The native hands took down sail and the schooner nosed up to a rickety pier that jutted out from the beach. Lines were made fast to palm trees. From the fringe of jungle above the beach a white man came down, walking briskly in the noonday heat.

He was very tall and thin, with knobby knees and elbows. The fierce Melanesian sun had burned out but not tanned him, and his nose and cheekbones were peeling. His horn-rimmed glasses had broken at the hinge and been repaired with a piece of tape. He looked eager, boyish, and curiously naive.

One hell-of-a-looking treasure-hunter, the mate thought.

"Glad to see you!" the man called out. "We'd about given you up for lost."

"Not likely," the skipper said. "Mr. Sorensen, I'd like you to meet my new mate, Mr. Willis."

"Glad to meet you, Professor," the mate said.

"I'm not a professor," Sorensen said, "but thanks anyhow."

"Where are the others?" the skipper asked.

"Out in the jungle," Sorensen said. "All except Drake, and he'll be down here shortly. You'll stay a while, won't you?"

"Only to unload," the skipper said. "Have to catch the tide out of here. How's the treasure-hunting?"

"We've done a lot of digging," Sorensen said. "We still have our hopes."

"But no doubloons yet?" the skipper asked. "No pieces of eight?"

"Not a damned one," Sorensen said wearily. "Did you bring the newspapers, Skipper?"

"That I did," Sorensen replied. "They're in the cabin. Did you hear about that second space-ship going to Mars?"

"Heard about it on the short wave," Sorensen said. "It didn't bring back much, did it?"

"Practically nothing. Still, just think of it. *Two* spaceships to Mars, and I hear they're getting ready to put one on Venus."

The three men looked around them and grinned.

"Well," the skipper said, "I guess maybe the space age hasn't reached the Southwest Pacific yet. And it certainly hasn't gotten to *this* place. Come on, let's unload the cargo."

THIS PLACE WAS the island of Vuanu, southern-most of the Solomons, almost in the Louisade Archipelago. It was a fair-sized volcanic island, almost twenty miles long and several wide. Once it had supported half a dozen native villages. But the population had begun to decline after the depredations of the blackbirders in the 1850s. Then a measles epidemic wiped out almost all the rest, and the survivors emigrated to New Georgia. A ship-watcher had been stationed here during the Second World War, but no ships had come this way. The Japanese invasion had poured across New Guinea and the upper Solomons, and further north through Micronesia. At the end of the war Vuanu was still deserted. It was not made into a bird sanctuary like Canton Island, or a cable station like Christmas Island, or a refueling point like Cocos-Keeling. No one even wanted to explode alphabet bombs on it. Vuanu was a worthless, humid, jungle-covered piece of land, free to anyone who wanted it.

William Sorensen, general manager of a chain of liquor stores in California, decided he wanted it.

Sorensen's hobby was treasure-hunting. He had looked for Lafitte's treasure in Louisiana and Texas, and for the Lost Dutchman Mine in Arizona. He had found neither. His luck had been better on the wreck-strewn Gulf coast, and on an expedition to Dagger Cay in the Caribbean he had found a double handful of Spanish coins in a rotting canvas bag. The coins were worth about three thousand dollars. The expedition had cost very much more, but Sorensen felt amply repaid.

For many years he had been interested in

the Spanish treasure galleon *Santa Teresa*. Contemporary accounts told how the ship, heavily laden with bullion, sailed from Manila in 1689. The clumsy ship, caught in a storm, had run off to the south and been wrecked. Eighteen survivors managed to get ashore with the treasure. They buried it, and set sail for the Phillipines in the ship's pinnacle. Two of them were alive when the boat reached Manila.

The treasure island was tentatively identified as one of the Solomons. But which one?

No one knew. Treasure-hunters looked for the cache on Bougainville and Buka. There was a rumor about it on Malaita, and even Ontong Java received an expedition. But no treasure was recovered.

Sorensen, researching the problem thoroughly, decided that the *Santa Teresa* had sailed completely through the Solomons, almost to the Louisades. The ship must have escaped destruction until it crashed into the reef at Vuanu.

His desire to search for the treasure might have remained only a dream if he hadn't met Dan Drake. Drake was also an amateur treasure-hunter. More important, he owned a fifty-five-foot Hanna ketch.

Over an evening's drinks the Vuanu expedition was born.

Additional members were recruited. Drake's ketch was put into seagoing condition, equipment and money saved or gathered. Several other possible treasure sites in the Southwest Pacific were researched. Finally, vacation time was synchronized and the expedition got under way.

They had put in three months' work on Vuanu already. Their morale was high, in spite of inevitable conflicts between members. This schooner, bringing in supplies from Sydney and Rabaul, was the last civilized contact they would have for another six months.

WHILE SORENSEN nervously supervised, the crew of the schooner unloaded the cargo. He didn't want any of the equipment, some of it shipped over six thousand miles, to be broken now. No replacements were possible; whatever they didn't have, they would have to do without. He breathed out in relief when the last crate, containing a metal detector, was safely hoisted over the side and put on the beach above the high-water mark.

There was something odd about that box. He examined it and found a quarter-sized hole in one end. It had not been properly sealed.

Dan Drake, the co-manager of the expedition, joined him. "What's wrong?" Drake asked.

"Hole in that crate," Sorensen said. "Salt water might have gotten in. We'll be in tough shape if this detector doesn't work."

Drake nodded. "We better open it and see." He was a short, deeply tanned, broad-chested man with close-cropped black hair and a straggly mustache. He wore an old yachting cap jammed down over his eyes, giving his face a tough bulldog look. He pulled a big screwdriver from his belt and inserted it into the crack.

"Wait a moment," Sorensen said. "Let's get it up to the camp first. Easier to carry the crate than something packed in grease."

"Right," Drake said. "Take the other end."

The camp was built in a clearing a hundred yards from the beach, on the site of an abandoned native village. They had been able to re-thatch several huts, and there was an old copra shed with a galvanized iron roof where they stored their supplies. Here they got the benefit of any breeze from the sea. Beyond the clearing, the gray-green jungle sprang up like a solid wall.

Sorensen and Drake set the case down. The skipper, who had accompanied them with the newspapers, looked around at the bleak huts and shook his head.

"Would you like a drink, Skipper?" Sorensen asked. "Afraid we can't offer any ice."

"A drink would be fine," the skipper said. He wondered what drove men to a godforsaken place like this in search of imaginary Spanish treasure.

Sorensen went into one of the huts and brought out a bottle of Scotch and a tin cup. Drake had taken out his screwdriver and was vigorously ripping boards off the crate.

"How does it look?" Sorensen asked.

"It's OK," Drake said, gently lifting out the

metal detector. "Heavily greased. Doesn't seem like there was any damage—"

He jumped back. The skipper had come forward and stamped down heavily on the sand.

"What's the matter?" Sorensen asked.

"Looked like a scorpion," the skipper said. "Damned thing crawled right out of your crate there. Might have bit you."

Sorensen shrugged. He had gotten used to the presence of an infinite number of insects during his three months on Vuanu. Another bug more or less didn't seem to make much difference.

"Another drink?" he asked.

"Can't do it," the skipper said regretfully. "I'd better get started. All your party healthy?"

"All healthy so far," Sorensen said. He smiled. "Except for some bad cases of gold fever."

"You'll never find gold in this place," the skipper said seriously. "I'll look in on you in about six months. Good luck."

After shaking hands, the skipper went down to the beach and boarded his ship. As the first pink flush of sunset touched the sky, the schooner was under way. Sorensen and Drake watched it negotiate the pass. For a few minutes its masts were visible above the reef. Then they had dipped below the horizon.

"That's that," Drake said. "Us crazy American treasure-hunters are alone again."

"You don't think he suspected anything?" Sorensen asked.

"Definitely not. As far as he's concerned, we're just crackpots."

Grinning, they looked back at their camp. Under the copra shed was nearly fifty thousand dollars worth of gold and silver bullion, dug out of the jungle and carefully reburied. They had located a part of the *Santa Teresa* treasure during their first month on the island. There was every indication of more to come. Since they had no legal title to the land, the expedition was not eager to let the news get out. Once it was known, every gold-hungry vagabond from Perth to Papeete would be heading to Vuanu.

"The boy'll be in soon," Drake said. "Let's get some stew going."

"Right," Sorensen said. He took a few steps and stopped. "That's funny."

"What is?"

"That scorpion the skipper squashed. It's gone."

"Maybe he missed it," Drake said. "Or maybe he just pushed it down into the sand. What difference does it make?"

"None, I guess," Sorensen said.

II

EDWARD EAKINS WALKED through the jungle with a long-handled spade on his shoulder, sucking reflectively on a piece of candy. It was the first he'd had in weeks, and he was enjoying it to the utmost. He was in very good spirits. The schooner yesterday had brought in not only machinery and replacement parts, but also candy, cigarettes and food. He had eaten scrambled eggs this morning, and real bacon. The expedition was becoming almost civilized.

Something rustled in the bushes near him. He marched on, ignoring it.

He was a lean, sandy-haired man, amiable and slouching, with pale blue eyes and an unprepossessing manner. He felt very lucky to have been taken on the expedition. His gas station didn't put him on a financial par with the others, and he hadn't been able to put up a full share of the money. He still felt guilty about that. He had been accepted because he was an eager and indefatigable treasure-hunter with a good knowledge of jungle ways. Equally important, he was a skilled radio operator and repairman. He had kept the transmitter on the ketch in working condition in spite of salt water and mildew.

He could pay his full share now, of course. But *now*, when they were practically rich, didn't really count. He wished there were some way he could—

There was that rustle in the bushes again.

Eakins stopped and waited. The bushes trembled. And out stepped a mouse.

Eakins was amazed. The mice on this island, like most wild animal life, were terrified of man. Although they feasted off the refuse of the camp—when the rats didn't get it first—they carefully avoided any contact with humans.

"You better get yourself home," Eakins said to the mouse.

The mouse stared at him. He stared back. It was a pretty little mouse, no more than four or five inches long, and colored a light tawny brown. It didn't seem afraid.

"So long, mouse," Eakins said. "I got work to do." He shifted his spade to the other shoulder and turned to go. As he turned, he caught a flash of brown out of the corner of his eye. Instinctively he ducked. The mouse whirled past him, turned, and gathered itself for another leap.

"Mouse, are you out of your head?" Eakins asked.

The mouse bared its tiny teeth and sprang. Eakins knocked it aside.

"Now get the hell out of here," he said. He was beginning to wonder if the rodent was crazy. Did it have rabies, perhaps?

The mouse gathered itself for another charge. Eakins lifted the spade off his shoulders and waited. When the mouse sprang, he met it with a carefully timed blow. Then carefully, regretfully, he battered it to death.

"Can't have rabid mice running around," he said.

But the mouse hadn't seemed rabid; it had just seemed very determined.

Eakins scratched his head. Now what, he wondered, had gotten into that little mouse?

In the camp that evening, Eakins' story was greeted with hoots of laughter. It was just like Eakins to be attacked by a mouse. Several men suggested that he go armed in case the mouse's family wanted revenge. Eakins just smiled sheepishly.

TWO DAYS LATER, Sorensen and Al Cable were finishing up a morning's hard work at Site 4, two miles from the camp. The metals detector had shown marked activity at this spot. They were seven feet down and nothing had been produced yet except a high mound of yellow-brown earth.

"That detector must be wrong," Cable said, wiping his face wearily. He was a big, pinkish man. He had sweated off twenty pounds on

Vuanu, picked up a bad case of prickly heat, and had enough treasure-hunting to last him a lifetime. He wished he were back in Baltimore taking care of his used-car agency. He didn't hesitate to say so, often and loudly. He was one member who had not worked out well.

"Nothing wrong with the detector," Sorensen said. "Trouble is, we're digging in swampy ground. The cache must have sunk."

"It's probably a hundred feet down," Cable said, stabbing angrily at the gluey mud.

"Nope," Sorensen said. "There's volcanic rock under us, no more than twenty feet down."

"Twenty feet? We should have a bulldozer."

"Might be costly bringing one in," Sorensen said mildly. "Come on, Al, let's get back to camp."

Sorensen helped Cable out of the excavation. They cleaned off their tools and started toward the narrow path leading back to the camp. They stopped abruptly.

A large, ugly bird had stepped out of the brush. It was standing on the path, blocking their way.

"What in hell is that?" Cable asked.

"A cassowary," Sorensen said.

"Well, let's boot it out of the way and get going."

"Take it easy," Sorensen said. "If anyone does any booting, it'll be the bird. Back away slowly."

The cassowary was nearly five feet high, a black-feathered ostrich-like bird standing erect on powerful legs. Each of its feet was three-toed, and the toes curved into heavy talons. It had a yellowish, bony head and short, useless wings. From its neck hung a brilliant wattle colored red, green, and purple.

"It is dangerous?" Cable asked.

Sorensen nodded. "Natives on New Guinea have been kicked to death by those birds."

"Why haven't we seen it before?" Cable asked.

"They're usually very shy," Sorensen said. "They stay as far from people as they can."

"This one sure isn't shy," Cable said, as the cassowary took a step toward them. "Can we run?"

"The bird can run a lot faster," Sorensen

said. "I don't suppose you have a gun with you?"

"Of course not. There's been nothing to shoot."

Backing away, they held their spades like spears. The brush crackled and an anteater emerged. It was followed by a wild pig. The three beasts converged on the men, backing them toward the dense wall of the jungle.

"They're herding us," Cable said, his voice going shrill.

"Take it easy," Sorensen said. "The cassowary is the only one we have to watch out for."

"Aren't anteaters dangerous?"

"Only to ants."

"The hell you say," Cable said. "Bill, the animals on this island have gone crazy. Remember Eakins' mouse?"

"I remember it," Sorensen said. They had reached the far edge of the clearing. The beasts were in front of them, still advancing, with the cassowary in the center. Behind them lay the jungle—and whatever they were being herded toward.

"We'll have to make a break for it," Sorensen said.

"That damned bird is blocking the trail."

"We'll have to knock him over," Sorensen said. "Watch out for his feet. Let's go!"

They raced toward the cassowary, swinging their spades. The cassowary hesitated, unable to make up its mind between targets. Then it turned toward Cable and its right leg lashed out. The partially deflected blow sounded like the flat of a meat cleaver against a side of beef. Cable grunted and collapsed, clutching his ribs.

Sorensen stabbed, and the honed edge of his spade nearly severed the cassowary's head from its body. The wild pig and the anteater were coming at him now. He flailed with his spade, driving them back. Then, with a strength he hadn't known he possessed, he stooped, lifted Cable across his shoulders and ran down the path.

A quarter of a mile down he had to stop, completely out of breath. There were no sounds behind him. The other animals were apparently not following. He went back to the wounded man.

Cable had begun to recover consciousness. He was able to walk, half-supported by Sorensen. When they reached the camp, Sorensen called everybody in for a meeting. He counted heads while Eakins taped up Cable's side. Only one man was missing.

"Where's Drake?" Sorensen asked.

"He's across the island at North Beach, fishing," said Tom Recetich. "Want me to get him?"

Sorensen hesitated. Finally he said, "No. I'd better explain what we're up against. Then we'll issue the guns. *Then* we'll try to find Drake."

"Man, what's going on?" Recetich asked.

Sorensen began to explain what had happened at Site 4.

FISHING PROVIDED an important part of the expedition's food and there was no work Drake liked better. At first he had gone out with face mask and spear gun. But the sharks in this corner of the world were numerous, hungry and aggressive. So, regretfully, he had given up skin diving and set out handlines on the leeward side of the island.

The lines were out now, and Drake lay in the shade of a palm tree, half asleep, his big forearms folded over his chest. His dog, Oro, was prowling the beach in search of hermit crabs. Oro was a good-natured mutt, part Airedale, part terrier, part unknown. He was growling at something now.

"Leave the crabs alone," Drake called out. "You'll just get nipped again."

Oro was still growling. Drake rolled over and saw that the dog was standing stiff-legged over a large insect. It looked like some kind of scorpion.

"Oro, leave that blasted—"

Before Drake could move, the insect sprang. It landed on Oro's neck and the jointed tail whipped out. Oro yelped once. Drake was on his feet instantly. He swatted at the bug, but it jumped off the dog's neck and scuttled into the brush.

"Take it easy, old boy," Drake said. "That's a nasty-looking wound. Might be poisoned. I better open it up."

He held the panting dog firmly and drew his

boat knife. He had operated on the dog for snake bite in Central America, and in the Adirondacks he had held him down and pulled porcupine quills out of his mouth with a pair of pliers. The dog always knew he was being helped. He never struggled.

This time, the dog bit.

"Oro!" Drake grabbed the dog at the jaw hinge with his free hand. He brought pressure to bear, paralyzing the muscles, forcing the dog's jaws open. He pulled his hand out and flung the dog away. Oro rolled to his feet and advanced on him again.

"Stand!" Drake shouted. The dog kept coming, edging around to get between the ocean and the man.

Turning, Drake saw the bug emerge from the jungle and creep toward him. His dog had circled around and was trying to drive him toward the bug.

Drake didn't know what was going on, and he decided he'd better not stay to find out. He picked up his knife and threw it at the bug. He missed. The bug was almost within jumping distance.

Drake ran toward the ocean. When Oro tried to intercept him, he kicked the dog out of the way and plunged into the water.

He began to swim around the island to the camp, hoping he'd make it before the sharks got him.

III

AT THE CAMP, rifles and revolvers were hastily wiped clean of cosmoline and passed around. Binoculars were taken out and adjusted. Cartridges were divided up, and the supply of knives, machetes and hatchets quickly disappeared. The expedition's two walkie-talkies were unpacked, and the men prepared to move out in search of Drake. Then they saw him, swimming vigorously around the edge of the island.

He waded ashore, tired but uninjured. He and the others put their information together and reached some unhappy conclusions.

"Do you mean to say," Cable demanded, "that a *bug* is doing all this?"

"It looks that way," Sorensen said. "We have to assume that it's able to exercise some kind of thought control. Maybe hypnotic or telepathic."

"It has to sting first," Drake said. "That's what it did with Oro."

"I just can't imagine a scorpion doing all that," Recetich said.

"It's not a scorpion," Drake said. "I saw it close up. It's got a tail like a scorpion, but its head is damn near four times as big, and its body is different. Up close, it doesn't look like anything you ever saw before."

"Do you think it's native to this island?" asked Monty Byrnes, a treasure-seeker from Indianapolis.

"I doubt it," Drake said. "If it is, why did it leave us and the animals alone for three months?"

"That's right," Sorensen said. "All our troubles began just after the schooner came. The schooner must have brought it from somewhere.... Hey!"

"What is it?" Drake asked.

"Remember that scorpion the skipper tried to squash? It came out of the detector crate. Do you think it could be the same one?"

Drake shrugged his shoulders. "Could be. Seems to me our problem right now isn't finding out where it came from. We have to figure out what to do about it."

"If it can control animals," Byrnes said, "I wonder if it can control men."

They were all silent. They had moved into a circle near the copra shed, and while they talked they watched the jungle for any sign of insect or animal life.

Sorensen said, "We'd better radio for help."

"If we do that," Recetich said, "somebody's going to find out about the *Santa Teresa* treasure. We'll be overrun in no time."

"Maybe so," Sorensen said. "But at the worst, we've cleared expenses. We've even made a small profit."

"And if we don't get help," Drake said, "we may be in no condition to take anything out of here."

"The problem isn't as bad as all that," Byrnes said. "We've got guns. We can take care of the animals."

"You haven't seen the bug yet," Drake said. "We'll squash it."

"That won't be easy," Drake said. "It's faster than hell. And how are you going to squash it if it comes into your hut some night while you're asleep? We could post guards and they wouldn't even see the thing."

Brynes shuddered involuntarily. "Yeah, I guess you're right. Maybe we'd better radio for help."

Eakins stood up. "Well, gents," he said, "I guess that means me. I just hope the batteries on the ketch are up to charge."

"It'll be dangerous going out there," Drake said. "We'll draw lots."

Eakins was amused. "We will? How many of you can operate a transmitter?"

Drake said, "I can."

"No offense meant," Eakins said, "but you don't operate that set of yours worth a damn. You don't even know Morse for key transmission. And can you fix the set if it goes out?"

"No," Drake said. "But the whole thing is too risky. We all should go."

Eakins shook his head. "Safest thing all around is if you cover me from the beach. That bug probably hasn't thought about the ketch yet."

Eakins stuck a tool kit in his pocket and strapped one of the camp's walkie-talkies over his shoulder. He handed the other one to Sorensen. He hurried down the beach past the launch and pushed the small dinghy into the water. The men of the expedition spread out, their rifles ready. Eakins got into the dinghy and started rowing across the quiet lagoon.

They saw him tie up to the ketch and pause a moment, looking around. Then he climbed aboard. Quickly he slid back the hatch and went inside.

"Everything all right?" Sorensen asked.

"No trouble yet," Eakins said, his voice sounding thin and sharp over the walkie-talkie. "I'm at the transmitter now, turning it on. It needs a couple of minutes to warm up."

Drake nudged Sorensen. "Look over there."

On the reef, almost hidden by the ketch, something was moving. Using binoculars, Sorensen could see three big gray rats slipping into the water. They began swimming toward the ketch.

"Start firing!" Sorensen said. "Eakins, get out of there!"

"I've got the transmitter going," Eakins said. "I just need a couple of minutes more to get a message off."

Bullets sent up white splashes around the swimming rats. One was hit; the other two managed to put the ketch between them and the riflemen. Studying the reef with his binoculars, Sorensen saw an anteater cross the reef and splash into the water. It was followed by a wild pig.

There was a crackle of static from the walkie-talkie. Sorensen called, "Eakins, have you got that message off?"

"Haven't sent it," Eakins called back. "Listen, Bill. We *mustn't* send any messages! That bug wants—" He stopped abruptly.

"What is it?" Sorensen asked. "What's happening?"

Eakins had appeared on deck, still holding the walkie-talkie. He was backing toward the stern.

"Hermit crabs," he said. "They climbed up the anchor line. I'm going to swim to shore."

"Don't do it," Sorensen said.

"Gotta do it," Eakins said. "They'll probably follow me. All of you come out here and *get that transmitter*. Bring it ashore."

Through his binoculars, Sorensen could see a solid gray carpet of hermit crabs crawling down the deck and waterways of the ketch. Eakins jumped into the water. He swam furiously toward shore, and Sorensen saw the rats turn and follow him. Hermit crabs swarmed off the boat, and the wild pig and the anteater paddled after him, trying to head him off before he reached the beach.

"Come on," Sorensen said. "I don't know what Eakins figured out, but we better get that transmitter while we have a chance."

They ran down the beach and put the launch into the water. Two hundred yards away, Eakins had reached the far edge of the beach with the animals in close pursuit. He broke into the jungle, still clinging to his walkie-talkie.

"Eakins?" Sorensen asked into the walkie-talkie.

"I'm all right," Eakins said, panting hard for air. "Get that transmitter, and don't forget the batteries!"

The men boarded the ketch. Working furiously, they ripped the transmitter off its bulkhead and dragged it up the companionway steps. Drake came last, carrying a twelve-volt battery. He went down again and brought up a second battery. He hesitated a moment, then went below for a third time.

"Drake!" Sorensen shouted. "Quit holding us up!"

Drake reappeared, carrying the ketch's two radio direction finders and the compass. He handed them down and jumped into the launch.

"OK," he said. "Let's go."

They rowed to the beach. Sorensen was trying to re-establish contact with Eakins on the walkie-talkie, but all he could hear was static. Then, as the launch grounded on the beach, he heard Eakins' voice.

"I'm surrounded," he said, very quietly. "I guess I'll have to see what Mr. Bug wants. Maybe I can swat him first, though."

There was a long silence. Then Eakins said, "It's coming toward me now. Drake was right. It sure isn't like any bug *I've* ever seen. I'm going to swat hell out of—"

They heard him scream, more in surprise than pain.

Sorensen said, "Eakins, can you hear me? Where are you? Can we help?"

"It sure *is* fast," Eakins said, his voice conversational again. "Fastest damned bug I've ever seen. Jumped on my neck, stung me and jumped off again."

"How do you feel?" Sorensen asked.

"Fine," Eakins said. "Hardly felt the sting."

"Where is the bug now?"

"Back in the bush."

"The animals?"

"They went away. You know," Eakins said, "maybe this thing doesn't work on humans. Maybe—"

"What?" Sorensen asked. "What's happening now?"

There was a long silence. Then Eakins' voice, low-pitched and calm, came over the walkie-talkie.

"We'll speak with you again later," Eakins said. "We must take consultation now and decide what to do with you."

"Eakins!"

There was no answer from the other end of the walkie-talkie.

IV

RETURNING TO THEIR CAMP, the men were in a mood of thorough depression. They couldn't understand what had happened to Eakins and they didn't feel like speculating on it. The ravaging afternoon sun beat down, reflecting heat back from the white sand. The damp jungle steamed, and appeared to creep toward them like a huge and sleepy green dragon, trapping them against the indifferent sea. Gun barrels grew too hot to touch, and the water in the canteens was as warm as blood. Overhead, thick gray cumulus clouds began to pile up; it was the beginning of the monsoon season.

Drake sat in the shade of the copra shed. He shook off his lethargy long enough to inspect the camp from the viewpoint of defense. He saw the encircling jungle as enemy territory. In front of it was an area fifty yards deep which they had cleared. This no man's land could perhaps be defended for a while.

Then came the huts and the copra shed, their last line of defense, leading to the beach and the sea.

The expedition had been in complete control of this island for better than three months. Now they were pinned to a small and precarious beachhead.

Drake glanced at the lagoon behind him and remembered that there was still one line of retreat open. If the bug and his damned menagerie pressed too hard, they could still escape in the ketch. With luck.

Sorensen came over and sat down beside him. "What are you doing?" he asked.

Drake grinned sourly. "Planning our master strategy."

"How does it look?"

"I think we can hold out," Drake said. "We've got plenty of ammo. If necessary, we'll interdict the cleared area with gasoline. We certainly aren't going to let that bug push us off the island." He thought for a moment. "But it's going to be damned hard digging for treasure."

Sorensen nodded. "I wonder what the bug wants."

"Maybe we'll find out from Eakins," Drake said.

THEY HAD TO WAIT half an hour. Then Eakins' voice came, sharp and shrill over the walkie-talkie.

"Sorensen? Drake?"

"We're here," Drake said. "What did that damned bug do to you?"

"Nothing," Eakins said. "You are talking to that bug now. My name is the Quedak."

"My God," Drake said to Sorensen, "that bug must have hypnotized him!"

"No. You are not speaking to a hypnotized Eakins. Nor are you speaking to a creature who is simply using Eakins as a mouthpiece. Nor are you speaking to the Eakins who was. You are speaking to many individuals who are one."

"I don't get that," Drake said.

"It's very simple," Eakins' voice replied. "I am the Quedak, the totality. But my totality is made up of separate parts, which are Eakins, several rats, a dog named Oro, a pig, an anteater, a cassowary—"

"Hold on," Sorensen said. "Let me get this straight. This is *not* Eakins I'm speaking to. This is the—the Quedak?"

"That is correct."

"And you control Eakins and the others? You speak through Eakins' mouth?"

"Also correct. But that doesn't mean that the personalities of the others are obliterated. Quite the contrary, the Quedak state is a federation in which the various member parts retain their idiosyncrasies, their individual needs and desires. They give their knowledge, their power, their special outlook to the Quedak whole. The Quedak is the coordinating and command center; but the individual parts supply the knowledge, the insights, the special skills. And together we form the Great Cooperation."

"Cooperation?" Drake said. "But you did all this by force!"

"It was necessary in the beginning. Otherwise, how would other creatures have known about the Great Cooperation?"

"Would they stay if you released your control over them?" Drake asked.

"That is a meaningless question. We form a single indivisible entity now. Would your arm return to you if you cut it off?"

"It isn't the same thing."

"It is," Eakins' voice said. "We are a single organism. We are still growing. And we welcome you wholeheartedly into the Great Cooperation."

"To hell with that," Drake said.

"But you must join," the Quedak told them. "It is the Quedak Mission to coordinate all sentient creatures into a single collective organism. Believe me, there is only the most trifling loss of the individuality you prize so highly. And you gain so much more! You learn the viewpoints and special knowledge of all other creatures. Within the Quedak framework you can fully realize your potentialities—"

"No!"

"I am sorry," the Quedak said. "The Quedak Mission must be fulfilled. You will not join us willingly?"

"Never," Drake said.

"Then *we* will join *you*," the Quedak said.

There was a click as he turned off the walkie-talkie.

FROM THE FRINGE of the jungle, several rats appeared. They hesitated, just out of rifle range. A bird of paradise flew overhead, hovering over the cleared area like an observation plane. As the men watched, the rats began to run forward in long zigzags.

"Start firing," Drake called out. "But go easy with the ammo."

The men began to fire. But it was difficult to sight on the quick-moving rats against the grayish-brown clearing. And almost immediately, the rats were joined by a dozen hermit crabs. They had an uncanny knack for moving when no one was watching them, darting forward, then freezing against the neutral background.

They saw Eakins appear on the fringe of the jungle.

"Lousy traitor," Cable said, raising his rifle.

Sorensen slapped the muzzle of the rifle aside. "Don't do it."

"But he's helping that bug!"

"He can't help it," Sorensen said. "And he's not armed. Leave him alone."

Eakins watched for a few moments, then melted back into the jungle.

The attack by the rats and crabs swept across half of the cleared space. Then, as they came closer, the men were able to pick their targets with more accuracy. Nothing was able to get closer than twenty yards. And when Recetich shot down the bird of paradise, the attack began to falter.

"You know," Drake said, "I think we're going to be all right."

"Could be," said Sorensen. "I don't understand what the Quedak is trying to accomplish. He knows we can't be taken like this. I should think—"

"Hey!" one of the men called out. "Our boat!"

They turned and saw why the Quedak had ordered the attack. While it had occupied their attention, Drake's dog had swum out to the ketch and gnawed through the anchor line. Unattended, the ketch was drifting before the wind, moving toward the reef. They saw it bump gently, then harder. In a moment it was heeled hard over, stuck in the coral.

There was a burst of static from the walkie-talkie. Sorensen held it up and heard the Quedak say, "The ketch isn't seriously damaged. It's simply immobilized."

"The hell you say," Drake growled. "For all you know, it's got a hole punched right through it. How do you plan on getting off the island, Quedak? Or are you just going to stay here?"

"I will leave at the proper time," the Quedak said. "I want to make sure that we all leave together."

V

THE WIND DIED. Huge gray thunderheads piled up in the sky to the southeast, their tops lost in the upper atmosphere, their black anvil bottoms pressing the hot still air upon the island. The sun had lost its fiery glare. Cherry-red, it slid listlessly toward the flat sea.

High overhead, a single bird of paradise circled, just out of rifle range. It had gone up ten minutes after Recetich had shot the first one down.

Monty Byrnes stood on the edge of the cleared area, his rifle ready. He had drawn the first guard shift. The rest of the men were eating a hasty dinner inside the copra shed. Sorensen and Drake were outside, looking over the situation.

Drake said, "By nightfall we'll have to pull everybody back into the shed. Can't take a chance on being exposed to the Quedak in the dark."

Sorensen nodded. He seemed to have aged ten years in a day's time.

"In the morning," Drake said, "we'll be able to work something out We'll.... What's wrong, Bill?"

"Do you really think we have a chance?" Sorensen asked.

"Sure we do. We've got a damned good chance."

"Be realistic," Sorensen said. "The longer this goes on, the more animals the Quedak can throw against us. What can we do about it?"

"Hunt him out and kill him."

"The damned thing is about the size of your thumb," Sorensen said irritably. "How can we hunt him?"

"We'll figure out something," Drake said. He was beginning to get worried about Sorensen. The morale among the men was low enough without Sorensen pushing it down further.

"I wish someone would shoot that damned bird," Sorensen said, glancing overhead.

About every fifteen minutes, the bird of paradise came darting down for a closer look at the camp. Then, before the guard had a chance to fire, he swept back up to a safe altitude.

"It's getting on my nerves, too," Drake said. "Maybe that's what it's supposed to do. One of these times we'll—"

He stopped abruptly. From the copra shed he could hear the loud hum of a radio. And he heard Al Cable saying, "Hello, hello, this is Vuanu calling. We need help."

Drake and Sorensen went into the shed. Cable was sitting in front of the transmitter, saying into the microphone, "Emergency, emergency, Vuanu calling, we need—"

"What in hell do you think you're doing?" Drake snapped.

Cable turned and looked at him, his pudgy pink body streaked with sweat. "I'm radioing for help, that's what I'm doing. I think I've picked up somebody. But they haven't answered me yet."

He readjusted the tuning. Over the receiver, they could hear a bored British voice saying, "Pawn to Queen four, eh? Why don't you ever try a different opening?"

There was a sharp burst of static. "Just move," a deep bass voice answered. "Just shut up and move."

"Sure," said the British voice. "Knight to king bishop three."

Drake recognized the voices. They were ham radio operators. One of them owned a plantation on Bougainville; the other was a shopkeeper in Rabaul. They came on the air for an hour of chess and argument every evening.

Cable tapped the microphone impatiently. "Hello," he said, "this is Vuanu calling, emergency call—"

Drake walked over and took the microphone out of Cable's hand. He put it down carefully.

"We can't call for help," he said.

"What are you talking about?" Cable cried. "We have to!"

Drake felt very tired. "Look, if we send out a distress call, somebody's going to come sailing right in—but they won't be prepared for this kind of trouble. The Quedak will take them over and then use them against us."

"We can explain what the trouble is," Cable said.

"*Explain?* Explain *what*? That a bug is taking over the island? They'd think we were crazy with fever. They'd send in a doctor on the inter-island schooner."

"Dan's right," Sorensen said. "Nobody would believe this without seeing it for himself."

"And by then," Drake said, "it'd be too late. Eakins figured it out before the Quedak got him. That's why he told us not to send any messages."

Cable looked dubious. "But why did he want us to take the transmitter?"

"So that *he* couldn't send any messages after the bug got him," Drake said. "The more people trampling around, the easier it would be for the Quedak. If he had possession of the transmitter, he'd be calling for help right now."

"Yeah, I suppose so," Cable said unhappily. "But, damn it, we can't handle this *alone*."

"We have to. If the Quedak ever gets us and then gets off the island, that's it for Earth. Period. There won't be any big war, no hydrogen bombs or fallout, no heroic little resistance groups. Everybody will become part of the Quedak Cooperation."

"We ought to get help somehow," Cable said stubbornly. "We're alone, isolated. Suppose we ask for a ship to stand offshore—"

"It won't work," Drake said. "Besides, we couldn't ask for help even if we wanted to."

"Why not?"

"Because the transmitter's not working," Drake said. "You've been talking into a dead mike."

"It's receiving OK," Cable said.

Drake checked to see if all the switches were on. "Nothing wrong with the receiver. But we must have joggled something taking the transmitter out of the ship. It isn't working."

Cable tapped the dead microphone several times, then put it down. They stood around the receiver, listening to the chess game between the man in Rabaul and the man in Bougainville.

"Pawn to queen bishop four."

"Pawn to king three."

"Knight to Queen bishop three."

There was a sudden staccato burst of static. It faded, then came again in three distinct bursts.

"What do you suppose that is?" Sorensen asked.

Drake shrugged his shoulders. "Could be anything. Storm's shaping up and—"

He stopped. He had been standing beside the door of the shed. As the static crackled, he saw the bird of paradise dive for a closer look. The static stopped when the bird returned to its slow-circling higher altitude.

"That's strange," Drake said. "Did you see that, Bill? The bird came down and the static went on at the same time."

"I saw it," Sorensen said. "Think it means anything?"

"I don't know. Let's see." Drake took out his field glasses. He turned up the volume of the receiver and stepped outside where he could observe the jungle. He waited, hearing the sounds of the chess game three or four hundred miles away.

"Come on now, move."

"Give me a minute."

"A minute? Listen, I can't stand in front of this bleeding set all night. Make your—"

Static crackled sharply. Drake saw four wild pigs come trotting out of the jungle, moving slowly, like a reconnaissance squad probing for weak spots in an enemy position. They stopped; the static stopped. Byrnes, standing guard with his rifle, took a snap shot at them. The pigs turned, and static crackled as they moved back into the jungle. There was more static as the bird of paradise swept down for a look, then climbed out of range. After that, the static stopped.

Drake put down his binoculars and went back inside the shed. "That must be it," he said. "The static is related to the Quedak. I think it comes when he's operating the animals."

"You mean he has come sort of radio control over them?" Sorensen asked.

"Seems like it," Drake said. "Either radio control or something propagated along a radio wavelength."

"If that's the case," Sorensen said, "he's like a little radio station, isn't he?"

"Sure he is. So what?"

"Then we should be able to locate him on a radio direction finder," Sorensen said.

Drake nodded emphatically. He snapped off the receiver, went to a corner of the shed and took out one of their portable direction finders. He set it to the frequency at which Cable had picked up the Rabaul-Bougainville broadcast. Then he turned it on and walked to the door.

The men watched while Drake rotated the loop antenna. He located the maximum signal, then turned the loop slowly, read the bearing and converted it to a compass course. Then he sat down with a small-scale chart of the Southwest Pacific.

"Well," Sorensen asked, "is it the Quedak?"

"It's got to be," said Drake. "I located a good null almost due south. That's straight ahead in the jungle."

"You're sure it isn't a reciprocal bearing?"

"I checked that out."

"Is there any chance the signal comes from some other station?"

"Nope. Due south, the next station is Sydney, and that's seventeen hundred miles away. Much too far for this RDF. It's the Quedak, all right."

"So we have a way of locating him," Sorensen said. "Two men with direction finders can go into the jungle—"

"—and get themselves killed," Drake said. "We can position the Quedak with RDFs, but his animals can locate us a lot faster. We wouldn't have a chance in the jungle."

Sorensen looked crestfallen. "Then we're no better off than before."

"We're a lot better off," Drake said. "We have a chance now."

"What makes you think so?"

"He controls the animals by radio," Drake said. "We know the frequency he operates on. We can broadcast on the same frequency. We can jam his signal."

"Are you sure about that?"

"Am I *sure*? Of course not. But I do know that two stations in the same area can't broadcast over the same frequency. If we tuned in to the frequency the Quedak uses, made enough noise to override his signal—"

"I see," Sorensen said. "Maybe it would work! If we could interfere with his signal, he wouldn't be able to control the animals. And then we could hunt him down with the RDFs."

"That's the idea," Drake said. "It has only one small flaw—our transmitter isn't working. With no transmitter, we can't do any broadcasting. No broadcasting, no jamming."

"Can you fix it?" Sorensen asked.

"I'll try," Drake said. "But we'd better not hope for too much. Eakins was the radio man on this expedition."

"We've got all the spare parts," Sorensen said. "Tubes, manual, everything."

"I know. Give me enough time and I'll figure out what's wrong. The question is, how much time is the Quedak going to give us?"

The bright copper disk of the sun was half submerged in the sea. Sunset colors touched the massing thunderheads and faded into the brief tropical twilight. The men began to barricade the copra shed for the night.

VI

DRAKE REMOVED the back from the transmitter and scowled at the compact mass of tubes and wiring. Those metal boxlike things were probably condensers, and the waxy cylindrical gadgets might or might not be resistors. It all looked hopelessly complicated, ridiculously dense and delicate. Where should he begin?

He turned on the set and waited a few minutes. All the tubes appeared to go on, some dim, some bright. He couldn't detect any loose wires. The mike was still dead.

So much for visual inspection. Next question: was the set getting enough juice?

He turned it off and checked the battery cells with a voltmeter. The batteries were up to charge. He removed the leads, scraped them and put them back on, making sure they fit snugly. He checked all connections, murmured a propitiatory prayer, and turned the set on.

It still didn't work.

Cursing, he turned it off again. He decided to replace all the tubes, starting with the dim ones. If that didn't work, he could try replacing condensers and resistors. If that didn't work, he could always shoot himself. With this cheerful thought, he opened the parts kit and went to work.

The men were all inside the copra shed, finishing the job of barricading it for the night. The door was wedged shut and locked. The two windows had to be kept open for ventilation; otherwise everyone would suffocate in the heat. But a double layer of heavy mosquito netting was nailed over each window, and a guard was posted beside it.

Nothing could get through the flat galvanized-iron roof. The floor was of pounded earth, a possible danger point. All they could do was keep watch over it.

The treasure-hunters settled down for a long night. Drake, with a handkerchief tied around his forehead to keep the perspiration out of his eyes, continued working on the transmitter.

AN HOUR LATER, there was a buzz on the walkie-talkie. Sorensen picked it up and said, "What do you want?"

"I want you to end this senseless resistance," said the Quedak, speaking with Eakins' voice. "You've had enough time to think over the situation. I want you to join me. Surely you can see there's no other way."

"We don't want to join you," Sorensen said.

"You must," the Quedak told him.

"Are you going to make us?"

"That poses problems," the Quedak said. "My animal parts are not suitable for coercion. Eakins is an excellent mechanism, but there is only one of him. And I must not expose myself to unnecessary danger. By doing so I would endanger the Quedak Mission."

"So it's a stalemate," Sorensen said.

"No. I am faced with difficulty only in taking you over. There is no problem in killing you."

The men shifted uneasily. Drake, working on the transmitter, didn't look up.

"I would rather *not* kill you," the Quedak said. "But the Quedak Mission is of primary importance. It would be endangered if you didn't join. It would be seriously compromised if you left the island. So you must either join or be killed."

"That's not the way I see it," Sorensen said. "If you killed us—assuming that you can—you'd never get off this island. Eakins can't handle that ketch."

"There would be no need to leave in the ketch," the Quedak said. "In six months, the inter-island schooner will return. Eakins and I will leave then. The rest of you will have died."

"You're bluffing," Sorensen said. "What makes you think you could kill us? You didn't do so well today." He caught Drake's attention and gestured at the radio. Drake shrugged his shoulders and went back to work.

"I wasn't trying," the Quedak said. "The time for that was at night. *This* night, before you have a chance to work out a better system of defense. You must join me tonight or I will kill one of you."

"One of us?"

"Yes. One man an hour. In that way, perhaps the survivors will change their minds about joining. But if they don't, all of you will be dead by morning."

Drake leaned over and whispered to Sorensen, "Stall him. Give me another ten minutes. I think I've found the trouble."

Sorensen said into the walkie-talkie, "We'd like to know a little more about the Quedak Cooperation."

"You can find out best by joining."

"We'd rather have a little more information on it first."

"It is an indescribable state," the Quedak said in an urgent, earnest, eager voice. "Can you imagine yourself as *yourself* and yet experiencing an entirely new series of sensory networks? You would, for example, experience the world through the perceptors of a dog as he goes through the forest following an odor which to him —and to you—is as clear and vivid as a painted line. A hermit crab senses things differently. From him you experience the slow interaction of life at the margin of sea and land. His time-sense is very slow, unlike that of a bird of paradise, whose viewpoint is spatial, rapid, cursory. And there are many others, above and below the earth and water, who furnish their own specialized viewpoints of reality. Their outlooks, I have found, are not essentially different from those of the animals that once inhabited Mars."

"What happened on Mars?" Sorensen asked.

"All life died," the Quedak mourned. "All except the Quedak. It happened a long time ago. For centuries there was peace and prosperity on the planet. Everything and everyone was part of the Quedak Cooperation. But the dominant race was basically weak. Their breeding rate went down; catastrophes happened. And finally there was no more life except the Quedak."

"Sounds great," Sorensen said ironically.

"It was the fault of the race," the Quedak protested. "With sturdier stock—such as you have on this planet—the will to live will remain intact. The peace and prosperity will continue indefinitely."

"I don't believe it. What happened on Mars will happen again on Earth if you take over. After a while, slaves just don't care very strongly about living."

"You wouldn't be slaves. You would be functional parts of the Quedak Cooperation."

"Which would be run by you," Sorensen said. "Any way you slice it, it's the same old pie."

"You don't know what you're talking about," the Quedak said. "We have talked long enough. I am prepared to kill one man in the next five minutes. Are you or are you not going to join me?" Sorensen looked at Drake. Drake turned on the transmitter.

Gusts of rain splattered on the roof while the transmitter warmed up. Drake lifted the microphone and tapped it, and was able to hear the sound in the speaker.

"It's working," he said.

At that moment something flew against the netting-covered window. The netting sagged; a fruit bat was entangled in it, glaring at them with tiny red-rimmed eyes.

"Get some boards over that window!" Sorensen shouted.

As he spoke, a second bat hurtled into the netting, broke through it and tumbled to the floor. The men clubbed it to death, but four more bats flew in through the open window. Drake flailed at them, but he couldn't drive them away from the transmitter. They were diving at his eyes, and he was forced back. A wild blow caught one bat and knocked it to the floor with a broken wing. Then the others had reached the transmitter.

They pushed it off the table. Drake tried to catch the set, and failed. He heard the glass tubes shattering, but by then he was busy protecting his eyes.

In a few minutes they had killed two more bats, and the others had fled out the window. The men nailed boards over both windows, and Drake bent to examine the transmitter.

"Any chance of fixing it?" Sorensen asked.

"Not a hope," Drake said. "They ripped out the wiring while they were at it."

"What do we do now?"

"I don't know."

Then the Quedak spoke to them over the walkie-talkie. "I must have your answer right now."

Nobody said a word.

"In that case," the Quedak said, "I'm deeply sorry that one of you must die now."

VII

RAIN PELTED the iron roof and the gusts of wind increased in intensity. There were rumbles of distant thunder. But within the copra shed, the air was hot and still. The gasoline lantern hanging from the center beam threw a harsh yellow light that illuminated the center of the room but left the corners in deep shadow. The treasure-hunters had moved away from the walls. They were all in the center of the room facing outward, and they made Drake think of a herd of buffalo drawn up against a wolf they could smell but could not see.

Cable said, "Listen, maybe we should try this Quedak Cooperation. Maybe it isn't so bad as—"

"Shut up," Drake said.

"Be reasonable," Cable argued. "It's better than dying, isn't it?"

"No one's dying yet," Drake said. "Just shut up and keep your eyes open."

"I think I'm going to be sick," Cable said. "Dan, let me out."

"Be sick where you are," Drake said. "Just keep your eyes open."

"You can't give me orders," Cable said. He started toward the door. Then he jumped back.

A yellowish scorpion had crept under the inch of clearance between the door and the floor. Recetich stamped on it, smashing it to pulp under his heavy boots. Then he whirled, swinging at three hornets which had come at him through the boarded windows.

"Forget the hornets!" Drake shouted. "Keep watching the ground!"

There was movement on the floor. Several hairy spiders crawled out of the shadows. Drake and Recetich beat at them with rifle butts. Byrnes saw something crawling under the door. It looked like some kind of huge flat centipede. He stamped at it, missed, and the centipede was on his boot, past it, on the flesh of his leg. He screamed; it felt like a ribbon of molten metal. He was able to smash it flat before he passed out.

Drake checked the wound and decided it was not fatal. He stamped on another spider, then felt Sorensen's hand clutching his shoulder. He looked toward the corner Sorensen was pointing at.

Sliding toward them were two large, dark-coated snakes. Drake recognized them as black adders. These normally shy creatures were coming forward like tigers.

The men panicked, trying to get away from the snakes. Drake pulled out his revolver and dropped to one knee, ignoring the hornets that buzzed around him, trying to draw a bead on the slender serpentine targets in the swaying yellow light.

Thunder roared directly overhead. A long flash of lightning suddenly flooded the room, spoiling his aim. Drake fired and missed, and waited for the snakes to strike.

They didn't strike. They were moving away from him, retreating to the rat hole from which they had emerged. One of the adders slid quickly through. The other began to follow, then stopped, half in the hole.

Sorensen took careful aim with a rifle. Drake pushed the muzzle aside. "Wait just a moment."

The adder hesitated. It came out of the hole and began to move toward them again....

And there was another crash of thunder and a vivid splash of lightning. The snake turned away and squirmed through the hole.

"What's going on?" Sorensen asked. "Is the thunder frightening them?"

"No, it's the lightning!" Drake said. "That's why the Quedak was in such a rush. He saw that a storm was coming, and he hadn't consolidated his position yet."

"What are you talking about?"

"The lightning," Drake said.

"The electrical storm! It's jamming that radio control of his! And when he's jammed, the beasts revert to normal behavior. It takes him time to re-establish control."

"The storm won't last forever," Cable said.

"But maybe it'll last long enough," Drake said. He picked up the direction finders and handed one to Sorensen. "Come on, Bill. We'll hunt out that bug right now."

"Hey," Recetich said, "isn't there something I can do?"

"You can start swimming if we don't come back in an hour," Drake said.

IN SLANTING LINES the rain drove down, pushed by the wild southwest wind. Thunder rolled continually and each flash of lightning seemed aimed at them. Drake and Sorensen reached the edge of the jungle and stopped.

"We'll separate here," Drake said. "Gives us a better chance of converging on him."

"Right," Sorensen said. "Take care of yourself, Dan."

Sorensen plunged into the jungle. Drake trotted fifty yards down the fringe and then entered the bush.

He pushed forward, the revolver in his belt, the radio direction finder in one hand, a flashlight in the other. The jungle seemed to be animated by a vicious life of its own, almost as if the Quedak controlled it. Vines curled cunningly around his ankles and the bushes reached out thorny hands toward him. Every branch took a special delight in slapping his face.

Each time the lightning flashed, Drake's direction finder tried to home on it. He was having a difficult time staying on course. But, he reminded himself, the Quedak was undoubtedly having an even more difficult time. Between flashes, he was able to set a course. The further he penetrated into the jungle, the stronger the signal became.

After a while he noticed that the flashes of lightning were spaced more widely apart. The storm was moving on toward the north, leaving the island behind. How much longer would he have the protection of the lightning? Another ten or fifteen minutes?

He heard something whimper. He swung his flashlight around and saw his dog, Oro, coming toward him.

His dog—or the Quedak's dog?

"Hey there, boy," Drake said. He wondered if he should drop the direction finder and get the revolver out of his belt. He wondered if the revolver would still work after such a thorough soaking.

Oro came up and licked his hand. He was Drake's dog, at least for the duration of the storm.

They moved on together, and the thunder rumbled distantly in the north. The signal on his RDF was very strong now. Somewhere around here....

He saw light from another flashlight. Sorensen, badly out of breath, had joined him. The jungle had ripped and clawed at him, but he still had his rifle, flashlight and direction finder.

Oro was scratching furiously at a bush. There was a long flash of lightning, and in it they saw the Quedak.

DRAKE REALIZED, in those final moments, that the rain had stopped. The lightning had stopped, too. He dropped the direction finder. With the flashlight in one hand and his revolver in the other, he tried to take aim at the Quedak, who was moving, who had jumped—

To Sorensen's neck, just above the right collarbone.

Sorensen raised his hands, then lowered them again. He turned toward Drake, raising his rifle. His face was perfectly calm. He looked as though his only purpose in life was to kill Drake.

Drake fired from less than two feet away. Sorensen spun with the impact, dropped his rifle and fell.

Drake bent over him, his revolver ready. He saw that he had fired accurately. The bullet had gone in just above the right collarbone. It was a bad wound. But it had been much worse for the Quedak, who had been in the direct path of the bullet. All that was left of the Quedak was a splatter of black across Sorensen's chest.

Drake applied hasty first aid and hoisted Sorensen to his shoulders. He wondered what he would have done if the Quedak had been standing above Sorensen's heart, or on his throat, or on his head.

He decided it was better not to think about that.

He started back to camp, with his dog trotting along beside him.

"Meeting of the Minds" first appeared in the February 1960 issue of Galaxy Magazine, *with illustrations by artist Dick Francis (not to be confused with the British jockey turned mystery novelist).*

Robert Sheckley (1928–2005) was a prolific American writer best known for his witty and unpredictable stories and novels, which were either directly adapted (or served as the source material) for numerous radio, movie, and television projects, including the Italian SF film The Tenth Victim *(1965) and Disney's* Condorman *(1981).*

FIRST TWO ISSUES STILL AVAILABLE!

PURCHASE ONLINE AT AMAZON OR BN.COM
—OR ORDER THROUGH YOUR LOCAL BOOKSTORE.

Strange science, weird worlds, hostile aliens, renegade robots ... and the cold vacuum of space.

200 oversized pages packed with exciting stories and art by some of the best writers of yesterday, today and tomorrow. Each issue features fiction, weird science, comics and retro movie reviews, all focusing on a different theme familiar to fans of SF in both print and celluloid.

***Black Infinity: Deadly Planets* (#1):** Fiction by award-winning authors Douglas Smith and Simon Strantzas; Kurt Newton, Clifford D. Simak and more; a complete novel by Harry Harrison; a classic comics story by Jack Kirby; plus, science and retro movie reviews—all celebrating one of the darker sides of SF: the often-deadly exploration of hostile alien worlds! • ISBN: 978-0996693677

***Black Infinity: Blobs, Globs, Slime and Spores* (#2):** New fiction by Rhys Hughes, Gregory L. Norris, Marc Vun Kannon; classic tales by Robert Sheckley, William Hope Hodgson, Joseph Payne Brennan and more; an overview of blobs, slime and spores in the entertainment media; weird science, retro movies, and a creepy SF comics story! • ISBN: 978-0996693684

DRAWING IN

BY RAMSEY CAMPBELL

NO WONDER THE RENT WAS SO LOW. THERE WERE CRACKS EVERYWHERE; NEW ONES HAD BROKEN OUT DURING THE NIGHT—one passed above the foot of his bed, through the elaborate moulding, then trailed towards the parquet floor. Still, the house didn't matter; Thorpe hadn't come here for the house.

He parted the curtains. Act one, scene three. Mist lingered; the lake was overlapped by a ghost of itself. Growing sunlight renewed colours from the mist: the green fur of the hills, the green spikes of pines. All this was free. He'd little reason to complain.

As always when he emerged from his room, the height of the ceiling made him glance up. Above the stairs, another new crack had etched the plaster. Suppose the house fell on him while he was asleep? Hardly likely—the place looked far too solid.

He hesitated, staring at the door that stood ajar. Should he give into curiosity? It wasn't as simple as that: he'd come here to recuperate, he could scarcely do so if curiosity kept him awake. Last night he'd lain awake for hours wondering. Feeling rather like a small boy who'd crept into this deserted house for a dare, he pushed open the door.

The room was smaller than his, and darker—though perhaps all that was because of the cabinets, high as the ceiling and black as drowned timber, that occupied all the walls. The cabinets were padlocked shut, save one whose broken padlock dangled from the half-open door. Beyond the door was darkness, dimly crowded. Speculations on the nature of that crowding had troubled his sleep.

He ventured forward. Again, as the cabinet loured over him, he felt like a small boy. Ignoring doubts, he tugged the door wide. The padlock fell, loud in the echoing room—and from high in the cabinet, dislodged objects toppled. Some

opened as they fell, and their contents scuttled over him.

The containers rattled on the parquet as he flinched back. They resembled pillboxes of transparent plastic. They were inscribed in a spidery handwriting, which seemed entirely appropriate, for each had contained a spider. A couple of dark furry blotches clung with long legs to his sleeve. He picked them off, shuddering. He couldn't rid himself of an insidious suspicion that some of the creatures were not quite dead.

He peered reluctantly at them. Bright pinheads of eyes peered back, dead as metal; beside them palpi bristled. The lifeless fur felt unpleasantly cold on his palm. Eventually he'd filled all the containers, God only knew how correctly. If he were an audience watching himself, this would be an enjoyable farce. As he replaced the boxes on the high shelf, he noticed a padlocked container, large as a hatbox, lurking at the back of the cabinet. Let it stay there. He'd had enough surprises for one day.

Besides, he must report the cracks. Eventually the bus arrived, laden with climbers. Some of their rucksacks occupied almost as much space as they did. Camps smoked below the hills.

Outside the estate agent's office, cows plodded to market. The agent listened to the tale of the cracks. "You surprise me. I'll look in tomorrow." His fingertips brushed his hair gently, abstractedly. He glanced up as Thorpe hesitated. "Something else?"

"The owner of the house—what line is he in?"

"Anarach—narach—" The agent shook his head irritably to clear it of the blockage. "*An arachnologist*," he pronounced at last.

"I thought it must be something of the kind. I looked in one of the cabinets—the one with the broken lock."

"Ah yes, his bloodsuckers. That's what he likes to call them. All these writers are eccentric in some way, I suppose. I should have asked you not to touch anything," he said reprovingly.

Thorpe had been glad to confess, but felt embarrassed now. "Well, perhaps no harm's done," the agent said. "He went to Eastern Europe six months ago, in search of some rarity—having fixed the amount of the rent."

Was that comment a kind of reproof? It sounded wistful. But the agent stood up smiling. "Anyway, you look better for the country," he said. "You've much more colour now."

And indeed Thorpe felt better. He was at his ease in the narrow streets; he was able to make his way between cars without flinching—without feeling jagged metal bite into him, the windscreen shatter into his face. The scars of his stitches no longer plucked at his cheeks. He walked part of the way back to the house, until weakness overtook him.

He sat gazing into the lake. Fragmented reflections of pines wavered delicately. When mist began to descend the hills he headed back, in time to glimpse a group of hikers admiring the house. Pleased, he scanned it himself. Mist had settled on the chimney stacks. The five squat horned blurs looked as though they were playing a secret game, trying to hide behind one another. One, the odd man out, lacked horns.

After dinner Thorpe strolled through the house, sipping malt whisky. Rooms resounded around him. They sounded like an empty stage, where he was playing owner of the house. He strode up the wide stairs, beneath the long straight crack, and halted outside the door next to his.

He wouldn't be able to sleep unless he looked. Besides, he had found the agent's disapproval faintly annoying. If Thorpe wasn't meant to look in the cabinets, why hadn't he been told? Why had one been left ajar?

He strode in, among the crowd of dark high doors. This time, as he opened the cabinet he made sure the padlock didn't slip from its hold. Piled shelves loomed above him as he stooped into the dimness, to peer at the hatbox or whatever it was.

It wasn't locked. It had been, but its fastening was split: a broken padlock lay on top. On the lid, wisps of handwriting spelled *Carps: Trans: C. D.* The obscure inscription was dated three months ago.

Thorpe frowned. Then, standing back, he poked gingerly at the lid with his foot. As he did so, he heard a shifting. It was the padlock, which landed with a thud on the bottom of the cabinet. Unburdened, the lid sprang up at once. Within was nothing but a crack in the metal of the container. He closed the cabinet and then the room, wondering why the metal box appeared to have been forced open.

And why was the date on the lid so recent? Was the man so eccentric that he could make such a mistake? Thorpe lay pondering that and the inscription. Half-dosing, he heard movement in one of the rooms: a trapped bird scrabbling in a chimney? It troubled him almost enough to make him search. But the whisky crept up on him, and he drifted with his thoughts.

How did the arachnologist bring his prizes home—in his pocket, or stowed away with the rest of the livestock on the voyage? Thorpe stood on a dockside, awaiting a package that was being lowered on a rope. Or was it a rope? No, for as it swung close the package unclenched and grabbed him. As its jaws closed on his face he awoke gasping.

In the morning he searched the house, but the bird seemed to have managed to fly. The cracks had multiplied; there was at least one in every room, and two now above the stairs. The scattering of plaster on the staircase looked oddly like earth.

When he heard the agent's car he buttoned his jacket and gave his hair a rapid severe brushing. Damn it, the bird was still trapped; he heard it stir behind him, though there was no hint of it in the mirror. It must be in the chimney, for it sounded far too large to be otherwise invisible.

The agent scrutinised the rooms. Was he looking only for cracks, or for evidence that Thorpe had been peeking? "This is most unexpected," he said as though Thorpe might be responsible. "I don't see how it can be subsidence. I'll have it looked at, though I don't think it's anything serious."

He was dawdling in Thorpe's room, perhaps to reassure himself that Thorpe had done it no injury. "Ah, here he is," he said without warning, and stooped to grope beneath the bed. Who had been skulking there while Thorpe was asleep? The owner of the house, it seemed— or at least a photograph of him, which the agent propped curtly on the bedside table, to supervise the room.

When the agent had left, Thorpe peered up the chimneys. Their furred throats looked empty, but were very dark. The flickering beam of the flashlight he'd found groped upwards. A soft dark mass plummeted towards him. It missed him, and proved to be a fall of soot, but was discouraging enough. In any case, if the bird was still up there, it was silent now.

He confronted the photograph. So that was what an arachnologist looked like: a clump of hair, a glazed expression, an attempt at a beard—the man seemed hypnotised, but no doubt was preoccupied. Thorpe found his dusty presence disconcerting.

Why stand here challenging the photograph? He felt healthy enough to make a circuit of the lake. As he strolled, the inverted landscape drifted with him. He could feel his strength returning, as though he were absorbing it from the hills. For the first time since he left the hospital, his hands looked enlivened by blood.

From the far end of the lake he admired the house. Its inverted chimneys swayed, rooted deep in the water. Suddenly he frowned and squinted. It must be an effect of the distance, that was all—but he kept glancing at the house as he returned along the lakeside. Once he was past the lake he had no chance to doubt. There were only four chimney stacks.

It must have been yesterday's mist that had produced the appearance of a fifth stack, lurking. Nevertheless it was odd. Doubts clung to his mind as he climbed the stairs, until his start of surprise demolished his thoughts. The glass of the photograph was cracked from top to bottom.

He refused to be blamed for that. The agent ought to have left it alone. He laid it carefully on its back on the bedside table. Its crack had made him obsessively aware of the others; some, he was sure, were new—including one in a downstairs window, a crack which, curiously, failed to pass right through the thickness of the pane. The staircase was sprinkled again; the scattering not only looked like, but seemed to smell like, earth. That night, as he lay in bed, he thought he heard dust whispering down from the cracks.

Though he ridiculed thoughts that the house was unsafe, he felt vulnerable. The shifting shadow of a branch looked like a new crack, digging into the wall. In turn, that made the entire room appear to shift. Whenever he woke from fitful dozing, he seemed to glimpse a stealthy movement of the substance of the room. It must be an optical effect, but it reminded him of the way a quivering ornament might betray the presence of an intruder.

Once he awoke, shocked by an image of a tufted face that peered upside down through the window. It infuriated him to have to sit up to make sure the window was blank. Its shutter of night was not reassuring. His subconscious must have borrowed the image of the inversion from the lake, that was all. But the room seemed to be trembling, as he was.

Next day he waited impatiently for the surveyor, or whoever the agent was sending. He rapidly grew irritable. Though it could be nothing but a hangover from his insomnia, to stay in the house made him nervous. Whenever he glanced in a mirror, he felt he was being invisibly watched. The dark fireplaces looked ominous, prosceniums awaiting a cue. At intervals he heard a pattering in other rooms: not of tiny feet, but of the fall of debris from new cracks.

Why was he waiting? He hadn't felt so nervously aimless since the infancy of his career, when he'd loitered, clinging to a single line, in the wings of a provincial theatre. The agent should have given his man a key to let himself in; if he hadn't, that was his problem. Thorpe strode over the slopes that surrounded the lake. He enjoyed the intricately true reflections in the still water, and felt a great deal healthier.

Had the man let himself in? Thorpe seemed to glimpse a face, groping into view at a twilit window. But the only sound in the house was a feeble scraping, which he was unable to locate. The face must have been a fragment of his dream, tangled in his lingering insomnia. His imagination, robbed of sleep, was everywhere now. As he climbed the stairs, he thought a face was spying on him from a dark corner of the ceiling.

When he descended, fallen debris crunched underfoot. During his meal he drank a bottle of wine, as much for distraction as for pleasure. Afterwards he surveyed the house. Yes, the cracks were more numerous; there was one in every surface now, except the floors. Had the older cracks deepened? Somehow he was most disturbed by the dust beneath the cracked windows. It looked like earth, not like pulverised glass at all.

He wished he'd gone into town to stay the night. It was too late now—indeed, the last bus had gone by the time he returned to the house. He was too tired to walk. He certainly couldn't sit outside all night with the mists. It was absurd to think of any other course than going to bed, to try and sleep. But he drained the bottle of whisky before doing so.

He lay listening. Yes, the trapped bird was still there. It sounded even feebler now; it must be dying. If he searched for it he would lose his chance of sleep. Besides, he knew already that he couldn't locate it. Its sounds were so weak that they seemed to shift impossibly, to be fumbling within the fabric of the walls.

He was determined to keep his eyes closed, for the dim room appeared to be jerking. Perhaps this was a delayed effect of his accident. He let his mind drift him out of the room, into memories: the wavering of trees and of their reflections, the comedy sketch of his encounter with the piled cabinet, Carps, Trans.

Darkness gathered like soot on his eyes. A dark mass sank towards him, or he was sinking into dark. He was underground. Around him, unlit corridors dripped sharply. The beam of his flashlight explored the figure that lay before him on dank stone. The figure was pale as a spider's cocoon. As the light fastened on it, it scuttled apart.

When he awoke, he was crying out not at the dream but at his stealthy realisation. He'd solved the inscription in his sleep, at least in part. Eastern Europe was the key. Carps meant Carpathians, Trans was Transylvania. But C. D.—no, what he was thinking was just a bad joke. He refused to take it seriously.

Nevertheless it had settled heavily on his mind. Good God, he'd once had to keep a straight face throughout a version of the play, squashed into a provincial stage: the walls of Castle Dracula had quaked whenever anyone had opened a door, the rubber bat had plummeted into the stalls. C. D. could mean anything—anything except that. Wouldn't it be hilarious if that was what the bemused old spider-man had meant? But in the dark it seemed less than hilarious, for near him in the room, something was stirring.

He groped for the cord of the bedside lamp. It was long and furry, and seemed unexpectedly fat. When he pulled it the light went on, and he saw at once that the cracks were deeper; he had been hearing the fall of debris. Whether the walls had begun to jerk rhythmically, or whether that was a delayed symptom of his accident, he had no time to judge. He must get out while he had the chance. He swung his feet to the floor, and knocked the photograph from the table.

Too bad, never mind, come on! But the shock of its fall delayed him. He glanced at the photograph, which had fallen upside down. The inverted tufted face stared up at him.

All right, it was the face he had dreamed in the window; why shouldn't it be? Just let him drag clothes over his pyjamas—he'd spend the night outside if need be. Quickly, quickly—he thought he could hear the room twitching. The

twitches reminded him not of the stirring of ornaments, but of something else: something of which he was terrified to think.

As he stamped his way into his trousers, refusing to think, he saw that now there were cracks in the floor. Perhaps worse, all the cracks in the room had joined together. He froze, appalled, and heard the scuttling.

What frightened him most was not how large it sounded, but the fact that it seemed not to be approaching over floors. Somehow he had the impression that it hardly inhabited the space of the house. Around him the cracks stood out from their surfaces. They looked too solid for cracks.

The room shook repetitively. The smell of earth was growing. He could hardly keep his balance in the unsteady room; the lines that weren't cracks at all were jerking him towards the door. If he could grab the bed, drag himself along to the window—His mind was struggling to withdraw into itself, to deny what was happening. He was fighting not only to reach the window but to forget the image that had seized his mind: a spider perched at the centre of its web, tugging in its prey.

"Drawing In" originally appeared in the author's 1982 collection *Dark Companions*. The illustration above is from the story's 2004 appearance in the second issue of *Allen K's Inhuman Magazine*.

The *Oxford Companion to English Literature* describes Ramsey Campbell as "Britain's most respected living horror writer". He has been given more awards than any other writer in the field, including the Grand Master Award of the World Horror Convention, the Lifetime Achievement Award of the Horror Writers Association, the Living Legend Award of the International Horror Guild and the World Fantasy Lifetime Achievement Award. In 2015 he was made an Honorary Fellow of Liverpool John Moores University for outstanding services to literature. Among his novels are *The Face That Must Die*, *Incarnate*, *Midnight Sun*, *The Count of Eleven*, *Silent Children*, *The Darkest Part of the Woods*, *The Overnight*, *Secret Story*, *The Grin of the Dark*, *Thieving Fear*, *Creatures of the Pool*, *The Seven Days of Cain*, *Ghosts Know*, *The Kind Folk*, *Think Yourself Lucky*, *Thirteen Days by Sunset Beach* and *The Wise Friend*. He recently brought out his Brichester Mythos trilogy, consisting of *The Searching Dead*, *Born to the Dark* and *The Way of the Worm*. *Needing Ghosts*, *The Last Revelation of Gla'aki*, *The Pretence*, *The Booking* and *The Enigma of the Flat Policeman* are novellas. His collections include *Waking Nightmares*, *Alone with the Horrors*, *Ghosts and Grisly Things*, *Told by the Dead*, *Just Behind You*, *Holes for Faces*, *By the Light of My Skull* and a two-volume retrospective roundup (*Phantasmagorical Stories*). His non-fiction is collected as *Ramsey Campbell, Probably* and *Ramsey's Rambles* (video reviews). *Limericks of the Alarming and Phantasmal* is a history of horror fiction in the form of fifty limericks. (CONTINUED AT BOTTOM OF NEXT PAGE.)

THE HANGING STRANGER

BY

PHILIP K. DICK

AT FIVE O'CLOCK ED LOYCE WASHED UP, TOSSED ON HIS HAT AND COAT, GOT HIS CAR OUT AND HEADED ACROSS TOWN TOWARD HIS TV SALES STORE. HE WAS TIRED. HIS BACK AND SHOULDERS ached from digging dirt out of the basement and wheeling it into the back yard. But for a forty-year-old man he had done okay. Janet could get a new vase with the money he had saved; and he liked the idea of repairing the foundations himself!

It was getting dark. The setting sun cast long rays over the scurrying commuters, tired and grim-faced, women loaded down with bundles and packages, students swarming home from the university, mixing with clerks and businessmen and drab secretaries. He stopped his Packard for a red light and then started it up again. The store had been open without him; he'd arrive just in time to spell the help for dinner, go over the records of the day, maybe even close a couple of sales himself. He drove slowly past the small square of green in the center of the street, the town park. There were no parking places in front of LOYCE TV SALES AND SERVICE. He cursed under his breath and swung the car in a U-turn. Again he passed the little square of green with its lonely drinking fountain and bench and single lamppost.

From the lamppost something was hanging. A shapeless dark bundle, swinging a little with the wind. Like a dummy of some sort. Loyce

(BIO OF RAMSEY CAMPBELL CONTINUED FROM PREVIOUS PAGE.)

His novels *The Nameless*, *Pact of the Fathers* and *The Influence* have been filmed in Spain, where a television series based on *The Nameless* is in development. He is the President of the Society of Fantastic Films.

Ramsey Campbell lives on Merseyside with his wife Jenny. His pleasures include classical music, good food and wine, and whatever's in that pipe. His web site is at www.ramseycampbell.com.

rolled down his window and peered out. What the hell was it? A display of some kind? Sometimes the Chamber of Commerce put up displays in the square.

Again he made a U-turn and brought his car around. He passed the park and concentrated on the dark bundle. It wasn't a dummy. And if it was a display it was a strange kind. The hackles on his neck rose and he swallowed uneasily. Sweat slid out on his face and hands.

It was a body. A human body.

"Look at it!" Loyce snapped. "Come on out here!"

Don Fergusson came slowly out of the store, buttoning his pin-stripe coat with dignity. "This is a big deal, Ed. I can't just leave the guy standing there."

"See it?" Ed pointed into the gathering gloom. The lamppost jutted up against the sky—the post and the bundle swinging from it. "There it is. How the hell long has it been there?" His voice rose excitedly. "What's wrong with everybody? They just walk on past!"

Don Fergusson lit a cigarette slowly. "Take it easy, old man. There must be a good reason, or it wouldn't be there."

"A reason! What kind of a reason?"

Fergusson shrugged. "Like the time the Traffic Safety Council put that wrecked Buick there. Some sort of civic thing. How would I know?"

Jack Potter from the shoe shop joined them. "What's up, boys?"

"There's a body hanging from the lamppost," Loyce said. "I'm going to call the cops."

"They must know about it," Potter said. "Or otherwise it wouldn't be there."

"I got to get back in." Fergusson headed back into the store. "Business before pleasure."

Loyce began to get hysterical. "You see it? You see it hanging there? A man's body! A dead man!"

"Sure, Ed. I saw it this afternoon when I went out for coffee."

"You mean it's been there all afternoon?"

"Sure. What's the matter?" Potter glanced at his watch. "Have to run. See you later, Ed."

Potter hurried off, joining the flow of people moving along the sidewalk. Men and women, passing by the park. A few glanced up curiously at the dark bundle—and then went on. Nobody stopped. Nobody paid any attention.

"I'm going nuts," Loyce whispered. He made his way to the curb and crossed out into traffic, among the cars. Horns honked angrily at him. He gained the curb and stepped up onto the little square of green.

The man had been middle-aged. His clothing was ripped and torn, a gray suit, splashed and caked with dried mud. A stranger. Loyce had never seen him before. Not a local man. His face was partly turned, away, and in the evening wind he spun a little, turning gently, silently. His skin was gouged and cut. Red gashes, deep scratches of congealed blood. A pair of steel-rimmed glasses hung from one ear, dangling foolishly. His eyes bulged. His mouth was open, tongue thick and ugly blue.

"For Heaven's sake," Loyce muttered, sickened. He pushed down his nausea and made his way back to the sidewalk. He was shaking all over, with revulsion—and fear.

Why? Who was the man? Why was he hanging there? What did it mean?

And—why didn't anybody notice?

He bumped into a small man hurrying along the sidewalk. "Watch it!" the man grated, "Oh, it's you, Ed."

Ed nodded dazedly. "Hello, Jenkins."

"What's the matter?" The stationery clerk caught Ed's arm. "You look sick."

"The body. There in the park."

"Sure, Ed." Jenkins led him into the alcove of LOYCE TV SALES AND SERVICE. "Take it easy."

Margaret Henderson from the jewelry store joined them. "Something wrong?"

"Ed's not feeling well."

Loyce yanked himself free. "How can you stand here? Don't you see it? For God's sake—"

"What's he talking about?" Margaret asked nervously.

"The body!" Ed shouted. "The body hanging there!"

More people collected. "Is he sick? It's Ed Loyce. You okay, Ed?"

"The body!" Loyce screamed, struggling to get past them. Hands caught at him. He tore loose. "Let me go! The police! Get the police!"

"Ed—"

"Better get a doctor!"

"He must be sick."

"Or drunk."

Loyce fought his way through the people. He stumbled and half fell. Through a blur he saw rows of faces, curious, concerned, anxious. Men and women halting to see what the disturbance was. He fought past them toward his store. He could see Fergusson inside talking to a man, showing him an Emerson TV set. Pete Foley in the back at the service counter, setting up a new Philco. Loyce shouted at them frantically. His voice was lost in the roar of traffic and the murmur around him.

"Do something!" he screamed. "Don't stand there! Do something! Something's wrong! Something's happened! Things are going on!"

The crowd melted respectfully for the two heavyset cops moving efficiently toward Loyce.

"Name?" the cop with the notebook murmured.

"Loyce." He mopped his forehead wearily. "Edward C. Loyce. Listen to me. Back there—"

"Address?" the cop demanded. The police car moved swiftly through traffic, shooting among the cars and buses. Loyce sagged against the seat, exhausted and confused. He took a deep shuddering breath.

"1368 Hurst Road."

"That's here in Pikeville?"

"That's right." Loyce pulled himself up with a violent effort. "Listen to me. Back there. In the square. Hanging from the lamppost—"

"Where were you today?" the cop behind the wheel demanded.

"Where?" Loyce echoed.

"You weren't in your shop, were you?"

"No." He shook his head. "No, I was home. Down in the basement."

"In the *basement?*"

"Digging. A new foundation. Getting out the dirt to pour a cement frame. Why? What has that to do with—"

"Was anybody else down there with you?"

"No. My wife was downtown. My kids were at school." Loyce looked from one heavyset cop to the other. Hope flicked across his face, wild hope. "You mean because I was down there I missed—the explanation? I didn't get in on it? Like everybody else?"

After a pause the cop with the notebook said: "That's right. You missed the explanation."

"Then it's official? The body—it's *supposed* to be hanging there?"

"It's supposed to be hanging there. For everybody to see."

Ed Loyce grinned weakly. "Good Lord. I guess I sort of went off the deep end. I thought maybe something had happened. You know, something like the Ku Klux Klan. Some kind of violence. Communists or Fascists taking over." He wiped his face with his breast-pocket handkerchief, his hands shaking. "I'm glad to know it's on the level."

"It's on the level." The police car was getting near the Hall of Justice. The sun had set. The streets were gloomy and dark. The lights had not yet come on.

"I feel better," Loyce said. "I was pretty excited there, for a minute. I guess I got all stirred up. Now that I understand, there's no need to take me in, is there?"

The two cops said nothing.

"I should be back at my store. The boys haven't had dinner. I'm all right, now. No more trouble. Is there any need of—"

"This won't take long," the cop behind the wheel interrupted. "A short process. Only a few minutes."

"I hope it's short," Loyce muttered. The car slowed down for a stoplight. "I guess I sort of disturbed the peace. Funny, getting excited like that and—"

Loyce yanked the door open. He sprawled out into the street and rolled to his feet. Cars were moving all around him, gaining speed as the light changed. Loyce leaped onto the curb and raced among the people, burrowing into the swarming crowds. Behind him he heard sounds, shouts, people running.

They weren't cops. He had realized that right away. He knew every cop in Pikeville. A man couldn't own a store, operate a business in a small town for twenty-five years without getting to know all the cops.

They weren't cops—and there hadn't been any explanation. Potter, Fergusson, Jenkins, none of them knew why it was there. They didn't know—and they didn't care. *That* was the strange part.

Loyce ducked into a hardware store. He raced toward the back, past the startled clerks and customers, into the shipping room and through the back door. He tripped over a garbage can and ran up a flight of concrete steps. He climbed over a fence and jumped down on the other side, gasping and panting.

There was no sound behind him. He had got away.

He was at the entrance of an alley, dark and strewn with boards and ruined boxes and tires. He could see the street at the far end. A street light wavered and came on. Men and women. Stores. Neon signs. Cars.

And to his right—the police station.

He was close, terribly close. Past the loading platform of a grocery store rose the white concrete side of the Hall of Justice. Barred windows. The police antenna. A great concrete wall rising up in the darkness. A bad place for him to be near. He was too close. He had to keep moving, get farther away from them.

Them?

Loyce moved cautiously down the alley. Beyond the police station was the City Hall, the old-fashioned yellow structure of wood and gilded brass and broad cement steps. He could see the endless rows of offices, dark windows, the cedars and beds of flowers on each side of the entrance.

And—something else.

Above the City Hall was a patch of darkness, a cone of gloom denser than the surrounding night. A prism of black that spread out and was lost into the sky.

He listened. Good God, he could hear something. Something that made him struggle frantically to close his ears, his mind, to shut out the sound. A buzzing. A distant, muted hum like a great swarm of bees.

Loyce gazed up, rigid with horror. The splotch of darkness, hanging over the City Hall. Darkness so thick it seemed almost solid. *In the vortex something moved.* Flickering shapes. Things, descending from the sky, pausing momentarily above the City Hall, fluttering over it in a dense swarm and then dropping silently onto the roof.

Shapes. Fluttering shapes from the sky. From the crack of darkness that hung above him.

He was seeing—them.

FOR A LONG TIME Loyce watched, crouched behind a sagging fence in a pool of scummy water.

They were landing. Coming down in groups, landing on the roof of the City Hall and disappearing inside. They had wings. Like giant insects of some kind. They flew and fluttered and came to rest—and then crawled crab-fashion, sideways, across the roof and into the building.

He was sickened. And fascinated. Cold night wind blew around him and he shuddered. He was tired, dazed with shock. On the front steps of the City Hall were men, standing here and there. Groups of men coming out of the building and halting for a moment before going on.

Were there more of them?

It didn't seem possible. What he saw descending from the black chasm weren't men. They were alien—from some other world, some other dimension. Sliding through this slit, this break in the shell of the universe. Entering through this gap, winged insects from another realm of being.

On the steps of the City Hall a group of men broke up. A few moved toward a waiting car. One of the remaining shapes started to re-enter the City Hall. It changed its mind and turned to follow the others.

Loyce closed his eyes in horror. His senses reeled. He hung on tight, clutching at the sagging fence. The shape, the man-shape, had abruptly fluttered up and flapped after the others. It flew to the sidewalk and came to rest among them.

Pseudo-men. Imitation men. Insects with ability to disguise themselves as men. Like other insects familiar to Earth. Protective coloration. Mimicry.

Loyce pulled himself away. He got slowly to his feet. It was night. The alley was totally dark. But maybe they could see in the dark. Maybe darkness made no difference to them.

He left the alley cautiously and moved out onto the street. Men and women flowed past, but not so many, now. At the bus-stops stood waiting groups. A huge bus lumbered along the street, its lights flashing in the evening gloom.

Loyce moved forward. He pushed his way among those waiting and when the bus halted he boarded it and took a seat in the rear, by the door. A moment later the bus moved into life and rumbled down the street.

LOYCE RELAXED A LITTLE. He studied the people around him. Dulled, tired faces. People going home from work. Quite ordinary faces. None of them paid any attention to him. All sat quietly, sunk down in their seats, jiggling with the motion of the bus.

The man sitting next to him unfolded a newspaper. He began to read the sports section, his lips moving. An ordinary man. Blue suit. Tie. A businessman, or a salesman. On his way home to his wife and family.

Across the aisle a young woman, perhaps twenty. Dark eyes and hair, a package on her lap. Nylons and heels. Red coat and white angora sweater. Gazing absently ahead of her.

A high school boy in jeans and black jacket.

A great triple-chinned woman with an immense shopping bag loaded with packages and parcels. Her thick face dim with weariness.

Ordinary people. The kind that rode the bus every evening. Going home to their families. To dinner.

Going home—with their minds dead. Controlled, filmed over with the mask of an alien being that had appeared and taken possession of them, their town, their lives. Himself, too. Except that he happened to be deep in his cellar instead of in the store. Somehow, he had been overlooked. They had missed him. Their control wasn't perfect, foolproof.

Maybe there were others.

Hope flickered in Loyce. They weren't omnipotent. They had made a mistake, not got control of him. Their net, their field of control, had passed over him. He had emerged from his cellar as he had gone down. Apparently their power-zone was limited.

A few seats down the aisle a man was watching him. Loyce broke off his chain of thought. A slender man, with dark hair and a small mustache. Well-dressed, brown suit and shiny shoes. A book between his small hands. He was watching Loyce, studying him intently. He turned quickly away.

Loyce tensed. One of *them*? Or—another they had missed?

The man was watching him again. Small dark eyes, alive and clever. Shrewd. A man too shrewd for them—or one of the things itself, an alien insect from beyond.

The bus halted. An elderly man got on slowly and dropped his token into the box. He moved down the aisle and took a seat opposite Loyce.

The elderly man caught the sharp-eyed man's gaze. For a split second something passed between them.

A look rich with meaning.

Loyce got to his feet. The bus was moving. He ran to the door. One step down into the well. He yanked the emergency door release. The rubber door swung open.

"Hey!" the driver shouted, jamming on the brakes. "What the hell—"

Loyce squirmed through. The bus was slowing down. Houses on all sides. A residential district, lawns and tall apartment buildings. Behind him, the bright-eyed man had leaped up. The elderly man was also on his feet. They were coming after him.

Loyce leaped. He hit the pavement with terrific force and rolled against the curb. Pain lapped over him. Pain and a vast tide of blackness. Desperately, he fought it off. He struggled to his knees and then slid down again. The bus had stopped. People were getting off.

Loyce groped around. His fingers closed over something. A rock, lying in the gutter. He crawled to his feet, grunting with pain. A shape loomed before him. A man, the bright-eyed man with the book.

Loyce kicked. The man gasped and fell. Loyce brought the rock down. The man screamed and tried to roll away. "*Stop!* For God's sake listen—"

He struck again. A hideous crunching sound. The man's voice cut off and dissolved in a bubbling wail. Loyce scrambled up and back. The others were there, now. All around him. He ran, awkwardly, down the sidewalk, up a driveway. None of them followed him. They had stopped and were bending over the inert body of the man with the book, the bright-eyed man who had come after him.

Had he made a mistake?

But it was too late to worry about that. He had to get out—away from them. Out of Pikeville, beyond the crack of darkness, the rent between their world and his.

"ED!" JANET LOYCE backed away nervously. "What is it? What—"

Ed Loyce slammed the door behind him and came into the living room. "Pull down the shades. Quick."

Janet moved toward the window. "But—"

"Do as I say. Who else is here besides you?"

"Nobody. Just the twins. They're upstairs in their room. What's happened? You look so strange. Why are you home?"

Ed locked the front door. He prowled around the house, into the kitchen. From the drawer under the sink he slid out the big butcher knife and ran his finger along it. Sharp. Plenty sharp. He returned to the living room.

"Listen to me," he said. "I don't have much time. They know I escaped and they'll be looking for me."

"Escaped?" Janet's face twisted with bewilderment and fear. "Who?"

"The town has been taken over. They're in control. I've got it pretty well figured out. They started at the top, at the City Hall and police department. What they did with the *real* humans they—"

"What are you talking about?"

"We've been invaded. From some other universe, some other dimension. They're insects. Mimicry. And more. Power to control minds. Your mind."

"My mind?"

"Their entrance is *here*, in Pikeville. They've taken over all of you. The whole town—except me. We're up against an incredibly powerful enemy, but they have their limitations. That's our hope. They're limited! They can make mistakes!"

Janet shook her head. "I don't understand, Ed. You must be insane."

"Insane? No. Just lucky. If I hadn't been down in the basement I'd be like all the rest of you." Loyce peered out the window. "But I can't stand here talking. Get your coat."

"My coat?"

"We're getting out of here. Out of Pikeville. We've got to get help. Fight this thing. They *can* be beaten. They're not infallible. It's going to be close—but we may make it if we hurry. Come on!" He grabbed her arm roughly. "Get your coat and call the twins. We're all leaving. Don't stop to pack. There's no time for that."

White-faced, his wife moved toward the closet and got down her coat. "Where are we going?"

Ed pulled open the desk drawer and spilled the contents out onto the floor. He grabbed up a road map and spread it open. "They'll have the highway covered, of course. But there's a back road. To Oak Grove. I got onto it once. It's practically abandoned. Maybe they'll forget about it."

"The old Ranch Road? Good Lord—it's completely closed. Nobody's supposed to drive over it."

"I know." Ed thrust the map grimly into his coat. "That's our best chance. Now call down the twins and let's get going. Your car is full of gas, isn't it?"

Janet was dazed.

"The Chevy? I had it filled up yesterday afternoon." Janet moved toward the stairs. "Ed, I—"

"Call the twins!" Ed unlocked the front door and peered out. Nothing stirred. No sign of life. All right so far.

"Come on downstairs," Janet called in a wavering voice. "We're—going out for awhile."

"Now?" Tommy's voice came.

"Hurry up," Ed barked. "Get down here, both of you."

Tommy appeared at the top of the stairs. "I was doing my home work. We're starting fractions. Miss Parker says if we don't get this done—"

"You can forget about fractions." Ed grabbed his son as he came down the stairs and propelled him toward the door. "Where's Jim?"

"He's coming."

Jim started slowly down the stairs. "What's up, Dad?"

"We're going for a ride."

"A ride? Where?"

Ed turned to Janet. "We'll leave the lights on. And the TV set. Go turn it on." He pushed her toward the set. "So they'll think we're still—"

He heard the buzz. And dropped instantly, the long butcher knife out. Sickened, he saw it coming down the stairs at him, wings a blur of motion as it aimed itself. It still bore a vague resemblance to Jimmy. It was small, a baby one. A brief glimpse—the thing hurtling at him, cold, multi-lensed inhuman eyes. Wings, body still clothed in yellow T-shirt and jeans, the mimic outline still stamped on it. A strange half-turn of its body as it reached him. What was it doing?

A stinger.

Loyce stabbed wildly at it. It retreated, buzzing frantically. Loyce rolled and crawled toward the door. Tommy and Janet stood still as statues, faces blank. Watching without expression. Loyce stabbed again. This time the knife connected. The thing shrieked and faltered. It bounced against the wall and fluttered down.

Something lapped through his mind. A wall of force, energy, an alien mind probing into him. He was suddenly paralyzed. The mind entered his own, touched against him briefly, shockingly. An utterly alien presence, settling over him—and then it flickered out as the thing collapsed in a broken heap on the rug.

It was dead. He turned it over with his foot. It was an insect, a fly of some kind. Yellow T-shirt, jeans. His son Jimmy.... He closed his mind tight. It was too late to think about that. Savagely he scooped up his knife and headed toward the door. Janet and Tommy stood stone-still, neither of them moving.

The car was out. He'd never get through. They'd be waiting for him. It was ten miles on foot. Ten long miles over rough ground, gullies and open fields and hills of uncut forest. He'd have to go alone.

Loyce opened the door. For a brief second he looked back at his wife and son. Then he slammed the door behind him and raced down the porch steps.

A moment later he was on his way, hurrying swiftly through the darkness toward the edge of town.

THE EARLY MORNING sunlight was blinding. Loyce halted, gasping for breath, swaying back and forth. Sweat ran down in his eyes. His clothing was torn, shredded by the brush and thorns through which he had crawled. Ten miles—on his hands and knees. Crawling, creeping through the night. His shoes were mud-caked. He was scratched and limping, utterly exhausted.

But ahead of him lay Oak Grove.

He took a deep breath and started down the hill. Twice he stumbled and fell, picking himself up and trudging on. His ears rang. Everything receded and wavered. But he was there. He had got out, away from Pikeville.

A farmer in a field gaped at him. From a house a young woman watched in wonder. Loyce reached the road and turned onto it. Ahead of him was a gasoline station and a drive-in. A couple of trucks, some chickens pecking in the dirt, a dog tied with a string.

The white-clad attendant watched suspiciously as he dragged himself up to the station. "Thank God." He caught hold of the wall. "I didn't think I was going to make it. They followed me most of the way. I could hear them buzzing. Buzzing and flitting around behind me."

"What happened?" the attendant demanded. "You in a wreck? A hold-up?"

Loyce shook his head wearily. "They have the whole town. The City Hall and the police station. They hung a man from the lamppost. That was the first thing I saw. They've got all the roads blocked. I saw them hovering over the cars coming in. About four this morning I got beyond them. I knew it right away. I could feel them leave. And then the sun came up."

The attendant licked his lip nervously. "You're out of your head. I better get a doctor."

"Get me into Oak Grove," Loyce gasped. He sank down on the gravel. "We've got to get started—cleaning them out. Got to get started right away."

THEY KEPT a tape recorder going all the time he talked. When he had finished the Commissioner snapped off the recorder and got to his feet. He stood for a moment, deep in thought. Finally he got out his cigarettes and lit up slowly, a frown on his beefy face.

"You don't believe me," Loyce said.

The Commissioner offered him a cigarette. Loyce pushed it impatiently away. "Suit yourself." The Commissioner moved over to the window and stood for a time looking out at the town of Oak Grove. "I believe you," he said abruptly.

Loyce sagged. "Thank God."

"So you got away." The Commissioner shook his head. "You were down in your cellar instead of at work. A freak chance. One in a million."

Loyce sipped some of the black coffee they had brought him. "I have a theory," he murmured.

"What is it?"

"About them. Who they are. They take over one area at a time. Starting at the top—the highest level of authority. Working down from there in a widening circle. When they're firmly in control they go on to the next town. They spread, slowly, very gradually. I think it's been going on for a long time."

"A long time?"

"Thousands of years. I don't think it's new."

"Why do you say that?"

"When I was a kid.... A picture they showed us in Bible League. A religious picture—an old print. The enemy gods, defeated by Jehovah. Moloch, Beelzebub, Moab, Baalim, Ashtaroth—"

"So?"

"They were all represented by figures." Loyce looked up at the Commissioner. "Beelzebub was represented as—a giant fly."

The Commissioner grunted. "An old struggle."

"They've been defeated. The Bible is an account of their defeats. They make gains—but finally they're defeated."

"Why defeated?"

"They can't get everyone. They didn't get me. And they never got the Hebrews. The Hebrews carried the message to the whole world. The realization of the danger. The two men on the bus. I think they understood. Had escaped, like I did." He clenched his fists. "I killed one of them. I made a mistake. I was afraid to take a chance."

The Commissioner nodded. "Yes, they undoubtedly had escaped, as you did. Freak accidents. But the rest of the town was firmly in control." He turned from the window. "Well, Mr. Loyce. You seem to have figured everything out."

"Not everything. The hanging man. The dead man hanging from the lamppost. I don't understand that. *Why?* Why did they deliberately hang him there?"

"That would seem simple." The Commissioner smiled faintly. *"Bait."*

Loyce stiffened. His heart stopped beating. "Bait? What do you mean?"

"To draw you out. Make you declare yourself. So they'd know who was under control—and who had escaped."

Loyce recoiled with horror. "Then they *expected* failures! They anticipated—" He broke off. "They were ready with a trap."

"And you showed yourself. You reacted. You made yourself known." The Commissioner abruptly moved toward the door. "Come along, Loyce. There's a lot to do. We must get moving. There's no time to waste."

Loyce started slowly to his feet, numbed. "And the man. *Who was the man?* I never saw him before. He wasn't a local man. He was a stranger. All muddy and dirty, his face cut, slashed—"

There was a strange look on the Commissioner's face as he answered. "Maybe," he said softly, "you'll understand that, too. Come along with me, Mr. Loyce." He held the door open, his eyes gleaming. Loyce caught a glimpse of the street in front of the police station. Policemen, a platform of some sort. A telephone pole—and a rope! "Right this way," the Commissioner said, smiling coldly.

As THE SUN SET, the vice-president of the Oak Grove Merchants' Bank came up out of the vault, threw the heavy time locks, put on his hat and coat, and hurried outside onto the sidewalk. Only a few people were there, hurrying home to dinner.

"Good night," the guard said, locking the door after him.

"Good night," Clarence Mason murmured. He started along the street toward his car. He was tired. He had been working all day down in the vault, examining the layout of the safety deposit boxes to see if there was room for another tier. He was glad to be finished.

At the corner he halted. The street lights had not yet come on. The street was dim. Everything was vague. He looked around—and froze.

From the telephone pole in front of the police station, something large and shapeless hung. It moved a little with the wind.

What the hell was it?

Mason approached it warily. He wanted to get home. He was tired and hungry. He thought of his wife, his kids, a hot meal on the dinner table. But there was something about the dark bundle, something ominous and ugly. The light was bad; he couldn't tell what it was. Yet it drew him on, made him move closer for a better look. The shapeless thing made him uneasy. He was frightened by it. Frightened—and fascinated.

And the strange part was that nobody else seemed to notice it.

"The Hanging Stranger" first appeared in the December 1953 issue of Science Fiction Adventures Magazine, *along with an illustration by H. R. Smith.*

Award-winning American author Philip K. Dick is perhaps better known to film buffs for several movies adapted from his inventive SF tales, most notably Blade Runner *and* Total Recall. *Dick often explored philosophical, social and political themes in a body of work encompassing 44 novels and 121 short stories. Dick was greatly interested in metaphysics, religion and the nature of identity.*

TABBY

By WINSTON MARKS

APRIL 18, 1956

DEAR BEN: IT BREAKS MY HEART YOU DIDN'T SIGN ON FOR THIS TRIP. YOUR REPLACEMENT, WHO *CALLS* HIMSELF AN ICHTHYOLOGIST, HAS ONLY ONE TALENT THAT PERTAINS TO FISH—HE DRINKS LIKE ONE. There are nine of us in the expedition, and every one of us is fed up with this joker, Cleveland, already. We've only been on the island a week, and he's gone native, complete with beard, bare feet and bone laziness. He slops around the lagoon like a beachcomber and hasn't brought in a decent specimen yet.

The island is a bit of paradise, though. Wouldn't be hard to let yourself relax under the palms all day instead of collecting blisters and coral gashes out in the bright sun of the atoll. No complaints, however. We aren't killing ourselves, and our little camp is very comfortable. The portable lab is working out fine, and the screened sleeping tent-houses have solved the one big nuisance we've suffered before: *Insects.* I think an entomologist would find more to keep him busy here than we will.

Your ankle should be useable by the time our next supply plane from Hawaii takes off. If you apply again at the Foundation right now I'm sure Sellers and the others will help me get rid of Cleveland, and there'll be an open berth here.

Got to close now. Our amphib jets off in an hour for the return trip. Hope this note is properly seductive. Come to the isles, boy, and live!

—Cordially, Fred

MAY 26, 1956

DEAR BEN: Now, aren't you sorry you didn't take my advice?!!!! I'm assuming you read the papers, and also, that too tight a censorship hasn't clamped down on this thing yet. Maybe I'm assuming too much on the latter. Anyhow, here's a detailed version from an actual eyewitness.

That's right! I was right there on the beach when the "saucer" landed. Only it looked more like a king-size poker chip. About six feet across and eight inches thick with a little hemispherical dome dead center on top. It hit offshore about seventy-five yards with a splash that sounded like a whale's tail. Jenner and I dropped our seine, waded to shore and started running along the beach to get opposite it. Cleveland came out of the shade and helped us launch a small boat.

We got within twenty feet of the thing when it started moving out, slowly, just fast enough to keep ahead of us. I was in the bow looking right at it when the lid popped open with a sound like a cork coming out of a wine bottle. The little dome had split. Sellers quit rowing and we all hit the bottom of the boat. I peeked over the gunwale right away, and it's a good thing. All that came out of the dome was a little cloud of flies, maybe a hundred or so, and the breeze picked them up and blew them over us inshore so fast that Cleveland and Sellers never did see them.

I yelled at them to look, but by then the flies were in mingling with the local varieties of sudden itch, and they figured I was seeing things. Cleveland, though, listened with the most interest. It develops that his specialty *is* entomology. He took this job because he was out of work. Don't know how he bluffed his way past the

Foundation, but here he is, and it looks like he might be useful after all.

He was all for going ashore, but Sellers and I rowed after the white disk for awhile until it became apparent we couldn't catch it. It's a good thing we didn't. A half hour later, Olafsen caught up to it in the power launch. We were watching from shore. It was about a half mile out when Ole cut his speed. Luckily he was alone. We had yelled at him to pick us up and take us along, but he was too excited to stop. He passed us up, went out there and—boom!

It wasn't exactly an A-bomb, but the spray hit us a half mile away, and the surface wave swamped us.

Sellers radioed the whole incident to Honolulu right away, and they are sending out a plane with a diver, but we don't think he'll find anything. Things really blew! So far we haven't even found any identifiable driftwood from the launch, let alone Ole's body or traces of the disk.

Meanwhile, Cleveland has come to believe my story, and he's out prowling around with an insect net. Most energy he's shown in weeks.

MAY 28—Looks like this letter will be delayed a bit. We are under quarantine. The government plane came this morning. They sent along a diver, two reporters and a navy officer. The diver went down right away, but it's several hundred feet deep out there and slants off fast. This island is the tip of a sunken mountain, and the diver gave up after less than an hour. Personally I think a couple of sharks scared him off, but he claims there's so much vegetable ruck down there he couldn't expect to find anything smaller than the launch's motor.

Cleveland hasn't found anything unusual in his bug net, but everyone is excited here, and you can guess why.

When the "saucer" reports stopped cold about a year ago, you'll remember, it made almost as much news for a while as when they were first spotted. Now the people out here are speculating that maybe this disc thing came from the same source as the saucers, after they had a chance to look us over, study our ecology and return to their base. Cleveland is the one who started this trend of thought with his obsession that the flies I reported seeing are an attack on our planet from someone out in space.

Commander Clawson, the navy officer, doesn't know what to think. He won't believe Cleveland until he produces a specimen of the "fly-from-Mars," but then he turns around and contradicts himself by declaring a temporary quarantine until he gets further orders from Honolulu.

The reporters are damned nuisances. They're turning out reams of Sunday supplement-type stuff and pestering the devil out of Sparks to let them wire it back, but our radio is now under navy control, too.

Sure is crowded in the bunk-house with the six additional people, but no one will sleep outside the screen.

MAY 29—Cleveland thinks he has his specimen. He went out at dawn this morning and came in before breakfast. He's quit drinking but he hasn't slept in three days now and looks like hell. I thought he was getting his fancy imagination out of the bottle, but the soberer he got the more worried he looked over this "invasion" idea of his.

Now he claims that his catch is definitely a sample of something new under our particular sun. He hustled it under a glass and started classifying it. It filled the bill for the arthropods, class *Insecta*. It looked to me, in fact, just like a small, ordinary blowfly, except that it has green wings. And I mean *green*, not just a little iridescent color.

Cleve very gently pulled one wing off and we looked at it under low power. There is more similarity to a leaf than to a wing. In the bug's back is a tiny pocket, a sort of reservoir of the green stuff, and Cleve's dissection shows tiny veins running up into the wings. It seems to be a closed system with no connection with the rest of the body except the restraining membrane.

Cleveland now rests his extraterrestrial origin theory on an idea that the green stuff is chlorophyll. If it *is* chlorophyll, either Cleve is right or else he's discovered a new class of arthropods. In other respects, the critter is an ordinary biting and sucking bug with the potentials of about a deerfly for making life miserable. The high-power lens showed no sign of unusual or malignant microscopic life inside or out of the thing. Cleve can't say how bad a bite would be, because he doesn't have his entomologist kit with him, and he can't analyze the secretion from the poison gland.

The commander has let him radio for a botanist and some micro-analysis equipment.

Everyone was so pitched up that Cleve's findings have been rather anti-climactic. I guess we were giving more credence to the space-invader theory than we thought. But even if Cleve has proved it, this fly doesn't look like much to be frightened over. The reporters are clamoring to be let loose, but the quarantine still holds.

JUNE 1—By the time the plane with the botanist arrived we were able to gather all the specimens of *Tabanidae viridis* (Cleveland's designation) that he wanted. Seems like every tenth flying creature you meet is a green "Tabby" now.

The botanist helped Cleve and me set up the bio kit, and he confirmed Cleve's guess. The green stuff is chlorophyll. Which makes Tabby quite a bug.

Kyser, the youngest reporter, volunteered to let a Tabby bite him. It did without too much coaxing. Now he has a little, itchy bump on his wrist, and he's happily banging away at his typewriter on a story titled, "I Was Bitten by the Bug from Space!" That was hours ago, and we haven't learned anything sinister about the green fly except that it does have a remarkable breeding ability.

One thing the reporter accomplished: we can go outside the screened quarters now without wondering about catching space-typhus.

JUNE 2—The quarantine was probably a pretty good idea. Cleve has turned up some dope on Tabby's life cycle that makes us glad all over that we are surrounded by a thousand miles of salt water. Tabby's adult life is only a couple of days, but she is viviparous, prolific (some thousand young at a sitting), and her green little microscopic babies combine the best survival features of spores and plankton, minus one: they

don't live in salt water. But they do very well almost anyplace else. We have watched them grow on hot rocks, leaves, in the sand and best of all, filtered down a little into the moist earth.

They grow incredibly fast with a little sun, so the chlorophyll is biologically justified in the life-cycle. This puzzled us at first, because the adult Tabby turns into a blood-sucking little brute. Deprived of any organic matter, our bottled specimens die in a short time, in or out of the sunlight, indicating the green stuff doesn't provide them with much if any nourishment after they are full-grown.

Now we are waiting for a supply of assorted insecticides to find the best controls over the pests. The few things we had on hand worked quite well, but I guess they aren't forgetting our sad experience with DDT a few years back.

The Tabbies now outnumber all the other insects here, and most outside work has been halted. The little green devils make life miserable outside the tent-houses. We have built another screened shelter to accommodate the latest arrivals. We are getting quite a fleet of amphibian aircraft floating around our lagoon. No one will be allowed to return until we come up with all the answers to the question of controlling our insect invasion.

Cleveland is trying to convince Sellers and the commander that we should get out and send in atomic fire to blow the whole island into the sea. They forwarded his suggestion to the U. N. committee which now has jurisdiction, but they wired back that if the insect is from space, we couldn't stop other discs from landing on the mainlands. Our orders are to study the bug and learn all we can.

Opinion is mixed here. I can't explain the flying disc unless it's extraterrestrial, but why would an invader choose an isolated spot like this to attack? Cleve says this is just a "test patch" and probably under surveillance. But why such an innocuous little fly if they mean business?

The newsmen are really bored now. They see no doom in the bugs, and since they can't file their stories they take a dim view of the quarantine. They have gotten up an evening fishing derby with the crew members of the planes. Have to fish after dusk. The Tabbies bite too often as long as the sun is up.

Cleve has turned into a different man. He is soft-spoken and intense. His hands tremble so much that he is conducting most of his work by verbal directions with the botanist and me to carry them out. When his suggestion about blowing up the atoll was turned down he quit talking except to conduct his work. If things were half as ominous as he makes out we'd be pretty worried.

JUNE 4—The spray planes got here and none too soon. We were running out of drinking water. The Tabbies got so thick that even at night a man would get stung insane if he went outside the screen.

The various sprays all worked well. This evening the air is relatively clear. Incidentally, the birds have been having a feast. Now the gulls are congregating to help us out like they did the Mormons in the cricket plague. The spiders are doing all right for themselves, too. In fact, now that we have sprayed the place, the spiders and their confounded webs are the biggest nuisance we have to contend with. They are getting fat and sassy. Spin their webs between your legs if you stand still a minute too long. Remind me of real

estate speculators in a land boom, the little bastardly opportunists. As you might gather, I don't care for brothers *Arachnidae*. They make everyone else nervous, too. Strangely, Cleveland, the entomologist, gets the worst jolt out of them. He'll stand for minutes at the screen watching them spin their nasty webs and skipping out to

de-juice a stray Tabby that the spray missed. And he'll mutter to himself and scowl and curse them. It is hard to include them as God's creatures.

Cleve still isn't giving out with the opinions. He works incessantly and has filled two notebooks full of data. Looks to me like our work is almost done.

AUGUST 7, YEAR OF OUR LORD 1956—To whom it will never concern: I can no longer make believe this is addressed to my friend, Ben Tobin. Cleveland has convinced me of the implications of our tragedy here. But somehow it gives me some crazy, necessary ray of hope to keep this journal until the end.

I think the real horror of this thing started to penetrate to me about June 6. Our big spray job lasted less than 24 hours, and on that morning I was watching for the planes to come in for a second try at it when I noticed the heavy spider webbing in the upper tree foliage. As I looked a gull dove through the trees, mouth open, eating Tabbies. Damned if the webs didn't foul his wings. At first he tore at them bravely and it looked like he was trying to swim in thin mud—sort of slow motion. Then he headed into a thick patch, slewed around at right angles and did a complete flip. Instantly three mammoth spiders the size of my fist pounced out on him and trussed him up before he could tear loose with his feet.

His pitiful squawking was what made me feel that horror for the first time. And the scene was repeated more and more often. The planes dusted us with everything they had, and it cut down the Tabbies pretty well again, but it didn't touch the spiders, of course.

And then our return radio messages started getting very vague. We were transmitting Cleve's data hourly as he compiled it, and we had been getting ordinary chatter and speculation from the Honolulu operator at the end of our message. That stopped on the sixth of June. Since then, we've had only curt acknowledgements of our data and sign-offs.

At the same time, we noticed that complete censorship on news of our situation and progress apparently hit all the long-wave radio broadcasts. Up to that time the newscasts had been feeding out a dilute and very cautious pablum about our fight against Tabby. Immediately when we noticed this news blindspot, Cleve went all to pieces and started drinking again.

Cleve, Sellers, and I had the lab tent to ourselves, having moved our bunks in there, so we got a little out of touch with the others. It wasn't the way Sellers and I liked it, but none of us liked the trip from lab to living quarters any more, although it was only fifty feet or so.

Then Sparks moved in, too. For the same reason. He said it was getting on his nerves running back and forth to the lab to pick up our outgoing bulletins. So he shifted the generator, radio gear and all over to a corner of the lab and brought in his bunk.

By the tenth of June we could see that the spraying was a losing battle. And it finally took the big tragedy to drive home the truth that was all about us already. When the crew got ready to go out to their planes on the eleventh, everyone except the four of us in the lab tent was drafted to help clear webs between the tents and the beach. We could hear them shouting from tent to tent as they made up their work party. We could no longer see across the distance. Everywhere outside, vision was obscured by the grayish film of webs on which little droplets caught the tropical sun like a million tiny mirrors. In the shade it was like trying to peer through thin milk, with the vicious, leggy little shadows skittering about restlessly.

As usual in the morning, the hum of the Tabbies had risen above the normal jungle buzzing, and this morning it was the loudest we'd heard it.

Well, we heard the first screen door squeak open, and someone let out a whoop as the group moved out with brooms, palm fronds and sticks to snatch a path through the nightmare of spider webs. The other two doors opened and slammed, and we could hear many sounds of deep disgust voiced amid the grunts and thrashings.

They must have been almost to the beach when the first scream reached us. Cleve had been listening in fascination, and the awful sound tore him loose of his senses. He screamed back. The rest of us had to sit on him to quiet him. Then the others outside all began screaming—not words, just shattering screams of pure terror, mixed with roars of pain and anger. Soon there was no more anger. Just horror. And in a few minutes they died away.

Sellers and Sparks and I looked at each other. Cleve had vomited and passed out. Sparks got out Cleve's whiskey, and we spilled half of it trying to get drinks into us.

Sparks snapped out of it first. He didn't try to talk to us. He just went to his gear, turned on the generator and warmed up the radio. He told Honolulu what had happened as we had heard it.

When he finished, he keyed over for an acknowledgment. The operator said to hold on for a minute. Then he said they would *try* to dispatch an air task force to get us off, but they couldn't be sure just when.

While this was coming in Cleve came to his senses and listened. He was deadly calm now, and when Honolulu finished he grabbed the mike from Sparks, cut in the TX and asked, "Are they landing discs on the mainlands?"

The operator answered, "Sorry, that's classified."

"For God's sake," Cleve demanded, "if you are ready to write us off you can at least answer our questions. Are there any of the green sonsofbitches on the mainland?"

There was another little pause, and then, "Yes."

That was all. Sparks ran down the batteries trying to raise them again for more answers, but no response. When the batteries went dead he checked the generator that had kicked off. It was out of gasoline. The drums were on the beach. Now we were without lights, power, and juice for our other radios.

We kept alive the first few days by staying half drunk. Then Cleve's case of whiskey gave out and we began to get hungry. Sparks and Sellers set fire to one of our straw-ticking mattresses and used it as a torch to burn their way over to the supply tent about thirty feet away. It worked fairly well. The silky webs flashed into nothing as the flames hit them, but they wouldn't support the fire, and other webs streamed down behind the two. They had to burn another mattress to get back with a few cases of food.

Then we dug a well under the floor of our tent. Hit water within a few feet. But when we cut through the screen floor it cost us sentry duty. We had to have one person awake all night long to stamp on the spiders that slipped in around the edge of the well.

Through all of this Cleveland has been out on his feet. He has just stood and stared out through the screen all day. We had to force him to eat. He didn't snap out of it until this morning.

Sparks couldn't stand our radio silence any longer, so he talked Sellers into helping him make a dash for the gas drums on the beach. They set fire to two mattresses and disappeared into the tunnel of burned webs that tangled and caved in behind them.

When they were gone, Cleveland suddenly came out of his trance and put a hand on my shoulder. I thought for a moment he was going to jump me, but his eyes were calm. He said, "Well, Fred, are you convinced now that we've been attacked?"

I said, "It makes no sense to me at all. Why these little flies?"

Cleve said, "They couldn't have done better so easily. They studied our ecology well. They saw that our greatest potential enemy was the insect population, and the most vicious part of it was the spider. *Tabanidae viridis* was not sent just to plague us with horsefly bites. Tabby was sent to multiply and feed the arachnids. There are durable species in all climates. And if our botanist were still alive he could explain in detail how long our plant life can last under this spider infestation.

"Look for yourself," he said pointing outside. "Not only are the regular pollenating insects doomed, but the density of those webs will choke out even wind pollinated grains."

He stared down our shallow well hole and stamped on a small, black, flat spider that had slithered under the screening. "I suppose you realize the spiders got the others. Down here in the tropics the big varieties could do it by working together. Sellers and Sparks won't return. Sounds like they got through all right, but they'll be bitten so badly they won't try to get back."

And even as he spoke we heard one of the aircraft engines start up. The sound was muffled as under a bed quilt.

Cleve said, "I don't blame them. I'd rather die in the sun, too. The beach should be fairly clear of webs. We've got one mattress left. What do you say?"

He's standing there now holding the mattress with the ticking sticking out. I don't think one torch will get us through. But it will be worth a try for one more look at the sun.

👽 👽 👽

"Tabby" first appeared in the March 1954 issue of IF: Worlds of Science Fiction, *with an illustration by Rudolph Palais.*

Winston K. Marks (1915–1979) wrote over five dozen short stories, nearly all of which were published in science fiction digests during a brief period from 1953 to 1959. In regards to his writing, he once stated that in the eyes of his neighbors, he was unemployed; which is ironic because, when it came to jobs, Marks seems to have done it all. "I was not born a writer," Marks wrote, "unless you would say also that I was born a grocery clerk, bellhop, sales-manager, aircraft pilot, soldier, sailor, trade-paper editor, huckster, advertising man, columnist, linoleum layer, electronics technician, political campaign manager, chemical-sacker, typist, sugar-loader, timekeeper, amateur semanticist and public speaker, fencing enthusiast, Lion, Elk and Episcopal—for I am or have been all these things. What I intended to be … was a doctor. My studies were interrupted by lack of money, brains or devotion to study—I forget which, but it was some such trivial thing."

COMPLETE YOUR COLLECTION!

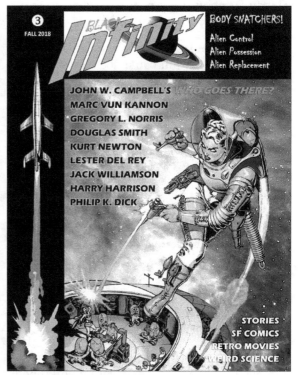

Black Infinity: Body Snatchers (#3) ISBN-13: 978-1732434424
Black Infinity: Strange Dimensions (#4) ISBN-13: 978-1732434431

WAXWORMS
BY JAMES DORR

HIS HEADACHES HAD COME BACK. HE'D ALWAYS HAD HEADACHES, OFF AND ON, EVER SINCE THAT SUMMER WHEN THEIR PARENTS DIED. WHEN THEY'D SEEN THE FLYING SAUCERS—WHATEVER IT *WAS* THEY'D SEEN. THEN, LATER ON, HIS TOUR IN THE ARMY HADN'T HELPED EITHER.

Nor was the fact that his sister was dying.

And Roger Sexton could see she was dying even before he climbed down from his rented jeep to greet her. She stood, half shadowed, on the ramshackle porch of her farmhouse, dressed in a '60s-style print blouse and skirt, not offering to help him unload his gear. He saw how pale she was, how thin—she'd always been slender, but, before, he would have considered her figure athletic. Now it was just thin.

"Marina," he called to her. "I got your letter."

"Yes," she said. Her still dark brown hair floated on the mountain breeze as she finally stepped down to the pathway. "Thank you for coming."

"Have you seen a doctor?"

His sister laughed.

LATER SHE DID DESCRIBE seeing a doctor as they sat at the kitchen table drinking herb tea—another holdover from their young childhood. Their parents, in turn, had grown up in the 1940s and '50s, the years of the saucer fear.

Lived with accounts of alien pilots found in the desert, of close encounters, of air force coverups. Told their children.

So much was forgotten, so much repressed really, but now he remembered more. He and Marina would laugh, of course—children born in the '60s, raised in the '70s, sophisticated even if sharing their parents' values. He'd dreamed of the priesthood back then in high school, for when he grew up. She'd wanted to be a nurse, or else get married straight out of college, even if she was somewhat of a tomboy. And their parents told of the saucer they'd seen once when they were first dating, high in the sky. He and his sister had been in the back seat, watching the car's headlights pierce through the darkness, illuminating clouds of tiny moths hovering just above the road's surface. And their father continued about how, in a farmer's field several days after, he'd come across the circle of burned crops, flattened and withered— what he called a "second kind" encounter— where he was convinced the saucer had landed.

But dreams never came true.

"I said, 'waxy discharges.'"

"I beg your pardon?"

Marina laughed. "You haven't been listening. You've been remembering, haven't you, Roger? That night. The car crash. How we were thrown clear. More will come back later, as it's been doing with me since I came here. But what I was saying, I went to the doctor. I told him about the sounds I was hearing, the ringing sensations. He looked at my ears, but all he said was I had waxy discharges. Too much wax in them—so much it was flowing out. He cleaned them for me and gave me medicine, but three weeks later the wax was back. And the sounds—and sights with them."

She laughed again, then her voice turned serious. "Roger, I know I'm going to die. I can feel myself weakening. But from that point on I was through with doctors."

Roger nodded. "What kinds of sights and sounds?"

"You'll hear them too, Roger. I'm sure you'll hear them. They come with the memories."

He strained his ears as she smiled in encouragement. Now he heard—sort of a sound of crunching? A kind of eating noise, so faint as to be almost imperceptible, coming from outside. From within the rich West Virginia soil beneath Marina's garden.

A sound of crops growing.

"Yes," he whispered.

"Why did you want me here?" he asked the next day. He and Marina were outside, working, she dressed now in jeans and a halter top. "I mean, I know, I *should* be here with you. But is it just to help with your garden?"

"Roger," she said, "do you remember? How I first found this place? How it was so cheap? And then how you helped me out with the payments?"

"Yes," he said. He'd been in the army, being trained to fly helicopters, when she'd written. He'd almost seen it when he read her letters. The damage. The reason the farmer was selling.

Tent caterpillars—webworms, the local people called them—had laid waste the area maybe two years before Marina found it. They'd come like an army—like an Old Testament plague from the Bible—eating—destroying. Weaving their silken shrouds over the fruit trees. Stripping the branches.

He'd looked them up afterward, after he'd completed his hitch and gone back to civilian life. How the worms *did* come like Biblical plagues, every ten years or so. Periodically, like with people and new generations.

He'd looked up, on geological maps, the section of country his sister would live in, only then realizing where it was.

But at the time, he'd sent her his army pay when she'd convinced him she was determined to buy the land anyway. Not to farm it, but just to be alone—she'd never married, despite her own dreams—and plant a small garden just for her own use. To be independent.

And he'd had a vision of what it had looked like. How she'd described it. The webworms long passed on, but the apple and pear and cherry trees lying shattered. The truck crops still withered. The land all in brownness, like some distant desert. Like the grain circle their father had claimed to have seen that day so long ago, except that this "landing" had covered acres.

And now he saw, also, the memory they both shared. The night on the mountain, the winding highway scarcely ten miles away from where they now stood. Their father's voice droning on, filling the car as they drove east to where they would spend their vacation, keeping to back roads because their father felt the Interstates ruined the scenery.

His voice. The moths outside. His stories of *other* sightings than his and their mother's, some involving actual creatures that flew in the saucers. The Flatwoods Monster in 1952, here in *these* mountains, in Braxton County. The 1961 encounter in Portsmouth, New Hampshire, of Barney and Betty Hill. The Pascagoula Creatures of 1973, in Mississippi....

His and Marina's trying to sleep, not wanting to listen. The woods, dark, on either side of their privately lit double-tunnel, seeming to close in...

...when *it* rose before them. Glowing, pulsing, as big as a football field. Up, from a notch between two ridge lines, it straddled the highway, seemingly missing them only by inches as it passed overhead.

Jarring them with its sound.

Shrill. Ululating.

The car's front wheels twisting—their father battling to stay on the road.

And the *second* one louder still, after he and Marina had left the wreck site, still in a daze, climbing the eastern slope—more memory came back—thinking somehow it might help to find out where the first of the huge, glowing disks had come from.

Both of them screaming....

"Are you okay, Roger?"

He blinked. He opened his eyes. He gazed at the lush trees that surrounded his sister's garden. New growth. New greenery.

He *heard* the growing.

His sister's voice called again. "Roger," she said, "I was just asking you. Do you remember? How, even after you left the army, you sent your reserve pay?"

"Yes," he said. "And later, my combat pay."

"That's why I need you here with me now," she said. She jumped up from the crop row she'd been weeding and kissed him on the cheek. "Roger, I told you the memories come back here. But only in pieces. I want you to help me remember it *all*."

THE FOLLOWING WEEKS they collaborated, sharing their memories along with the farm work. The work was hard, especially now with his sister weakening, less and less able to do her full share. He remembered Marina as she'd been back then, nearly two years older than him, and the family's athlete, while he'd been the bookworm. He'd tried to compete with her— baseball, hiking, even touch football during the autumns when they were growing up. But whatever they did that was physical, she took the lead in.

Until that summer—she'd just finished her first year of college while he was already sending his applications out, hoping to get a scholarship to Notre Dame—when they woke up in the full light of morning on top of the ridge. They looked around them—the trees, the ivy, the windswept branches. They didn't remember....

Frightened, they crashed back down the ridge, getting hopelessly lost, knowing only that *something* had happened. A vague recollection ... their parents ... the highway....

And then, two days later, him in the lead now, practically falling into the arms of the state policeman. An aunt and uncle called in from Kansas. The funeral. Closed coffins. Then the long trip west with their relatives to stay at their farm outside of Emporia.

That he remembered. The oats and barley. Helping with chores—their aunt and uncle were getting along and the work was hard. Plans for college forgotten.

And it didn't matter. He felt a peace farming. Helping the plants grow.

Until three years later.

His uncle had spotted it first—something that covered the land, not the sky.

"Roger," he shouted. "Run to the shed! Get a couple of shovels. Call in the house and get your aunt and your sister here too."

"What is it?" he asked.

"Just *do* it, Roger!"

And he found out soon enough. When they got to the edge of the far field and put their backs into digging ditches.

Armyworms. Cutworms. A living carpet, undulating across the landscape, overrunning their barrier ditches before they were even halfway finished. Two-inch long monsters—appearing in cycles, his uncle said later, much like the webworms of West Virginia—stripping the fields bare.

UNLIKE HIS SISTER'S GARDEN, however, the land did not come back. Before the next summer, their uncle had died and, not being able to work it herself, their aunt had been forced to sell the farm. Marina had gotten a job in Emporia as a medical records technician while he, with just his high school education, had joined the army.

They stayed in touch. He took to army life well enough—after all, there weren't any wars, unless one counted things like Grenada, and no one really expected the Russians to start World

War III. In spite of the talks their officers gave them.

But as for Marina, it started to be clear she still searched for something. Her moves, her changes of jobs, ever eastward. A Saint Louis hospital, then, later, Evansville, Indiana. Then, briefly, Louisville. Then another hospital in Wheeling.

And then her garden. Him, after the army, living in Raleigh, North Carolina. The active reserves.

Operation Desert Storm.

And, then, *this* letter—

His work in the garden now. Sharing memories. Hearing—the sounds of growth in the moist earth. His sister's visions.

"*Don't* you see?" she'd demand as they sweated, side by side. "Look. That tree over there. The apple tree. Squint your eyes *just* right."

He tried. He squinted. Still he saw nothing like what she described.

"The bark. If you look at it right, it seems like it's almost transparent. Try it again—you can see how it's growing. The sap, slowly flowing like blood through veins. You can see the nutrients. See how they're gathering to form the tree's fruit."

And once in a while, as the summer drew on, he had the feeling he almost *did* see. But he saw, also, what had become of the land when the webworms had taken it over. White, like a snowfield, except the hillocks and ridges weren't iceformed, but rather were nets of translucent silk.

Like the camouflage netting they'd used in the desert.

But silent. Ghostlike. And then a new sound within the soil, but not of plants growing. Rather, an animal sound now, of sleeping.

And memories. Flashes. Their leaving the accident, thrown from their parents' car. Marina leading them up the ridge....

"Marina," he said. "Tomorrow I've got to use the jeep. Take a trip into town."

"Why?" she asked. Her voice had become so weak by now that he had to strain his ears to hear her.

He looked at her face—her own ears encrusted. The wax discharges her doctor had

treated her for had become so bad by now that, even with his help, she could no longer completely clear them.

He raised his voice slightly. "To get some supplies—we need those anyway. Also, though, I want to buy some hiking equipment."

IT WAS MARINA who had insisted *they climb the ridge.* The memory came back, after he'd pulled his jeep off the highway and now was attempting to retrace their steps. It had been she who had led the way up, saying they *had* to see. Telling him they had to see it alone.

Now, however, he climbed by himself. Marina had been too weak that morning to even get out of bed. So weak her flesh had seemed almost transparent—so weak he could see the wasting away, the bones outlined starkly beneath the taut skin.

But he recognized now—a pine tree they'd blundered against in the darkness. A glade. A clearing, the grass flattened down as if animals used it. Above, the ridge peak.

He climbed to reach it and saw the sign, the letters faded by sun and rain. *U.S. WEATHER STATION.* The barracks below on the other side, abandoned, crumbling. The platform, its surface cracked. Rusted out Quonset huts.

Except he'd looked up the maps of the area back in Raleigh—maps dating back to the year they'd seen *it*, the second UFO, rising, balloonlike, up above the ridge top to meet them. Pinned by searchlights, trails of dust filling the air like moths swarming.

When he and his sister had heard the sirens —the sirens and more than that. Shrill ululation. The sounds so high they could no longer hear them, but answered instead with their own high shrieks as they clung to each other.

Except that the maps—the 1982 U.S. Government Survey Charts—showed that nothing had been there...

...and memories came crashing back...

...swarms of flies in the heat of the desert, even at night when he and his copilot/gunner lifted. Rising above them. Pinning Iraqi tanks with their own huge light, playing the tape their colonel had given them through the loud-speaker.

First, the rotor sounds of their Apache, then weird … *inhuman* … sounds. He and his gunner wore ear protectors, yet still they could hear them.

And afterward, crashing. The tanks, now abandoned, the enemy soldiers no longer in them. Riddled with tiny holes…

…his uncle's beehives, the autumn before the cutworm invasion. "Look," his uncle said, holding the ruined comb up so he could see it. The tiny, silk-lined tunnels that riddled it.

"Wax moths," his uncle said. "Larvae of wax moths live in the hives, burrowing through them. Only the older hives—and weakened colonies. They eat the nitrogen that the bees leave as well as the wax itself. Still, though, when you can't afford to get new queens."

He squeezed the honeycomb in his hand and watched it crumble, as if it were so much dust…

…his sister lying, wax-stained, shrunken, when he'd left that morning. He *did* see beneath her skin. Tissue attacked and destroyed by … by *something* … that tunneled within it. Eroding the blood vessels, piercing her lungs.

Her constant headaches—his own headaches worse now. Her having to spit blood. Her pallor. Her fevers…

…*Maria per aurem impregnata est.* The words of Saint Anselm, memorized in his high school Advanced Latin class—that the Virgin Mary must have become with child through the act of her hearing the words of the angel.

And flying saucers … "third kind" encounters. Involving the actual sightings of creatures. And fourth kinds—abductions. And were there then *fifth* kinds…?

Their waking up, alone on the ridge, their clothes disheveled. Clasped in each other's arms.

His dreams of becoming a priest forever shattered…

…and his own ears filled with wax—for the past year his hearing had been going out intermittently. After the Gulf War.

Perhaps it took longer for him than Marina.

HE WALKED BACK to the farm, not hurrying, not surprised to hear no answer when he called his sister's name. Not surprised at all by the smell that greeted him when he went upstairs.

He went into her bedroom and saw the tents already beginning to form on her body. The silken, shroud-like tubes that enveloped her, pulsating softly, covering whatever shards and pieces might be left of flesh.

He pulled up a chair and sat by her bedside the whole night through, he didn't know how long, until he could stay awake no longer. Twelve hours? A full day? Sitting and watching until sleep came to him.

And dreaming of angels. And helicopters. Of weather balloons rising in darkness, flooded with light. Of the sound of wings beating—increasing in amplitude. Shrill. Ululating.

Of flying saucers.

And, waking to the glow of the moon through his sister's east window, he saw that the room was filled with tiny moths.

"Waxworms" first appeared in the July-September 2003 issue of ChiZine. *(Illustration by Allen Koszowski.)*

Indiana author James Dorr's most recent book is a novel-in-stories from Elder Signs Press, Tombs: A Chronicle of Latter-Day Times of Earth. *Working mostly in dark fantasy/horror with some forays into science fiction and mystery, his* The Tears of Isis *was a 2013 Bram Stoker Award® finalist for Superior Achievement in a Fiction Collection, while other books include* Strange Mistresses: Tales of Wonder and Romance, Darker Loves: Tales of Mystery and Regret, *and his all-poetry* Vamps (A Retrospective). *He has also been a technical writer, an editor on a regional magazine, a full-time non-fiction freelancer, and a semi-professional musician, and currently harbors a Goth cat named Triana. An Active Member of SFWA and HWA, Dorr invites readers to visit his blog at jamesdorrwriter.wordpress.com*

THE OUTER LIMITS

A REMEMBRANCE

BY GARY GERANI

WITH ILLUSTRATIONS BY ALLEN KOSZOWSKI

WHAT IS IT about a movie or TV series that makes such an impression, it remains a force in your life forever? Something about the experience sticks in your psyche: it might be a certain character played by a certain actor, or maybe an endearingly absurd central premise. In the case of *The Outer Limits*, it was the sheer audaciousness of style that grabbed me. This wasn't often the case with network-produced television product, especially shows fabricated during the relatively superficial, escapist-driven early '60s.

So, who or what was responsible for the special style of *The Outer Limits*, and how might one define it? I believe it was the lightning-in-a-bottle pairing of screenwriter-producer Joseph Stefano, *Psycho*'s famed scribe and therefore a Hitchcock-related creative force, and cinematographer Conrad Hall, who would soon shoot major movies, win an Oscar and become, by popular consensus, one of the greatest directors of photography in the history of motion pictures.

This is not to underrate the contributions of other significant creative artists who worked on the show. There'd be no *Outer Limits* at all if it weren't for executive producer/creator Leslie Stevens, a feisty maverick who rattled the Hollywood establishment in the early-to-mid '60s; he ultimately managed to co-exist with it. Then there's composer Dominic Frontiere, whose original music for the series is considered his finest work. One should also mention the

contribution of director Gerd Oswald, helmer of a handful of interesting feature movies, but never more impressive than on this offbeat, relentlessly experimental series that provided the perfect platform for his neurotic brand of intellectual melodrama.

But it's with Stefano and Hall that the show reached beyond mere impressiveness and ventured into the realm of sublime surrealism, an odd combination of German Expressionism, film noir, sci-fi thriller monster movies, and early '60s social angst. And it's this aspect of *The Outer Limits* that sets it apart and above almost all made-for-TV fare. Even Rod Serling's more accessible *The Twilight*

Academy Award-winning cinematographer Conrad Hall stylishly led viewers down the dark corridors of First-Season writer/producer Stefano's "inner mind," as in the expressionist, noir episode "The Forms of Things Unknown" (1964). Above: Warren Oates, in "The Mutant" ('64). Previous page: Season Two's "Keeper of the Purple Twilight" ('64) and (inset) "The Zanti Misfits" ('63). *The Outer Limits* and associated photographic images are © Metro-Goldwyn-Mayer.

Zone, the single most significant practical inspiration for *Limits*, pushes more conventional buttons. When *Zone* featured sophisticated visuals, they were almost always motivated by the demands of the plot—in "Third from the Sun," for example, the celebrated twist is that we're actually on another planet for most of the story, so camera angles are subtly cocked to suggest an alien environment. When *The Outer Limits* gives us Conrad Hall's up angles and warped-lens choices, it's because the inner paranoia of the mixed-up characters or the profound heaviness of the theme are being artfully explored. *Zone* and *Limits* are clearly related, yet different in significant ways.

Producer Joseph Stefano was rather famously in analysis during the writing of *Psycho* and *The Outer Limits*. How lucky a fellow was he to have an ingenious young cinematographer visualize his rumbling "inner mind," images which, when combined with Frontiere's equally relentless music, amounted to a therapeutic psych session each and every Monday night. Never before was a network television series so consistently an artistic reflection of the man in charge's subconscious. Since its inception, TV had traditionally been viewed as a writer and actor's medium. *The Outer Limits* sought to expand this creative potential, giving us flamboyant cinematic subtext on the small screen at a time when displaced hillbillies and Raymond Burr's legal gabfests were the norm.

Of course, we're really talking only about OL Season One, the Stevens-Stefano-Hall-Frontiere batch of shows. Not to minimize the importance of Harlan Ellison's Season Two teleplays and a few other worthy S2 episodes, it is the inaugural year that has the true juice. And because *The Outer Limits* was a spooky show as much as it was imaginative and visionary, the dark recesses of the mind could easily congeal into an honest-to-gosh, rubber-suited Hollywood monster per installment, or "Bear" as Stefano classified them. These dream

Light and shadows, angles and angst, courtesy of Conrad Hall; with Barry Atwater as an alien-possessed scientist, in the creepy Season One episode "Corpus Earthling" ('63).

demons were often metaphors, rather eloquently pointing out the error of human ways in tales that were only nominally science fiction. In truth, Stefano and company had other fish to deep fry. These guys were interested in producing avant-garde television, Chiller Theatre with a message and a high-brow approach to visual style that not only resembled feature films, but sophisticated foreign films, which Stefano loved. Influences of French new wave and Ingmar Bergman's moody existential drama are evident throughout, with Orson Welles-like cinematography informing much of Hall's early work.

As long as an unspeakable monstrosity lumbered at the audience every week, ABC left the show's creators to their own mysterious, pretentious-in-a-good-way devices. Dense ideas and sharp wordplay elevated *The Outer Limits*, because what these filmmakers were doing really wasn't pretending... they were legitimately enhancing intelligent questions and conclusions by uniting the high end (pithy philosophy) with the low (rubber monsters). This was a combination that perplexed Greatest Generation mainstreamers,

A typical *TOL* bear, from "The Children of Spider County" (1964).

Satisfyingly weird, from "Counterweight" (S2: 1964).

between *Zone* and *Trek*. Meanwhile, significant new movies inspired by OL began popping up (*Altered States*, *The Terminator*, etc.), as filmmakers who watched *The Outer Limits* as kids were now old enough to do their own spin on similar ideas.

Like everyone else of my generation, I watched endless network promos for *The Outer Limits* before the series premiered in 1963, then sat down and got a big charge out of the debut episode. The Galaxy Being was an awesome science fiction monster with a lot of admirable things to say, a glowing, clawed combination of Michael Rennie's eloquent Klaatu and his implacably destructive robot, Gort. It was a terrific way to begin this series, establishing its heady intellectual tone and "monster of the week" formula. Oddly, OL's formula was briefly interrupted by the second episode aired, a sharp *Manchurian Candidate*-like thriller called "The Hundred Days of the Dragon" that offered some agreeably weird effects, but no rubber-suited gargoyle. We kids originally thought "Okay, we got that cool Galaxy Being right out of the gate, but God knows when they'll roll out another great monster like that." By the third episode, "The Architects of Fear," we all realized that science fiction monsters of one

but fully satisfied young Boomers hungry for something weird and different. It's hardly surprising that the show was viewed as either an oddball semi-success or ambitious misfire by most professional observers in '63–'64. Only years later would the uniqueness of *The Outer Limits* be fully appreciated. A concentrated effort was made by young media historians like myself in the mid-'70s to remind people of this oh-so-interesting groundbreaker. *Star Trek*'s popularity enabled *Limits* to be reexamined, viewed favorably by many fans as a kind of missing link

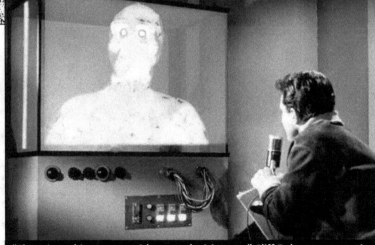

"There is nothing wrong with your television set." Cliff Robertson tunes in a fellow explorer from Andromeda, in creator Leslie Stevens' pilot episode "The Galaxy Being" (1963).

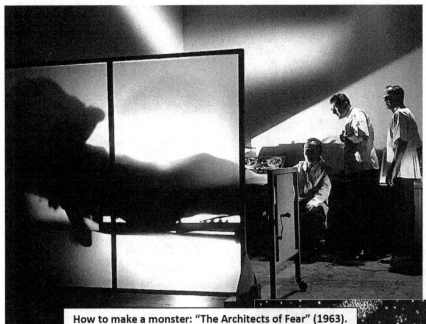

How to make a monster: "The Architects of Fear" (1963).

of cinematographer Conrad Hall's sweetest visuals, and you have a genuine, full-fledged *Outer Limits* classic... a great episode among many great ones, as things would turn out.

We didn't have to wait long for another super-classic, "The Sixth Finger" featuring pre-*Man from U.N.C.L.E.* David McCallum as the high-domed Man from Tomorrow... in truth, an ordinary human evolved into his future self by a guilt-ridden scientist in a remote mining community.

sort or another had found a permanent home on *The Outer Limits*.

"The Man with the Power" with Donald Pleasance in an Id-gone-amok scenario was okay as the fourth episode broadcast, but it was the next entry, "The Man Who Was Never Born," that proved the real game-changer. Arguably the most satisfying episode of Season One, "Man" dazzled viewers with one heck of a compelling sci-fi premise: change the screwed-up past in order to reshape and safeguard the imperiled future. It's a notion producer/director James Cameron would famously re-visit in his Terminator films years later. Guest star Martin Landau was given quite a showcase as *OL*'s weekly "Bear," a horribly mutated but gentle, poetic time-traveling soul from a microbe-ravaged tomorrow who must somehow reverse humanity's dark destiny. Add to these assets an empathetic performance by leading lady Shirley Knight, the biggest orchestra yet for Dominic Frontiere's heartfelt and exciting music, and some

"Nightmare" gave us what I first thought was a weird imitation of *The Twilight Zone*'s "Where is Everybody?" as scientists and the military put astronauts in a box of sorts to test their endurance under extreme psychological pressure. Because the sets were so spare and artificial-looking, I mistakenly thought the whole ordeal—including the glowering "aliens" —was a lie cooked up by the U.S. government. In truth, the Ebonites were indeed real aliens who accidentally caused tragedy on Earth, and were looking for a way to make amends. The notion that our government would cover-up the truth in our first contact with an off-world

"The Man Who Was Never Born" (1963).

race and use this accident as an excuse for secret training maneuvers was amazingly bold and subversive in its day, perhaps even more so than script writer Joseph Stefano even realized at the time.

The middle of *The Outer Limits* Season One was distinguished by a number of extremely weird, highly personal episodes, most of them written by Stefano, shot by Hall, and directed by Gerd Oswald. I remember a bunch of female-centric shows ("The Bellero Shield," "Don't Open Till Doomsday," and "ZZZZZ," with a high-testosterone entry, "The Invisibles," sandwiched between them.) All were breathtaking Stefano fever-dreams come to life, making full use of their ace cinematographer's esoteric creative gifts and composer Frontiere's penchant for the downright hysterical. His score for "Doomsday" pushed high-strung urgency to the max, mirroring the oh-so-mad "Baby Jane"-type character played by Miriam Hopkins.

As Season One started winding down, I remember two particularly

Allen K's portrait of David McCallum as a man fully evolved, from "The Sixth Finger." (1963).

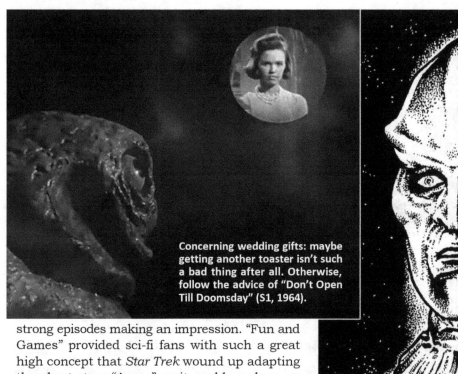

Concerning wedding gifts: maybe getting another toaster isn't such a bad thing after all. Otherwise, follow the advice of "Don't Open Till Doomsday" (S1, 1964).

The Ebonite, from "Nightmare" (1963). —ALLEN K. '81

strong episodes making an impression. "Fun and Games" provided sci-fi fans with such a great high concept that *Star Trek* wound up adapting the short story "Arena" so it could produce an episode of its own that would semi-emulate what Stefano and company accomplished just a few years earlier. As a matter of fact, the gnarly Calico aliens of "Fun and Games" and *Star Trek*'s scaly Gorn could be reptilian cousins. In any event, the notion of an ordinary man and woman

Martin Sheen faces an alien interrogation, in "Nightmare" (1963).

pitted against an alien monster and his mate with Earth's survival hanging in the balance was irresistible. In bitter, shoulder-tensing Nick Adams and unhappily married Nancy Malone, OL's casting director found the perfect unlikely saviors.

Also making an indelible impression around this time was "A Feasibility Study." It was the first *Outer Limits* script written by Joe Stefano and his first to be filmed, but concerns about its mass-suicide finale held it back from broadcast until the end of the season. Probably OL's most humanistic tale, it is built around a noble act of self-sacrifice (from a bunch of Beverly Hills suburbanites, no less) that saves our species from mass-enslavement on another world. In a way, this dark but ultimately optimistic study of human selflessness is something of an answer to Rod Serling's ultra-cynical "The Monsters

Playing for keeps, in "Fun and Games" (S1, 1964).

truth a slightly altered version of the pilot for a new anthology series Joe Stefano was hoping to sell, *The Unknown*. ABC politely declined, but not before this astonishing mix of film noir, *The Old Dark House*, European art films, and weird science was beamed into our lives. To the very Euronotion of two beautiful women poisoning their sadistic male lover, Stefano added a possibly mad, possibly back-from-the-dead time traveling misfit (David McCallum) who promptly restores the murdered scoundrel. Directed by OL veteran Gerd Oswald and containing some of DP Conrad Hall's most astonishing compositions, "Forms" was truly a unique moment in network television broadcasting as we knew it. More than anything, this aggressively strange melodrama was telling viewers where producer/writer/creator Joseph Stefano intended to take us after a year of

are Due on Maple Street." Celebrating humanity at its most altruistic, Stefano's alien-imperiled community sticks together, anonymously saves the human race, and outsmarts the smug, hellish monsters that abducted it. Being an early episode, "Feasibility" also benefits from a healthy budget and some impressive fx/set designs—the nightmarish Lumanoid "think" gatherings play like a sci-fi take on Dante's Inferno. On the aural side, Frontiere's inspirational music for that all-important self-sacrifice scene, set in a shadowy church, was originally composed as the Gary Merrill-Sally Kellerman love theme for "The Human Factor," but reaches its dramatic fruition here.

As a kid, I didn't know what to make of "The Forms of Things Unknown," Season One's final episode. It was in

Welcome to our nightmare, from "A Feasibility Study" (S1, 1964).

bug-eyed monsters and electromagnetic explosions on *The Outer Limits*. This was decidedly weirder, wilder, more sophisticated anthology territory, Hitchcock and the French New Wave combined. "The Forms of Things Unknown" relied on stylized characters/visuals and exaggerated situations to evoke an emotional response. Fearlessly experimental, it ended OL Season One on exactly the right creative note.

The corpse of a rogue, played by Scott Marlowe, tilted back in time, in "The Forms of Things Unknown" (S1, 1964).

had run its course.

Interestingly, *The Outer Limits* went into nationwide TV syndication the very same season ('64–'65) it was still playing on ABC. That's an amazingly fast, perhaps unprecedented turnaround. I always suspected UA-TV wanted another package of '50s-style sci-fi monster movies to serve all those *Chiller Theatre* and *Creature Feature* shows on syndie channels across the country, and couldn't wait to get their

Truth to tell, my relationship with Season Two *Outer Limits*, produced by Ben Brady, was a bit more distanced than the primal love affair I seemed to have had with the Leslie Stevens/Joe Stefano regime, axed by the network in '64. Like everyone else, I marveled at the ingenuity of writer Harlan Ellison's work on "Soldier" and "Demon with a Glass Hand." The two-part episode "The Inheritors," with Bob Duvall and Steve Ihnat, is one of the classiest science fiction stories ever made for television. But the cinematic flavors of Season One appeared to have been deliberately muted, and with even bigger budget cuts and fewer monsters, it was pretty clear the series

Robert Duvall and Steve Ihnat (inset), in "The Inheritors" (1964).

gargoyle-infested *Outer Limits* into the marketplace. And there it remained, in grainy 16mm form, for the next couple of decades.

Flash forward to the mid-'70s and the "Star Trek Lives!" phenomenon. Never a ratings hit on the NBC network, *Trek* surprised just about everyone by becoming a phenomenon in syndication. This enabled die-hard fans of *The Outer Limits* to draw attention to their semi-forgotten favorite show by using ST's success as a reason to explore *all* TV sci-fi. For me, this journey into the recent past soon took on a very personal flavor. After seeking out and befriending living legends Joseph Stefano and Harlan Ellison, I began interviewing these gentlemen in public and writing articles about OL for whatever pop

Considered the finest Season Two episode: Harlan Ellison's iconic "Demon With a Glass Hand" (1964), starring Robert Culp and Arlene Martel.

anthology series that lasted only a year and a half has somehow managed to survive the test of time, becoming more influential and revered than ever before.

In the final analysis, and with all due respect to the Galaxy Being, there is no "end of transmission" when it comes to *The Outer Limits*.

At least, there isn't for me.

Gary Gerani, 2020

👽 👽 👽 👽 👽 👽 👽

Fantastic Television, The Card King, Dinosaurs Attack!, Pumpkinhead, Bram Stoker's Death Ship, Top 100 Horror Movies…

Gary Gerani is a professional fiction/non-fiction writer and film critic. As a screenwriter, he is best known for creating and co-authoring the screenplay for (multiple Oscar winner) Stan Winston's Pumpkinhead, *a cult horror film starring Lance Henriksen that has spawned three sequels and a planned big-budget remake. Gerani also scripted Showtime's adaptation of the popular* Vampirella *comic book (starring Roger Daltrey), and also co-wrote the 2019 John Travolta racing car drama,* Trading Paint.

(CONTINUED ON NEXT PAGE)

New life for OL in syndication allowed viewers to continue tuning in to stylish and imaginative SF—not to mention all those cool bears. Above, Jeff Corey in "O.B.I.T." (S1, 1963).

publication would have them (*Starlog*, etc.). That culminated in something of an OL love letter for my 1977 book *Fantastic Television* … a book that was sold to Crown/Harmony Press on the strength of *Trek*'s resurgence.

And so it goes. *The Outer Limits* was and always will be a significant part of my pop culture heritage. First and foremost, it's an artful TV series that deserves to be remembered and appreciated. But for us misfit Boomers, it also epitomized the wonderful "monster movie craze" of the early '60s, a period of hopeful innocence that is fondly remembered. Forry Ackerman's *Famous Monsters* mag was at its height, the Aurora plastic model kits were busy revitalizing Universal's classic creatures, and both *The Munsters* and *The Addams Family* were only a year away. *The Outer Limits* was smack in the middle of all this, God bless it. Over the decades, ABC's badly-reviewed

Monstrous insects from outer space, from "The Zanti Misfits" (S1, 1963).

"Keeper of the Purple Twilight" (S2, 1964)

published by various youth-oriented manufacturers, including Upper Deck, Artbox, Comic Images, Rittenhouse Archives, and Inkworks.

Non-fiction author Gerani has also written a number of books/articles dealing with the movie and TV industry. His celebrated 1976 tome Fantastic Television was the very first book to explore science fiction, horror and fantasy on the small screen. George Lucas himself wrote the introduction to one of Gerani's non-fiction trade paperbacks.

In 2010, a number of Gary Gerani projects surfaced. He was at the helm of a new IDW graphic novel, Bram Stoker's Death Ship, released on a monthly basis (starting in June) as a four-part comic book series before the complete version hit bookstores. This spooky tale provided the "lost facts" of what happened on the fateful sea voyage that brought a ravenous Count Dracula from Transylvania to the shores of Whitby, England. Gerani also became president of Fantastic Press (a moniker inspired by his first trade paperback success), which is an independent imprint of parent company IDW. Between 2011 and 2018, four full-color trade paperbacks were published: Top 100 Horror Movies, Top 100 Sci-Fi Movies, Top 100 Fantasy Movies, and Top 100 Comic Book Movies. All were written, edited, designed, and photo-edited by Gerani. Also during this period, Abrams Books published several hard-cover tomes reprinting Gary Gerani's classic trading card sets for Topps. Gerani was called in to write lengthy "making of" introductions and also served as commentator on the specific cards.

Apart from screenwriting, Gerani has 35 years experience creating, developing and producing countless items for the youth market. He worked on staff at Topps for over 20 years, writing and editing all movie/TV-related products (including cards, books and magazines), in addition to creating brand new franchises. In the early '80s, Gerani designed an approved prototype for the phenomenally successful Garbage Pail Kids, and also helmed the sci-fi cult property Dinosaurs Attack!, which was later optioned for a movie property by Tim Burton and Joe Dante. His work has appeared in similar products

Although retired from Topps, Gary Gerani continues to write all of the company's Star Wars *trading card sets, as he has done since the movie first appeared in 1977. He has a new book coming out in 2020,* The Art of Joe Smith *(famed Hollywood movie poster painter), and is completing a feature-length documentary called* Romantic Mysticism: The Music of Billy Goldenberg, *produced with the involvement of Universal Studios. Ongoing articles and Blu-ray commentaries are also on Gerani's creative agenda for 2020-21, and John Travolta retains the rights to another original screenplay he has co-authored, a road comedy with a pool-playing theme.*

For the record, Gerani has won various awards over the decades, as have many of the projects he created and/or worked on. He has been honored by the Society of Illustrators as an art director, won numerous "Gummie" awards for his trading card sets, a Saturn Certificate of Achievement for Pumpkinhead *(Stan Winston took home the trophy), and three Rondo Awards for fiction and non-fiction projects… so far.*

Note: A Google search will provide a more thorough list of Gerani's various creations.

DON'T MISS OUR NEXT BIG ISSUE FEATURING

RENEGADE ROBOTS

YOUR MECHANICAL FRIENDS WOULD NEVER FORGIVE YOU!

LEININGEN
VERSUS THE ANTS
BY CARL STEPHENSON

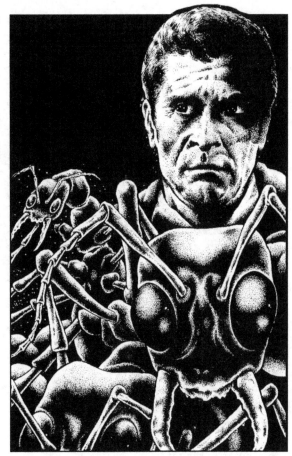

"**U**NLESS THEY ALTER THEIR COURSE, AND THERE'S NO REASON WHY THEY SHOULD, THEY'LL REACH YOUR PLANTATION IN TWO DAYS AT THE LATEST."

Leiningen sucked placidly at a cigar about the size of a corncob and for a few seconds gazed without answering at the agitated District Commissioner. Then he took the cigar from his lips, and leaned slightly forward. With his bristling grey hair, bulky nose, and lucid eyes, he had the look of an aging and shabby eagle.

"Decent of you," he murmured, "paddling all this way just to give me the tip. But you're pulling my leg, of course, when you say I must do a bunk. Why, even a herd of saurians couldn't drive me from this plantation of mine."

The Brazilian official threw up lean and lanky arms and clawed the air with wildly distended fingers. "Leiningen!" he shouted. "You're insane! They're not creatures you can fight—they're an elemental—an 'act of God!' Ten miles long, two miles wide—ants, nothing but ants! And every single one of them a fiend from hell; before you can spit three times they'll eat a full-grown buffalo to the bones. I tell you if you don't clear out at once there'll he nothing left of you but a skeleton picked as clean as your own plantation."

Leiningen grinned. "Act of God, my eye! Anyway, I'm not an old woman; I'm not going to run for it just because an elemental's on the way. And don't think I'm the kind of fathead who tries to fend off lightning with his fists either. I use my intelligence, old man. With me, the brain isn't a second blind gut; I know what it's there for. When I began this model farm and plantation three years ago, I took into account all that could conceivably happen to it. And now I'm ready for anything and everything—including your ants."

The Brazilian rose heavily to his feet. "I've done my best," he gasped. "Your obstinacy endangers not only yourself, but the lives of your four hundred workers. You don't know these ants!"

Leiningen accompanied him down to the river, where the Government launch was moored. The vessel cast off. As it moved downstream, the exclamation mark neared the rail and began waving its arms frantically. Long after the launch had disappeared round the bend, Leiningen thought he could still hear that dimming imploring voice, "You don't know them, I tell you! You don't know them!"

But the reported enemy was by no means

unfamiliar to the planter. Before he started work on his settlement, he had lived long enough in the country to see for himself the fearful devastations sometimes wrought by these ravenous insects in their campaigns for food. But since then he had planned measures of defense accordingly, and these, he was convinced, were in every way adequate to withstand the approaching peril.

Moreover, during his three years as a planter, Leiningen had met and defeated drought, flood, plague and all other "acts of God" which had come against him—unlike his fellow-settlers in the district, who had made little or no resistance. This unbroken success he attributed solely to the observance of his life-long motto: The human brain needs only to become fully aware of its powers to conquer even the elements. Dullards reeled senselessly and aimlessly into the abyss; cranks, however brilliant, lost their heads when circumstances suddenly altered or accelerated, and ran into stone walls; sluggards drifted with the current until they were caught in whirlpools and dragged under. But such disasters, Leiningen contended, merely strengthened his argument that intelligence, directed aright, invariably makes man the master of his fate.

Yes, Leiningen had always known how to grapple with life. Even here, in this Brazilian wilderness, his brain had triumphed over every difficulty and danger it had so far encountered. First he had vanquished primal forces by cunning and organization, then he had enlisted the resources of modern science to increase miraculously the yield of his plantation. And now he was sure he would prove more than a match for the "irresistible" ants.

That same evening, however, Leiningen assembled his workers. He had no intention of waiting till the news reached their ears from other sources. Most of them had been born in the district; the cry "The ants are coming!" was to them an imperative signal for instant, panic-stricken flight, a spring for life itself. But so great was the Indians' trust in Leiningen, in Leiningen's word, and in Leiningen's wisdom, that they received his curt tidings, and his

orders for the imminent struggle, with the calmness with which they were given. They waited, unafraid, alert, as if for the beginning of a new game or hunt which he had just described to them. The ants were indeed mighty, but not so mighty as the boss. Let them come!

They came at noon the second day. Their approach was announced by the wild unrest of the horses, scarcely controllable now, either in stall or under rider, scenting from afar a vapor instinct with horror.

It was announced by a stampede of animals, timid and savage, hurtling past each other; jaguars and pumas flashing by nimble stags of the pampas, bulky tapirs, no longer hunters, themselves hunted, outpacing fleet kinkajous, maddened herds of cattle, heads lowered, nostrils snorting, rushing through tribes of loping monkeys, chattering in a dementia of terror; then followed the creeping and springing denizens of bush and steppe, big and little rodents, snakes, and lizards.

Pell-mell the rabble swarmed down the hill to the plantation, scattered right and left before the barrier of the water-filled ditch, then sped onwards to the river, where, again hindered, they fled along its bank out of sight.

This water-filled ditch was one of the defense measures which Leiningen had long since prepared against the advent of the ants. It encompassed three sides of the plantation like a huge horseshoe. Twelve feet across, but not very deep, when dry it could hardly be described as an obstacle to either man or beast. But the ends of the "horseshoe" ran into the river which formed the northern boundary, and fourth side, of the plantation. And at the end nearer the house and outbuildings in the middle of the plantation, Leiningen had constructed a dam by means of which water from the river could be diverted into the ditch.

So now, by opening the dam, he was able to fling an imposing girdle of water, a huge quadrilateral with the river as its base, completely around the plantation, like the moat encircling a medieval city. Unless the ants were clever enough to build rafts. they had no hope of reaching the plantation, Leiningen concluded.

The twelve-foot water ditch seemed to afford in itself all the security needed. But while awaiting the arrival of the ants, Leiningen made a further improvement. The western section of the ditch ran along the edge of a tamarind wood, and the branches of some great trees reached over the water. Leiningen now had them lopped so that ants could not descend from them within the "moat."

The women and children, then the herds of cattle, were escorted by peons on rafts over the river, to remain on the other side in absolute safety until the plunderers had departed. Leiningen gave this instruction, not because he believed the non-combatants were in any danger, but in order to avoid hampering the efficiency of the defenders. "Critical situations first become crises," he explained to his men, "when oxen or women get excited."

Finally, he made a careful inspection of the "inner moat"—a smaller ditch lined with concrete, which extended around the hill on which stood the ranch house, barns, stables and other buildings. Into this concrete ditch emptied the inflow pipes from three great petrol tanks. If by some miracle the ants managed to cross the water and reached the plantation, this "rampart of petrol," would be an absolutely impassable protection for the besieged and their dwellings and stock. Such, at least, was Leiningen's opinion.

He stationed his men at irregular distances along the water ditch, the first line of defense. Then he lay down in his hammock and puffed drowsily away at his pipe until a peon came with the report that the ants had been observed far away in the South.

Leiningen mounted his horse, which at the feel of its master seemed to forget its uneasiness, and rode leisurely in the direction of the threatening offensive. The southern stretch of ditch—the upper side of the quadrilateral—was nearly three miles long; from its center one could survey the entire countryside. This was destined to be the scene of the outbreak of war between Leiningen's brain and twenty square miles of life-destroying ants.

It was a sight one could never forget. Over the range of hills, as far as eye could see, crept a darkening hem, ever longer and broader, until the shadow spread across the slope from east to west, then downwards, downwards, uncannily swift, and all the green herbage of that wide vista was being mown as by a giant sickle, leaving only the vast moving shadow, extending, deepening, and moving rapidly nearer.

When Leiningen's men, behind their barrier of water, perceived the approach of the long-expected foe, they gave vent to their suspense in screams and imprecations. But as the distance began to lessen between the "sons of hell" and the water ditch, they relapsed into silence. Before the advance of that awe-inspiring throng, their belief in the powers of the boss began to steadily dwindle.

Even Leiningen himself, who had ridden up just in time to restore their loss of heart by a display of unshakable calm, even he could not free himself from a qualm of malaise. Yonder were thousands of millions of voracious jaws bearing down upon him and only a suddenly insignificant, narrow ditch lay between him and his men and being gnawed to the bones "before you can spit three times."

Hadn't this brain for once taken on more than it could manage? If the blighters decided to rush the ditch, fill it to the brim with their corpses, there'd still be more than enough to destroy every trace of that cranium of his. The planter's chin jutted; they hadn't got him yet, and he'd see to it they never would. While he could think at all, he'd flout both death and the devil.

The hostile army was approaching in perfect formation; no human battalions, however well-drilled, could ever hope to rival the precision of that advance. Along a front that moved forward as uniformly as a straight line, the ants drew nearer and nearer to the water ditch. Then, when they learned through their scouts the nature of the obstacle, the two outlying wings of the army detached themselves from the main body and marched down the western and eastern sides of the ditch.

This surrounding maneuver took rather more than an hour to accomplish; no doubt the ants expected that at some point they would find a crossing.

During this outflanking movement by the wings, the army on the center and southern front remained still. The besieged were therefore able to contemplate at their leisure the thumb-long, reddish black, long-legged insects; some of the Indians believed they could see, too, intent on them, the brilliant, cold eyes, and the razor-edged mandibles, of this host of infinity.

It is not easy for the average person to imagine that an animal, not to mention an insect, can think. But now both the European brain of Leiningen and the primitive brains of the Indians began to stir with the unpleasant foreboding that inside every single one of that deluge of insects dwelt a thought. And that thought was: Ditch or no ditch, we'll get to your flesh!

NOT UNTIL FOUR O'CLOCK did the wings reach the "horseshoe" ends of the ditch, only to find these ran into the great river. Through some kind of secret telegraphy, the report must then have flashed very swiftly indeed along the entire enemy line. And Leiningen, riding—no longer casually—along his side of the ditch, noticed by energetic and widespread movements of troops that for some unknown reason the news of the check had its greatest effect on the southern front, where the main army was massed. Perhaps the failure to find a way over the ditch was persuading the ants to withdraw from the plantation in search of spoils more easily attainable.

An immense flood of ants, about a hundred yards in width, was pouring in a glimmering-black cataract down the far slope of the ditch. Many thousands were already drowning in the sluggish creeping flow, but they were followed by troop after troop, who clambered over their sinking comrades, and then themselves served as dying bridges to the reserves hurrying on in their rear.

Shoals of ants were being carried away by the current into the middle of the ditch, where gradually they broke asunder and then, exhausted by their struggles, vanished below the surface. Nevertheless, the wavering, floundering hundred-yard front was remorselessly if slowly advancing towards the besieged on the other bank. Leiningen had been wrong when he supposed the enemy would first have to fill the ditch with their bodies before they could cross; instead, they merely needed to act as stepping-stones, as they swam and sank, to the hordes ever pressing onwards from behind.

Near Leiningen a few mounted herdsmen awaited his orders. He sent one to the weir—the river must be dammed more strongly to increase the speed and power of the water coursing through the ditch.

A second peon was dispatched to the outhouses to bring spades and petrol sprinklers. A third rode away to summon to the zone of the offensive all the men, except the observation posts, on the nearby sections of the ditch, which were not yet actively threatened.

The ants were getting across far more quickly than Leiningen would have deemed possible. Impelled by the mighty cascade behind them, they struggled nearer and nearer to the inner bank. The momentum of the attack was so great that neither the tardy flow of the stream nor its downward pull could exert its proper force; and into the gap left by every submerging insect, hastened forward a dozen more.

When reinforcements reached Leiningen, the invaders were halfway over. The planter had to admit to himself that it was only by a stroke of luck for him that the ants were attempting the crossing on a relatively short front: had they assaulted simultaneously along the entire length of the ditch, the outlook for the defenders would have been black indeed.

Even as it was, it could hardly be described as rosy, though the planter seemed quite unaware that death in a gruesome form was drawing closer and closer. As the war between his brain and the "act of God" reached its climax, the very shadow of annihilation began to pale to Leiningen, who now felt like a champion in a new Olympic game, a gigantic and thrilling contest, from which he was determined to emerge victor. Such, indeed, was his aura of confidence that the Indians forgot their stupefied fear of the peril only a yard or two away; under the planter's supervision, they began fervidly digging up to the edge of the bank and throwing clods of earth and spadefuls of sand into the midst of the hostile fleet.

The petrol sprinklers, hitherto used to destroy pests and blights on the plantation, were also brought into action. Streams of evil-reeking oil now soared and fell over an enemy already in disorder through the bombardment of earth and sand.

The ants responded to these vigorous and successful measures of defense by further developments of their offensive. Entire clumps of huddling insects began to roll down the opposite bank into the water. At the same time, Leiningen noticed that the ants were now attacking along an ever-widening front. As the numbers both of his men and his petrol sprinklers were severely limited, this rapid extension of the line of battle was becoming an overwhelming danger.

To add to his difficulties, the very clods of earth they flung into that black floating carpet often whirled fragments toward the defenders' side, and here and there dark ribbons were already mounting the inner bank. True, wherever a man saw these they could still be driven back into the water by spadefuls of earth or jets of petrol. But the file of defenders was too sparse and scattered to hold off at all points these landing parties, and though the peons toiled like madmen, their plight became momentarily more perilous.

One man struck with his spade at an enemy clump, but did not draw it back quickly enough from the water; in a trice the wooden shaft swarmed with upward scurrying insects. With a curse, he dropped the spade into the ditch; too late, they were already on his body. They lost no time; wherever they encountered bare flesh they bit deeply; a few, bigger than the rest, carried in their hind-quarters a sting which injected a burning and paralyzing venom. Screaming, frantic with pain, the peon danced and twirled like a dervish.

Realizing that another such casualty, yes, perhaps this alone, might plunge his men into confusion and destroy their morale, Leiningen roared in a bellow louder than the yells of the victim: "Into the petrol, idiot! Douse your paws in the petrol!" The dervish ceased his pirouette as if transfixed, then tore of his shirt and plunged his arm and the ants hanging to it up to the shoulder in one of the large open tins of petrol. But even then the fierce mandibles did not slacken; another peon had to help him squash and detach each separate insect.

Distracted by the episode, some defenders had turned away from the ditch. And now cries of fury, a thudding of spades, and a wild trampling to and fro, showed that the ants had made full use of the interval, though luckily only a few had managed to get across. The men set to work again desperately with the barrage of earth and sand. Meanwhile an old Indian, who acted as medicine-man to the plantation workers, gave the bitten peon a drink he had prepared some hours before, which, he claimed, possessed the virtue of dissolving and weakening ants' venom.

Leiningen surveyed his position. A dispassionate observer would have estimated the odds against him at a thousand to one. But then such an on-looker would have reckoned only by what he saw—the advance of myriad battalions of ants against the futile efforts of a few defenders—and not by the unseen activity that can go on in a man's brain.

For Leiningen had not erred when he decided he would fight elemental with elemental. The water in the ditch was beginning to rise; the stronger damming of the river was making itself apparent.

Visibly the swiftness and power of the masses of water increased, swirling into quicker and quicker movement its living black surface, dispersing its pattern, carrying away more and more of it on the hastening current.

Victory had been snatched from the very jaws of defeat. With a hysterical shout of joy, the peons feverishly intensified their bombardment of earth clods and sand.

And now the wide cataract down the opposite bank was thinning and ceasing, as if the ants were becoming aware that they could not attain their aim. They were scurrying back up the slope to safety.

All the troops so far hurled into the ditch had

been sacrificed in vain. Drowned and floundering insects eddied in thousands along the flow, while Indians running on the bank destroyed every swimmer that reached the side.

Not until the ditch curved towards the east did the scattered ranks assemble again in a coherent mass. And now, exhausted and half-numbed, they were in no condition to ascend the bank. Fusillades of clods drove them round the bend towards the mouth of the ditch and then into the river, wherein they vanished without leaving a trace.

The news ran swiftly along the entire chain of outposts, and soon a long, scattered line of laughing men could be seen hastening along the ditch towards the scene of victory.

For once they seemed to have lost all their native reserve, for it was in wild abandon now they celebrated the triumph—as if there were no longer thousands of millions of merciless, cold and hungry eyes watching them from the opposite bank, watching and waiting.

The sun sank behind the rim of the tamarind wood and twilight deepened into night. It was not only hoped but expected that the ants would remain quiet until dawn. "But to defeat any forlorn attempt at a crossing, the flow of water through the ditch was powerfully increased by opening the dam still further.

In spite of this impregnable barrier, Leiningen was not yet altogether convinced that the ants would not venture another surprise attack. He ordered his men to camp along the bank overnight. He also detailed parties of them to patrol the ditch in two of his motor cars and ceaselessly to illuminate the surface of the water with headlights and electric torches.

After having taken all the precautions he deemed necessary, the farmer ate his supper with considerable appetite and went to bed. His slumbers were in no wise disturbed by the memory of the waiting, live, twenty square miles.

DAWN FOUND A thoroughly refreshed and active Leiningen riding along the edge of the ditch. The planter saw before him a motionless and unaltered throng of besiegers. He studied the wide belt of water between them and the plantation,

and for a moment almost regretted that the fight had ended so soon and so simply. In the comforting, matter-of-fact light of morning, it seemed to him now that the ants hadn't the ghost of a chance to cross the ditch. Even if they plunged headlong into it on all three fronts at once, the force of the now powerful current would inevitably sweep them away. He had got quite a thrill out of the fight—a pity it was already over.

He rode along the eastern and southern sections of the ditch and found everything in order. He reached the western section, opposite the tamarind wood, and here, contrary to the other battle fronts, he found the enemy very busy indeed. The trunks and branches of the trees and the creepers of the lianas, on the far bank of the ditch, fairly swarmed with industrious insects. But instead of eating the leaves there and then, they were merely gnawing through the stalks, so that a thick green shower fell steadily to the ground.

No doubt they were victualing columns sent out to obtain provender for the rest of the army. The discovery did not surprise Leiningen. He did not need to be told that ants are intelligent, that certain species even use others as milch cows, watchdogs and slaves. He was well aware of their power of adaptation, their sense of discipline, their marvelous talent for organization.

His belief that a foray to supply the army was in progress was strengthened when he saw the leaves that fell to the ground being dragged to the troops waiting outside the wood. Then all at once he realized the aim that rain of green was intended to serve.

Each single leaf, pulled or pushed by dozens of toiling insects, was borne straight to the edge of the ditch. Even as Macbeth watched the approach of Birnam Wood in the hands of his enemies, Leiningen saw the tamarind wood move nearer and nearer in the mandibles of the ants. Unlike the fey Scot, however, he did not lose his nerve; no witches had prophesied his doom, and if they had he would have slept just as soundly. All the same, he was forced to admit to himself that the situation was far more ominous than that of the day before.

He had thought it impossible for the ants to build rafts for themselves—well, here they were, coming in thousands, more than enough to bridge the ditch. Leaves after leaves rustled down the slope into the water, where the current drew them away from the bank and carried them into midstream. And every single leaf carried several ants. This time the farmer did not trust to the alacrity of his messengers. He galloped away, leaning from his saddle and yelling orders as he rushed past outpost after outpost: "Bring petrol pumps to the southwest front! Issue spades to every man along the line facing the wood!" And arrived at the eastern and southern sections, he dispatched every man except the observation posts to the menaced west.

Then, as he rode past the stretch where the ants had failed to cross the day before, he witnessed a brief but impressive scene. Down the slope of the distant hill there came towards him a singular being, writhing rather than running, an animal-like blackened statue with shapeless head and four quivering feet that knuckled under almost ceaselessly. When the creature reached the far bank of the ditch and collapsed opposite Leiningen, he recognized it as a pampas stag, covered over and over with ants.

It had strayed near the zone of the army. As usual, they had attacked its eyes first. Blinded, it had reeled in the madness of hideous torment straight into the ranks of its persecutors, and now the beast swayed to and fro in its death agony.

With a shot from his rifle Leiningen put it out of its misery. Then he pulled out his watch. He hadn't a second to lose, but for life itself he could not have denied his curiosity the satisfaction of knowing how long the ants would take—for personal reasons, so to speak. After six minutes the white polished bones alone remained. That's how he himself would look before you can—Leiningen spat once, and put spurs to his horse.

The sporting zest with which the excitement of the novel contest had inspired him the day before had now vanished; in its place was a cold and violent purpose. He would send these vermin back to the hell where they belonged, somehow, anyhow. Yes, but *how* was indeed the question; as things stood at present it looked as if the devils would raze him and his men from the earth instead. He had underestimated the might of the enemy; he really would have to bestir himself if he hoped to outwit them.

The biggest danger now, he decided, was the point where the western section of the ditch curved southwards. And arrived there, he found his worst expectations justified. The very power of the current had huddled the leaves and their crews of ants so close together at the bend that the bridge was almost ready.

True, streams of petrol and clumps of earth still prevented a landing. But the number of floating leaves was increasing ever more swiftly. It could not be long now before a stretch of water a mile in length was decked by a green pontoon over which the ants could rush in millions.

Leiningen galloped to the weir. The damming of the river was controlled by a wheel on its bank. The planter ordered the man at the wheel first to lower the water in the ditch almost to vanishing point, next to wait a moment, then suddenly to let the river in again. This maneuver of lowering and raising the surface, of decreasing then increasing the flow of water through the ditch was to be repeated over and over again until further notice.

This tactic was at first successful. The water in the ditch sank, and with it the film of leaves. The green fleet nearly reached the bed and the troops on the far bank swarmed down the slope to it. Then a violent flow of water at the original depth raced through the ditch, overwhelming leaves and ants, and sweeping them along.

This intermittent rapid flushing prevented just in time the almost completed fording of the ditch. But it also flung here and there squads of the enemy vanguard simultaneously up the inner bank. These seemed to know their duty only too well, and lost no time accomplishing it. The air rang with the curses of bitten Indians. They had removed their shirts and pants to detect the quicker the upwards-hastening insects; when they saw one, they crushed it; and fortunately, the onslaught as yet was only by skirmishers. Again and again, the water sank and rose, carrying leaves and drowned ants away with it. It lowered once more nearly to its bed; but this time the exhausted defenders waited in vain for the flush of destruction. Leiningen sensed disaster; something must have gone wrong with the machinery of the dam. Then a sweating peon tore up to him—

"They're over!"

While the besieged were concentrating upon the defense of the stretch opposite the wood, the seemingly unaffected line beyond the wood had become the theatre of decisive action. Here the defenders' front was sparse and scattered; everyone who could be spared had hurried away to the south.

Just as the man at the weir had lowered the water almost to the bed of the ditch, the ants on a wide front began another attempt at a direct crossing like that of the preceding day. Into the emptied bed poured an irresistible throng. Rushing across the ditch, they attained the inner bank before the slow-witted Indians fully grasped the situation. Their frantic screams dumbfounded the man at the weir. Before he could direct the river anew into the safeguarding bed he saw himself surrounded by raging ants. He ran like the others, ran for his life.

When Leiningen heard this, he knew the plantation was doomed. He wasted no time bemoaning the inevitable. For as long as there was the slightest chance of success, he had stood his ground, and now any further resistance was both useless and dangerous. He fired three revolver shots into the air—the prearranged signal for his men to retreat instantly within the "inner moat." Then he rode towards the ranch house.

This was two miles from the point of invasion. There was therefore time enough to prepare the second line of defense against the advent of the ants. Of the three great petrol cisterns near the house, one had already been half emptied by the constant withdrawals needed for the pumps during the fight at the water ditch. The remaining petrol in it was now drawn off through underground pipes into the concrete trench which encircled the ranch house and its outbuildings.

And there, drifting in twos and threes, Leiningen's men reached him. Most of them were obviously trying to preserve an air of calm and indifference, belied, however, by their restless glances and knitted brows. One could see their belief in a favorable outcome of the struggle was already considerably shaken.

The planter called his peons around him.

"Well, lads," he began, "we've lost the first round. But we'll smash the beggars yet, don't you worry. Anyone who thinks otherwise can draw his pay here and now and push off. There are rafts enough to spare on the river and plenty of time still to reach 'em."

Not a man stirred.

Leiningen acknowledged his silent vote of confidence with a laugh that was half a grunt. "That's the stuff, lads. Too bad if you'd missed the rest of the show, eh? Well, the fun won't start till morning. Once these blighters turn tail, there'll be plenty of work for everyone and higher wages all round. And now run along and get something to eat; you've earned it all right."

In the excitement of the fight the greater part of the day had passed without the men once pausing to snatch a bite. Now that the ants were for the time being out of sight, and the "wall of petrol" gave a stronger feeling of security, hungry stomachs began to assert their claims.

The bridges over the concrete ditch were removed. Here and there solitary ants had reached the ditch; they gazed at the petrol meditatively, then scurried back again. Apparently, they had little interest at the moment for what lay beyond the evil-reeking barrier; the abundant spoils of the plantation were the main attraction. Soon the trees, shrubs and beds for miles around were hulled with ants zealously gobbling the yield of long weary months of strenuous toil.

As twilight began to fall, a cordon of ants marched around the petrol trench, but as yet made no move towards its brink. Leiningen posted sentries with headlights and electric torches, then withdrew to his office, and began to reckon up his losses. He estimated these as large, but, in comparison with his bank balance, by no means unbearable. He worked out in some detail a scheme of intensive cultivation which would enable him, before very long, to more than compensate himself for the damage now being wrought to his crops. It was with a contented mind that he finally betook himself to bed where he slept deeply until dawn, undisturbed by any thought that next day little more might be left of him than a glistening skeleton.

He rose with the sun and went out on the flat roof of his house. And a scene like one from Dante lay around him; for miles in every direction there was nothing but a black, glittering multitude, a multitude of rested, sated, but none the less voracious ants: yes, look as far as one might, one could see nothing but that rustling black throng, except in the north, where the great river drew a boundary they could not hope to pass. But even the high stone breakwater, along the bank of the river, which Leiningen had built as a defense against inundations, was, like the paths, the shorn trees and shrubs, the ground itself, black with ants.

So their greed was not glutted in razing that vast plantation? Not by a long shot; they were all the more eager now on a rich and certain booty—four hundred men, numerous horses, and bursting granaries.

At first it seemed that the petrol trench would serve its purpose. The besiegers sensed the peril of swimming it, and made no move to plunge blindly over its brink. Instead they devised a better maneuver; they began to collect shreds of bark, twigs and dried leaves and dropped these into the petrol. Everything green, which could have been similarly used, had long since been eaten. After a time, though, a long procession could be seen bringing from the west the tamarind leaves used as rafts the day before.

Since the petrol, unlike the water in the outer ditch, was perfectly still, the refuse stayed where it was thrown. It was several hours before the ants succeeded in covering an appreciable part of the surface. At length, however, they were ready to proceed to a direct attack.

Their storm troops swarmed down the concrete side, scrambled over the supporting surface of twigs and leaves, and impelled these over the few remaining streaks of open petrol until they reached the other side. Then they began to climb up this to make straight for the helpless garrison.

During the entire offensive, the planter sat peacefully, watching them with interest, but not stirring a muscle. Moreover, he had ordered his men not to disturb in any way whatever the advancing horde. So they squatted listlessly along the bank of the ditch and waited for a sign from the boss. The petrol was now covered with ants. A few had climbed the inner concrete wall and were scurrying towards the defenders.

"Everyone back from the ditch!" roared Leiningen. The men rushed away, without the slightest idea of his plan. He stooped forward and cautiously dropped into the ditch a stone which split the floating carpet and its living freight, to reveal a gleaming patch of petrol. A match spurted, sank down to the oily surface— Leiningen sprang back; in a flash a towering rampart of fire encompassed the garrison.

This spectacular and instant repulse threw the Indians into ecstasy. They applauded, yelled and stamped, like children at a pantomime. Had it not been for the awe in which they held the boss, they would infallibly have carried him shoulder high.

It was some time before the petrol burned down to the bed of the ditch, and the wall of smoke and flame began to lower. The ants had retreated in a wide circle from the devastation, and innumerable charred fragments along the outer bank showed that the flames had spread from the holocaust in the ditch well into the ranks beyond, where they had wrought havoc far and wide.

Yet the perseverance of the ants was by no means broken; indeed, each setback seemed only to whet it. The concrete cooled, the flicker of the dying flames wavered and vanished, petrol from the second tank poured into the trench— and the ants marched forward anew to the attack.

The foregoing scene repeated itself in every detail, except that on this occasion less time was needed to bridge the ditch, for the petrol was now already filmed by a layer of ash. Once again they withdrew; once again petrol flowed into the ditch. Would the creatures never learn that their self-sacrifice was utterly senseless? It really was senseless, wasn't it? Yes, of course it was senseless—provided the defenders had an unlimited supply of petrol.

When Leiningen reached this stage of reasoning, he felt for the first time since the arrival of the ants that his confidence was deserting him. His skin began to creep; he loosened his collar. Once the devils were over the trench there wasn't a chance in hell for him and his men. God, what a prospect, to be eaten alive like that!

For the third time the flames immolated the attacking troops, and burned down to extinction. Yet the ants were coming on again as if nothing had happened. And meanwhile Leiningen had made a discovery that chilled him to the bone—petrol was no longer flowing into the ditch. Something must be blocking the outflow pipe of the third and last cistern—a snake or a dead rat? Whatever it was, the ants could be held off no longer, unless petrol could by some method be led from the cistern into the ditch.

Then Leiningen remembered that in an outhouse nearby were two old disused fire engines. Spry as never before in their lives, the peons dragged them out of the shed, connected their pumps to the cistern, uncoiled and laid the hose. They were just in time to aim a stream of petrol at a column of ants that had already crossed and drive them back down the incline into the ditch. Once more an oily girdle surrounded the garrison, once more it was possible to hold the position—for the moment.

It was obvious, however, that this last resource meant only the postponement of defeat and death. A few of the peons fell on their knees and began to pray; others, shrieking insanely, fired their revolvers at the black, advancing masses, as if they felt their despair was pitiful enough to sway fate itself to mercy.

At length, two of the men's nerves broke: Leiningen saw a naked Indian leap over the north side of the petrol trench, quickly followed by a second. They sprinted with incredible speed towards the river. But their fleetness did not save them; long before they could attain the rafts, the enemy covered their bodies from head to foot.

In the agony of their torment, both sprang blindly into the wide river, where enemies no less sinister awaited them. Wild screams of mortal anguish informed the breathless onlookers that crocodiles and sword-toothed piranhas were no less ravenous than ants, and even nimbler in reaching their prey.

In spite of this bloody warning, more and more men showed they were making up their minds to run the blockade. Anything, even a fight midstream against alligators, seemed better than powerlessly waiting for death to come and slowly consume their living bodies.

Leiningen flogged his brain till it reeled. Was there nothing on earth could sweep this devil's spawn back into the hell from which it came?

Then out of the inferno of his bewilderment rose a terrifying inspiration. Yes, one hope remained, and one alone. It might be possible to dam the great river completely, so that its waters would fill not only the water ditch but overflow into the entire gigantic "saucer" of land in which lay the plantation.

The far bank of the river was too high for the waters to escape that way. The stone breakwater ran between the river and the plantation; its only gaps occurred where the "horseshoe" ends of the water ditch passed into the river. So its waters would not only be forced to inundate into the plantation, they would also be held there by the breakwater until they rose to its own high level. In half an hour, perhaps even earlier, the plantation and its hostile army of occupation would be flooded.

The ranch house and outbuildings stood upon rising ground. Their foundations were higher than the breakwater, so the flood would not reach them. And any remaining ants trying to ascend the slope could be repulsed by petrol.

It was possible—yes, if one could only get to the dam! A distance of nearly two miles lay between the ranch house and the weir—two miles of ants. Those two peons had managed only a fifth of that distance at the cost of their lives. Was there an Indian daring enough after that to run the gauntlet five times as far? Hardly likely; and if there were, his prospect of getting back was almost nil.

No, there was only one thing for it, he'd have to make the attempt himself; he might just as well be running as sitting still, anyway, when the ants finally got him. Besides, there was a bit of a chance. Perhaps the ants weren't so almighty, after all; perhaps he had allowed the mass suggestion of that evil black throng to hypnotize him, just as a snake fascinates and overpowers.

The ants were building their bridges. Leiningen got up on a chair. "Hey, lads, listen to me!" he cried. Slowly and listlessly, from all sides of the trench, the men began to shuffle towards him, the apathy of death already stamped on their faces.

"Listen, lads!" he shouted. "You're frightened of those beggars, but you're a damn sight more frightened of me, and I'm proud of you. There's still a chance to save our lives—by flooding the plantation from the river. Now one of you might manage to get as far as the weir— but he'd never come back. Well, I'm not going to let you try it; if I did I'd be worse than one of those ants. No, I called the tune, and now I'm going to pay the piper.

"The moment I'm over the ditch, set fire to the petrol. That'll allow time for the flood to do the trick. Then all you have to do is wait here all snug and quiet till I'm back. Yes, I'm coming back, trust me"—he grinned—"when I've finished my slimming-cure."

He pulled on high leather boots, drew heavy gauntlets over his hands, and stuffed the spaces between breeches and boots, gauntlets and arms, shirt and neck, with rags soaked in petrol. With close-fitting mosquito goggles he shielded his eyes, knowing too well the ants' dodge of first robbing their victim of sight. Finally, he plugged his nostrils and ears with cotton-wool, and let the peons drench his clothes with petrol.

He was about to set off, when the old Indian medicine man came up to him. He had a wondrous salve, he said, prepared from a species of chafer whose odor was intolerable to ants. Yes, this odor protected these chafers from the attacks of even the most murderous ants. The Indian smeared the boss' boots, his gauntlets, and his face over and over with the extract.

Leiningen then remembered the paralyzing effect of ants' venom, and the Indian gave him a gourd full of the medicine he had administered to the bitten peon at the water ditch. The planter drank it down without noticing its bitter taste; his mind was already at the weir.

He started off towards the northwest corner of the trench. With a bound he was over—and among the ants.

The beleaguered garrison had no opportunity to watch Leiningen's race against death. The ants were climbing the inner bank again— the lurid ring of petrol blazed aloft. For the fourth time that day the reflection from the fire shone on the sweating faces of the imprisoned men, and on the reddish-black cuirasses of their oppressors. The red and blue, dark-edged flames leaped vividly now, celebrating what? The funeral pyre of the four hundred, or of the hosts of destruction? Leiningen ran. He ran in long, equal strides, with only one thought, one sensation, in his being—he must get through. He dodged all trees and shrubs. Except for the split seconds his soles touched the ground the ants should have no opportunity to alight on him. That they would get to him soon, despite the salve on his boots, the petrol in his clothes, he realized only too well, but he knew even more surely that he must, and that he would, get to the weir.

Apparently the salve was some use after all; not until he reached halfway did he feel ants under his clothes, and a few on his face. Mechanically, in his stride, he struck at them, scarcely conscious of their bites. He saw he was drawing appreciably nearer the weir—the distance grew less and less—sank to five hundred —three—two—one hundred yards.

Then he was at the weir and gripping the ant-hulled wheel. Hardly had he seized it when a horde of infuriated ants flowed over his hands, arms and shoulders. He started the wheel— before it turned once on its axis the swarm covered his face. Leiningen strained like a madman, his lips pressed tight; if he opened them to draw breath....

He turned and turned; slowly the dam lowered until it reached the bed of the river.

Already the water was overflowing the ditch. Another minute, and the river was pouring through the nearby gap in the breakwater. The flooding of the plantation had begun.

Leiningen let go the wheel. Now, for the first time, he realized he was coated from head to foot with a layer of ants. In spite of the petrol his clothes were full of them, several had got to his body or were clinging to his face. Now that he had completed his task, he felt the smart raging over his flesh from the bites of sawing and piercing insects.

Frantic with pain, he almost plunged into the river. To be ripped and splashed to shreds by paranhas? Already he was running the return journey, knocking ants from his gloves and jacket, brushing them from his bloodied face, squashing them to death under his clothes.

One of the creatures bit him just below the rim of his goggles; he managed to tear it away, but the agony of the bite and its etching acid drilled into the eye nerves. He saw now through circles of fire into a milky mist, then he ran for a time almost blinded, knowing that if he once tripped and fell.... The old Indian's brew didn't seem much good; it weakened the poison a bit, but didn't get rid of it. His heart pounded as if it would burst; blood roared in his ears; a giant's fist battered his lungs.

Then he could see again, but the burning girdle of petrol appeared infinitely far away; he could not last half that distance. Swift-changing pictures flashed through his head, episodes in his life, while in another part of his brain a cool and impartial onlooker informed this ant-blurred, gasping, exhausted bundle named Leiningen that such a rushing panorama of scenes from one's past is seen only in the moment before death.

A stone in the path ... to weak to avoid it ... the planter stumbled and collapsed. He tried to rise ... he must be pinned under a rock ... it was impossible ... the slightest movement was impossible....

Then all at once he saw, starkly clear and huge, and, right before his eyes, furred with ants, towering and swaying in its death agony, the pampas stag. In six minutes—gnawed to the bones. God, he couldn't die like that! And something outside him seemed to drag him to his feet. He tottered. He began to stagger forward again.

Through the blazing ring hurtled an apparition which, as soon as it reached the ground on the inner side, fell full length and did not move. Leiningen, at the moment he made that leap through the flames, lost consciousness for the first time in his life. As he lay there, with glazing eyes and lacerated face, he appeared a man returned from the grave. The peons rushed to him, stripped off his clothes, tore away the ants from a body that seemed almost one open wound; in some paces the bones were showing. They carried him into the ranch house.

As the curtain of flames lowered, one could see in place of the illimitable host of ants an extensive vista of water. The thwarted river had swept over the plantation, carrying with it the entire army. The water had collected and mounted in the great "saucer," while the ants had in vain attempted to reach the hill on which stood the ranch house. The girdle of flames held them back.

And so imprisoned between water and fire, they had been delivered into the annihilation that was their god. And near the farther mouth of the water ditch, where the stone mole had its second gap, the ocean swept the lost battalions into the river, to vanish forever.

The ring of fire dwindled as the water mounted to the petrol trench and quenched the dimming flames. The inundation rose higher and higher, because its outflow was impeded by the timber and underbrush it had carried along with it, its surface required some time to reach the top of the high stone breakwater and discharge over it the rest of the shattered army.

It swelled over ant-stippled shrubs and bushes, until it washed against the foot of the knoll whereon the besieged had taken refuge. For a while an alluvial of ants tried again and again to attain this dry land, only to be repulsed by streams of petrol back into the merciless flood.

LEININGEN LAY ON HIS BED, his body swathed from head to foot in bandages. With fomentations and salves, they had managed to stop the bleeding, and had dressed his many wounds. Now they thronged around him, one question in every face. Would he recover? "He won't die," said the old man who had bandaged him, "if he doesn't want to."

The planter opened his eyes. "Everything in order?" he asked.

"They're gone," said his nurse. "To hell." He held out to his master a gourd full of a powerful sleeping draught. Leiningen gulped it down.

"I told you I'd come back," he murmured, "even if I am a bit streamlined." He grinned and shut his eyes. He slept.

♦ ♦ ♦

"Leiningen Versus the Ants" first appeared in Germany, in 1937, as "Leiningens Kampf mit den Ameisen." The story's first appearance in English was in the December 1938 issue of Esquire *Magazine. The accompanying illustration is by Allen Koszowski.*

Austrian-born author Carl Stephenson (November 3, 1893 until sometime shortly after 1960), who also wrote pseudonymously as Stefan Sorel, is best known for this memorable and frequently reprinted tale of attacking army ants. "Leiningen..." was dramatized several times for radio: for the anthology shows Escape, *in 1948 and again in '49, and* Suspense, *in 1957 and '59. In 1954, producer George Pal premiered a big-screen adaptation,* The Naked Jungle, *starring Charlton Heston, and directed by Byron Haskin. The year before, Pal and Haskin had collaborated on the box-office hit* The War of the Worlds. *Pal's other films include* Destination Moon *(1950) and* The Time Machine *(1961). Also, "Von Mohl Vs. the Ants," a comic book story obviously inspired by Stephenson's tale, appeared in the August 1954 issue of Charlton's* Strange Suspense. *The story, illustrated by Steve Ditko, does not credit a writer, nor does it acknowledge the now legendary "Leiningen Versus the Ants."*

MIVE

BY CARL JACOBI

CARLING'S MARSH, SOME CALLED IT, BUT MORE OFTEN IT WAS KNOWN BY THE NAME OF MIVE. STRANGE NAME THAT—MIVE. AND IT WAS A STRANGE PLACE. FIVE WILD, DESOLATE MILES OF THICK WATER, GREEN MASSES OF SOME KIND OF KELP, AND VIOLENT VEGETABLE GROWTH. To the east the cypress trees swelled more into prominence, and this district was vaguely designated by the villagers as the Flan. Again a strange name, and again I offer no explanation. A sense of depression, of isolation perhaps, which threatened to crush any buoyancy of feeling possessed by the most hardened traveler, seemed to emanate from this lonely wasteland. Was it any wonder that its observers always told of seeing it at night, before a storm, or in the spent afternoon of a dark and frowning day? And even if they had wandered upon it, say on a bright morning in June, the impression probably would have been the same, for the sun glittering upon the surface of the olive water would have lost its exuberant brilliance and become absorbed in the roily depths below. However, the presence of this huge marsh would have interested no one, had not the east road skirted for a dismal quarter-mile its melancholy shore

The east road, avoided, being frequently impassable because of high water, was a roundabout connection between the little towns of Twellen and Lamarr. The road seemed to have been irresistibly drawn toward the Mive, for it cut a huge half-moon across the country for seemingly no reason at all. But this arc led through a wilderness of an entirely different aspect from the land surrounding the other trails. Like the rest it started among the hills, climbed the hills, and rambled down the hills, but after passing Echo Lake, that lowering tarn locked in a deep ravine, it straggled up a last hillock and swept down upon a large flat. And as one proceeded, the flat steadily sank lower; it forgot the hills, and the ground, already damp, became sodden and quivering under the feet.

And then looming up almost suddenly— Mive! ... a morass at first, a mere bog, then a jungle of growth repulsive in its over-luxuriance, and finally a sea of kelp, an inland Sargasso.

Just why I had chosen the east road for a long walk into the country I don't really know. In fact, my reason for taking such a hike at all was rather vague. The day was certainly anything but ideal; a raw wind whipping in from the south, and a leaden sky typical of early September lent anything but an inviting aspect to those rolling Rentharpian hills. But walk I did, starting out briskly as the inexperienced all do, and gradually slowing down until four o'clock found me plodding almost mechanically along the flat. I dare say every passer-by, no matter how many times he frequented the road, always stopped at exactly the same spot I did and suffered the same feeling of awe and depression that came upon me as my eyes fell upon that wild marsh. But instead of hurrying on, instead of quickening my steps in search of the hills again, I for some unaccountable reason which I have always laid to curiosity, left the trail and plunged through oozing fungi to the water's very edge.

A wave of warm humid air, heavy with the odor of growth, swept over me as though I had suddenly opened the door of some monstrous hothouse. Great masses of vines with fat creeping tendrils hung from the cypress trees. Razor-edged reeds, marsh grass, long waving cattails, swamp vegetation of a thousand kinds flourished here with luxuriant abundance. I went on along the shore; the water lapped steadily the sodden earth at my feet, oily-looking water, grim-looking, reflecting a sullen and overcast sky.

There was something fascinating in it all, and while I am not one of those adventurous souls who revel in the unusual, I gave no thought of turning back to the road, but plodded through the soggy, clinging soil, and over rotting logs as though hurrying toward some destination. The very contrast, the voluptuousness of all the growth seemed some mighty lure, and I came to a halt only when gasping for breath from exertion.

For perhaps half an hour I stumbled forward at intervals, and then from the increasing number of cypress trees I saw that I was approaching that district known as the Flan. A large lagoon lay here, stagnant, dark, and entangled among the rip-grass and reeds, reeds that rasped against each other in a dry, unpleasant manner like some sleeper constantly clearing his throat.

All the while I had been wondering over the absolute absence of all animate life. With its dank air, its dark appeal, and its wildness, the Eden recesses of the Mive presented a glorious place for all forms of swamp life. And yet not a snake, not a toad, nor an insect had I seen. It was rather strange, and I looked curiously about me as I walked.

And then ... and then as if in contradiction to my thoughts it fluttered before me.

With a gasp of amazement, I found myself staring at an enormous, a gigantic ebony-black butterfly. Its jet coloring was magnificent, its proportions startling, for from wing tip to wing tip it measured fully fifteen inches. It approached me slowly, and as it did I saw that I was wrong in my classification. It was not a butterfly; neither was it a moth; nor did it seem to belong to the order of the *Lepidoptera* at all. As large as a bird, its great body came into prominence over the wings, disclosing a huge proboscis, ugly and repulsive.

I suppose it was instinctively that I stretched out my hand to catch the thing as it suddenly drew nearer. My fingers closed over it, but with a frightened whir it tore away, darted high in the air, and fluttered proudly into the undergrowth. An exclamation of disappointment burst from me, and I glanced ruefully at my hand where the prize should have been.

It was then that I became aware that the first two fingers and a part of my palm were lightly coated with a powdery substance that had rubbed off the delicate membrane of the insect's wings. The perspiration of my hand was fast changing this powder into a sticky bluish substance, and I noticed that this gave off a delightfully sweet odor. The odor grew heavier; it changed to a perfume, an incense, luring, exotic, fascinating. It seemed to fill the air, to crowd my lungs, to create an irresistible desire to taste it. I sat down on a log; I tried to fight it off, but like a blanket it enveloped me, tearing down my resistance in a great attraction as magnet to steel. Like a sword it seared its way into my nostrils, and the desire became maddening, irresistible.

At length I could stand it no longer, and I slowly brought my fingers to my lips. A horribly bitter taste which momentarily paralyzed my entire mouth and throat was the result. It ended in a long coughing spell.

Disgusted at my lack of will-power and at this rather foolish episode, I turned and began to retrace my steps toward the road. A feeling of nausea and of sluggishness began to seep into me, and I quickened my pace to get away from the stifling air. But at the same time I kept watch for a reappearance of that strange butterfly. No sound now save the washing of the heavy water against the reeds and the sucking noise of my steps.

I had gone farther than I realized, and I cursed the foolish whim that had sent me here. As for the butterfly—whom could I make believe the truth of its size or even of its existence? I had nothing for proof, and ... I stopped suddenly!

A peculiar formation of vines had attracted my attention—and yet not vines either. The thing was oval, about five feet in length, and appeared to be many weavings or coils of some kind of hemp. It lay fastened securely in a lower crotch of a cypress. One end was open, and the whole thing was a grayish color like a cocoon ... a cocoon! An instinctive shudder of horror swept over me as the meaning of my thoughts struck me with full force.

With a cocoon as large as this, the size of the butterfly would be enormous. In a flash I saw the reason for the absence of all other life in the Mive. These butterflies, developed as they were to such proportions, had evolved into some strange order and become carnivorous. The fifteen-inch butterfly which had so startled me before faded into insignificance in the presence of this cocoon.

I seized a huge stick for defense and hurried on toward the road. A low muttering of thunder from somewhere off to the west added to my discomfort. Black threatening clouds, harbingers of an oncoming storm, were racing in from the horizon, and my spirits fell even lower with the deepening gloom. The gloom blurred into a darkness, and I picked my way forward along the shore with more and more difficulty. Suddenly the mutterings stopped, and there came that expectant, sultry silence that precedes the breaking of a storm.

But no storm came. The clouds all moved slowly, lava-like, toward a central formation directly above me, and there they stopped, became utterly motionless, engraved upon the sky. There was something ominous about that monstrous cloud bank, and in spite of the growing feeling of nausea, I watched it pass through a series of strange color metamorphoses, from a black to a greenish black, and from a decided green to a yellow, and from a yellow to a blinding, glaring red.

And then as I looked those clouds gradually opened; a ray of peculiar colorless light pierced through as the aperture enlarged, disclosing an enormous vault-shaped cavern cut through the stratus. The whole vision seemed to move nearer, to change from an indistinguishable blur as though magnified a thousand times. And then towers, domes, streets, and walls took form, and these coagulated into a city painted stereoscopically in the sky. I forgot everything and lost myself in a weird panorama of impossible happenings above me.

Crowds, mobs, millions of men clothed in mediæval armor of chain mail with high helmets were hurrying on, racing past in an endless procession of confusion. Regiment upon regiment, men and more men, a turbulent sea of marching humanity were fleeing, retreating as if from some horrible enemy!

And then it came, a swarm, a horde of butterflies ... enormous, ebony-black, carnivorous butterflies, approaching a doomed city. They met—the men and that strange form of life. But the defensive army and the gilded city seemed to be swallowed up, to be dissolved under this terrible force of incalculable power. The entire scene began to disintegrate into a mass, a river of molten gray, swirling and revolving like a wheel—a wheel with a hub, a flaming, fantastic, colossal ball of effulgence.

I was mad! My eyes were mad! I screamed in horror, but like Cyprola turned to stone, stood staring at this blasphemy in the heavens.

Again it began to coalesce; again a picture took form, but this time a design, gigantic, magnificent. And there under tremendous proportions with its black wings outspread was the butterfly I had sought to catch. The whole sky was covered by its massive form, a mighty repulsive tapestry.

It disappeared! The thunder mutterings, which had become silenced before, now burst forth without warning in unrestrained simultaneous fury. The clouds suddenly raced back again, erasing outline and detail, devouring the sight, and there was only the blackness, the gloom of a brooding, overcast sky.

With a wild cry, I turned and ran, plunged through the underbrush, my sole thought being to escape from this insane marsh. Vines and creepers lashed at my face as I tore on; knife reeds and swamp grass penetrated my clothing, leaving stinging burns of pain. Streak lightning of blinding brilliance, thunderations like some volcanic upheaval belched forth from the sky. A wind sprang up, and the reeds and long grasses undulated before it like a thousand writhing serpents. The sullen water of the Mive was black now and racing in toward the shore in huge waves, and the thunder above swelled into one stupendous crescendo.

Suddenly I threw myself flat upon the oozing

ground and with wild fear wormed my way deep into the undergrowth. It was coming!

A moment later, with a loud flapping, the giant butterfly raced out of the storm toward me. Scarcely ten feet away I could see its enormous, sword-like proboscis, its repulsive, disgusting body, and I could hear its sucking inhalations of breath. A wave of horror seared its way through my very brain; the pulsations of my heart throbbed at my temples and at my throat, and I continued to stare helplessly at it. *A thing of evil it was, trans-normal, bred in a leprous, feverish swamp, a hybrid growth from a paludinous place of rot and over-luxuriant vegetation.*

But I was well hidden in the reeds. The monstrosity passed on unseeing. In a flash I was up and lunging on again. The crashing reverberations of the storm seemed to pound against me as if trying to hold me back. A hundred times I thought I heard that terrible flapping of wings behind me, only to discover with a prayer of thanks that I was mistaken. But at last the road! Without stopping, without slackening speed, I tore on, away from the Mive, across the quivering flat, and on and on to the hills. I climbed; I stumbled; I ran; my sole thought was to go as far as possible. At length exhaustion swept over me, and I fell gasping to the ground.

It seemed hours that I lay there, motionless, unheeding the driving rain on my back, and yet fully conscious. My brain was wild now. It pawed over the terrible events that had crowded themselves into the past few hours, re-pictured them, and strove for an answer.

What had happened to me? What had happened to me? And then suddenly I gave an exclamation. I remembered now, fool that I was. The fifteen-inch butterfly which had so startled me near the district of the Flan ... I had tried to catch the thing, and it had escaped, leaving in my hand only a powderish substance that I had vainly fought off and at last brought to my lips. That was it. What had happened after that? A feeling of nausea had set in, a great inward sickness like the immediate effects of a powerful drug. A strange insect of an unknown order, a thing resembling and yet differing from all forms of the *Lepidopiera*, a butterfly and yet not

a butterfly.... Who knows what internal effect that powder would have on one? Had I been wandering in a delirium, a delirium caused by the tasting of that powder from the insect's wings? And if so, where did the delirium fade into reality? The vision in the sky ... a vagary of a poisoned brain perhaps, but the monstrosity which had pursued me and the telltale cocoon ... again the delirium? No, and again no! That was too real, too horrible, and yet everything was all so strange and fantastic.

But what master insect was this that could play with a man's brain at will? What drug, what unknown opiate existed in the membrane of its ebony-black wings?

And I looked back, confused, bewildered, expecting perhaps an answer. There it lay, far below me, vague and indistinct in the deepening gloom, the black outlines of the cypress trees writhing in the night wind, silent, brooding, mysterious—the Mive.

👽 👽 👽

American journalist and author Carl Jacobi's second published story, "The Mive," first appeared in the Fall 1928 issue of his University's literary magazine, the Minnesota Quarterly. Both H. P. Lovecraft and August Derleth highly praised the story when it was reprinted in the January 1932 issue of Weird Tales, signaling the beginning of Jacobi's long association with "the Unique Magazine."

Of his university days, Jacobi (1908–1997) wrote, "I tried to divide my time between rhetoric courses and the geology lab. As an underclassman I was somewhat undecided whether future life would find me studying rocks and fossils or simply pounding a typewriter. The typewriter won." Jacobi went on to produce over a hundred tales for the leading pulp magazines of his day.

Author Jack Adrian writes, "Jacobi had a useful knack for dreaming up memorable milieu against which to set his tales, and bizarre situations that stayed in the mind long after the magazine the story itself was in had been finished and tossed away."

INSECT SUMMER

BY KURT NEWTON

AUGUST NIGHT. RADIO PLAYING. DAVID LITTLE WATCHED THE ROAD AHEAD, THE HEADLIGHTS OF HIS CHEVY PICK-UP STABBING AT THE DARKNESS LIKE A JOGGER WITH A FLASHLIGHT. HE WAS ALREADY TWO HOURS LATE FOR DINNER, BUT HIS wife, Kerri, already knew he was putting in the OT. Work had him stretched thin and tired. End-of-the-fiscal-year business crunch approaching. It was crazy. Corporations and universities spending their government funding like monopoly money. But that's what it was like in the laser business these days. The age of Buck Rogers and Star Wars had finally come to pass.

David didn't really care whose age was here, as long as it paid the bills and he wasn't so tired at night that he and Kerri couldn't turn back the sheets and get some much needed quality time.

The radio erupted in static. "Damn it!" David turned the knob down and clicked it off. Ahead, in the glare of his headlights, he saw them—two of those PESTS—alien machines that looked like armor-plated VW Beetles sitting along the side of the road.

David slowed his truck as he passed by. They never ceased to amaze and disgust him at the same time. One was half-climbed up the back end of the other and was slowly pumping its pistons. David made a snorting noise and laid on his horn. "Get a room!" he yelled out the window, and drove on.

POLYMORPHIC EXTRA-TERRESTRIAL SILICON-BASED TRANSIENTS. Or PESTS. They weren't really machines at all. They were more stone than metal, but their smooth grey skins, a result of atmospheric burn, lent them the appearance of machines. Moving machines. Slow-moving machines. Completely harmless, except if one were to latch onto your building's foundation, or start chewing up your driveway.

They had arrived two years earlier. Scientists theorized that these creatures, like Columbus, had missed their mark, perhaps aiming for Mercury or even Venus. It created quite a stir when it happened. E.T. phone home, and all that hype. Except in the movie, E.T. came solo. These guys showered down by the thousands during "Insect Summer," as it became known. Crashing into expensive hillside Californian homes. Taking out Caesar's Palace during a pay-per-view boxing event. Landing on the fifty-yard line at the Meadowlands. (The Giants had to split their home games between Buffalo's Ralph Wilson Stadium and New England's Foxboro that winter.) The excitement lasted until people realized just how useless they were. It took special cranes to lift them, so most of them just stayed where they landed. You couldn't kill them. Dynamiting them only gave you more than what you started with. They were self-replicating on a cellular level. Cut off a finger and you grow a hand. So, after a while, except for the nature lovers and the I-told-you-so scientists, most people considered them a nuisance. Space garbage tossed out of the passenger-side window of a free-wheeling cosmos.

But new fears were beginning to crop up. Six months ago, the PESTS began to reproduce on their own. New ones were being born at a rate of about a hundred a day. With a gestation period of 18 months, and a life expectancy of who knows how long, it didn't take a Stephen Hawking to figure out that in several years time our slow-moving rock buddies were going to eat us out of house and home—quite literally. And that had some people worried.

DAVID PULLED INTO HIS DRIVEWAY. He turned off the truck's engine. It died after two ticks and a rattle. Inside the house, the kitchen lights were off. The next window over David saw the dull neon glow of the television set. At least the front light was on, a good sign. He grabbed the six-pack off the front seat and stepped out of the truck.

It was a beautiful clear night. The stars were out in force, all sharply sprayed across the heavens like a fine crystalline mist. It could be worse, David thought to himself, picturing in his mind the two PESTS he had passed down on lover's lane resting up against the foundation of his home—the world's largest termites!

Around the front porch light, a clot of mosquitoes and night flies greeted David as he entered the house.

"Kerri?" He placed the six-pack on the kitchen island.

The TV was blasting, some announcer's voice deep and low and serious. David walked into the den. "Hi, hon."

"Shhh," his wife said, holding up a finger. Her eyes were focused on the television set.

"...and the debate continues: ancient monolithic messengers, or polymorphic pests? I'm Stone Drawbridge. Goodnight."

"What are they saying now?"

David's wife looked up at him. Her eyes were wide. "Fleas."

"What—no spiders?" David tried to make light of the subject. He knew his wife hated anything creepy crawly.

"David, it's not funny. I've never liked them. Something is just not right. Why are they here?"

"Kerri, honey, they're the size of elephants and move as slow as snails."

"But one scientist is now saying that he thinks they're parasites. Like 'fleas on the back of a dog' was how he put it."

David shook his head. "They don't know. They're just guessing." He leaned over and gave her a kiss. "Hey, I heard something that ought to make you happy. The guys up at MIT are close to finding a way to disintegrate the silicon suckers—without regeneration. They're working on a new high-frequency laser separator that just might do the trick. And guess who's providing the lenses?"

Kerri's eyes lit up. But the momentary brightness was quickly diffused. Her face turned moody again. "But what if that scientist is right? What if they are just pests? Did you know that in three years there could be nearly as many of them as there are of us?"

David nestled in beside his wife and held her in his arms. "Don't worry. They're working on it. It'll never happen." He stroked her hair.

Outside, the night was quiet. David had almost forgotten. One of the effects of the PESTS's presence was that the crickets no longer chirruped in the night. He missed that sound, that peaceful, monotonous drone that let you know the world had its own voice. That it was alive and breathing. Now, it was as if the night were empty. Silent. Waiting. Holding its breath.

THAT NIGHT, David and Kerri made love. Afterward, as he lay in bed, David thought about the PESTS. He wished he could have been there at MIT to see the test firing of that new laser system. He felt good about his company's work, proud to be part of such an important technology. He imagined one of the stone creatures melting like plastic beneath the invisible ray of the separator.

A smile swept across his face. Man had faced worse problems in the past, had conquered greater foes. Disease and disaster. And through it all, Man had always come out on top. Look at

Noah and his Ark? The best damn example of Man's technology coming out on top.

David let himself settle into his pillow, content with his species' superiority, and soon fell off to sleep.

That night he dreamed of hot summer nights, playing outside with his childhood friends. Hide-and-go-seek. The sound of the crickets playing up a storm, loud as fire sirens...

...so loud, in fact, they woke him up.

It was early morning, dawn just breaking on the horizon. David's arm was numb, lost beneath his wife's body. Kerri shifted slightly and he slid his arm out with a grimace. The sirens were real. "What the hell?"

David sat up. The sirens were whooping it up all across town. He got out of bed and went to the window.

The sky was an ominous grey overcast, just the hint of morning sun beginning to burn through. The sirens rose and fell. The last time David had heard sirens like these was when the old Sunoco Station burned down in the center of town. That was a five-alarm fire. This sounded more like a ten-alarm.

He turned to his wife, who was now awake. She was looking up at him.

"Something's going on," he said. "Sounds like a fire." David grabbed his clothes and got dressed. "Can't see any smoke, though." A nervous chitter began to creep into his gut. "You coming?"

His wife simply lay there. She stared out the window and shook her head slowly. A tear ran down the slope of her cheek.

A rumble now. A sound like thunder beneath the sirens. David ran outside.

The religious fanatics had called Insect Summer one of God's plagues, space locust signaling the end of the world. Environmentalists smugly regarded the visitors as our mirror—that, in fact, Man was the real parasite, sucking the world dry of its resources, and these bugs were here to illustrate that point.

But none of that mattered now. For they were all wrong.

David stood in his front yard and looked up in awe. The sky was full of sound. His stomach shook with a reverberant sub-frequency. The clouds were breaking apart. He could see them, now. Huge. Wings spread wide as oil tankers. Bodies the size of Hindenburgs. Immense, monstrous, stone-like creatures. Descending from the heavens in search of food. To pick the fleas off the back of this dog called Earth.

David's wife screamed, but he barely heard her above the din, as the sun's light blazed across the threshold of this new dawn.

"Insect Summer" first appeared in issue #8 of Burning Sky Magazine *(2001).*

As a child, Kurt Newton was weaned on episodes of The Twilight Zone *and* The Outer Limits, *and* Chiller Theater *(which showed many of the classic sci-fi horror movies of the '50s and '60s), laying the groundwork for his fertile imagination. His stories have appeared in numerous publications over the last twenty years, including* Weird Tales, Weirdbook, Space and Time, Dark Discoveries, Daily Science Fiction, The Arcanist *and* Hinnom Magazine. *He lives in Connecticut.*

THE ASH-TREE

By M. R. JAMES

EVERYONE WHO HAS TRAVELLED OVER EASTERN ENGLAND KNOWS THE SMALLER COUNTRY-HOUSES WITH WHICH IT IS STUDDED—THE RATHER DANK LITTLE buildings, usually in the Italian style, surrounded with parks of some eighty to a hundred acres. For me they have always had a very strong attraction, with the grey paling of split oak, the noble trees, the meres with their reed-beds, and the line of distant woods. Then, I like the pillared portico—perhaps stuck on to a red-brick Queen Anne house which has been faced with stucco to bring it into line with the "Grecian" taste of the end of the eighteenth century; the hall inside, going up to the roof, which hall ought always to be provided with a gallery and a small organ. I like the library, too, where you may find anything from a Psalter of the thirteenth century to a Shakespeare quarto. I like the pictures, of course; and perhaps most of all I like fancying what life in such a house was when it was first built, and in the piping times of landlords' prosperity, and not least now, when, if money is not so plentiful, taste is more varied and life quite as interesting. I wish to have one of these houses, and enough money to keep it together and entertain my friends in it modestly.

But this is a digression. I have to tell you of a curious series of events which happened in such a house as I have tried to describe. It is Castringham Hall in Suffolk. I think a good deal has been done to the building since the period of my story, but the essential features I have sketched are still there—Italian portico, square block of white house, older inside than out, park with fringe of woods, and mere. The one feature that marked out the house from a score of others is gone. As you looked at it from the park, you saw on the right a great old ash-tree growing within half a dozen yards of the wall, and almost or quite touching the building with its branches. I suppose it had stood there ever since Castringham ceased to be a fortified place, and since the moat was filled in and the Elizabethan dwelling-house built. At any rate, it had well-nigh attained its full dimensions in the year 1690.

In that year the district in which the Hall is situated was the scene of a number of witch-trials. It will be long, I think, before we arrive at a just estimate of the amount of solid reason—if there was any—which lay at the root of the universal fear of witches in old times. Whether the persons accused of this offence really did imagine that they were possessed of unusual power of any kind; or whether they had the will at least, if not the power, of doing mischief to their neighbours; or whether all the confessions, of which there are so many, were extorted by the cruelty of the witch-finders—these are questions which are not, I fancy, yet solved. And the present narrative gives me pause. I cannot altogether sweep it away as mere invention. The reader must judge for himself.

Castringham contributed a victim to the *auto-da-fé*. Mrs Mothersole was her name, and she differed from the ordinary run of village witches only in being rather better off and in a more influential position. Efforts were made to save her by several reputable farmers of the parish. They did their best to testify to her character, and showed considerable anxiety as to the verdict of the jury.

But what seems to have been fatal to the woman was the evidence of the then proprietor of Castringham Hall—Sir Matthew Fell. He deposed to having watched her on three different occasions from his window, at the full of the moon, gathering sprigs "from the ash-tree near my house." She had climbed into the branches, clad only in her shift, and was cutting off small twigs with a peculiarly curved knife, and as she did so she seemed to be talking to herself. On each occasion Sir Matthew had done his best to capture the woman, but she had always taken alarm at some accidental noise he had made, and all he could see when he got down to the garden was a hare running across the path in the direction of the village.

On the third night he had been at the pains to follow at his best speed, and had gone straight to Mrs Mothersole's house; but he had had to wait a quarter of an hour battering at her door, and then she had come out very cross, and apparently very sleepy, as if just out of bed; and he had no good explanation to offer of his visit.

Mainly on this evidence, though there was much more of a less striking and unusual kind from other parishioners, Mrs Mothersole was found guilty and condemned to die. She was hanged a week after the trial, with five or six more unhappy creatures, at Bury St Edmunds.

Sir Matthew Fell, then Deputy-Sheriff, was present at the execution. It was a damp, drizzly March morning when the cart made its way up the rough grass hill outside Northgate, where the gallows stood. The other victims were apathetic or broken down with misery; but Mrs Mothersole was, as in life so in death, of a very different temper. Her "poysonous Rage," as a reporter of the time puts it, "did so work upon the Bystanders—yea, even upon the Hangman—that it was constantly affirmed of all that saw her that she presented the living Aspect of a mad Divell. Yet she offer'd no Resistance to the Officers of the Law; only she looked upon those that laid Hands upon her with so direfull and venomous an Aspect that—as one of them afterwards assured me—the meer Thought of it preyed inwardly

upon his Mind for six Months after."

However, all that she is reported to have said were the seemingly meaningless words: "There will be guests at the Hall." Which she repeated more than once in an undertone.

Sir Matthew Fell was not unimpressed by the bearing of the woman. He had some talk upon the matter with the Vicar of his parish, with whom he travelled home after the assize business was over. His evidence at the trial had not been very willingly given; he was not specially infected with the witch-finding mania, but he declared, then and afterwards, that he could not give any other account of the matter than that he had given, and that he could not possibly have been mistaken as to what he saw. The whole transaction had been repugnant to him, for he was a man who liked to be on pleasant terms with those about him; but he saw a duty to be done in this business, and he had done it. That seems to have been the gist of his sentiments, and the Vicar applauded it, as any reasonable man must have done.

A few weeks after, when the moon of May was at the full, Vicar and Squire met again in the park, and walked to the Hall together. Lady Fell was with her mother, who was dangerously ill, and Sir Matthew was alone at home; so the Vicar, Mr Crome, was easily persuaded to take a late supper at the Hall.

Sir Matthew was not very good company this evening. The talk ran chiefly on family and parish matters, and, as luck would have it, Sir Matthew made a memorandum in writing of certain wishes or intentions of his regarding his estates, which afterwards proved exceedingly useful.

When Mr Crome thought of starting for home, about half past nine o'clock, Sir Matthew and he took a preliminary turn on the gravelled walk at the back of the house. The only incident that struck Mr Crome was this: they were in sight of the ash-tree which I described as growing near the windows of the building, when Sir Matthew stopped and said:

"What is that that runs up and down the stem of the ash? It is never a squirrel? They will all be in their nests by now."

The Vicar looked and saw the moving creature, but he could make nothing of its colour in the moonlight. The sharp outline, however, seen for an instant, was imprinted on his brain, and he could have sworn, he said, though it sounded foolish, that, squirrel or not, it had more than four legs.

Still, not much was to be made of the momentary vision, and the two men parted. They may have met since then, but it was not for a score of years.

Next day Sir Matthew Fell was not downstairs at six in the morning, as was his custom, nor at seven, nor yet at eight. Hereupon the servants went and knocked at his chamber door. I need not prolong the description of their anxious listenings and renewed batterings on the panels. The door was opened at last from the outside, and they found their master dead and black. So much you have guessed. That there were any marks of violence did not at the moment appear; but the window was open.

One of the men went to fetch the parson, and then by his directions rode on to give notice to the coroner. Mr Crome himself went as quick as he might to the Hall, and was shown to the room where the dead man lay. He has left some notes among his papers which show how genuine a respect and sorrow was felt for Sir Matthew, and there is also this passage, which I transcribe for the sake of the light it throws upon the course of events, and also upon the common beliefs of the time:

"There was not any the least Trace of an Entrance having been forc'd to the Chamber: but the Casement stood open, as my poor Friend would always have it in this Season. He had his Evening Drink of small Ale in a silver vessel of about a pint measure, and tonight had not drunk it out. This Drink was examined by the Physician from Bury, a Mr Hodgkins, who could not, however, as he afterwards declar'd upon his Oath, before the Coroner's quest, discover that any matter of a venomous kind was present in it. For, as was natural, in the great Swelling and Blackness of the Corpse, there was talk made among the Neighbours of Poyson. The Body was very much Disorder'd as it laid in the Bed, being twisted after so extream a sort as gave too probable Conjecture that my worthy Friend and Patron had expir'd in great Pain and Agony. And what is as yet unexplain'd, and to myself the Argument of some Horrid and Artfull Designe in the Perpetrators of this Barbarous Murther, was this, that the Women which were entrusted with the laying-out of the Corpse and washing it, being both sad Pearsons and very well Respected in their Mournfull Profession, came to me in a great Pain and Distress both of Mind and Body, saying, what was indeed confirmed upon the first View, that they had no sooner touch'd the Breast of the Corpse with their naked Hands than they were sensible of a more than ordinary violent Smart and Acheing in their Palms, which, with their whole Forearms, in no long time swell'd so immoderately, the Pain still continuing, that, as afterwards proved, during many weeks they were forc'd to lay by the exercise of their Calling; and yet no mark seen on the Skin.

"Upon hearing this, I sent for the Physician, who was still in the House, and we made as carefull a Proof as we were able by the Help of a small Magnifying Lens of Crystal of the condition of the Skinn on this Part of the Body: but could not detect with the Instrument we had any Matter of Importance beyond a couple of small Punctures or Pricks, which we then concluded were the Spotts by which the Poyson might be introduced, remembering that Ring of *Pope Borgia*, with other known Specimens of the Horrid Art of the Italian Poysoners of the last age.

"So much is to be said of the Symptoms seen on the Corpse. As to what I am to add, it is meerly my own Experiment, and to be left to Posterity to judge whether there be anything of Value therein. There was on the Table by the Beddside a Bible of the small size, in which my Friend—punctuall as in Matters of less Moment, so in this more weighty one—used nightly, and upon his First Rising, to read a sett Portion. And I taking it up—not without a Tear duly paid to him wich from the Study of this poorer Adumbration was now pass'd to the contemplation of its great Originall—it came into my

Thoughts, as at such moments of Helplessness we are prone to catch at any the least Glimmer that makes promise of Light, to make trial of that old and by many accounted Superstitious Practice of drawing the *Sortes;* of which a Principall Instance, in the case of his late Sacred Majesty the Blessed Martyr King *Charles* and my Lord *Falkland*, was now much talked of. I must needs admit that by my Trial not much Assistance was afforded me: yet, as the Cause and Origin of these Dreadfull Events may hereafter be search'd out, I set down the Results, in the case it may be found that they pointed the true Quarter of the Mischief to a quicker Intelligence than my own.

"I made, then, three trials, opening the Book and placing my Finger upon certain Words: which gave in the first these words, from Luke xiii. 7, *Cut it down*; in the second, Isaiah xiii. 20, *It shall never be inhabited*; and upon the third Experiment, Job xxxix. 30, *Her young ones also suck up blood.*"

This is all that need be quoted from Mr Crome's papers. Sir Matthew Fell was duly coffined and laid into the earth, and his funeral sermon, preached by Mr Crome on the following Sunday, has been printed under the title of "The Unsearchable Way; or, England's Danger and the Malicious Dealings of Antichrist," it being the Vicar's view, as well as that most commonly held in the neighbourhood, that the Squire was the victim of a recrudescence of the Popish Plot.

His son, Sir Matthew the second, succeeded to the title and estates. And so ends the first act of the Castringham tragedy. It is to be mentioned, though the fact is not surprising, that the new Baronet did not occupy the room in which his father had died. Nor, indeed, was it slept in by anyone but an occasional visitor during the whole of his occupation. He died in 1735, and I do not find that anything particular marked his reign, save a curiously constant mortality among his cattle and live-stock in general, which showed a tendency to increase slightly as time went on.

Those who are interested in the details will find a statistical account in a letter to the *Gentleman's Magazine* of 1772, which draws the facts from the Baronet's own papers. He put an end to it at last by a very simple expedient, that of shutting up all his beasts in sheds at night, and keeping no sheep in his park. For he had noticed that nothing was ever attacked that spent the night indoors. After that the disorder confined itself to wild birds, and beasts of chase. But as we have no good account of the symptoms, and as all-night watching was quite unproductive of any clue, I do not dwell on what the Suffolk farmers called the "Castringham sickness."

The second Sir Matthew died in 1735, as I said, and was duly succeeded by his son, Sir Richard. It was in his time that the great family pew was built out on the north side of the parish church. So large were the Squire's ideas that several of the graves on that unhallowed side of the building had to be disturbed to satisfy his requirements. Among them was that of Mrs Mothersole, the position of which was accurately known, thanks to a note on a plan of the church and yard, both made by Mr Crome.

A certain amount of interest was excited in the village when it was known that the famous witch, who was still remembered by a few, was to be exhumed. And the feeling of surprise, and indeed disquiet, was very strong when it was found that, though her coffin was fairly sound and unbroken, there was no trace whatever inside it of body, bones, or dust. Indeed, it is a curious phenomenon, for at the time of her burying no such things were dreamt of as resurrection-men, and it is difficult to conceive any rational motive for stealing a body otherwise than for the uses of the dissecting-room.

The incident revived for a time all the stories of witch-trials and of the exploits of the witches, dormant for forty years, and Sir Richard's orders that the coffin should be burnt were thought by a good many to be rather foolhardy, though they were duly carried out.

Sir Richard was a pestilent innovator, it is certain. Before his time the Hall had been a fine block of the mellowest red brick; but Sir Richard had travelled in Italy and become infected with the Italian taste, and, having more money than his predecessors, he determined to leave an Italian palace where he had found an English house. So stucco and ashlar masked the brick; some indifferent Roman marbles were planted about in the entrance-hall and gardens; a reproduction of the Sibyl's temple at Tivoli was erected on the opposite bank of the mere; and Castringham took on an entirely new, and, I must say, a less engaging, aspect. But it was much admired, and served as a model to a good many of the neighbouring gentry in after-years.

ONE MORNING (it was in 1754) Sir Richard woke after a night of discomfort. It had been windy, and his chimney had smoked persistently, and yet it was so cold that he must keep up a fire. Also something had so rattled about the window that no man could get a moment's peace. Further, there was the prospect of several guests of position arriving in the course of the day, who would expect sport of some kind, and the inroads of the distemper (which continued among his game) had been lately so serious that he was afraid for his reputation as a game-preserver. But what really touched him most nearly was the other matter of his sleepless night. He could certainly not sleep in that room again.

That was the chief subject of his meditations at breakfast, and after it he began a systematic examination of the rooms to see which would suit his notions best. It was long before he found one. This had a window with an eastern aspect and that with a northern; this door the servants would be always passing, and he did not like the bedstead in that. No, he must have a room with a western look-out, so that the sun could not wake him early, and it must be out of the way of the business of the house. The housekeeper was at the end of her resources.

"Well, Sir Richard," she said, "you know that there is but the one room like that in the house."

"Which may that be?" said Sir Richard.

"And that is Sir Matthew's—the West Chamber."

"Well, put me in there, for there I'll lie to-night," said her master. "Which way is it? Here, to be sure"; and he hurried off.

"Oh, Sir Richard, but no one has slept there these forty years. The air has hardly been changed since Sir Matthew died there."

Thus she spoke, and rustled after him.

"Come, open the door, Mrs Chiddock. I'll see the chamber, at least."

So it was opened, and, indeed, the smell was very close and earthy. Sir Richard crossed to the window, and, impatiently, as was his wont, threw the shutters back, and flung open the casement. For this end of the house was one which the alterations had barely touched, grown up as it was with the great ash-tree, and being otherwise concealed from view.

"Air it, Mrs Chiddock, all today, and move my bed-furniture in in the afternoon. Put the Bishop of Kilmore in my old room."

"Pray, Sir Richard," said a new voice, breaking in on this speech, "might I have the favour of a moment's interview?"

Sir Richard turned round and saw a man in black in the doorway, who bowed.

"I must ask your indulgence for this intrusion, Sir Richard. You will, perhaps, hardly remember me. My name is William Crome, and my grandfather was Vicar in your grandfather's time."

"Well, sir," said Sir Richard, "the name of Crome is always a passport to Castringham. I am glad to renew a friendship of two generations' standing. In what can I serve you? for your hour of calling—and, if I do not mistake you, your bearing—shows you to be in some haste."

"That is no more than the truth, sir. I am riding from Norwich to Bury St Edmunds with what haste I can make, and I have called in on my way to leave with you some papers which we have but just come upon in looking over what my grandfather left at his death. It is thought you may find some matters of family interest in them."

"You are mighty obliging, Mr Crome, and, if you will be so good as to follow me to the parlour, and drink a glass of wine, we will take a first look at these same papers together. And you, Mrs Chiddock, as I said, be about airing this chamber.... Yes, it is here my grandfather died.... Yes, the tree, perhaps, does make the place a little dampish.... No; I do not wish to listen to any more. Make no difficulties, I beg. You have your orders—go. Will you follow me, sir?"

They went to the study. The packet which young Mr Crome had brought—he was then just become a Fellow of Clare Hall in Cambridge, I may say, and subsequently brought out a respectable edition of Polyaenus—contained among other things the notes which the old Vicar had made upon the occasion of Sir Matthew Fell's death. And for the first time Sir Richard was confronted with the enigmatical *Sortes Biblicae* which you have heard. They amused him a good deal.

"Well," he said, "my grandfather's Bible gave one prudent piece of advice—*Cut it down*. If that stands for the ash-tree, he may rest assured I shall not neglect it. Such a nest of catarrhs and agues was never seen."

The parlour contained the family books, which, pending the arrival of a collection which Sir Richard had made in Italy, and the building of a proper room to receive them, were not many in number.

Sir Richard looked up from the paper to the bookcase.

"I wonder," says he, "whether the old prophet is there yet? I fancy I see him."

Crossing the room, he took out a dumpy Bible, which, sure enough, bore on the flyleaf the inscription: "To Matthew Fell, from his Loving Godmother, Anne Aldous, 2 September 1659."

"It would be no bad plan to test him again, Mr Crome. I will wager we get a couple of names in the Chronicles. H'm! what have we here? "Thou shalt seek me in the morning, and I shall not be." Well, well! Your grandfather would have made a fine omen of that, hey? No more prophets for me! They are all in a tale. And now, Mr Crome, I am infinitely obliged to you for your packet. You will, I fear, be impatient to get on. Pray allow me—another glass."

So with offers of hospitality, which were genuinely meant (for Sir Richard thought well of the young man's address and manner), they parted.

In the afternoon came the guests—the Bishop of Kilmore, Lady Mary Hervey, Sir William Kentfield, etc. Dinner at five, wine, cards, supper, and dispersal to bed.

Next morning Sir Richard is disinclined to take his gun with the rest. He talks with the Bishop of Kilmore. This prelate, unlike a good many of the Irish Bishops of his day, had visited his see, and, indeed, resided there, for some considerable time. This morning, as the two were walking along the terrace and talking over the alterations and improvements in the house, the Bishop said, pointing to the window of the West Room:

"You could never get one of my Irish flock to occupy that room, Sir Richard."

"Why is that, my lord? It is, in fact, my own."

"Well, our Irish peasantry will always have it that it brings the worst of luck to sleep near an ash-tree, and you have a fine growth of ash not two yards from your chamber window. Perhaps," the Bishop went on, with a smile, "it has given you a touch of its quality already, for you do not seem, if I may say it, so much the fresher for your night's rest as your friends would like to see you."

"That, or something else, it is true, cost me my sleep from twelve to four, my lord. But the tree is to come down tomorrow, so I shall not hear much more from it."

"I applaud your determination. It can hardly be wholesome to have the air you breathe strained, as it were, through all that leafage."

"Your lordship is right there, I think. But I had not my window open last night. It was rather the noise that went on—no doubt from the twigs sweeping the glass—that kept me open-eyed."

"I think that can hardly be, Sir Richard. Here—you see it from this point. None of these nearest branches even can touch your casement unless there were a gale, and there was none of that last night. They miss the panes by a foot."

"No, sir, true. What, then, will it be, I wonder, that scratched and rustled so—ay, and covered the dust on my sill with lines and marks?"

At last they agreed that the rats must have come up through the ivy. That was the Bishop's idea, and Sir Richard jumped at it.

So the day passed quietly, and night came, and the party dispersed to their rooms, and wished Sir Richard a better night.

And now we are in his bedroom, with the light out and the Squire in bed. The room is over the kitchen, and the night outside still and warm, so the window stands open.

There is very little light about the bedstead, but there is a strange movement there; it seems as if Sir Richard were moving his head rapidly to and fro with only the slightest possible sound. And now you would guess, so deceptive is the half-darkness, that he had several heads, round and brownish, which move back and forward, even as low as his chest. It is a horrible illusion. Is it nothing more? There! something drops off the bed with a soft plump, like a kitten, and is out of the window in a flash; another—four—and after that there is quiet again.

Thou shall seek me in the morning, and I shall not be.

As with Sir Matthew, so with Sir Richard—dead and black in his bed!

A pale and silent party of guests and servants gathered under the window when the news was known. Italian poisoners, Popish emissaries, infected air—all these and more guesses were hazarded, and the Bishop of Kilmore looked at the tree, in the fork of whose lower boughs a white tom-cat was crouching, looking down the hollow which years had gnawed in the trunk. It was watching something inside the tree with great interest.

Suddenly it got up and craned over the hole. Then a bit of the edge on which it stood gave way, and it went slithering in. Everyone looked up at the noise of the fall.

It is known to most of us that a cat can cry; but few of us have heard, I hope, such a yell as came out of the trunk of the great ash. Two or three screams there were—the witnesses are not sure which—and then a slight and muffled noise of some commotion or struggling was all that came. But Lady Mary Hervey fainted outright, and the housekeeper stopped her ears and fled till she fell on the terrace.

The Bishop of Kilmore and Sir William Kentfield stayed. Yet even they were daunted, though it was only at the cry of a cat; and Sir William swallowed once or twice before he could say:

"There is something more than we know of in that tree, my lord. I am for an instant search."

And this was agreed upon. A ladder was brought, and one of the gardeners went up, and, looking down the hollow, could detect nothing but a few dim indications of something moving. They got a lantern, and let it down by a rope.

"We must get at the bottom of this. My life upon it, my lord, but the secret of these terrible deaths is there."

Up went the gardener again with the lantern, and let it down the hole cautiously. They saw the yellow light upon his face as he bent over, and saw his face struck with an incredulous terror and loathing before he cried out in a dreadful voice and fell back from the ladder—where, happily, he was caught by two of the men—letting the lantern fall inside the tree.

He was in a dead faint, and it was some time before any word could be got from him.

By then they had something else to look at. The lantern must have broken at the bottom, and the light in it caught upon dry leaves and rubbish that lay there, for in a few minutes a dense smoke began to come up, and then flame; and, to be short, the tree was in a blaze.

The bystanders made a ring at some yards' distance, and Sir William and the Bishop sent men to get what weapons and tools they could; for, clearly, whatever might be using the tree as its lair would be forced out by the fire.

So it was. First, at the fork, they saw a round body covered with fire—the size of a man's head—appear very suddenly, then seem to collapse and fall back. This, five or six times; then a similar ball leapt into the air and fell on the grass, where after a moment it lay still. The Bishop went as near as he dared to it, and saw—what but the remains of an enormous spider, veinous and seared! And, as the fire burned lower down

more terrible bodies like this began to break out from the trunk, and it was seen that these were covered with greyish hair.

All that day the ash burned, and until it fell to pieces the men stood about it, and from time to time killed the brutes as they darted out. At last there was a long interval when none appeared, and they cautiously closed in and examined the roots of the tree.

"They found," says the Bishop of Kilmore, "below it a rounded hollow place in the earth, wherein were two or three bodies of these creatures that had plainly been smothered by the smoke; and, what is to me more curious, at the side of this den, against the wall, was crouching the anatomy or skeleton of a human being, with the skin dried upon the bones, having some remains of black hair, which was pronounced by those that examined it to be undoubtedly the body of a woman, and clearly dead for a period of fifty years."

👽 👽 👽

"The Ash-Tree" first appeared in the author's 1904 collection Ghost Stories of an Antiquary. *The story illustration is by Allen Koszowski.*

Although English author and medievalist scholar Montague Rhodes James (1862–1936) variously held from 1905–1936 the offices of provost of King's College, Cambridge, and of Eton College, and Vice-Chancellor of the University of Cambridge, he is best remembered today as the originator of the antiquarian ghost story. His creepy tales, which were collected in four volumes during his lifetime, greatly influenced several generations of horror writers who followed. "...In the opinion of many," E. F. Bleiler wrote in his 1983 book The Guide to Supernatural Literature, *[James is] "the foremost modern writer of supernatural fiction."*

James wrote many of his ghost stories as Christmas Eve entertainments, which he would read by the fire to friends and students.

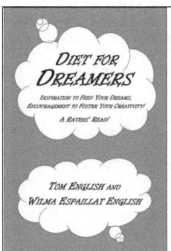

A HANDFUL OF DUST

By Tom English

...I will show you something different....
Your shadow at morning striding behind you
Or your shadow at evening rising to meet you;
I will show you fear in a handful of dust.

—T. S. Eliot
The Waste Land

ALL HIS LIFE OLD MAN BRUMSTEAD HAD LIVED IN FEAR. AS A CHILD HE HAD BEEN TERRIFIED OF THE DARK, AND HIS OVERINDULGENT MOTHER HAD ALLOWED him to sleep with the light on in his room until he was a senior at Dinsmore High School, back in 1956.

When he was fourteen, three of his "friends" locked him up in a rotting tool shed behind Grady's Feed Store. It was typical of the pranks Mill Hurst boys were constantly pulling on each other. They stood by the door smoking cigarettes and repeating dirty jokes they'd heard in the locker room, all the while looking about nervously, as poor Brumstead, crouching amid a clutter of hanging harnesses, castoff tractor parts, busted barrels and hay forks, first yelled obscenities, then pleaded for mercy, then started screaming like a frightened girl.

By the time his hysterical cries finally got to them, and his friends dragged his limp, sweat-drenched body from the cluttered shed, Brumstead was sobbing uncontrollably. He'd been locked in that cramped shack for just a few minutes, but a fear of confined spaces stayed with him for the rest of his life.

Brunstead was afraid of heights and crowds, speaking in public and the opposite sex; running out of gas in the middle of nowhere, and being audited by the IRS. He once even told me that the drone of a Hoover vacuum cleaner gave him nightmares. Perhaps some of his fears were silly and unfounded. Obviously, others were not.

"BUT THERE WAS one thing in particular he feared, which affected him more than all the others," I said. "Something caused by an extremely unpleasant experience he had the year his mother died. One of those stupid and unlikely things you often hear about but can never imagine happening to you."

I paused in my story just long enough to brush away an annoying little insect buzzing about my ear. The room was stuffy, the air musty with the smell of old fabric and mildew. I leaned forward in the overstuffed wing chair and scanned the room where Brumstead had died late one Friday night nearly two months ago.

The old man had managed to dial 911 before going into respiratory arrest, but the fire department was located on the other side of the county and manned totally by volunteers. They had arrived too late to do anything but find Brumstead's dead body slumped against the front door. The coroner wrote the old man's death off as the result of a weakened physical condition: Brumstead had had a bout of flu a couple weeks before, and at seventy-seven he just seemed worn out.

Worn out, I imagined, from too many years spent dreading one thing or another.

My twelve-year-old daughter sat across from me, wide-eyed with anticipation. "What happened?" Beth asked, eager for me to finish the story of Brumstead's neuroses.

I stood up and walked to the window. Chuck Harper's kids were playing in the yard across the street. "Old man Brumstead had an accident," I continued, but then stopped again while I struggled to raise the window. The thing had been nailed shut—like all the other windows in the house.

When I was a teenager, Brumstead's airtight house had been one of the many peculiar things that fascinated me about the old man. When other kids had begun to shun his place, I became a frequent visitor; while other kids were mocking him, I was lending a respectful, sympathetic ear to all his fearful woes.

"Dad!" Beth whined. Like most kids, she loved a good story, and the weirder the better.

"It happened just outside this two-story farmhouse. Brumstead inherited the place when his mother died, in 1977."

"And now it's ours," Beth said in childish awe.

"Yes," I said slowly.

Evidently, the old man hadn't had anyone else to leave it to. So he left it the skinny kid who used to come by and drink the weak beer Brumstead brewed in his cellar. And listen to the horror stories of all the old man's fears.

I swiped at the buzzing sound near my ear again, and continued: "Forty years ago, this house sat in the middle of a field—this was all farm land. After the accident, Brumstead began selling off the surrounding land. At first, a few homes were built. Then Hurst Street was extended through.

"Then this housing development sprang up," I said, gesturing to the row of almost uniform houses across the street. "Brumstead had always loved the farm ... nature ... walking through the fields. But after the accident he didn't care about any of that. He was glad to see other people living nearby—relieved to see fields give way to asphalt, and trees to street lights."

"But *why*?" Beth asked impatiently. "What happened?"

"Shortly after the death of his mother, Brumstead went for a walk through a section of field that had lain fallow for two years and was now overgrown with thick weeds. This would have been behind the house," I added, "but still in plain view of it.

"He had been devastated by his mother's death. Brumstead was almost forty years old at the time, and he had still been living with her when she died. He couldn't remember a time when she hadn't been there for him. She'd been his shelter from the dangers of the world; and hers had been the voice that calmed all his fears.

"Wondering if he could ever live without his mother, Brumstead wandered across the field, lost in his thoughts, scuffing his feet over the dry crust. Never before in his life had he felt so alone. Never before had he been so overwhelmed with doubt, so sick with uncertainty. As he walked along he could feel the brittle ground crumbling beneath his shoes; and he gave no thought at all when a small section of the crust gave a bit more than usual, collapsing and caving in an inch or so, accompanied by an unsettling crunch.

"He took several more languorous paces through the rising cloud of dust he'd kicked up before looking down at his feet. They were covered with something black and yellow; something moving—something creeping up his trouser legs.

"A rush of horror surged through his chest. He felt several bursts of pain on his legs, which felt like they were on fire. He slapped at his trousers, stomping and shaking his feet to dislodge the angry mass swarming up his body. Out of the corner of his eye, he could see the dust cloud about his feet thicken, blacken—and quickly rise. He lurched backward, then sideways, his arms flailing violently as he ineffectually grabbed first at one, then another, stab of searing pain. He screamed like he'd never heard himself scream before, stopping just long enough to slap mercilessly at his own face and head, both of which felt like they were burning up.

"When he ran, at first blindly, mindlessly, the seething cloud moved with him, enveloping him—hundreds of winged furies seeking vengeance for their destroyed nest in the dry earth, and each one of them gifted with the ability to sting again and again and again. When at last—after an eternity of mere seconds—a voice inside Brumstead screamed 'Get inside!' and he ran toward the promised safety of the house, the boiling mass chased him.

"With every yard he covered, the number of aggressors dropped and the swarm thinned. But when Brumstead reached the back porch and slammed the screened door shut, there were still several crawling through his hair and clinging to his blue denim.

"His face was a red swollen mask of pain, his body barely better. He managed to drive himself to a doctor who practiced out of his home four or five miles from here."

Beth was starting to feel the itch of some imagined intruder creeping across the back of her neck, her legs, her scalp. As I was soon to learn, she had a particular aversion to crawling insects. "What happened then?" she asked, drawing the collar of her shirt up tight around her neck, and shuddered.

"Brumstead was lucky. Some people have severe reactions to the venom of yellow jackets. Even one or two stings can trigger an allergic reaction that can swell the throat shut. Brumstead was one of those people. But he made it to the doctor in time.

"When he got there, he was in severe pain, and he could barely breathe. He passed out on the doctor's front porch, and Kearney had to drag him inside."

I sat down again, on an old trunk tucked in a corner of the room. Beth had moved to the overstuffed wing chair, and was sitting with her bare feet on the edge of the cushion, hugging her knees to her chest.

"Which couldn't have been an easy task," I said. "I think Dr. Kearney was around seventy at the time—still making house calls, still x-raying broken bones on an old machine in the back-room of his two-story duplex.

"Anyway, as soon as he got Brumstead stabilized, the doctor phoned Drury County Rescue to send over an ambulance, and had the poor man transported to the hospital. I think Brumstead stayed there a couple nights or so. Kearney told him, later, that if he'd delayed getting there, even a few minutes, he might have died. He also told Brumstead to avoid getting stung again, because his body was now 'sensitized' to the venom. Another dose could perhaps be fatal.

"Needless to say, Brumstead didn't need a new phobia to worry about. But he got one

anyway. He stopped going for walks, started staying indoors. Other than driving to the courthouse, where he worked as a clerk, or to Haskin's Food-Mart, the old man hardly strayed from this house.

"He read up on yellow jackets: their life-cycle, their habits, their diet. He learned far more than he needed to know; too much for his own peace of mind. Like honeybees, yellow jackets are communal insects. When their nest is disturbed, or even threatened, they attack as a well-coordinated army to defend the hive. But honeybees die after stinging once. Their stingers break off and become embedded in the flesh. Yellow jackets were not cursed with such a limitation. They're capable of repeatedly stinging an enemy, with no harm to themselves.

"And swatting one of them only incites their fury: a smashed yellow jacket releases a scent that alerts the other members of the communal nest. Sensing that one of their numbers has been killed, the others will attack with a vengeance. But that was an extremely painful experience Brumstead didn't need to learn from a book.

"Again, a little bit of knowledge is a dangerous thing. As Brumstead mulled over the facts, and licked his wounds, he grew increasingly fearful of being stung again. Initially, he kept all the windows shut—no matter how stuffy the house got. But ultimately, he *nailed* them shut."

"I'm glad he had AC," Beth said, scratching hard at her scalp. "Do you think there's any still around here?"

"I doubt it. A few days after being released from the hospital, he paid Mike Fenton's sons to destroy the nest in the backyard. Yellow jackets are supposed to be least active at night, so the two boys waited till dusk, after most of the hive had flown back to the nest. They crept up to a respectful distance of the nest and one of them threw a pail of kerosene on it. The other one flicked a match at it. And then they both ran like mad.

"The kerosene burned long and hot. By the light of the flames rising from the dust, the boys could see dark shapes flying into the heart of the inferno. It was the stragglers returning to the nest—driven by instinct to try and save the hive. Flying to their death.

"Standing at the kitchen window, Brumstead watched the glow of the burning nest until the last ember had disappeared against the blackness of night. Years later, he continued to recount the whole affair, each time rubbing his hands together somewhat fiendishly—peculiarly comforted that vengeance had been served."

I finished my tale in an appropriately solemn tone, but unlike other occasions when Beth would clap and ask for another story, she was unusually quiet. I watched her head tilt slowly back as her eyes rose to the corner above my head.

"Dad," she said in a low, *anxious* voice, "There's one in here!"

I stood and looked around. There was nothing flying about the room but Beth's overworked imagination. She loved a good scare, and my stories—even the more ghoulish ones—rarely caused her even a moment of unease. But perhaps this time, owing to the truth of Brumstead's story, I'd gone too far.

"We don't have to worry about yellow jackets in *this* house, Beth. All the windows are shut. And nothing flew in when we had the door open." I threw my arm around her and squeezed her tightly. Outside, the late summer day had faded, and flashes of heat lightning illuminated the darkening eastern sky.

"We had a long drive today. I bet you're tired," I said, and she nodded in agreement. "Enough excitement for one day. Why don't you go upstairs and get ready for bed. I'll come up in a bit and tuck you in."

She nodded again.

"Tomorrow we'll go treasure hunting. There's tons of neat junk in this old house."

She smiled, scratching her sides and neck. "Maybe I'll find some old skeleton keys for my collection," she said.

"Probably so. We'll go into town and get some pancakes first."

"Yes!"

"Go brush your teeth." I said.

"And Beth," I added before she left the room, "We don't need to tell mom about this story."

She nodded in agreement.

I went to the window and studied the heads of the large nails driven into the sides of the frame. It wasn't going to be easy removing them. But it needed to be done soon. Old houses were firetraps and the idea of not being able to raise a single window wasn't exactly comforting.

The whole place would need repainting before I could put it on the market, and I had serious doubts the electrical wiring was up to code. I'd have to climb into the attic tomorrow and take a look at it. Joan would be driving down in a few days, and she'd help me clean the place out. Still, the amount of work involved....

I caught myself. How often do we dream of someone putting us in their will, let alone leaving us everything? It wasn't fair to treat this unexpected blessing from Brumstead as though it were a curse. So I quietly thanked him for my windfall, and then began to wonder if the old man had feared banks as much as he'd feared just about everything else. Was he one of those eccentrics who'd hidden money behind a wall or under the floorboards? What treasures would I find for *my* collection?

I sat musing over this fanciful notion, and over Brumstead's cloistered way of life. He'd lived alone in this old house for close to four decades—with only his fears to occupy him. Not the healthy fear that keeps us from doing stupid things; not the entertaining scare you get from a rollercoaster ride or a really good horror movie; but the kind of fear that has the power to cripple and choke the life out of a man; a genuine and palpable fear.

I yawned and checked my watch. It was a little past ten, and starting to rain. I could hear the soft clatter of the rain striking the house's tin roof, accompanied by occasional rumblings of distant thunder. I switched off the light and headed upstairs. When I reached the landing, I stopped at the first room, where Beth was staying, and gently turned the knob.

Her room was impenetrably dark. I had unthinkingly put her in a room at the back of the house, sheltered from the streetlights. The faint glow of a lamp in the corner of the landing did little to banish the darkness in her room.

Neither was there a single shaft of moonlight in the storm-blackened sky.

I stood in the doorway, waiting for my eyes to adjust to the darkness, trying to perceive Beth's shape upon the bed. I stepped softly into the room and was swallowed up in its darkness. If Beth were asleep, I didn't want to awaken her, but I felt a foolish need to reassure myself of her presence in the room. I moved carefully across the room, feeling my way blindly, one hand gently searching for her sleeping form.

I felt something, like a feather, sweep lightly past my nose, my ear—got the impression of frantic movement in the room, of something not quite right in the thick, stale air.

I fumbled for the lamp on the night table, then switched it on. For a moment I thought the sudden brightness that flooded the room had me seeing spots before my eyes—spots that circled, dipped, shot past my head. The whole room was crawling with yellow jackets.

There were dozens swarming about Beth's bed, perhaps hundreds more seething across the walls and clinging to the ceiling above her. The surface of the night table was completely covered over with them, the lampshade crawling with them, the water glass bristling with their winged bodies. I have never had a fear of yellow jackets, knowing that they attack only when provoked; but the sheer multitude of their numbers—forced upon me without warning—combined with some natural revulsion at seeing the things clinging to every available surface and object, sent a rush of utter panic through me.

I lurched back, knocking something from the night table, and stirred up a cloud of moving bodies. Beth sprang up in her bed. She was disorientated from being jarred awake. She squinted at me, puzzled, and rubbed her eyes. Before I could think or speak—before I could warn her and lessen the shock—she saw them. She screamed repeatedly, her legs kicking violently at the sheets.

"Beth!" I said hoarsely, "Be still! They're swarming, not attacking."

Almost as if stimulated by the intensity of her horror, the numbers of black and yellow bodies swarming about the room increased significantly. As the cloud of flying insects swirled around us, moving as a single, intelligent entity, I saw one of them alight on Beth's arm. She flinched in revulsion.

"No, Beth!" I screamed, as her hand arced across her face, and she slapped at the spot, crushing the tiny insect beneath her palm.

I cringed at the sight, like a soldier who's had a grenade tossed at his feet, and knows it's too late to do anything but wait for the explosion.

Nothing happened. Nothing changed.

And then they were on her.

I jerked the sheet over her head, and swept her from the bed. She was screaming and writhing in agony. I wrapped the flapping edges of the sheet about her twisting form and bundled her from the room, slamming the door shut behind me.

PACING OUTSIDE THE DOUBLE doors marked EMERGENCY, I kept wondering: Why hadn't *I* been stung. There had been hundreds of them, and I had been at the heart of their fury.

When the doors parted, I hurried to intercept Dr. Sam Travis as he walked out. "How is she?" I asked.

"Her breathing is no longer constricted. She's resting now."

Sam and I had attended Pratt University together, and I was glad he was on duty. He studied me for a moment, then said, "Let's get some coffee."

It sounded more like a command than an invitation. I followed him into the staff lounge. "Grab a chair," he said, pointing to a table at the back of the room. He poured two cups, then sat down across from me. "Rob," he said, hesitating long enough to sip his coffee, "what the hell are you trying to pull here?"

It took a moment for the implication of his question to sink in. "What are you talking about?"

"You bring your daughter in with all the symptoms of envenomation. Yet there's not a mark on her."

"Are you kidding?" I said. "She was *covered* with swollen stings when I brought her in."

"Yeah, I know she was." He stared at the

Styrofoam cup in his hand. "They're gone now; there's no trace of wasp stings."

"How...? Is that normal?"

He shook his head and leaned back in his chair.

"Sam," I said, "do you believe in the power of suggestion?"

"Why? What's that got to do with anything?"

"Beth went to bed tonight thinking about yellow jackets," I said. "We drove down today to work on the farmhouse I inherited from Ray Brumstead. Did you know him?"

"No. But I remember you talking about him. He was phobic."

"*Phobic* is putting it mildly. He was scared to death of just about everything."

"What's your point, Rob?"

"Brumstead stepped on a ground nest of yellow jackets, years ago, and had to be hospitalized. It was something that changed his life. He sold his fields, stopped going for walks. And he had all the windows in the house nailed shut. I wanted Beth to know why, so I told her the whole story—in all its macabre splendor, unfortunately."

I stood and started pacing about the table. "Could the power of suggestion—hearing the details, seeing the windows nailed shut, being in the very house where it happened—trigger her imagination?"

"You think she conjured up a swarm of wasps out of her head. Got stung," he said, "and her initial symptoms were all psychosomatic?"

"Imagination is a powerful force, Sam."

"Interesting. But that would take *some* imagination." He put his cup down, and leaned back in his chair. "And you saw them, too. Were you seeing the phantoms of a child's overworked imagination?"

"Yeah, I know," I said, realizing how ridiculous the whole thing sounded once it was verbalized. "But Beth *had* seen something that wasn't there: earlier, before bed, right after hearing the story. She said there was a yellow jacket buzzing about my head. I *didn't* see it."

I leaned on the table, and stared at his smug expression. "How else can you explain why *I* wasn't stung?"

"That's what I'm trying to find out," he said. He drummed his index finger against his empty cup. "It's possible. Emotional stress can induce a variety of illnesses, including allergic reaction. There *are* precedents of psychosomatic injury in individuals who too closely identify with a particular situation or person. The wounds in the hands of stigmatics, for instance, may somehow be mentally induced by a close identification with the crucified Christ."

He shook his head. "But this would go way beyond anything I've ever read about psycho-physiological disorders. There's so much we don't understand about the power of the mind—the power of human emotion."

He pushed himself up from his chair. "But you saw it, too." He tossed the Styrofoam cup at the trashcan, but missed it. "This sounds more like a case of mass hysteria," he said. "In fact, the whole thing sounds like the weird stuff you used to write for the college journal."

"That was fiction," I said brusquely, "meant to entertain. I'm talking about my daughter now."

"Whose care you've entrusted to me. That's why we're having this conversation." He glanced at his watch. "It's an interesting theory, Rob, but if I were you, I'd call an exterminator—pronto. Old houses can harbor a lot of things. You could have a nest in the attic or behind a wall. They probably have a way to get inside, a crack or hole somewhere."

"Yeah," I nodded.

"Mack Loomis is an exterminator. Call *him*."

"*Slack* Mack? The guy who quit high school? Haven't seen him in ages."

"Yeah, well, he bummed around for awhile, but I stopped thumbing my nose at him several years ago. He owns his own company now, and he probably makes more money than I do."

"I guess this will give me a chance to see him, again," I said. "Can I take Beth home now?"

"I want to keep her for observation, at least overnight. Besides," he said, "if that house *has* triggered some emotional problems, she shouldn't go back there. And if you *do* have a wasp infestation, she shouldn't be there. Her body's now sensitized to the venom. Another sting, even one, could cause a severe allergic reaction."

I thanked Sam for his time and care, and then hustled upstairs to Beth's room. She was sleeping peacefully. The night-duty nurse reassured me that she would be checking on Beth throughout the night, and that the best thing for me to do was go home and get some rest.

I got back to the Brumstead place a little past midnight, and walked about the empty house, examining the walls, ceiling and floors till almost one in the morning.

Nothing. No cracks, no holes, no hidden passages leading to secret rooms.

I fell asleep with my clothes on, and woke up early with the sun blasting through a curtain-less window. At eight o'clock sharp, I called Loomis Pest Control. When Mack heard it was me, he said he'd come out personally, and less than an hour later he pulled into the gravel driveway.

Mack had gained a great deal of weight since high school—probably from lounging in the air-conditioned office where he dispatched his crew of "hard-working professionals." As he clambered up the stepladder he'd placed under the attic door, it wobbled and groaned under his not insignificant mass; and I started wondering if he'd even be able to fit through the narrow opening in the ceiling.

"Yeah, buddy-boy," he bellowed, squirming through the opening. "Business has been good. Mind handing me that flashlight?"

I passed the light to him, and he took another step up the ladder, wedging himself up to the waist. "You gotta dusty attic, buddy-boy," he said, shining the light into one corner of the roof beams. "Yessir, old and dusty. But if you got bugs up here—and I'm sure ya do—your old buddy Mack's gonna fix you up. Yessiree," he said, slowly twisting in the attic doorway as the beam of his flashlight stripped the darkness from each succeeding rafter. "You bastards can forget about Raid, 'cause there's a *new* sheriff in town. Nope. When I find you, you're in for a helluva lot more than a little raid—this is gonna be a full-scale *Mack Attack*."

He had almost completed a half-circle turn in the too-tight opening when his flashlight clattered to the floor. "Shit!" he yelled in a husky voice, and I heard the thud of his elbows against the doorframe as he yanked his upper torso from the attic. The stepladder rocked from side to side, and he almost kicked it over as he stumbled down the rungs, skipping the last two and landing heavily on the floor.

"Outside!" he said, pushing me out the door and onto the landing. "Go, go, go!" he yelled, urging me downstairs. He cleared the front door, leapt from the porch, and ran to the street.

I walked to the sidewalk, where he stood bent over, his hands resting on his thighs, his chest heaving as he gasped for breath.

"You okay?" I asked.

He looked up and nodded, then straightened and walked slowly to the van at the end of the driveway. He pulled the rear doors open and sat down on the back of the truck. "Buddy-boy," he said, still breathing hard and wiping sweat from his reddened face, "you gotta big wasp nest up there."

"Yeah, well, isn't that what you're here for?"

"Listen, smartass, I've been doing this for over twelve years. I've gone into barns and silos and rotted-out warehouses, and I've never seen anything like what you got up there!"

He sat there at the back of the van, staring at the ground around his feet, while he caught his breath. "I'm sorry, Rob," he said finally, wiping his face on his sleeve. "I started out in this business because I needed the cash and I couldn't find anything else. But I *do not* like insects, Rob, I hate 'em!" He rubbed the back of his neck. "Maybe that's where my success comes from—I love killing 'em. It's a passion, you understand. But when I run across a bad infestation...." His voice trailed off as he scanned the roofline of the old farmhouse.

"Rob," he said, still looking up, "you got a nest up there the size of ... Hell, it takes up two-thirds of the attic space." He looked me in the eye. "It must be home to thousands."

I finally convinced Mack to come back inside with me. He cautiously followed me back upstairs, no doubt motivated more by shame than courage, and then steadied the ladder as I climbed into the attic to see for myself.

I was glad he had prepared me for what I saw.

The beam of the flashlight moved across foot after foot, yard after yard, of dark grey, paper-like shell. The nest stretched from the attic floor to the highest point in the rafters, from the back of the house to the front; and it extended at least half the length of the hipped roof.

It looked like a bloated cocoon, anchored to the heavy beams by a muddy substance the same sickly grey color as the outer shell. Half of the end facing me was honeycombed with thousands of dark holes—tiny tunnels extending deep into the heart of the nest.

I eased myself into the attic and knelt on a joist a few feet from the swollen mass. "What's this thing made of," I called down to Mack.

"Uh, cellulose," he said. "It's pretty much just regurgitated paper. They make it out of plant debris. Old trash, wood shavings … and dust."

"It looks empty," I said.

A couple minutes later, Mack slowly put his head through the attic door. "There's a lot of stuff I may not know, but I *do* know about this," he said. "This thing has all the signs of being an active nest."

"Come on, Mack. There's no sign of them."

"You wanna see 'em?" he said hatefully. "Go rap on it with the flashlight—just gimme a chance to clear out first."

"No, I don't," I said in a wave of anger. "But I do need to know. My daughter was stung last night, repeatedly, by … something I can't explain."

"Well there you have it," he said, pointing to the grey mass.

"But where are they *now*?"

"They probably all left the nest to scavenge. They feed on garbage, you know. Me, I'm glad they're not here. We better clear out too, before some of 'em fly back to the nest."

"Mack. I need to know if I've got a problem with wasps or if last night I was seeing something that wasn't there."

"Something that wasn't there? Are you crazy? Look at the size of this monster. You're lucky to be alive!"

"There's nothing here but an empty shell. What evidence do you have that this thing's inhabited?"

"Evidence?" Mack cried. "There's your evidence!"

"I can see the nest," I said hotly, "That doesn't mean the house is infested with yellow jackets."

"For God's sake, Rob, come on out. Let's shut the door. Do you hafta personally see everything before you believe it. Hell, didn't you ever go to Sunday school? Why can't you trust my judgment? I've been at this for years. I'm telling you the nest is active. Have a little faith in me, will ya?"

"Faith?" I said.

"Yeah, some things you just hafta take on faith."

I stared at the empty grey cocoon rising up before me, but my mind was somewhere else, searching through a jumble of memories for something I'd forgotten—something someone once told me. I felt an urgency to remember it. But *what* was it?

"Hold the ladder," I said, crawling from the attic.

"Now you're talking, buddy-boy," Mack said. "You need to decide what you're gonna do about this thing quick."

"Any suggestions?"

"We can saturate the thing with enough chemical to kill anything that returns to it for weeks. But you'll hafta leave the house. Give the fumes time to clear."

I nodded.

"That's the easy part. I wasn't sure if you noticed, but the damn thing runs down inside the walls. There's probably not a void space in the whole house that's not plugged with paper. And with the old copper wire running behind these walls, you have the potential for one hell of an electrical fire."

"Can it be removed?" I asked.

"If you have enough money you can do anything," Mack said. "But is it worth it?" He shrugged. "You definitely need to have someone pull the stuff outta the attic. But I doubt you can get to the crap behind the walls—not without tearing them out."

I told Mack I needed time to think about it. He said he'd enjoyed seeing me again, despite the circumstances, then warned me not to put off having the nest treated. I watched him back the van out of the drive, and speed away—back to his air-conditioned office, probably.

Then I drove to the hospital to visit Beth. She was sore and a bit sluggish from all the antihistamines, but otherwise she seemed in good spirits. To her delight, I promised her we'd go to the beach before summer vacation was over, and that she could spend the whole day treasure hunting with her metal detector.

I also promised her she'd never have to go inside the old Brumstead house again. I could read the relief in her young eyes.

I walked down to the cafeteria and bought her a chocolate milkshake. When I got back to her room she was sitting up, watching television. I gave her a kiss, then left her happily sipping the shake and watching *Jeopardy*.

Heading back to the farmhouse, I kept replaying the events of the last couple days: that monstrosity in the attic; the terrifying scene in Beth's room; what Dr. Sam Travis had said about the power of human emotion; and the words Mack had bellowed at me through that narrow opening in the ceiling.

I thought about the wretchedness of Brumstead's existence in that lonely old house; how fear had been the old man's constant companion; how it had dominated his thoughts and haunted his dreams.

Suddenly the whole thing started to make sense.

I stopped at City Hall to pick up the permits I would need. I was sent from one office to the next, and spent four hours filling out forms. It hadn't hurt being something of a celebrity: the Mill Hurst boy who'd made it in the big city, and had returned to rub elbows with the folks he'd grown up with.

But by the time I had filed my last form it was too late to do anything but hire the work crew. I scheduled one to start promptly at 7:30

in the morning, then drove back to the Brumstead house.

I phoned Joan. She wouldn't have to drive down after all. Then I packed up Beth's and my things, and loaded up the SUV.

I didn't sleep that night. I sat in Brumstead's over-stuffed wing chair, staring at the walls, a constant stream of words and pictures swirling like flying insects through my brain. In fact, I was still pondering them when I heard the sound of a bulldozer cranking. I stepped from the house, gently closed the door behind me, and walked out to the street.

I stood on the sidewalk with the demolition crew, and watched as the bulldozer raised its blade and approached the house. Twenty minutes later, accompanied by a symphony of cracklings, crunches, and hand-clapping, the old farmhouse splintered and collapsed upon itself.

Through the swirling dust, I saw the grey form of the nest protruding through the pile of broken boards and bits of insulation. The demolition crew walked around the ruins, pointing at the cracked shell and swearing in angry tones, but no one ventured near it. No one touched it.

When I was a boy I used to walk to the old Mill Hurst Baptist Church every week to attend Sunday school. Pastor Barnes taught me many interesting things, but the one I remember now —triggered by the impatient words of an old friend—had to do with faith.

Faith, the pastor had taught us kids, was the evidence of things we cannot see; it was the substance of things we hope for. He also told us that fear was the opposite of faith, and that dread held almost as much power as hope.

I thought about the power of raw human emotions. All his life, Brumstead had lived in fear. Fear had shaped his habits. Fear had forged his destiny. Fear and dust and the dread of something that otherwise might never have happened.

Was the grey nest lying amidst these ruins a physical manifestation of everything Brumstead had dreaded? Was this monstrosity the *material* substance of all his fears?

There were no signs of activity about the nest. No stirrings of life from within. Nothing to indicate this was an active hive. At least, nothing in the natural realm.

I left the site for several hours—to visit Beth—and to take care of one last thing. But a little before five, I returned to the pile of rubble that had defined Brumstead's life; to the hideous cocoon reposing beneath the old man's broken dreams.

At 5:30 p.m. a pumper-truck from the local fire department arrived, without fanfare, and I was joined on the sidewalk by Steve Gaston, yet another friend from my youth. He had brought two other men with him, and after a few minutes of quietly conversing, the trio set fire to the pile of rubble.

We watched the flames as they licked and consumed the grey shell. It was the final episode in the long history of a lonely, frightened old man. His terrible legacy would soon return to a handful of dust.

The pile burned hot for three hours. We sat together on the truck, watching the flames, reminiscing as though we were simply gathered around the fireplace at Tall Timber Lodge.

Then, just before dusk, a black, swirling plume rose up from the flames. But it wasn't smoke.

It moved off into the darkening eastern sky, sweeping low over the rooftops of the houses across the street, until it disappeared into the blackness on the horizon.

We had all seen it. But not one of us commented.

👽 👽 👽

"A Handful of Dust" first appeared in issue #35 of Weirdbook Magazine. *The above illustration was created by Rocket Science Engineering.*

Tom English is an environmental chemist who loves watching old movies, reading vintage comic books, and writing strange tales of the supernatural. His work has appeared in various genre magazines and several print anthologies, including: Haunted House Short Stories *and* Detective Thrillers Short Stories *(both from Flame Tree Publishing);* Gaslight Arcanum: Uncanny Tales of Sherlock Holmes; Re-Haunt; Challenger Unbound; *and* Dead Souls. *Tom also edited* Bound for Evil: Curious Tales of Books Gone Bad, *a 2008 Shirley Jackson Award finalist for best anthology; and has written five inspirational books with his wife, Wilma Espaillat English, including* Spiritual Boot Camp for Creators & Dreamers, *which BookLife praised as "uniquely thorough, well-written, persuasive, and inspiring." (The BookLife Prize)*

He resides with Wilma, surrounded by books and beasts, deep in the woods of New Kent, Virginia.

SKINSECTS

By Gregory L. Norris

H E KNOWS THEY ARE INSIDE HIM. HE FEELS THEM ROOTING AROUND, A THIN BREEZE WHISPERING OVER HIS SKIN, ONLY IT'S ALSO UNDERNEATH. Mostly, the proof comes in the memories, and there's a song on his lips he wants to sing. A kid's kind of song. Something about a ladybird whose house is on fire.

The impetus to move, to *fly*, grips him. He can't fly, though part of him has started to believe he can. Maybe, soon he will. Maybe after the metamorphosis is complete he'll spread his wings and fly on home, because his house is on fire.

That's what they'd like him to believe, he thinks, still marginally able to think independently, which he guesses is a temporary condition. His house is on fire, his children all will burn. At twenty-eight, he doesn't have any children, and he knows this, but still he paces the garden apartment, anxious to save phantoms from imaginary licks of flame. He doesn't remember his name anymore—insects aren't given names, only titles. He's a worker. A drone.

First, Drone needs convincing. So, in order to get him flying, swarming with the rest of the new hive, the creatures scurrying beneath his skin and through his blood remind him of the good memories; seduce him while they make adjustments, tinker, transform.

HE IS FIVE in the mental snapshot, bouncing around the Rocking Horse Nursery School—a charming name for a place surrounded by chain link fence. Across the street, the busy double lane of Range Road, lurks the I-93 overpass. Sometimes, he wonders if the fence is to keep children in or undesirables out. That overpass has sheltered plenty of hitchhikers during interludes between Here and There.

A sunny September day set beneath sky the color of comfortable denim, no need for jackets. He and a dozen other shrieking urchins race around the playground, all happy except for the girl who brings butter sandwiches for lunch and cries during the structured naptime. He doesn't remember her name, either. Names no longer matter.

The rest dig—*burrow*—in the sandbox. He whisks higher and higher on one of the swings, kicking out with his little legs. If he let go on the ride up, spread his arms, and released his hold, he'd fly away, just like the ladybird in that hypnotic song.

A perfect sunny day, the children eat their lunches on the playground and then deposit the leftovers and wrappings into the big red oil drum garbage can. The girl with the butter sandwiches refuses to eat a single bite. The untouched remains, along with the crust of a grape jelly sandwich, attract a plump black and yellow bumblebee.

The bee dances up from the last of the weedy summer clover fading from pale purple to brown around the boundary of chain link. Its buzz doesn't crawl across his flesh, like the slithering songs of yellow jacket wasps. The bee is beautiful, gentle—with its body covered in soft fur, it reminds him of a tiny teddy bear, a friend. It would never hurt him; wouldn't sting him, like yellow jackets have in the past. Its only interest is in the sweet sticky lure of grape jelly before continuing on its way to the next ragged clump of clover blossoms.

Beautiful bee.

Follow me, it seems to beckon.

Higher and higher, almost flying now, he lets go. The sky spins overhead, the clearest blue.

Only cracks appear at the edges, and gravity drops him down hard, onto his spine. Drone gasps awake and realizes he is staring up at the fractured ceiling plaster of his bedroom in the apartment.

Summer heat bakes the place. He hears the weight of footfalls through the walls from 2-9, the apartment next door, and unintentionally licks his lips. When was the last time he ate? He can't remember, but the image of that purple smear from the past makes his stomach complain. He's so hungry he could eat—

Another happy memory, from not so long ago, rises to the forefront of his thoughts. A different autumn, Indian summer. Ladybugs are everywhere. Sweet little ladybugs, a bumper crop of tiny flying berries—they cover the windshields of the cars in the parking lot and find their way into his garden apartment. He remembers carefully scooping them up and releasing them out int the sunshine. Adorable, harmless little creatures, he recalls that ladybugs are a portent of good luck but glosses over the footnote that this particular infestation is of an invasive species from Asia; that these little red, black, and white creatures have been known to bite and exude a toxic yellow secretion. In England, ladybugs are known as *ladybirds*.

His house is on fire, he swears, and his children all in jeopardy of burning. It's time to fly. But first, he must eat.

THEY GOT INTO the food supply, and then the food chain, where they quickly leaped to the top through parasitic symbiosis. Popular belief was, during that other time and era not so long ago when such concepts as free will and thinking existed, that they were engineered as part of a government plan to spy on the general populace. Some government's plan; and now the global populace. Insects don't recognize borders. Just ask the Japanese beetle.

Stay indoors until the crisis has passed!

Locked doors don't keep out houseflies or silverfish. Ants and termites invade human houses through the tiniest of cracks in the mortar. Mosquitoes track people on sweat and scent. They find us and they feed.

A neighbor, moving about, behind the bedroom wall. The things skittering about under his skin and in his blood urge him to feed. When he resists, the hunger in his guts doubles then quadruples in intensity. And he remembers.

Remembers the time he picked up the elegant oddity on that long-ago summer day: a praying mantis, its skin a milky green, its pincers clasped together in worship of the Creator. So reverent a creature, surely it followed the same morals as other praying souls. Harm none. Hallelujah! Only the praying mantis jabbed its praying pincers, lightning-quick, into the meat of his young palm, and pain bloomed around a tiny dot of blood.

Insects pray to no deity and honor no ethic, he learned.

He remembers the house on the lake, a summer night when a mosquito that got past the window screens roused him with its buzz and then the maddening itch after it landed on his flesh, inserted its needle, and sipped. It drove him out of his bedroom to the living room sofa, where he hoped to find peace. But no, the bloodsucker pursued, following the tang of his perspiration, and drank some more. He remembers switching on the light. By then, the mosquito was engorged, its abdomen a bloated red obscenity moving slowly through the air, a clear target. Itching all over, he easily smashed it between his hands, though he found little satisfaction in the victory, because his flesh had been lit on fire.

As it is now, at this hungry hour in a world where the sirens have gone quiet, and the parasites beneath his skin pull invisible strings, making him do their work.

THE FOOD DELIVERIES dropped from planes have stopped. So have the flights, he assumes, by the relative stillness overhead. No contrails stain the sallow summer sky. It's possible there are still jets racing around up there, so high in altitude as to be invisible to the naked eye. The last one he saw was on fire and in pieces, falling out of the blue toward the general direction of Boston.

The first E.M. pulse knocked out the power, but not the intended target, because by that point they'd evolved, bonded with their hosts, gotten crafty at burrowing. They scramble deep inside body *and* soul, compelling him to eat, eat.

The days of this summer have all bled together. Perception alters. The pain grows so intense that Drone vomits, pitching the emptiness in his stomach onto the floor. Only his guts aren't really empty.

The wall above the bed is a perfect white canvas—in his lease, one of the 'thou-shalt-nots' spelled out stipulates no colors are to be painted, else that sweet security deposit is in jeopardy.

Jesus preached to love his neighbor. The new religion urges him to go over there, hammer down the door, and eat his fellow man. Eat as much of him as possible, because his house is on fire, his children are burning, and it's time to fly, fly, fly. He needs sustenance for the journey.

A perfect white canvas.

Only when he looks again, that white wall crawls with black and green splotches of color. The wall is covered in the writhing contents expelled from his stomach. In bugs.

WHEN HE WAS TEN, an uncle on his mother's side gave him a nature guide for his birthday. The cover was black and shiny. So, too, were the pages of *Insects of the World*. He scanned the book and, his fingers trembling, dropped it in disgust. The images contained within, such as *Zelus renardii* and *Scarabaeus sacer*, repulsed him so greatly and were presented in such clarity that he refused to pick up the book for fear the pictures would come alive.

It was a cruel gift from an uncle who'd routinely knocked him around when no one was looking, and who delighted in terrorizing him.

He walks out of the apartment, tromps over to the next door in the row of garden apartments, and makes a fist. Then he sees the back of his hand twitching with movement from something under his jaundiced skin. Another follows the first. He glances below his wrist to his forearm. They are everywhere inside him.

Knocking? He laughs, his voice emerging through a filter of phlegm, and drives his booted foot into the door.

"Get out of here!" his neighbor shrieks.

She's a woman, not the man he expects—perhaps his wife or girlfriend, though he's nowhere in the place, which stinks of sweat; is still a pale, pretty pink; doesn't have them inside her. Salivating, he ignores her command and drives his fist into the tender flesh of her throat, registering the crunch of cartilage beneath knuckles and the liquid gurgles of breaths coming in unnatural gasps after she spills across the floor.

The ragged pleas for mercy only fuel his hunger. How many days have passed since the last Meals Ready to Eat rationed to grains of rice quieted his stomach? A hand bats at his face. He seizes hold of it and chews one of the fingers down to bone. Screams fill the apartment, but his mind translates the din to chirrups, the lazy melody of a peaceful summer night.

A FOUL BURP shudders up his throat. He tastes bile, and his gorge threatens again to rise. He chokes it down and wipes his mouth with the back of his hand. The tops of his fingers come away damp and red.

Ladybird, Ladybird fly away...

Nothing in this new world is how he remembers it. Flames burn in all directions, and oily black plumes stain the horizon.

Your house is on fire...

He plods forward across the cracked pavement and through the tattered trees.

Drone did it—he actually went through with it. Walking with his hands in his pockets, he knows he should feel some remorse. No traces of horror stop him from advancing. He is driven by the magnetic forces and currents of air, like the Monarch butterfly making its annual pilgrimage to Mexico; like the cicada, which sleeps for seventeen years and then wakes, right on time. He marches forward.

Besides, insects are known to cannibalize one another. The praying mantis devours its mate's head during coitus. Worker ants shuffle all manner of food back to the nest, some of it still alive, some of it other dead worker ants. His tongue tingles. His teeth ache. He remembers plunging them into the soft skin of her belly and salivates.

HIS LAST TRUE HUMAN MEMORY involves Mister Hunt, his third-grade teacher. Math was never his strong suit, and he recalls sweating out being called upon during multiplication problems.

"What is six times six?"

Mister Hunt points at him in the vision. Somehow, he comes up with the correct answer. "Thirty-six."

Relief washes over him now, as it did then, in scintillating waves of electricity from panicked nerve endings. In that same classroom, either before or after his unwanted time in the spotlight, Mister Hunt—a handsome bachelor who wears burgundy socks with the ankles worn down to gauze, visible at the tops of his loafers—poses another baffling question.

"If you could gather up all the different groups of animals on the planet, which would weigh the most? Which would outweigh all the others?"

He really wants to say *Dinosaurs*, his favorites, but they're extinct so he settles for "The mammals, clearly." So many people, and when you add in elephants and giraffes and blue whales—

"Wrong," says Mister Hunt.

Those kids who suggest fish, birds, and lizards are wrong, too. Their teacher seems to delight in prolonging the correct answer; gloating over this horrible nugget of truth he alone among them knows. The answer is so obvious that it couldn't be gleaned by young minds thinking bigger, stronger, not *smaller*.

"They outnumber every other form of life combined," he says. "They'd tip the scale if you put all of them together. *Insects*."

HE CONNECTS WITH others along the way. They nod in silent agreement and form a line, marching single file a thousand-plus bodies deep over what used to be I-93. Moving ever forward, they lumber south, for the house has burned down and must be rebuilt.

They're building cities now. The closest rises above what was once Boston. The skyline has altered. Asymmetrical cones and honeycombs reflect the light of the setting sun. There are massive pens filled with screaming, terrified bodies—those who aren't yet host. Food, he knows. *Meat* for the colony.

He walks on, into the tunnels leading into their new city, ready to work and serve the colony, like a good drone.

"Skinsects" debuts in this issue of Black Infinity.

Raised on a healthy diet of creature double features and classic SF television, Gregory L. Norris is a full-time professional writer, with work appearing in numerous short story anthologies, national magazines, novels, the occasional TV episode, and, so far, one produced feature film (Brutal Colors, which debuted on Amazon Prime, January 2016). A former feature writer and columnist at Sci Fi, the official magazine of the Sci Fi Channel (before all those ridiculous Ys invaded), he once worked as a screenwriter on two episodes of Paramount's modern classic, Star Trek: Voyager. Two of his paranormal novels (written under his nom-de-plume, Jo Atkinson) were published by Home Shopping Network as part of their "Escape with Romance" line—the first time HSN has offered novels to their global customer base. He judged the 2012 Lambda Awards in the SF/F/H category. Three times now, his stories have notched Honorable Mentions in Ellen Datlow's Best-of books. In May 2016, he traveled to Hollywood to accept HM in the Roswell Awards in Short SF Writing. Follow Norris' literary adventures at www.gregorylnorris.blogspot.com

THE PLACE OF HAIRY DEATH
By Anthony M. Rud

AT LEAST NOT ALONE, SEÑOR! IF I WERE LIKE YOU, YOUNG, HANDSOME, AND WITH THE STRENGTH OF TWO MEN IN MY ARMS, I WOULD NOT VENTURE AT ALL DOWN INTO THOSE ANCIENT WORKINGS. I foresee trouble; and in those horrible dripping tunnels below Croszchen Pahna, where death may lurk in every slime-lined crevice, a comrade who will not flinch is even more necessary than your own great courage.

Ah, it is not a nice place down there! I have been part way, many years ago. I suppose every young *mozo* in all this district of Quintana Roo once could say as much. For there was a tale of treasure, of a room of gold and skeletons. Not this cheap ore that remains, and that costs more to mine than the ore will yield. A storeroom of the heavy nuggets found in rotten rock. And sealed up with that gold, the bodies of all the Indians who worked down in the bowels of the earth for their masters, the *Conquistadores*.

Not the first time I ventured there, but the second, death reached out with many hairy fingers and caught its prey. The first time I descended alone, and in terror. I returned to the blessed daylight very quickly—but not alone. A multitude of hairy horrors came with me! Even now after nearly thirty years, when I eat to a fullness of *carne* at nightfall, I know what will happen. Ever since then, in all my dreams I see—

But the señor shrugs. He is a hothead, like all *Americanos*. He wishes knowledge, not the fancies of an old man. It shall be so. Even today, the offer of fifty pesos is enough to tempt; for after all, one must eat. If the señor will get a good comrade, and both wish it, I shall guide them halfway. That is as far as my knowledge extends. I will build a fire, then, in the Room of Many Craters, and wait. But I will not go unless I judge the señor has a man of bravery for a comrade.

How do I know the Room of Many Craters is halfway? Well, it is a guess, Señor, but a good guess. I believe. The Indians who slaved in the mine for their Spanish masters never saw daylight. They dwelt in this huge room, which is a great bubble in the rock.

Also, a hundred or more of them worked here in this room. The round craters were worn in the floor by many men pushing against tree trunks, and walking endlessly in circles. This ground the rotten ore, and in time scoured out the craters in the floor.

According to old story, which has much sign of truth, the gold secured from the ore had to be stored many months. Ships came seldom, not every few weeks like today when steam drives ships as legs drive water beetles, wherever they wish to go. There were no strongholds above ground; so the gold was taken a long way through a secret passage, and stored in a barren room where guards watched night and day.

And that room once was found, though its unimaginable store of yellow gold still remains untouched. Unless more slides have come, it is probable that the señor will know the right passage or crevice, for before he may force a way it will be necessary to move a moldered skeleton.

That is not the short and rather frail bone frame of one of my people. That youth was strong, blue of eye like the señor himself. Yellow of hair. Easy to make smile or laugh. But he did not laugh once, from the time he, his companion, and I reached the Room of Craters, where I was to wait. There is a hot, wet atmosphere down there. And among the many things that hang in that heavy air is a queer, fetid stench that sends the heart of man down into his boots.

That time, when I saw the two men leave me by my fire in the Room of Craters, I crossed myself and prayed for their safe return. I did not even think of the gold, then, though they had promised me all I could carry, as my share. The one with blue eyes, the laughing one, was such as my mother's people worshipped in the old days, you understand. I was loyal to his companion, naturally; but to *him* I would render any service but one! I would not go farther into that place of hairy death! No, not even loyalty could take me there. That is why I caution the señor to choose his comrade with care.

Those two young men left me, and vanished into the wet dark. And only the wrong one returned. I must tell a little of those men and their story, so the señor can know how that could be. Usually it is the other way. In most struggles with darkness and evil, the strongest and most right it is who comes back to tell the tale. But not this time.

THE TALE, the señor must understand, is pieced together from fragments. It may not all be true exactly as I tell it. But the main facts are as I say. There is no need even to imagine a hatred or jealousy between the two men. There was none. One man was strong and poor. The other was weak—and the heir to millions of *Americano* gold. He, at least, should never have risked health and mind and life for more wealth. But thus it is in this world. No one is satisfied.

The blue-eyed, laughing man had been the superintendent of the great *jeniquen* rope factory in Valladolid, up north forty miles from here, in Yucatan. The señor doubtless knows the factory, for he came by narrow-gage railway, and Valladolid is the terminus.

The factory, and perhaps two hundred square miles of the great *jeniquen* plantations, were owned by the *Americano* father of the second man, the dark-skinned young fellow who was known as Señor Lester Ainslee.

It seems that the great father of Señor Lester did not approve of his boy. It was wished that Señor Lester get out into the jungle and what is called "rough it," drinking less wine, smoking fewer cigarettes, and learning to work hard with his hands. That was strange to me; for a sharp glance told me that one single day in the broiling sun, cutting *jeniquen*, would kill the delicate boy. But fathers are strange. They love and marry women who are delicate and nervous, and

who die young. Then they demand their own strength in their offspring—when it is well known that Nature orders it otherwise. No breeder of fine horses would be such a fool. He would look for the characteristics of the dam to appear in the male colt; and those of the sturdy sire to show themselves in the female get.

Señor Jim Coulter—he was the blond, laughing one—was perhaps twenty-eight, though he looked not so much older than his companion. The boy, a fortnight or so before, had got drunk to celebrate his twenty-first birthday, and there were purple saucers under his eyes remaining from that bad time.

Then it was that the rich father could endure no more. He sent the boy down from the United States to work in the rope factory, or in the fields. Alongside the most ignorant *peons*, you understand—mere beasts who have slaved for generations under the lash of the overseers of the *haciendados!*

It was asking the impossible. The factory superintendent, Señor Jim Coulter, sent many telegraph messages; for the unreasonable father would hold him responsible, and he knew that nothing save quick death could happen to the frail young man in his charge.

In the end it was agreed that Señor Jim would take one month of holiday from the rope factory, and accompany the boy from the north on a trip into the jungle. The Señor Jim somewhere had got hold of a story that told of the treasure vault still remaining deep in this Madre d'Oro Mine, two thousand feet below the ancient temple at Croszchen Pahna. The story was an old one to me, of course, and probably true.

When they came to me, hearing that I had ventured down into these old workings at much risk to my life, and I assured them that no one ever had dared go far enough to find the treasure room, they nearly burst with excitement. What to them were walls that fell at a touch? What were a few deadly vipers, a thousand ten-inch scorpions waving their armored tails, or the horrible hosts of *conechos*—those great, leaping spiders that *Americanos* call tarantulas?

True, Señor, you frown impatiently. You will say to me, ah, but everyone knows a tarantula is not deadly poison. Well, perhaps that is true. I once knew a man who was bitten in the lobe of the ear, and lived. But he had a sharp knife. And after all, part of an ear is not so much to sacrifice, when life itself is in hazard.

The *conechos*, Señor, that dwell in the slimy crevices of this old Madre d'Oro Mine below the wettest cellars of Croszchen Pahna, are of a larger variety than those one finds feeding on bananas. Also they are whitish-pink in color, and sightless. They do not need the eyes. They leap surely through the dark at what they wish to bite....

The way down as far as the Room of Craters is not far, as miles are measured up here in the blessed sunshine. Perhaps there was a day when the bearded Spaniards walked safely enough from the broken shaft mouth, down the steep-slanted manways, helped here and there by rough ladders, in no more than one hour.

I know not if the way remains passable now. But if it is no worse than it was the day those two young *Americanos* and I descended to the Room of Craters, it will take three active, daring men more than ten times that space of time.

Roped to each other, we crawled and slid down the terrible passages. I led, and carried in my left hand a long and heavy broom of twigs bound with wire. With this I struck ahead before I placed my foot—or cleared a way of vipers and scorpions before lying down and wriggling feet foremost through narrow, low apertures where time and again my coming was the signal for a fall of wet, rotten rock.

I call to your attention, Señor, that the way to enter such unknown passages always is feet first. Then if there are creatures waiting unseen to strike or leap at one from the side, they are apt to waste their venom on the heavy boots, or on the thighs that are wrapped in many thicknesses of paper, under the heavy trousers.

Also it is easier to withdraw, if a serious slide occurs.

Señor Jim, who followed me, carried a strong lantern. Another, smaller one for my use in the Room of Craters was attached to his belt, near the taut rope. Señor Lester, who came last, bore a miner s pick, for use in breaking through walled-up passages.

Once I was knocked flat and pinned down by a flake of rock like a sheet of slate, which fell before I even touched it; jarred free, no doubt, by the vibrations of our footsteps.

With the pick, however, Señor Jim quickly released me. And while he was working there I heard him strike swiftly once, twice, thrice with the pick, though not on the rock which held me.

Then he cursed, and his voice held a note of wonderment.

"Fastest thing I ever saw!" he muttered; while behind him Señor Lester whimpered aloud. I knew he had viewed some frightful thing, and had failed to kill it with the pick.

That was the first of the sickly-white spiders, the *conechos*. I had warned the two young men, of course; but until one sees those horrible, sightless, hairy monsters, and learns how they can leap and dodge—even a swift bullet, some maintain!—there can be no understanding of the terror they inspire in men.

From then on the *conechos*, which never appear near the surface, became more numerous. It was necessary for us to shout, and to hurl small rocks ahead of us, to drive them into their crevices. Otherwise they might leap at us. And such is the weird soundless telegraphy of such creatures, that if any living thing is bitten by a spider, all the other spiders know it instantly, and come. Whatever the living thing may be, it is buried under an avalanche of horrid albino hunger.

LONG BEFORE WE REACHED the Room of Craters, Señor Lester—the weak one—was exhausted. He was a shivering wreck from terror, the foul air, and the heat, and was pleading with Señor Jim to go back.

The other one would not have it. He kept mocking the dangers, laughing shortly—and how soon that brave laugh was to be stilled! But Señor Lester got to stumbling; weeping as he staggered or crawled after us. He dropped the pick, and neither of us knew, until we reached a place where the enlargement of an opening had to be done. Then we had to retrace many weary steps to secure the tool.

At last we reached the Room of Craters, where a fire may be built from the old logs that were used by the Indian slaves in pushing the ore mill. There was comparative safety, and we rested, while Señor Jim did all he could to revive the courage of his companion.

I could have told him it was of no use; but in those days I too was young, and did not feel it my place to advise. Señor Lester quieted; but every minute or two his whole thin frame would be racked by a fit of shuddering. I was glad I had made it very plain I would go no farther, but would wait for them here. Señor Jim tried every inducement, but I held firm. The few pesos I had earned outright were enough. I did not care much whether or not they found gold. The one time before I had come this far, I had penetrated a few dozen yards farther, into a narrow passage I deemed might be the one leading to the treasure room. And I knew what that passage contained—white, hairy death!

So I huddled over my fire of punk logs, ate food from the small pack I carried, slept, and waited through the weary hours. I thought hideous things, though none was worse than reality. My knowledge of what happened, you understand, Señor, comes in great part from the ravings of a man to which I was forced to listen.

In the narrow, slide-obstructed passage that led on, those two young ones fought their way. How Señor Jim ever made the other follow as far as he did, is not for me to guess. But struggle on they did; and at length they reached a blank ending of the passage—a place where centuries before, the Spaniards had walled in their treasure, and with it the human slaves who had dug, ground, and carried the ore and gold.

There was one small hole pierced in this wall. *Quien sabe?* Perhaps the prisoners broke through that much. It is likely that the dons would have a swordsman waiting outside as a guard, ready to chop off the groping arms of those dying desperate ones.

But while Señor Lester sank on the rock floor, too spent now to help, Señor Jim set at the wall with the pick. In time, by dint of much sweat, and many pauses in which he used the broom to brush aside the spiders, which were numerous at this low level, he had broken in a hole large enough so that a man could crawl through feet first.

He flashed the lantern into the chamber which opened beyond the wall. *It was the treasure house!*

His yell at sight of the piles of gold, long since burst from their hide sacks and spilled together, aroused Señor Lester, who was able to stagger to his feet and look. They saw, besides the great mountain of gold, white traceries on the floor that might once have been the moldered human bones of the imprisoned slaves. Yes, it was the storehouse of treasure!

Frantically then, forgetting his caution that had brought him and his companion farther than any other white man, Señor Jim wriggled into the hole he had made. He would have got through, too—only there was a slight movement of the rock, just a subsidence of perhaps six inches.

It squeezed him at the waist! It held him horizontal and helpless, two feet from the rock floor!

Señor Lester cried out in weak terror, but Señor Jim did not lose his head.

"You'll have to break me out—quick!" he commanded. "It's slowly squeezing the insides out of me! Quick, the pick! Hit it right up above me—there!" He nodded with his head, both arms being pinioned so that he could not point.

Whimpering, whining, almost unable to lift the pick, the other tried to obey. But that was when the first hairy thing fell or leaped from above. It landed squarely on Señor Jim's upturned face. He screeched with horror—then with pain and realization that this was the end.

Almost before the sound had left his whitening lips, the *others* came, leaping, bounding, from the roof, along the walls, from the floor. The albino horde!

And from Señor Lester fled the last vestige of manhood. Jerking back on the rope that held him to his doomed companion, he sawed at it with his knife.

When it broke he fled, screaming himself to drown the awful, smothering sounds from the end of the passage....

* * *

THAT IS NOT QUITE ALL, SEÑOR. I heard the ghastly tale, though not until I had slept safely many hours, there in the Room of Many Craters. The young *Americano* had taken at least seven or eight hours to fight his way back to me. There was no hope for the other.

I brought Señor Lester up into the blessed daylight, though because of his complete collapse we were a whole day and night on the way.

Until his father could come from the United States, I cared for the young man, who could not leave his bed. A part of his mind had gone, it seemed, and he raved about the death of his friend, saying the same things over and over. I was very glad to surrender Señor Lester to his saddened father, who took his boy home where good doctors could care for him.

It was almost a year later when a scarecrow came to my hut. It was Señor Lester, dressed now in rags, but with a sheaf of money with which he tried to bribe me to descend with him again into the old mine!

Valgame Dios! I would not have gone then for a million million dollars, *Americano* gold! The fear was too lately on me. So then he threw back his head, his voice shaking, and said:

"Then I must go alone! I can never rest till I bring up Jim's body! I—I was a coward! I *am* a coward!"

"Well, that is the truth," I admitted, "but there are many cowards. What difference can it make now?"

But he was resolute—in words. In actions, not so resolute. He had made up his mind to go again, this time alone; but days dragged by. He lived in my hut. He jumped each time a game-cock crowed, every time a door was closed. He was a nervous shadow, not even as strong as he had been when I saw him first. He had escaped from a sanatorium up north, and come back here secretly, I discovered. I decided to send a message to his father. When that message did go it was somewhat different from what I intended.

I was a bachelor then, Señor. The little spiders, the *malichos*, spun their webs where they would on the rafters of my hut. I did not care. The mice played around freely at night; for my striped cat was old and fat, sleeping much and doing little.

To keep the young *Americano* from those sudden screeching fits, though, I had to climb up with a broom and wipe away the spider webs. They would build new ones. It did not matter.

"I can't *stand* them!" he would wail, shuddering all over. I thought to myself then there was little danger he ever would go again into the Madre d'Oro Mine. And that was true. He never went again.

That very night as I slept in my blankets on the floor, I was awakened suddenly. Señor Lester had leapt up, screaming as I hope I never hear another man or woman scream! He jumped around. I could not quiet him. I made a light hurriedly, hearing him fall to the floor.

He was stiffening then, head arched back.

"It *bit* me! I killed it!" he shrieked. Then came a final shudder, and he went limp—dead!

Now that was too fast even for the bite of a great pit-viper. I tried to find what had killed him. His two hands had been clenched together, but now in death they relaxed. I drew them apart. I knew the truth, and my heart went faint within me. He had been dreaming of the hairy spiders, when—

Crushed between the palms of his thin, nervous hands, was the dead body of a small mouse!

"The Place of Hairy Death" first appeared in the February 1934 issue of Weird Tales.

American author Anthony Melville Rud (1893–1942) penned eight novels as well as over two dozen stories which appeared in Argosy, Weird Tales, and a handful of other pulp genre magazines—occasionally writing under the pen names Ray McGillivary or Anson Piper. His Lovecraftian thriller "Ooze" was the cover story of the premiere issue of "the Unique Magazine" and was reprinted in Black Infinity: Blobs, Globs, Slime and Spores. *Rud also edited* Adventure *magazine during the late 1920s.*

ELYSIUM 4

BY JASON J. McCUISTON

HANK O'BRIAN WOKE WITH A START, ALL OF HIS SENSES ALERT, SIGNALING ONE WORD: *DANGER!*

His wife, Jean, stirred next to him. "Hm? What is it, Hank?"

"Someone's in the pod. Stay here."

She sat up. "The kids!"

Pulling on his jumpsuit, Hank signaled her to stay quiet. "I'll check."

Hank slipped through the sliding door into the tiny corridor separating the master suite from the hall bath and the kids' room. He wondered how anyone could get into the pod without setting off the alarms and activating 9N-Gen's defense protocols. He also wondered why anyone would bother. Hank knew he wasn't popular among the other colonists of Elysium 4, thanks to his service in the Space Force, but he never thought any of them might resort to terrorizing his newly-arrived family. The planet was still in the first stages of terraforming, so any serious vandalism or theft was tantamount to murder.

Hank opened the smaller bedroom door. Billy and Gail both slept peacefully in their bunks. He smiled. With the kids aged eight and ten, respectively, Hank still had a little time before he needed to add another room to the pod. Time he could ill afford to use if he was going to get their new homestead up to maximum efficiency. Especially since he and Jean would be doing it alone. Their nearest neighbors were almost forty kilometers away, and Sato Tanaka had shown absolutely no interest in extending a hand of friendship or welcome.

Another rustling sound came from the kitchen.

Hank activated the wall control just inside the small common room. "9N-Gen, enter the house. Defense Protocol Alpha." Confident that the general-purpose labor bot would follow the command and engage the intruder with non-lethal force, Hank moved to his "office," the tiny nook where his desk and computer were crammed. His service weapon was locked in the safe hidden behind the family portrait.

A skittering, clicking sound from the kitchen froze him in his tracks. The hair stood up on the back of his neck. That inner voice that was still screaming *Danger* now added a new, irrational phrase: *Not human!*

The kitchen door slid open and something large and misshapen moved through the portal. Hank smelled raw soil and something else, something organic and pungent. A knot formed in his belly. "Lights, maximum glow."

Suddenly Hank understood those rumors they had heard when they'd first arrived and learned of their allotment on E-4. He understood why this homestead had been abandoned by the previous tenants. He understood what Sato Tanaka had meant when he'd said, "Me and mine won't go out there, Captain. Even if you weren't tainted by the UE, there's nothing but ill luck in that place. Ill luck and *strange things....*"

The strange thing in the doorway made a chittering hiss and stood up on hind legs. In the sudden white light erupting from the domed ceiling, Hank beheld a roughly two-meter red-and-black insectoid creature. Each of its six articulated limbs ended in a three-pronged pincher. A shiny, chitinous exoskeleton covered its segmented body. Its head, slightly larger than his own, was dominated by two bulbous multi-faceted golden eyes, a pair of wispy antennae, and a mouth surrounded by cruel-bladed mandibles.

As it moved into the common room, Hank saw that it was not alone. At least two more skittered behind it.

Not having time to open the safe and recover his pistol, Hank snatched the heavy steel paperweight off his desk. Shaped like his old ship, the *UES Heinlein*, the item had been a wedding gift from Jean, the actual designer of the United Earth frigate. Grasping the impromptu weapon, he moved between the invaders and the bedrooms.

The first insectoid rushed him. As big as it was, it moved in a chittering, rustling blur. Hank fell back, avoiding the snapping mandibles aimed for his throat. He lashed out with the paperweight, heard the thing's exoskeleton crunch as it staggered away.

The outer door of the pod opened, admitting a gust of cool desert wind. 9N-Gen hovered into the front room on a jet of anti-G energy, its six articulated appendages extending from its central metallic orb and bristling with stun guns and strobe lights. Bright flashes and electric bolts filled the dome as the robot declared in a deep synthetic voice: "Do not resist. Do not resist."

One of the insectoids stumbled as it took a stun bolt to the head. It seemed momentarily dazed rather than incapacitated. A third bug-thing rushed past Hank and his opponent, making a beeline for the bedrooms.

"9N-Gen! Defense Protocol Omega!"

Hank's injured adversary swatted the paperweight from his hand with one pincer while clamping down on his left shoulder with its mandibles. The pain was sharp and rending, but there was also a stinging, burning aspect to it. Hank knew he had just been poisoned.

He slumped to the ground as bright crimson bolts of plasma replaced the blue strobes of electricity. The creature above him shuddered,

a glowing red hole in the center of its horrible face. Hank's world blurred, turned to darkness around the edges... Many multi-limbed shadows click-clacked around him... His body went limp and he forgot how to breathe... Enveloped in that foul earthy stench....

"Jean... Billy... Gail...."

* * *

"PLEASE BE ADVISED that you are injured and still recovering from low-level blood toxicity."

Hank blinked against the dull pain coursing through his body, something like the flu. 9N-Gen hovered above him, having dressed his wound and administered a dose of antitoxin. Hank sat up, aggravating the sickening pain, remembering. "Jean? The kids? What happened?"

"They have been taken." The robot ran another scan. "Regrettably, there were more enemies than I could neutralize on my own, sir."

Hank looked around the disheveled room, noting the broken furniture, blast marks and black ichor splattering the walls and floor. However, there were no insectoid corpses. He got to his feet and staggered to the bedrooms. Thankfully, there were no red bloodstains or human tissue evident in either room.

He slumped against the doorframe. "Taken? Taken where?"

"Underground, sir. The invaders carried off their dead and injured as well."

Hank followed the robot into the kitchen. In the middle of the second-largest room in the pod was a three-meter wide hole that went almost straight down. The insectoids had burrowed right up into the house, completely bypassing his security measures. "How long?"

"One hour, sixteen minutes, standard time, sir. I would have pursued but my programming forbade me from leaving you in such a delicate state. The bio-toxin is an unknown paralytic with indeterminate effects on the human physiology. Without my ministrations, it is entirely possible you would have succumbed to your wounds, sir."

Hank nodded, stepped to the communicator, and pounded in the code for the Tanaka pod. When the connection finally went through, he looked at the glowering face on the screen.

"Sato, I need help. Some kind of indigenous lifeform has taken my family underground. Can you round up some folks, get them equipped with weapons, lights, climbing gear, and meet me here within the hour?"

Tanaka frowned, rubbed his tired face. "Indigenous lifeforms? I'm sorry, Captain, but there's no record of such a thing on Elysium 4." He gave a bitter chuckle. "In fact, until we showed up, there was nothing in this entire system stupid enough to try and make a living on this waste of a rock. Of course, you know that, being a United Earth Space Forcer. You needed colonists here, to keep the Collective from encroaching too closely to UE space. Why else would your people offer such bonuses and give it such an attractive name? *Elysium*, hah! If you had wanted to be honest, you'd have called it Acheron or Jigoku."

"Dammit, Sato! This is my family we're talking about, not politics!"

Tanaka gave him a cruel smirk. "No, Captain. I'll not play a part in your alibi. I'm guessing you've cracked up just like the last man who lived out there, and you've done something horrible, and now you want me to help you cover it up. Well, I will send someone. I'm calling the constables. Just sit tight. They should be there by first dawn."

The line went dead and Hank yanked the com off the wall with a curse.

Forcing down the urge to vomit, he turned to 9N-Gen. "Scan that bio matter. Find out everything you can about these new lifeforms."

As the robot set to this task, Hank went out to his workshop to retrieve his gear. Before retiring from the Space Force to complete his doctorate in advanced robotics, he had been a survival instructor at the academy. Fortunately, he had brought his kit to this new home, on the off chance he might someday need it again.

He'd never imagined that need would be something like this. "Luck of the Irish, my Aunt Fanny...."

Wearing his HUD helmet and equipment harness, Hank returned to the house just as 9N-Gen completed his analysis. While the robot gave his report, Hank retrieved his blaster pistol and ammunition from the safe.

"There are strange anomalies in the DNA of these creatures, sir. Though 98.3 percent is insect, not too dissimilar from several subspecies of ants on Earth, there are some unidentifiable strands, as well as 0.4 percent human DNA."

Hank raised an eyebrow. "How's that?"

"It would seem to be a recent and incomplete addition to the creatures' makeup. Although these chromosomes are partially grafted onto the double helix, it does not appear to be an artificial graft, sir."

Hank chewed on this as he led the robot into the kitchen. "Something to ponder. But right now, we're heading down there, 9N-Gen. From here on out, I want you in Omega mode." He prayed that would be the deadliest setting he'd need from the robot on this venture.

"Yes, sir."

9N-Gen descended first, using his spotlight to illuminate the tunnel while Hank rappelled down from the kitchen. The shaft went down some thirty or forty meters before leveling off into a more-or-less horizontal tunnel. The robot's light revealed a world within a world. Where the surface of E-4 was almost universally desert sand and stone with a few rivers heavy in sulfur and salt, this underground realm was one of omnipresent moisture and bioluminescent fungus.

Hank marveled at this mystery. "How is this even possible? How is it that the mining projects never dug deep enough to find this? Maybe there's something about these ant-like things' biology that transforms the environment? Maybe they've made sure to avoid the mines? Something else to ponder...."

They followed the tunnel for approximately half an hour before 9N-Gen signaled caution. "Two of the creatures just ahead, sir. They are substantially larger than those that attacked the residence."

"Stealth mode." Hank and the robot crouched and crept closer. He switched the visor of his helmet to night-vision while 9N-Gen doused the spotlight.

Hank heard them before he saw them, just around a sloping curve in the tunnel wall. The clacking and chittering was louder and somehow more menacing than before, and once he saw the things, he understood why.

These two were half again as big as those in the first encounter, their carapaces glossy black and lined with bristling black fur. Stranger still, they wielded long, spear-like weapons. Their broad backs to Hank and the robot, they huddled around something affixed to the tunnel wall.

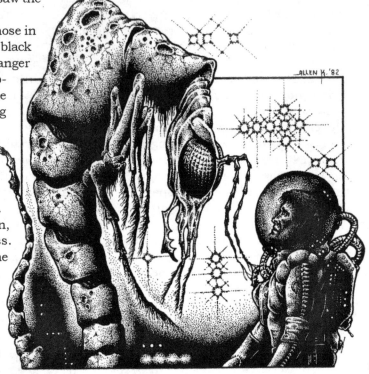

When one shifted, revealing what that something was, Hank gasped. The desiccated body of a man hung in gooey strands from the earthen wall, and these giant insects were eating it. The creatures spun at his exclamation, raising their weapons with a clicking hiss.

Recalling the ferocious speed of the drones above, Hank opened fire. 9N-Gen beat him to it. The tunnel blazed with six short bursts of plasma, and the two soldier bugs fell to the floor, sizzling and smoking. Breathing a sigh of relief, Hank holstered his weapon and inspected the scene.

"He's a colonist." Hank used his pocket vibroblade to cut away some of the goo to inspect the dead man's jumpsuit. Reading the nametag stitched above the torn breast, he took a deep breath. "Norris. He's the original claim holder of our pod. They said he disappeared with his family six months ago...."

"I am detecting a power source in these weapons, sir. They appear to be far more advanced than these creatures' apparent technological capabilities."

Hank picked up one of the spears, realizing it had a trigger designed for a three-clawed pincer. "Curiouser and curiouser...."

Hank and 9N-Gen continued deeper into the tunnel for about another hour before they came to a nexus of four more corridors. The robot scanned each opening and indicated the one to the far right. "I am detecting human DNA down this tunnel, sir."

"DNA, but no life signs?" Hank's blood ran cold at the thought....

"Not at present, sir. However, the abundance of bio-matter in the vicinity may be interfering with my sensors."

Hank clung to this thin strand of hope and set off down the smaller corridor. He had to crouch as the ceiling and walls closed in around him. Gripping his blaster firmly in his right hand, he steadied himself against the tunnel's smooth surface with his left. "Please let them be all right..."

Strong, segmented limbs dropped from the low ceiling, burying knife-like pincers into his shoulders. A deafening clacking-chittering sound filled his ears as mandibles pounded and scraped across his helmet. The blaster fell from his numbed fingers. His knees went weak. His heart thundered in his chest. Hank felt the stinging poison course through his system again.

Heat and light flashed behind him. 9N-Gen fired a plasma pulse and the ambushing insectoid fell from the overhead tunnel onto Hank's back. He was vaguely aware of how light it was in comparison to its sheer power. He struggled to breathe and remain conscious until the robot could tend his wounds. A sudden vibration broke through his dwindling consciousness.

Then he broke through the tunnel floor into freefall.

Hank was numb when he finally came to a bone-jarring stop. Sweat covered his body, ran into his eyes. Gasping for breath, he swatted at his HUD visor, trying to clear his vision. A moment of panic took hold as he felt the helmet suffocating him. With a surge of energy, he wrestled the headgear off and gulped in the moist and fetid earthy air. Finally clearing his vision, he wished he hadn't.

He was surrounded by death.

Hundreds of bones and desiccated corpses stretched out into the darkness bordering the dim glow of his lighting rig. Possibly thousands. This shock was almost too much to bear. At that moment all Hank O'Brian, former captain of the United Earth Space Force, wanted to do was close his eyes and join his family in eternal rest.

But a voice inside him, the same voice which had gotten him through the Battle of Oberon, the same voice which had kept him alive for ninety-six days of hunted isolation on Ganymede, the same voice which had alerted him to the dangers invading his home this very night, that voice whispered to him, *"They could still be alive. It's up to you to save them."*

More light filled the immense pit as 9N-Gen descended from the shaft above on a jet of anti-G. "You are still alive, sir. Hold still a moment and I will begin a medical assessment."

Hank struggled against the tightening in his chest, the burning in his veins. "Just give me another dose of anti-tox. Aside from the poison and the punctures in my shoulders, I'm fine. Just a few bumps and scrapes. Nothing to worry about."

"As you prefer, sir." 9N-Gen hovered beside him and administered the injection before sealing the wounds. "However, I must warn you that another dose of antitoxin within the next twenty-four hours may prove fatal, given your current condition."

Feeling the poison neutralized in his system and the mild euphoria from the local anesthetic, Hank breathed easier and turned his attention to his grisly surroundings. He noted a scattering of human remains, each wearing some portion of a colonial jumpsuit. A few dating back to the era of initial colonization a century before. But there were other things beneath them, the remnants of other life forms.

Once the robot had finished his ministrations, Hank donned his helmet and activated the visor's scanner. Pushing himself shakily to his feet, he began a hurried but detailed analysis of the various corpses.

"I do not believe this. Mankind has been exploring this part of the galaxy for almost three centuries and we have yet to come across so much as a sentient microbe or tardigrade, and yet at least half the things in this pit appear to have been intelligent. Look, that diminutive one over there is wearing what seems to be a flight suit. And this one with the elongated skull actually has some form of cybernetic enhancements! And that one with the reptilian appearance has equipment and weapons still strapped to its harness. This is absolutely incredible!"

9N-Gen's scanning grid washed over the remains. "It would appear that these creatures' DNA matches the unidentified grafts earlier detected on the insectoids, sir."

Hank thought about the two they had killed earlier, the ones eating the mummified Norris. "These things don't only prey on other species. They somehow use them to evolve." He picked up his blaster pistol and headed for the nearest tunnel. "Maybe that's why they took Jean and the kids instead of just...." He shook the thought away.

"But sir, my sensors cannot isolate any human DNA in this chaos."

"Forget it. Just look for massive heat signatures. Unless I miss my guess, they've taken my family into the heart of the hive. To their queen. Lord only knows what they'll do to them when they get there...."

But Hank had an idea, and he did not like it one little bit.

As they travelled deeper and deeper into the tunnels, Hank noticed that the walls were smoother and covered in a more solid form of the alien goo he had seen on Norris's mummy closer to the entrance. "9N-Gen, can you tell how old these tunnels are?"

The robot hummed in electronic thought. "It

would appear that our current location is approximately three hundred standard years older than the upper tunnels where we entered, sir. In fact, my scans indicate that there are three specific epochs of tunnels, each section having been dug out at roughly one-hundred-year intervals."

Hank chewed on this and kept walking. "That would make sense. As barren as this planet is, it could not sustain a large population of these creatures for any prolonged length of time. The insectoids must have a lengthy hibernation period where they wait for resources to replenish before they emerge, consume and evolve—probably something close to a century. Each generation prepares for the betterment of the next. But to what ultimate end?"

"End, sir?"

Hank shook his head. "Nothing. I've just got a notion that these things aren't native. And if that's the case, then who or what put them here? And why…?"

Hank trailed off as the beam of his helmet light fell across something disquietingly familiar. His belly filled with stones. Hot bile rose up in his throat. He reached down and picked up Jean's robe. He had given her the silk garment on her first Mother's Day after Gail's birth. It was filthy—spattered with the insectoid goop and mud—and torn ragged in places. Turning it over and over in his gloved hands, he could see no signs of blood, however.

"Thank God! Come on, at least we know we're heading in the right direction."

A few moments later, Hank and 9N-Gen came to the mouth of their tunnel. Roughly four meters above the chamber's floor, it looked out upon an immense cavern that appeared to be the nexus of a hundred tunnels. At least that number of giant ant-like things swarmed over every surface of the massive space. Most of these were the red-and-black variety that Hank thought of as drones. There were also a number of smaller, squirming, translucent creatures that must have been pupa or emerging larvae. But more than a few were the black-armored soldiers with the spear-like weapons.

"There, sir." 9N-Gen drew his attention to three still forms in the midst of the carapaced confusion. Jean and his children were swaddled in the ropy white strands of goo and secured to the backs of three of the drones. In a moment, they vanished into a large tunnel descending into the midst of the chamber floor.

Hank drew the blaster, checked the ammo pack and made sure he could get to the rest on his harness in a hurry. "All weapons on max charge, 9N-Gen. Focus on the armed ones. I'll take out the drones. Got it?"

"Yes, sir."

"Then let's go."

Hank leapt from the tunnel, filling the target-rich environment with plasma bolts. He knew he had killed or disabled half a dozen of the enemy by the time he hit the floor. The robot descended, its energy beams and bolts securing a perimeter around him and cutting a swath toward the central tunnel.

The insectoids rallied with ferocity. Some of them even used their dead and wounded companions as shields in order to get closer to the hive's invaders. "Keep pouring it on, 9N-Gen. We must be getting close to the queen."

A bolt of green energy flashed over Hank's head, blasting one of the robot's arms off at the jointed elbow. Hank returned fire, dropping one of the soldiers. A dozen more took its place.

"Are you all right, 9N-Gen?" Hank replaced the depleted pack on his pistol.

"Minimal damage, sir." The robot continued its harrowing assault on the insectoid swarm, but they had only advanced three or four meters into the central chamber. Hank feared he might run out of power packs or 9N-Gen might run out of arms before they reached the central tunnel into which his family had disappeared. He scanned the chamber for a sign of anything he could turn to their advantage before they were swallowed up by the monstrous insects.

"Desperate times…." Hank pulled one of his last fully charged packs. "When this lands, target it."

"Yes, sir."

Hank hurled the ammo pack into the phalanx of soldiers separating them from the tunnel entrance. "Now!"

9N-Gen didn't miss. The pack exploded in a

conflagration of electro-chemical fire, engulfing nearly a score of the enemy and igniting twice as many more. The blast's concussion toppled a comparable number, opening a narrow corridor to the tunnel's mouth.

Hank took off at a dead run, the robot behind him filling the burning air with more plasma bolts. A meter from the tunnel's entrance, he dove headfirst.

A green flash blinded him as something hit his helmet with the force of a wrecking ball. He was knocked senseless, but not unconscious. Hank cartwheeled like a ragdoll into the tunnel, skidding, tumbling, and rolling into sudden darkness.

When he finally came to rest, he thought he might have broken his neck. "9N-Gen!"

The robot hovered down beside him, half its serviceable limbs still firing up the tunnel behind them. Two more ran a scan over Hank's body. "You are not seriously injured, sir. It appears that your helmet took a glancing blow from one of the creatures' energy weapons."

Hank struggled onto his knees and removed the headgear. Examining it by the robot's spotlight, he saw a smoldering incision that had nearly split the helmet and his head in two. Taking a deep breath and acknowledging his Irish luck, Hank found his weapon, loaded his last ammo pack and got to his feet. "Come on, we've got to be close."

"They are not following us, sir."

"And just that much is right with the world, 9N-Gen. Let's go."

"I detect human life signs that way, sir."

Hank set off in that direction, the robot close behind. As they travelled deeper and deeper into the hive, he noted that some of these tunnels did not seem to be carved out by mandibles and pincers, but by elaborate tools. One vertical set of incisions on a corner drew his attention. They reminded him of the marks he used to chart the kids' growth on a doorframe of the family's apartment on Perseus Station. He picked up the pace.

"Could another civilization have evolved down here, and somehow created these things or been conquered by them?"

9N-Gen ran another scan. "It is not outside the realm of probability, sir, given what we have already seen."

"I hear something."

Two figures loomed out of the shadow, each holding a spotlight. "Hold up! Don't shoot!"

Hank frowned, blinked in surprise. He recognized the reinforced blue uniforms of the constables, dirty and torn as they were. He also recognized the two men wearing them. "Frank? Doug? What in blazes are you doing down here?"

Frank smoothed his moustache and glanced at his taller companion. "Tanaka called us. When we got to your pod, we saw the rappelling lines and figured we'd give chase. Long story short, here we are."

"But it wasn't easy," Doug added.

"I am still operating in Omega mode, sir. Shall I kill them?"

Hank shook his head. "No, 9N-Gen. I think they're on our side. Reserve Omega mode only for nonhuman targets."

"Yes, sir."

Doug smiled as the robot's plasma projectors lowered. "Man, am I glad you did that."

Hank raised an eyebrow at the constable's tone. But it was too late. Doug aimed his neural prod.

A bright flash of electricity and Hank smelled burning ozone. He slumped to the ground, stunned. Although his body was no longer under his control, he was conscious enough to see Frank hit 9N-Gen with an EMP pulse, dropping the inert robot to the ground beside him.

* * *

HANK REGAINED HIS SENSES. He was strapped to the chitinous back of one of the red-and-black drones. Raising his chin, he saw that he was in the rear of a procession of the things. He craned his neck around. Frank and Doug walked behind the giant insectoids, carrying their lights and dragging the disabled 9N-Gen between them like a trophy.

"Why? What's going on? Why are you doing this?"

The two constables smiled. "You'll see."

They emerged into a gigantic chamber that dwarfed the previous nexus of tunnels. The center of this cavern was occupied by a glistening pillar-like monstrosity—a gigantic winged and crested, mottled brown-and-green variation on the insectoid creatures. It was the hive's queen.

The colossal matriarch was fixed to the ceiling by a network of gooey, viscous tendrils that snaked outward and into every single tunnel above, and to the floor by a similar array descending into those caves below. Beneath her bulbous metasoma sprawled a nest of glowing greenish eggs numbering in the hundreds.

Jean, Billy, and Gail were attached to this horrific accumulation with the same alien goo binding him to the drone's back. Hank struggled, kicked, and shouted at the top of his lungs. "Get the hell away from my family, you abomination! Leave them alone!"

A wave of tittering chuckles washed over the chamber. Hank suddenly realized that he was not surrounded by the giant insects alone. As he strained to look around in the dim glow of the constables' lights, he recognized dozens of faces: the faces of the other colonists of Elysium 4. Covered in dirt and slime, these people seemed more akin to the scuttling monsters than to any human being he had ever known.

"You should be honored, spaceman." Sato Tanaka stepped in front of the titanic queen. Hank realized that it was his neighbor's voice, but the behemoth's words. Somehow these things had infected the colonists with their telepathic hive mind. "You and your family have been chosen to guide the hive into the next generation. And beyond."

Hank wrestled against the slimy ropes lashing him to the back of the drone. If he could just get his hand into his pocket.... "What does that mean? What are you talking about?"

"We—the hive—have existed for many millennia, as you Earthmen reckon time. We came here from the stars so long ago that we no longer remember our home world, or even how we achieved the travel. All we have is a memory of a dying world.... But now that you have come, with your knowledge of space travel and robotic production, we shall soon return to the heavens in search of a new home....

"With the taking of your knowledge and essence, I will pass it on to the hive's next

generation. Your mate will carry the larva of my successor, and your offspring shall serve us for the rest of their lives, just as these, your fellow Earthmen will. When next the hive wakes from its torpor, we shall be ready to build ships and launch them into the night sky. We will travel to new worlds and the hive will grow for untold generations to come."

Hank understood that there was much more at stake than the survival of his family. If these things learned how to build ships and pilot them, they would pose a very real threat to the entire galaxy and every sentient being that called it home.

The queen's grotesquely long forelimbs emerged from the slime cocooning her torso, extending down toward Jean and the children.

Hank's fingers reached the flap of his pocket. Clearing his throat, he shouted with all his might: *"9N-Gen, Protocol Wormwood!"*

Finding what he needed, Hank heard the robot's servos come back online. When he had built 9N-Gen, he had installed a Faraday shield on a small backup drive in the robotic brain. It responded to just the one voice command, which turned 9N-Gen into a simple-minded battle-bot that would fight and kill until it was rendered inoperative. At which time it would initiate a self-destruct sequence terminating in a low-yield thermonuclear detonation.

Hank had hoped for the best in his new life on Elysium 4, but, being an expert in survival as well as a veteran of the worst fighting in humanity's long and bellicose history, he had prepared for the worst.

As the drone to which he was attached turned to face this sudden threat, Hank grasped the vibro-blade in his pocket. With a flick of the wrist, he slashed the cords holding him in place and rolled from the creature's back just before it exploded in a flash of plasma.

Keeping low and running in a zig-zag pattern, Hank rushed into the chaos of the swarming insectoids and brainwashed colonists. Slashing his way through the throng with the glowing blade, Hank faced more danger from the robot's erratic fusillade than from the pincers and mandibles of the alien enemy. The hive focused on destroying the apparent greater threat to the queen, the berserk 9N-Gen.

Hank reached the egg clutch at the base of the stationary queen. A red plasma bolt arced over his head, exploding in the monster's armored abdomen in a shower of sparks and slime. The giant creature shook and hissed as Hank slashed at the gooey bonds holding his stunned family. "Jean! Wake up, honey! We've got to go!"

Jean blinked, recognition slowly filling her dark eyes. "Hank...? Where are we? What's happening?" The recognition was replaced with a look of sudden horror.

"I'll explain later. Just help me with the kids!"

"Hank!"

He turned at Jean's warning. Tanaka, covered in blood and ichor, held one of the alien spears in his hands, a look of inhuman hatred on his face. "I can still take your essence if you're dead, Earthman!"

Hank hurled the vibro-blade. It spun through the air and buried itself in the brainwashed colonist's forehead. As Tanaka fell to the cavern floor, Jean snatched up his dropped weapon.

Grabbing his children in his arms, Hank followed Jean as she clubbed a path through the maze of battle. He spared a glance at the fracas's epicenter and saw 9N-Gen, missing all but one arm, going down in a swarm of insectoids and hive-minded colonists.

"Hurry! We don't have much time!"

Jean picked an upper tunnel at random, and they ran for their lives. Hank heard the battle come to an abrupt end. He heard the hive set off in click-clacking, frenzied pursuit. He heard the swarm getting closer. He began counting down from one hundred, wondering what would kill his family first: giant insects or atomic fire.

"Give me the weapon, Jean. You take the kids and go. I'll try to buy you some time."

"No." Jean kept going. "We survive together or not at all."

Hank couldn't believe what he was hearing. "What?"

"Trust me. Just keep running!"

Hank did.

Somehow, they emerged from the tunnel into a mine shaft mere paces from the shielded elevator car. Even more surprisingly, Hank no longer heard the sounds of pursuit.

His mental countdown under ten, Hank hurried his family into the elevator and activated its ascent. A few seconds later they felt the tremendous shockwave and heard the muffled blast. Fortunately, the elevator's superstructure held and the O'Brians made it safely to the surface of Elysium 4. The secondary sun dawned bright and crimson over the orange desert.

"We made it." Hank crouched beside Jean and the kids, an exhausted smile on his face. "I don't know how, but we made it. I guess the four of us still have the luck of the Irish after all."

Jean smiled at him. "Five. The five of us."

Hank blinked, his heart filled with unexpected and sudden elation.

Gail smiled up at him, a strange sparkle in her big blue eyes. "We're gonna have a baby sister, Daddy!"

Billy hugged his mother tight, looking wisely at Hank. "And it's up to you, Dad, to make sure we all get back to Earth. You need to build more robots that can build us a ship."

Hank's elation dropped into a deep, dark pit in his belly as he stared at his family with a creeping doubt and dread. How did Jean know exactly which tunnel would lead them to the shielded mineshaft...?

"Elysium 4" debuts in this issue of Black Infinity *with an illustration by Allen Koszowski.*

Jason McCuiston has been a semi-finalist in the Writers of the Future contest and has studied under the tutelage of best-selling author Philip Athans. Jason's stories of fantasy, horror, science fiction, and crime have appeared in numerous anthologies, periodicals, websites, and podcasts. His first novel, Project Notebook, *is forthcoming. Connect with him on the internet at: https://www.facebook.com/ShadowCrusade. Jason occasionally tweets about his dogs, his stories, his likes, and his gripes @JasonJMcCuiston. You can find most of his publications on his Amazon page at: https://www.amazon.com/-/e/B07RN8HT98*

Matt Cowan's **Threat Watch**

YOU MAY NOW ACCESS THE FILES. THESE FILES CONTAIN DATA MODULES COMPILED FROM EVIDENCE PRESENTED IN MOVIES AND TELEVISION. EACH MODULE FOCUSES ON A SPECIFIC THREAT: DEADLY PLANETS, HOSTILE ALIENS, SCIENTIFIC ABOMINATIONS, MURDEROUS COMPUTERS AND ...

ACCESSING ... ACCESSING.... OPENING MODULE 6:

INSIDIOUS INSECTS

SPIDERS, FLIES, BEETLES AND SUCH SQUIRMY THINGS, WHAT IS IT ABOUT THEM THAT REPULSES US SO MUCH? THEY SCUTTLE, THEY SWARM AND THEY BUZZ about in segmented bodies that boast too many legs as they regard the world with bulbous, multifaceted eyes. If their travels chance to bring them into contact with our own bare skin, we react immediately with disgust and repulsion. Some are unsanitary, their bodies rife with diseases. Others inject poisons to render their prey helpless as they feast upon their captive bodies. I think what inspires such disdain in us is their utterly alien appearance. We find it impossible to picture what existence must be like for something so markedly at odds with ourselves. Despite the hideousness viewing them causes us, we usually see them as nothing more than minor irritants because they are so minuscule and powerless against us; but what

if they weren't? What if the roles were reversed, granting them the superior might? How would we deal with such a threat? The movies below explore that very concept—flipping the script by granting insects, worms, spiders and the like the upper hand against us.

CATEGORY: FLIES AND WASPS

THE FLY
(20th Century Fox, 1958)

Species:
Hybrid Human/Fly Amalgamation
Abnormalities:
A human with the head and left arm of a fly
Cause of Abnormality:
Experimental Scientific Accident
Location: Montreal, Quebec, Canada

Deadliness Factor: 5 out of 10
(While disturbing to look at and rather unbalanced, the human-fly hybrid doesn't possess extraordinary powers or abilities.)

Deadliest Aspect:
Savagery as its mental condition deteriorates

Necessities for Survival: He can be killed the same way as any normal man, so conventional weaponry should do the trick.

Favorite Scene: The scene at the film's end involving the discovery of the tiny, white-headed fly by François and Inspector Charas is truly unforgettable.

Synopsis: After scientist André Delambre's *(David "Al" Hedison)* body is discovered with both his head and arm crushed in a hydraulic press, his wife Hélène *(Patricia Owens)* calls his brother Francois Delambre *(played by the legendary Vincent Price)* and confesses to killing him but won't say why. François brings in an acquaintance of his, Police Inspector Charas *(Herbert Marshall)*, to help get to the bottom of what happened. When Hélène is pressed about the bizarre circumstances of her husband's death as well as her preoccupation with flies, specifically a white-headed one, she relates the whole bizarre tale of what exactly happened.

André had been working on building a teleportation device capable of disintegrating anything inside it long enough to send its atoms to another location where it would then be reintegrated, unharmed, back together again within a receiver. His obsession with perfecting this teleportation technology causes him to take dangerous risks which ultimately includes using himself as a subject. When he fails to notice the tiny fly that entered the chamber with him while testing the device on himself, he is transformed into a hideous creature.

My Take: Every time I watch a film starring Vincent Price I'm reminded why he was such an icon of the horror genre. He was a tremendous actor whose charisma always granted such believability to each of his films no matter how bizarre its premise might be. Patricia Owens is also excellent carrying a large portion of the film's narrative on her shoulders portraying Hélène. The atmosphere early on with Hélène's obsession with the white-headed fly and the peculiar nature of her husband's death is well done, creating an enticing mystery. The disembodied meows of the Delambre's pet cat Dandelo following André's ill-fated experiment adds a further unsettling aspect to the overall eerie mood of the film. I think this movie holds up well despite its age. It's well-written and well-acted, with lots of spooky hints at the strange mystery that's unfolding in the Delambre's house. If this one manages to properly whet your appetite for Fly-Man-oriented creature features, you might want to give its 1986 remake starring Jeff Goldblum a try. It's far more gory but definitely holds an appeal all its own.

Rating: 8 out of 10

THE WASP WOMAN
(Allied Artist Pictures, 1959)

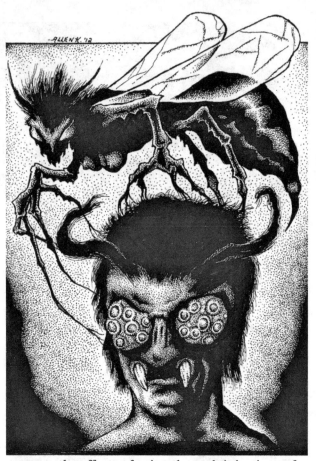

Species: Human/Wasp Hybrid
Abnormalities: Entire head and hands shift into human size-proportioned wasp features along with murderous impulses
Cause of Abnormality: Experimental, de-aging, wasp enzyme formula injections
Location: A city in the United States
Deadliness Factor: 6 out of 10
(While the Wasp Woman appears super-strong, this could be a result of her hyper-aggressive state. She is still capable of being killed by conventional means, however.)
Deadliest Aspect: Vicious aggressiveness
Necessities for Survival: Anything that can kill a normal human can kill her as well.
Favorite Scene: When the wasp-transformed Janice Starlin attacks the nurse in Dr. Zinthrop's hospital room

Synopsis: With her once prominent cosmetics company on the decline, its founder and namesake Janice Starlin *(Susan Cabot)* employs the services of Dr. Eric Zinthrop *(Michael Mark)* who claims to have created a serum which can reverse the effects of aging through injections of enzyme from the royal jelly of a queen wasp. She insists on being the first human subject for the process. When she becomes impatient with the slow occurrence of its results, Starlin begins to sneak into Zinthrop's lab to give herself additional doses. Although she does begin to grow swiftly younger and more beautiful, Dr. Zinthrop begins to notice his animal subjects becoming extremely violent. He goes to warn Starlin of this unexpected side effect but is badly injured in an accident before he can. Starlin soon finds herself transforming werewolf-style into a hideous human/wasp creature that attacks anyone she encounters, usually killing them.

My Take: This is an interesting black-and-white film with decently unsettling creature effects for its time. Directed by legendary camp-master Roger Corman, it's light on plot but remains an entertaining monster film nonetheless. Susan

Cabot carries her leading role well. Sadly, her life ended in a bizarre tragedy and her filmography is limited. I feel she could have gone on to excel in better roles if things had turned out differently. The film does make some effort at character development for Bill Lane *(Fred Eisley)*, Mary Dennison *(Barboura Morris)* and Arthur Cooper *(William Roerick)*, but it's limited at best. For a light horror watch, you could do worse than *The Wasp Woman*.   **Rating: 5 out of 10**

CATEGORY: ANTS

THEM! (Warner Bros. Pictures, 1954)

Species: Atomic Radiated Giant Ants
Abnormalities: Enormous enlargement
Cause of Abnormality: Mutation due to radiation exposure resulting from the first atomic bomb tests
Location: A dessert in New Mexico
Deadliness Factor: 7 out of 10
(If you know what to do and act quickly enough, they can be defeated.)
Deadliest Aspect: Their huge size which grants incredible strength and endurance
Necessities for Survival: The right plan and enough military firepower to pull off a coordinated assault on their nest
Favorite Scene: Honestly, I found Dr. Harold Medford's speech about the threat these huge ants pose to be the scariest scene. It doesn't have the impressive visual effects displayed

later on, but his description of what they are facing is quite chilling indeed.

Synopsis: Sgt. Ben Peterson *(James Whitmore)* and Trooper Ed Blackburn *(Chris Drake)* of the New Mexico State Police find a young girl wandering through the dessert who's apparently suffering from shock. Their subsequent investigation leads them to some startling discoveries, including the demolished trailer where the girl and her family had been staying, giant inhuman prints left in the sand, and a murder victim whose body is filled with large quantities of formic acid. FBI Special Agent Robert Graham *(James Arness)*, Department of Agriculture myrmecologist Dr. Harold Medford *(Edmund Gwenn)* and his daughter Dr. Pat Medford *(Joan Weldon)* are brought in to investigate these strange incidents. They soon encounter a nest of enormous ants, mutated into 8-foot tall killing machines after having been exposed to radiation from the first atomic bomb tests that took place there. While these gigantic creatures can be taken down with enough firepower, their

massive strength *(able to lift 20 times their own weight)* and aggressiveness is projected to eliminate man as the dominate Earth species within about a year's time. If a solution for this threat isn't found before the ants begin reproducing, the planet will be overwhelmed by them.

My Take: *"Ants are the only creatures on Earth, other than man who make war. They campaign, they are chronic aggressors and they make slave laborers of the captives they don't kill. None of the ants previously seen by man are more than an inch in length, most considerably under that size, but even the most minute of them have an instinct and talent for industry, social organization and savagery that make man look feeble by comparison."* These are the words Dr. Harold Medford uses to describe the threat they are up against, and given that these ants are exorbitantly larger and stronger than regular ants the situation looks dire indeed. By today's standards, the giant ant effects aren't particularly scary, but this was a very influential film in regards to the creation of future creature features and even garnered an Oscar nomination for special effects at the time.

Rating: 6 out of 10

From left: James Arness, Joan Weldon, James Whitmore, and Edmund Gwenn

THE NAKED JUNGLE
(Paramount Pictures, 1954)

Species: A huge swarm of ants referred to as a *marabunta*

Abnormalities: Their overwhelming numbers

Cause of Abnormality: Unknown, but something that occurs from time to time in that region

Location: South America, 1901

Deadliness Factor: 8 out of 10
(Their incredible number and destructive capability make them a terrifying force to combat.)

Deadliest Aspect: Their massive numbers as they devour everything in their path

Necessities for Survival: The ability to present a widely sweeping destructive force against the ants' vast numbers

Favorite Scene: The ant swarm devouring the heavyset native as they assail the plantation—His gray hand reaching for the wall with ants crawling over it displays the chilling fate our heroes are attempting to avoid.

Synopsis: Joanna *(Eleanor Parker)* travels from New Orleans to South America to meet her husband, Christopher Leiningen *(a young Charlton Heston)*, the owner of a

From left:
Charlton Heston,
Eleanor Parker,
& William Conrad

large cocoa plantation, for the first time. The marriage was arranged by Leiningen's brother with the ceremony taking place before she even arrived, the area's Commissioner *(William Conrad)* having stood in as his proxy. She's excited to meet her new husband but finds him stand-offish at first, as he's suspicious as to why a woman as beautiful and cultured as she is would agree to such an odd marriage arrangement. She soon reveals that she had been previously married but that her husband had died. Leiningen is angered by this fact, causing further strife between them. It's certainly not love at first sight, as Leiningen is surly and abusive.

Despite Leiningen's gruff exterior, he's popular with his native workers since he doesn't beat them the way his nefarious counterpart Gruber *(John Dierkes)* does his men.

When Leiningen decides to send Joanna back to America, he and the Commissioner embark to transport her, but they encounter an enormous hoard of ants numbering in the billions destroying everything in their path in route to his place. Joanna insists on staying with Leiningen who has decided to remain and defend his plantation against the seemingly unbeatable ant swarm.

My Take: Based on the classic 1938 short story *"Leiningen Versus the Ants"* by Carl Stephenson, the movie version does an excellent job letting us get to know the primary characters. The tension is thick from the start as it centers around the strained relationship between the lovely and kind Joanna who arrives as an outsider and endears herself to the locals quickly, but struggles to win over her generally hostile, new husband, Leiningen. He is a complex character in his own right, both stern, driven and prideful, but kind to his workers, as well. He's a damaged man who's been hardened by life but is ultimately good at his core. The ant swarm juggernaut doesn't even arrive until the final third of the film, but the character development is so well executed it retained my interest throughout. There are great performances put in by all the leads: Heston, Parker, Conrad and Abraham Sofaer as Leiningen's top man Incacha.

Rating: 8 out of 10

PHASE IV (Paramount Pictures, 1974)

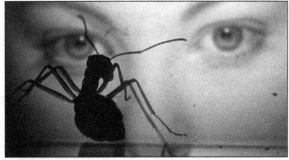

Species: Enhanced Intelligent *Formicidae*
Abnormalities: Cosmically endowed super-intelligence and cross-species hive mind abilities
Cause of Abnormality: An unidentified cosmic event
Location: An Arizona desert
Deadliness Factor: 5 out of 10
(While very intelligent, they're still ants which can be killed the same way as any other ant.)

inhabitants of the area. The two manage to rescue a young woman they find named Kendra Eldridge *(a young Lynne Frederick before her life went down a turbulent road)*. She assists them in combating the ants. The ants work together to isolate them as they sacrifice themselves to destroy communication equipment, air conditioning units and other electronic devices. These

Deadliest Aspect: Their high intelligence, devotion to their cause and large numbers

Necessities for Survival: Any large-area-effect weaponry should help clear a path to safety.

Favorite Scene: Early on, the scientists force open the hand of a corpse they find in the desert to reveal a stream of ants crawling out of three large gaping holes in it.

Synopsis: An anomalous cosmic event causes the Earth's ants to experience a hyper-evolutionary state. As a result, they begin to expand their hive mind abilities to communicate with other species and to build huge towers in the desert. A scientific base is set up in Arizona to examine these mutated ants. A couple of scientists Dr. Ernest D. Hubbs *(Nigel Davenport)* and James R. Lesko *(Michael Murphy)* are tasked with finding a solution to the growing ant menace which has begun attacking the few remaining

ants prove to be terrible adversaries, tormenting the scientists who must find a way to stop them or die trying.

My Take: An intriguing film, if not all that scary. I like the idea of a cosmic event altering the minds of the ants. It could almost be viewed in a Lovecraftian light. What is it that has brought about this altering of the ant's minds and for what purpose? In the end, the film doesn't quite reach that level for me, however. I did like the actors, the main three carry the vast bulk of the film, particularly Nigel Davenport who plays the intense, succeed-at-all-costs scientist brilliantly. Michael Murphy is effective as the down-to-Earth, empathetic protagonist. All in all, *Phase IV* isn't a bad film, but doesn't excel either.

Rating: 6 out of 10

SQUIRM
(American International Pictures, 1976)

Species: Invertebrate Phyla *(Worms)*
Abnormalities: Their ravenous hunger and flesh-eating ability
Cause of Abnormality: Power lines downed during a heavy storm
Location: Fly Creek, a rural sea coast area of Georgia
Deadliness Factor: 3 out of 10 *(It's relatively easy to evade these slow-moving creatures.)*
Deadliest Aspect: If they get on you in mass, they can devour you.
Necessities for Survival: Just keep your vigil up for them and be prepared to start stomping.
Favorite Scene: Mick's encounters with the massive worm invasion of Geri's house near the film's end

Synopsis: Taking place in 1975, heavy storms drop power lines into the muddy soil of the small Georgia town of Fly Creek, sending over 3,000 volts of electricity into the saturated ground. The town loses power as a result but far worse is how the supercharged soil affects the local worms, mutating and enraging them. It all unfolds through the eyes of beautiful young local Geri Sanders *(Patricia Pearcy)* who welcomes her boyfriend Mick *(Don Scardino)* into town from New York for a vacation. They realize something is wrong once they start uncovering skeletons *(not metaphorical skeletons but actual skeletons and quite a few of them)*. Geri witnesses an aggressive attack by bait worms on both Mick and Roger *(R. A. Dow in his only notable role as a local handyman whose father owns the worm farm and who has an obsessive infatuation with Geri)*. It eventually becomes apparent that these electrified worms have become ravenously aggressive creatures that devour anyone with whom they come into contact, which explains why they keep discovering so many skeletons. With the local blowhard sheriff *(Peter MacLean)* against them as well, Geri and Mick struggle to find a way to stop this bizarre act of frenzied violent nature.

My Take: This film has its work cut out for it in trying to portray worms as anything fear-worthy. They are slow moving and have no personality to inspire any chills. The special effects are weak and the acting barely serviceable. Add to that a lackluster plot and there isn't much left to praise here. There is some effort put forth in the character development department in the love triangle between Gerri, Mick and Roger, but not much outside of that. This one is kind of a snoozer.
Rating: 3 out of 10

THE INCREDIBLE SHRINKING MAN
(Universal Pictures, 1957)

Species: An arachnid

Abnormalities: A man's shrunken size versus a spider's normal size

Cause of Abnormality: A mysterious sea fog

Location: Inside his house

Deadliness Factor: 5 out of 10
(Size and strength are an issue)

Deadliest Aspect: The spider's superior power to his

Necessities for Survival: Intellect and weaponry

Favorite Scene: Scott's conflict with the spider in his diminutive state

Synopsis: While vacationing at sea, the boat carrying Scott Carey *(Grant Williams)* and his wife Louise *(Randy Stuart)* becomes enveloped by a mysterious fog that arises out of nowhere then vanishes just as quickly. It leaves Scott coated by strange, glittering dust-like particles all over his body. As his wife was inside when it happened, she was unaffected by it. Six months later he begins to notice his clothes becoming too large for him. After a series of tests, it's proven that he's been shrinking as a result of what happened on the boat, combined with an encounter he had with a large dose of insecticide previously. Unable to work as he continues to shrink, he's forced to sell the story of his precipitously diminishing size to the press in order to pay the bills. As doctors search for a cure, Scott recluses himself from the world, spending all his time in his house with his wife.

(to him), hairy spider, which he attempts to avoid but which keeps reappearing to torment him.

My Take: This film was produced from the first screenplay written by the great Richard Matheson and would by no means be the end of his scripting career. In fact, Matheson swiftly became a top-notch writer in his day, penning numerous television scripts, including a

After the shrinking is temporarily halted at 36.5 inches tall, Scott meets a female Little Person, who works in a circus sideshow, named Clarice *(April Kent)*. She helps him come to terms with his height by pointing out that he's still taller than her, but soon afterwards he notices that is no longer the case and that he's begun shrinking again. Eventually, he finds himself living in a doll house inside his home.

number of excellent episodes of *The Twilight Zone,* as well as films such as the superb adaptation of his novel, *The Legend of Hell House.* He was truly a master storyteller. Back to this film, I love how the spider is shown early on crawling away, then remains gone long enough you start to forget about it until it returns in all its terrifying glory when

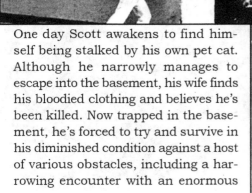

One day Scott awakens to find himself being stalked by his own pet cat. Although he narrowly manages to escape into the basement, his wife finds his bloodied clothing and believes he's been killed. Now trapped in the basement, he's forced to try and survive in his diminished condition against a host of various obstacles, including a harrowing encounter with an enormous

Species: A giant arachnid
Abnormalities: It's huge size
Cause of Abnormality: Unknown
Location: A small U.S. town
Deadliness Factor: 6 out of 10
(Their huge proportions are an issue, but they can be dealt with given enough proper supplies.)
Deadliest Aspect: Their size, strength and predilection for sucking the blood of their victims
Necessities for Survival: A large quantity of DDT, explosives and firearms
Favorite Scene: The discovery of Carol's father's body in the caves—its look is exceptionally bizarre and unsettling.

Synopsis: When Carol Flynn's *(June Kenney)* father doesn't come home one night, she convinces her boyfriend Mike Simpson *(Eugene Persson)* to take her out looking for him. They find his wrecked truck along with a bracelet he had purchased for Carol's birthday at the site, but his body is missing. They head out on foot to try and see if they can find him in the vicinity, which brings them to a vast cave network. While exploring inside it, they discover some human skeletal remains and fall into an enormous spider web where they narrowly avoid the giant creature that created it. They go

Scott begins his search for food. It's a stark reminder of how he no longer sits unchallenged atop the food chain and is the scene which lands this movie on our list at hand. The challenges Scott is forced to deal with at such a small size are well-realized here and you find yourself rooting for him to get back to his normal size and way of life. This is really a survival film as Scott fights to battle his way back to his wife against incredible odds. Matheson knew how to write characters and scenes which would draw you in and make you invested in them. This film is no exception. There's a reason he was such a successful writer of literature, television and films, and that's on display here.

Rating: 8 out of 10

EARTH VS. THE SPIDER
(American International, 1958)

into town and alert the authorities but aren't taken seriously.

Once the police and a posse of locals encounter and mange to kill one, all doubt of their existence is removed. Unfortunately, they discover that there's more than just one of them, and everyone is forced to deal with them once they begin crawling into town.

My Take: I found it difficult to understand why the noise emitted by the giant spider sounds like a horde of screeching harpies every time it appears. While it is definitely horrific sounding, it doesn't seem like a proper fit for the creature that's supposed to be bellowing it. The film is very basic overall. The special effects are dated, but at least most of the acting is well performed and there is some effort put forth involving the development of the characters who are forced to deal with these behemoth spiders. The cavern set pieces had a decent look to them which lent some interesting visuals. The plot here is paper thin, and there's not much in *Earth vs. the Spider* which hasn't been better done in other films. **Rating: 5 out of 10**

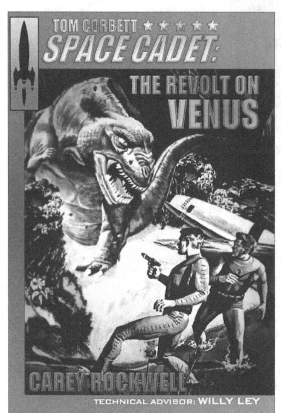

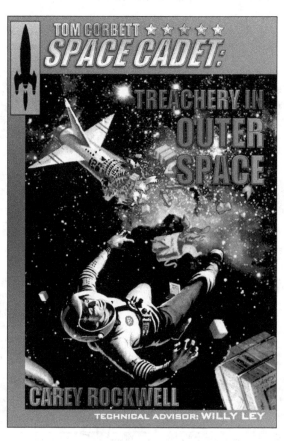

THE COLLECTIVE OF BLAQUE REACH

By Matt Cowan

IT WAS THE DREAM IN HIS UNCLE'S CABIN THAT LED KENNETH WHITHLOWE TO THE BOOK. HE HAD GONE THERE TO SPEND A WEEK ALONE. HIDDEN DEEP IN A secluded section of the massive Talbot Forest, it would be all but impossible for anyone to find him. Uncle Vincent was gone, reported missing over a year ago after failing to show up for work. There was no call, no note; he never even picked up his last week's paycheck. He just vanished. Eventually, he was given up for dead. Uncle Vincent had been on Ken's mind quite a bit lately. Memories of the good times of his youth spent at the cabin with his uncle, replaying in his mind. Uncle Vincent taking him on long walks through forest trails that surrounded the cabin to "commune with nature," as he liked to say. Often they would go to swim or fish in Willow Breen Pond on hot summer days. The constant reminders of those days went on for about a month before Ken finally decided to take a week's vacation and travel there. He hoped a stay at the cabin would get him back to feeling like he wasn't just sleep walking through his life. A few years ago Uncle Vincent had given Ken his own set of keys.

"You and I are the only two who have any interest in the place," he had told Ken on that day. "We are the only ones who can see the magic contained there, deep in the heart of the Talbot Forest."

The drive took several hours, with the last spent negotiating a narrow, heavily wooded, dirt road through the forest. Rich smells of oak and pine trees seeped in through the car vents. A sea of green tree limbs swayed in welcome as he drove along their borders. A narrow, rutted trail led to a small clearing where the cabin stood. Its walls were dull, gray and weather-beaten, showing its age and neglect. A set of murky windows, stained dark by tree sap, peered out from either side of its single rotting door. Ken pulled his car to the rear of the cabin and got out, stretching his stiff legs. The ground was layered with thousands of pine needles, fallen from trees that always seemed impossibly tall to him. Stacked up behind the cabin were several pieces of chopped firewood. They were blackened and covered in a thick layer of spider webs. A lone, rusting ax jutted up from a large chopping stump. The clearing did not reach far before being absorbed by the swell of trees beyond.

Inside the cabin, sunlight was barely able to penetrate the sap-blackened windows. Two rooms made up the entire cabin. The largest room held a fireplace, a moth-eaten couch, several wooden chairs, and a dusty oaken table, stacked high with an assortment of fishing and hunting gear. Ken smiled when he noticed his uncle's old hunting knife amidst the gear—it had been one of his uncle's most prized possessions. The side room contained a bed, a dresser and a narrow closet. A cluster of old clothes lay piled in one corner.

Ken spent the rest of the day straightening things up enough to get settled. There was no electricity, so he sorted through the woodpile until he found some good pieces for burning. That night he put new sheets on the bed before lying down to read. He enjoyed the sounds of the forest that wafted in from the window he had forced open, the hooting of owls, fluttering of wings, chirping of crickets, and most of all, the wind through the trees. He read for an hour before falling sleep.

THE NEXT MORNING, Ken awoke groggy. He had dreamt about his uncle. Most of the dream was hazy, but he remembered they had been walking through the forest. He tried to recall what they had spoken about, but it eluded him. The image of his uncle's face, full of concern, remained clear in his mind. Perhaps, wherever he was, his uncle knew what a mess Ken's life had become. His recent divorce from Tina, and the subsequent uneasiness he felt from their mutual friends, left him feeling like he had been excommunicated. He was not interested in talking about his feelings either, as some of his co-workers had suggested. Now only his daughter, Alice, cared for him, and Tina had custody of her most of the time. After a quick breakfast, he dressed and went outside. The sun shone bright through breaks in the trees. He had told his coworkers that the primary reason he wanted to stay at the cabin was to explore the forest, but really it was the seclusion.

Ken was going to take one of his uncle's favorite paths when he stumbled upon the vague remnants of a trail he did not recognize. The trail was overgrown with weeds and underbrush but had to have been made by something heading to, or from, his uncle's cabin. He decided to follow it. After hiking forty-five minutes Ken spotted a clearing a few feet off the trail.

"Looks like a good spot for a break," he said to himself, leaving the path and moving toward it. At the center of the clearing stood the large misshapen husk of a tree. It was thick, but stood just six feet tall, blackened and dead. It looked to have some sort of infestation. Protruding out of its center was a large split that looked vaguely organic. It was white, like dead flesh, a stark contrast with the blackness of the rest of the tree. He guessed it to be a fungus seeping up from a deep internal cavity. At first, the tree gave him the impression of something unnatural and obscene, but it riveted his attention so much the feeling soon faded. A band of thin, but taller trees formed a surrounding outer circle, as though they were attendants of the infected tree.

"You're a creepy-looking fellow, aren't you?" Ken said, running his fingers along the tree's wooden hide. While hiking, he had been unable to shake the loneliness that hung over him, but since moving into the clearing, an intense feeling of peacefulness washed it all away. For the first time in months, he did not feel alone. Thoughts of Tina, and his estranged friends were forgotten. He felt that perhaps he could be a part of something great, do important things. Maybe he *did* matter. He sat in the clearing for a long time before reluctantly deciding to head back.

It was late by the time Ken returned to the cabin. He read for a while before going to sleep. That was when he had the dream. In it he found himself leaving the cabin and traveling down the Tree-path. A twilight sun drifted from the sky. Wind, funneling through the trees, blew into his face like the breath of something vast. The further he went the more a damp smell of rain began to thicken on the cool breeze that swept over him. The sun completed its descent, plunging the forest into darkness. He moved along the path to the clearing at an inhumanly fast rate. He halted a few feet from the gnarled center tree in silence, observing it for a time. Then it began to pulse. The white fungus cavity became lined with purple veins. Ken got the vague impression that The Tree's huge gaping crevice was shifting together, as though it were an enormous mouth chewing on something. Feelings of peace and acceptance flowed from The Tree into Ken. A spasm rippled through the trunk, followed by a gurgling sound from somewhere within. Then the mouth opened, spewing forth a thick cloud of black insects. They fell to the ground, a mass of swarming bugs Ken could not identify. The throng surged toward the trail and disappeared. They stayed together the whole time, acting as though they were formed of a single entity. When Ken returned his attention to The Tree he noticed that the insects had dislodged something from inside it. At its base sat an oversized book, whose cover was made of wood. Ken reached down and picked it up. A set of words had been etched into it: *BLAQUE REACH.*

KEN AWOKE, the dream fresh in his mind. He got up, dressed, fixed breakfast, and thought about what he should do that day. He was not sure he wanted to return to the forest just yet. The dream had disturbed him, and he was becoming concerned with his own mental health. He was just finishing breakfast when he noticed some writing on a discarded envelope on the table. He picked it up. It read, "VILE WITHEN." Several other letters were scrawled, unconnected around the edges of the envelope. The letters were thick and upraised but looked to be his uncle's handwriting. He was trying to figure out what it meant when his cell phone rang. It startled him at first, as his phone service had been sporadic at best. He found his coat and dug through the pockets to retrieve it. The battery was down to one bar. He would need to charge it soon.

The name TINA GUILFORD was displayed as the incoming call. He had suspected her of cheating on him for several months before they separated. A week after the divorce became final she announced her engagement to a man named Barry.

"What?" He said flatly as he answered the phone.

"Daddy?" Came the tiny voice of his daughter on the other end of the line.

"Oh, hey darling, how are you?" he said, softening his tone.

"I'm good. Where are you at?"

"I'm just out at my Uncle Vincent's cabin. What are you up to?"

"Just playing with my new dolls Barry got me."

"That's nice," Ken said trying not to grit his teeth. "Hey, I have an idea. How would you like it if I brought you here to stay at the cabin with me this weekend? I think you'd like it. It's in a big forest with lots of trees and flowers and cute little animals. It's just like from the fairy tales I used to read you before bedtime. Would you like that?"

There was an awkward pause on the other end of the line. He heard someone talking to her in the background, most likely Tina. She returned a few moments later. "Well... I was wondering if it would be okay if I went with Mommy and Barry to Wonder World this weekend? Then I can go to the cabin with you next time." She said attempting to be diplomatic.

A torrent of rage tore through Ken. It was just like Tina and Barry to try and screw him out of his weekend with his daughter. He only got her every other weekend as it was. He knew it was their goal to cause her to not want to spend time with him, and they were doing a damn good job of it.

"I don't know about that, Alice. I haven't gotten to see you in over two weeks. Don't you want to spend some time with your old dad?" He said, hoping to shame her into coming to stay with him, then feeling guilty for the tactic.

"I do, but I also really want to go to Wonder World. I've never been there, and they have a ride named after me. It's called Alice in Wonder World, like from that story with the rabbit and the smiling cat!" The pleading was obvious, and Ken knew he had lost the battle before she even called.

"We'll see, Darling. Let me speak to your mother, please."

"Okay, Daddy, but I really, really want to go," Alice added before passing the phone off.

KEN SAT IN THE SILENT CABIN for over an hour, fuming. The conversation with Tina had erupted into a full-blown argument he had ultimately lost. If he refused to let Alice go with them to Wonder World, then she would be unhappy the whole time she was with him. If he let her go, then he had willingly given up his weekend with her, but at least she would be happy. He ended up deciding he did not want to stoop to their level by punishing Alice with his own selfishness. He was beginning to feel resigned to the fact they were going to eventually edge him out of her life altogether. He felt defeated and alone in the world. He slammed his fist on the table hard enough to knock off the envelope he had been examining before the call. When he retrieved it, the letters were gone. It was blank.

"I must be seriously losing it," he muttered, wadding the envelope into a ball, which he cast across the room.

PEACE PUSHED AWAY the turmoil that plagued Ken after the phone call as soon as he arrived at the clearing. He sat before The Tree, his pain and loneliness seemingly whisked away by the gentle breeze that flowed through the clearing. He was there for a while, kneeling down facing The Tree before he spoke.

"I wish I could stay here forever," he said to The Tree, but he knew that it was impossible. Soon he would have to leave the cabin, and the forest, and return to the relentless torments of the world. The peace Ken had enjoyed fled him. He slumped with his back against The Tree and began to sob.

A sharp pain pierced his hand. He snatched it up from the ground to examine what had caused it. A small chunk of flesh had been bitten out of his palm. He looked down where his hand had been to witness a strange looking ant-like thing skittering away, climbing up the base of The Tree. He tried to grab it, but it moved too quickly. He was unsure what it was. It certainly was not like any insect he had seen before. It was the correct size for one, but it was distorted, with a pair of unusual humps making up most of its body. Its movement reminded Ken of a fast-moving inchworm. Whatever it was, it disappeared into the crevice of The Tree before he could examine it closer.

With the distraction of the insect gone, Ken returned his attention to the bleeding hole in his hand. It stung and bled more than he thought it should. The bite must have been deep. Figuring he should return to the cabin to tend the wound, Ken started to exit the clearing. Then he remembered his dream from the previous night. He moved back to stand before The Tree once more, staring at its garish split. The thought of reaching inside it caused his stomach to turn. There was no telling what, if anything, the breach housed, but he was certain it would be unpleasant to find out. Still, the dream had seemed so poignant he felt he must at least try. Pulling a handkerchief out of his back pocket, Ken wrapped it around his uninjured hand as best he could and then gently eased into the white fungus opening. It was warm and damp inside, like something alive. He pushed his arm through layers of pulpy murk that he assumed must be mold. In his mind he imagined glistening snakes slithering about within, preparing to sink their fangs deep into his hand at any moment. It was almost enough to halt his attempt, but he closed his eyes and strove on. He stretched down as far as he could go. By the time he was in up to his shoulder, he could feel something wedged inside the orifice. He wrapped his fingers around it. It was solid, but slimy. After struggling awhile to try and free it, he succeeded and managed to pull the object up. In his hand, he held a wooden book covered in putrid smelling, greasy, dark fluid. It looked exactly the same as the one from his dream. He ran his fingers over the letters engraved in its cover.

"Blaque Reach," he said aloud, a smile breaking wide across his face.

It was getting too dark for him to read in the forest, so Ken tucked the book tight to his chest and left the clearing.

Tonight he would have something new to read.

BY THE TIME he made it back to the cabin, and settled into bed, it was after midnight. He had spent hours in the forest clearing. Now that he was away from it, he wondered why he had done so, and started to think it might be best if he left the cabin sooner than he had planned. It seemed to be having an effect on him that he did not think was particularly positive. Once he started to read the book, all of those thoughts dissipated.

Upon opening its wooden cover, he found large, black, handwritten words on age-browned paper. Green mold stained several parts of its surface. Still, for having been stored inside a dead tree for presumably a long time, it was remarkably well preserved. It looked to be about eighty pages long. Although obviously weathered, none of the pages appeared brittle. Ken flipped to the first page and began to read.

Those who wish to join The Collective of Blaque Reach must willingly cast aside their individual bodies, minds and souls. They must forget all that the world has taught them, purge themselves of their desires and sorrows, and be consumed by the words of Blaque Reach. Once you are joined to the whole, you will cease to be driven by your own wishes or fears and will instead, add all that you are to the Collective in order to continue spelling out the text of the great tome. Your thoughts, knowledge, skills and abilities will be added to those of the Collective, as will your fears, weaknesses and pain. They will be distributed amongst the whole of Blaque Reach. You will no longer have to shoulder your burdens alone, but will instead have the unwavering support of The Collective of Blaque Reach. Once you are joined to the Collective, your name will be added to the great tome.

The words resonated with Ken. All he felt anymore was heartache and loneliness, with the divorce, his loss of friends, and the inevitable loss of his daughter's love. To be rid of all of that pain would be worth whatever price would be required of him.

"I want to join the Collective," Ken said aloud.

"Please, I want to join the Collective of Blaque Reach," he implored louder.

When nothing happened he returned his attention to the book. The print on the pages was in several different handwriting styles, but was otherwise the same as those from the envelope message he had found before. The letters stood higher than any ink he had seen. He ran his fingers across the page. It hummed, vibrating vaguely warm at his touch, as though it had a pulse. He threw the book from him in shock. It landed with a loud thud beyond the foot of his bed, out of sight. Ken lay there, trying to comprehend what was happening. He had left the bedroom window open to combat the room's stuffiness. Through it he noticed the night was still. None of the sounds he had grown accustomed to hearing from the forest emerged. The silence unnerved him, made him feel watched by something furtive and dark just beyond the wall of trees. He had not thought it possible he could fall asleep, but a sudden wave of extreme exhaustion soon overwhelmed him.

His dreams returned him to the clearing. The sky, tainted by dark shades of red and orange, swirled to form a nexus centered above the infected Tree. It pulsated, as thick, black ooze poured from its stretched crevasse. The surrounding trees swayed in the strong wind, casting leaves aloft with menacing ferocity. From somewhere, a chant arose.

"Blaque Reach, Blaque Reach, Blaque Reach," the bodiless voices intoned. The black jumbled mass continued to swarm from The Tree, crawling through the forest, seemingly without end. The chant grew louder, and thunder rumbled through the night.

KEN AWOKE IN A SWEAT. He glanced at his watch: 9:27 a.m. He had not planned on sleeping so late. The book on the floor caught his eye as soon as he got out of bed. He felt a little foolish about how he reacted to it the previous night. After all, it was just an old book. He lifted it from the floor and flipped through the pages. The thought struck him that the raised letters were probably done that way so blind people could read it. He touched the page, but this time it felt like any other piece of paper. He flipped through a few more until he noticed something skitter across its surface. Ken jumped back, dropping the book to the floor. One of the strange insects that had bit him by The Tree moved across the floor. It was joined by a few others, which escaped the book and ran out of the room. Grabbing a discarded boot, Ken chased after them. When he entered the main room he saw some of them slip through a crack beside the attic trap door in the ceiling. Ken pulled the short rope that dangled from it. A set of folded wooden stairs extended down, followed by cascading dust and the stench of stale air. Ken wiped off as much of the dust from his head and shirt as he could and then snatched an electric lantern from the table and began to ascend the creaking steps.

The attic was floored, he was happy to learn, although he did have to walk hunched over due to the low ceiling. Through a haze of dust particles and stray cobwebs illuminated by his lantern, were the silhouettes of several stacked boxes, chests, and an occasional piece of furniture. There was a narrow walkway down the center of the stored items. Ken searched with his lantern until he spied the line of weird bugs along the edge of a wall at the far end of the attic.

"Got you now, you little bastards," Ken said raising the boot to bring it down on them. To his surprise, they all squeezed through a slim opening along the base of the wall. He knelt down with his lantern and soon came to the conclusion that there was a small, nearly invisible door made out of thin wood there. Upon further examination, Ken found that someone had fashioned a room at the end of the attic. Feeling along the gap revealed a tiny niche he could get his finger behind, which he used to pull open the secret door.

The sight beyond froze Ken. Inside was a tiny chamber that contained a single skeleton, slumped in a corner. It was devoid of flesh. Ken recognized the clothing that hung loosely on its frame as belonging to his uncle. Questions swarmed through Ken's mind. How could his uncle be dead inside a secret room with the door closed? Did someone murder him? If so, was the killer still nearby? And where was his flesh? Sure, it would be badly decayed, but there should still be something. The skeleton looked as though it had been picked clean, leaving only the bones behind. Ken staggered backwards out of the room, trying to come to grips with his discovery. He left the attic in a daze, the insects forgotten. He felt dizzy as he went to sit on the edge of his bed. Absently, Ken found his cell phone again, deciding he should call the police. The screen was blank. He had forgotten to charge it.

"Damn," he muttered to himself.

He sat there awhile, running various possible scenarios over in his head, when the sight of the book sparked a thought. He rose from the bed, grabbed it and flipped to the back. The last twenty pages were long lists of names. Each of them printed in different handwriting styles. The last name to appear in the book was Vincent Whithlowe. It was written in his uncle's handwriting. He touched Vincent's name in the book. The warmth had returned, and once again the page pulsed, but Ken did not feel fear this time. He had felt such peace and harmony in the

forest before, and had such fond memories of his uncle, he thought perhaps everything had been an attempt by his uncle to try and communicate with him—despite being dead.

It wasn't until the words on the page began to move that Ken started to feel the first inklings of fear. The letters that made up his uncle's name began to shift and scuttle across the browned page. In a clear spot they rearranged themselves to form a new sentence. The letters *W, N, C, T,* and *H* fell away and the words read "ONE WITH EVIL." Other letters on the page began to scatter and move about. More letters fell away to read "LEVE NOW." Even missing a letter, Ken was able to perceive the warning, as well as its urgency, but it was too late. The letters from the other names on the page swarmed around his thumb, which touched the strange paper. Ken tried to pull it free, but it would not budge. The letters formed a tight circle around his thumb, and seemed to be grasping it somehow.

"What the hell?" Ken said, perspiration beginning to form on his forehead. He pulled harder, but the effect was the same. Sharp pain arced up from his thumb as the letter insects started to bite into him. Ken watched in horror as blood flowed from his hand onto the book, only to be absorbed into thin veins that now swelled across the throbbing page. More three-dimensional letters began to pour out from the sides of the book, all making their way from the other rippling pages of text. When a new wave reached the other letters, they climbed atop each other, crawling higher up Ken's hand, trying to envelope him.

Panic gripped Ken. He leapt to his feet, attempting to throw the book, but it would not separate from him. His hand was rapidly becoming encased in the black, writhing mass. Pain lanced from it as though it were stuck inside a blender. He screamed in agony. The letters kept coming. Running from the room, the book still attached to his pain-wracked hand, Ken thrust the book against the bedroom doorframe. A few of the letters fell to the ground with a stream of blood and thick chunks of purple meat, but he was held fast. He saw a letter *E* followed by a couple of *R*'s scamper toward his fallen flesh and begin to feast on it. He screamed again as he searched in desperation for something to help free himself of the book and its frenzied letters. Squishing and slurping sounds from his forearm were becoming louder. The letters continued to devour him, moving higher up his arm. Ken started to feel he would soon pass out. He had to try and save himself before he lost consciousness. Stumbling across the cabin, he threw himself toward the cluttered table knocking most of its contents to the floor as he sprawled across its surface. Before his momentum carried him there as well, Ken managed to grab his uncle's large hunting knife with his free hand. Without thinking he savagely swept the sharp knife blade down the writhing black mass where his arm should be. He screamed again as a huge chunk of partially devoured flesh fell to the floor with a damp splat along with several of the ravenous letter-things. Several more disengaged themselves from his arm to pursue the separated meat. Enough of them

deserted him that the book fell free.

Holding his wounded arm aloft, Ken stared in horror at what remained. His forearm was slick with blood, a large swath of sheared flesh carved from it. At its end were the skeletal remains of his hand, red-soaked with a few clumps of mangled tissue still dangling from it. He let out a whimper of despair. His vision grew fuzzy, and his mind began to recede into unconsciousness. Before it did, Ken saw the swarm of insect-like, black letters massing towards his prone body. From somewhere in the forest, he heard a rumbling chant.

"Blaque Reach, Blaque Reach, Blaque Reach," the inhuman voices called in unison. With his last thought, Ken realized a new voice was emerging to join the drone that formed the chant, his own.

"BLAQUE REACH, BLAQUE REACH, BLAQUE REACH"

👽 👽 👽

"The Collective of Blaque Reach" was originally published as a chapbook premium to accompany the hardcover anthology Bound for Evil: Curious Tales of Books Gone Bad *(Dead Letter Press, 2008).*

Matt Cowan's love for the horror genre stretches back beyond his earliest childhood memories. At a young age he stopped having nightmares once he began enjoying them too much. Since their departure he's been forced to craft nightmares of his own devising on the printed page. He's had short stories published in various horror, science fiction and crime anthologies over the years, including regular entries in the Deathlehem *series of Christmas-themed horror stories. A few of his stories have been featured on podcasts including* Pod of Horror *and* Tales To Terrify. *In addition to writing fiction, Matt also writes the movie review column Matt Cowan's Threat Watch for* Black Infinity Magazine *from Rocket Science Books. Being a voracious fan of short horror fiction, he also explores works from classic and modern horror authors over at his blog, Horror Delve (horrordelve.com).*

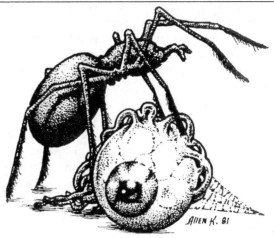

THE BEES FROM BORNEO
By Will H. Gray

S ILAS DONAGHY WAS BY FAR THE BEST BEEKEEPER AND QUEEN BREEDER IN THE UNITED STATES; NOT BECAUSE OF the amount of honey he produced, but because he had bred a strain of bees that produced records. Those two hundred hives consistently averaged three hundred pounds of honey each. Naturally enough, everyone who had read about his results in the different bee journals wanted queens from his yard, and his yearly production of two thousand queens was always bought up ahead of time at two dollars each, which is just double the usual price.

Silas was a keen student of biology besides an expert beekeeper. He had tried all the usual experiments with different races of bees before falling back on Italian stock, bred for many generations in the United States for honey-gathering qualities, gentleness, and color.

Although he had achieved commercial success, he still found the experimental side most fascinating, especially with regard to artificial fertilization of drone eggs—a comparatively simple matter, only requiring a little care. His greatest ambition was to cross-breed different species and even different genera. From his studies he found out that the freaks exhibited in sideshows were not crosses between dog and rabbit or cat and dog, as advertised, such things being impossible, owing, it is thought, to chemical differences in the life germs.

Every beekeeper knows that the queen bee lays fertile or unfertile eggs at will. One mating is sufficient for life, and after it the queen can lay a million or more fertile eggs at the rate of as many as two thousand a day in summer. The fertile eggs become females, either workers or queens, depending on how they are fed, while the unfertile eggs hatch out into drones, which are the big, clumsy, stingless males. For the most part they are useless, for they require the labor of five workers to keep them fed, and only a very few ever perform the services for which they were created. Nature is very bounteous when it comes to reproduction, but seems to desert her children once they are safely ushered into this wicked world.

All might have gone well if someone had not sent Silas Donaghy a queen bee from the wilds of Borneo. After careful examination, he introduced it to one of his hives which he had just deprived of its own queen. In a month's time the new brood had hatched and were on the wing; pretty bees they were, with a red tuft on the abdomen and long, graceful bodies with strong wings. Soon the honey began to come in and pile up on that hive, which was mounted on a weighing scale. Up and up crept the weight until Silas saw that he had something as far beyond his own strain as his own were above the ordinary black bee. In his enthusiasm for these new and beautiful creatures, he overlooked the source of their honey. Not alone did they gather from the flowers but from every plant that had sweet juice in its stems or leaves, and they did not hesitate to enter other hives and rob them of their stores. In fact, wherever there was a sign of sugar, they seemed to find it and carry it off.

When that hive had piled up a thousand pounds of honey, Silas took eggs from it and put them in every hive he had. Risking everything, he bought extra hives and equipment and raised five thousand of the new queens, which he sold for five dollars each. Soon his mail was flooded with letters of two kinds; one lot praising his queens as the most wonderful honey gatherers in the world, the other abusing him for scattering a race of robbers that were ruining crops and cleaning out all other hives within a radius of five miles.

Things might have righted themselves if it had not been for a California senator who owned two thousand hives and had them completely robbed out by another beekeeper who had only five hundred, all mothered by the new Borneo strain.

By means of influence at Washington, and without consulting the Bureau of Entomology, this senator had the mails closed to Silas Donaghy's queens. It was a dreadful shock to Silas because he had already begun refunding people their money and replacing the queens free of charge. Now he could no longer make amends, but the letters of abuse continued to come in by the hundred. He said nothing, but devoted himself more and more to his experiments.

IT WAS WITH AN ORDINARY wasp or yellow jacket that he succeeded in producing a creature that soon turned the continent upside down.

Under his super-microscope he was looking at an un-fertile egg of a Borneo queen. Something buzzed into the room and flew around the microscope, making a breeze that threatened to blow away the delicate egg from its glass slide. Impatiently he put out his hand and to his surprise caught something between his fingers. It was a drone wasp and he had partly crushed it. An idea suddenly struck him; he took a fine camel's-hair brush and touched it to the fluid containing the microscopic spermatazoa or life germs exuding from the dead wasp. With infinite care he applied the brush to the large end of the tiny, cucumber-shaped egg on the stage of the microscope. Presently he saw several minute, eel-like creatures burrowing into the egg. One outswam the others; its long tail was replaced by protoplasmic radiations and it united with the female pronucleus. With a tense look, the experimenter sat on with his eye rigidly glued to the microscope.

Had he succeeded? Would cleavage take place? He was called to lunch, but the call went unheeded. At last the pronucleus elongated, became narrow in the middle and finally split into two.

Wonderful! Extraordinary! It would seem that he had accomplished that which no other man had ever done.

Carefully he transferred the wonderful egg to a queen cup and covered it with royal jelly, that special food that in quantity would make it a queen.

Now he must trust it to the tender mercies of the bees, for no man knows the exact constituents of the food fed to the larvae day by day. Then there is always the chance that the bees will reject the egg thus offered to them; they show their disapproval by licking up the royal jelly and devouring the delicate egg.

Silas went through agonies in those three days that it takes the egg to hatch. Everything went as it should, and in fourteen days he had a perfect queen resembling a wasp except for a few reddish hairs on the abdomen. His anxieties were not yet over, for a week after hatching the queen goes on her wedding flight. High up into the air she soars with all the drones after her in a flock. To the strong goes the victory, but his joy is short lived, for after one embrace he falls to the ground, dead, his vitals torn from him and attached to the queen. Such is the queen's first flight, and after it she returns to the hive to lay countless thousands of eggs. Had he wished to, Silas could have fertilized the queen by the Sladen method, almost amounting to an operation, but he thought it wiser to let nature take her course.

On the seventh day the young queen came out of the hive, ran about the alighting board nervously for a minute, then took a short flight to get her bearings and finally shot into the air and out of sight while the drones followed in desperate haste.

Silas waited and watched, but she did not return. Days passed and his spirits fell to zero, for the chance of a lifetime had slipped from his grasp.

It was a month or so later that young Silas came running into his father's study one morning with the news: "Oh, Father! Come quick and bring the cyanide. There's a wasp's nest bigger than a pumpkin down on a tree in the wood lot."

"Now, Silas, I've often told you not to exaggerate. You know it isn't that size."

"Well, Father, it's enormous, anyway."

When Silas, senior, went down to investigate he found his son's description not in the least exaggerated. If anything, the size was underestimated. There, to his astonishment, hung the largest wasp's nest he had ever seen or heard about. The insects going in and out seemed different from the ordinary yellow jackets. Walking over to investigate, he received a sting that temporarily knocked him out. He was well inoculated to bee stings and they hardly affected him, but this was something quite different. Some way or other he reached the house and collapsed on the doorstep.

It was three days before he was about again, feeling very shaky on his legs. He did not lack courage, for he took a butterfly net and veil and went down to see how the new insects were getting along. The nest was bigger still and the numbers of bees coming in and out had greatly increased. He managed to capture one before he was chased home, and a sting on the hand, though very painful, did not incapacitate him so badly as the first had done.

To his astonishment the captured insect had the red tip to its abdomen. Here was a great discovery. His escaped queen had settled down on her own account and started a paper-pulp nest like ordinary wasps instead of returning to her own hive. Interest in the new species overcame everything else in his mind, even the severity of the sting.

Putting the captured specimen in a queen mailing cage, he posted it to the professor of entomology at the State University, who had been friendly to him through all his late troubles. Alas for the regulations which he had quite forgotten in his excitement. The Post Office people returned his specimen with a prosecution notice. He was summoned to court and heavily fined.

While he was away from home, little Silas was stung by one of the bees and died the same evening.

Something gave way in the poor man's mind and he hated the whole world with a deadly hatred.

Making himself a perfectly bee-tight costume, he sat near the great nest for hours at a time, capturing young queens as they emerged. Next he bought a gross of little rubber balloons and some cylinders of compressed hydrogen. Making small paper cages, he attached an inflated balloon to each, put in a young queen and started them off wherever the wind would take them. When the queen got tired of her paper prison, she chewed her way out to freedom and, singlehanded, started a new colony.

IT WAS GETTING LATE in the season and the new strain of insects did not make much headway before the cold weather set in.

Early the next spring the country papers began to complain of the prevalence of deaths from bee or wasp stings. Every year some people die of stings, but now the number was greatly increased. Animals also were frequently found dead without apparent reason. Many people got stung and recovered after a week in bed.

In the cities these constant accounts from the country became a sort of joke. The words "stung," "sting" and "stings" were used on every occasion, in season and out. When a man was away from work without permission, instead of saying he was burying his grandmother he said he had been laid up with a bee sting.

At last official notice was taken of the new menace and they were recognized as being descended from the famous Borneo queens. The bees from Borneo were now discussed in every state in the Union. The cities were still joking, but the country people were getting desperate. Many had sold out for what they could get and had moved to parts not yet infested with the new pest. Those that remained wore special clothes, had all doors and windows carefully screened, and took every precaution not to let the insects into the house. It was soon discovered that even the chimneys had to be covered when fires were not burning. The new insects had to have sugar as well as an insect or flesh diet, but they preferred to get their sweets in any other way rather than from the flowers. All beehives were quickly robbed and the bees killed off. Soon it was realized that there would be no fruit crop in many districts, for even if pickers could be found who would run the risk of being stung, the insects were always ahead of them devouring the fruit as soon as ripe.

The cities began to wake up when the new insects found that open fruit stalls and candy stores were theirs for the taking. They built their nests from waste paper or old wood or any fibrous material that they could find. The nests were built high up under cornices and gables where it was very difficult to find them and still more difficult to destroy them. The death toll was now greater, for the city people were not inoculated as many of the country folk were. One in every four died from the stings. The conversation became more serious, the papers had a special column for deaths from stings. A fellow worker would not turn up at the office; his friends looked at each other gravely and cast lots to see who should ring up to find out the sad news. If he did come back after being in a hospital he was hailed with enthusiasm.

All the leading scientists and doctors were working hard to devise a serum or antitoxin. Some brave men were undergoing a series of injections with formic acid to see if it would immunize them. Every newspaper had a list of so-called cures sent in by people who professed to have cured themselves or others. It was hard to judge these things, for it was impossible to know if the sting were really of a Borneo queen and not of some other hymenopterous insect. Panic alone killed many, so great was the fright of those stung by any insect. Those who recovered

from a sting practically never died when stung again; this fact was of great use when recruiting began later on in the year.

A dreadful catastrophe raised the menace of the bees to an importance exceeding everything else.

A trainload of molasses was entering a suburb of a great city where the bees had obtained quite a foothold. The engineer was stung in the face and staggered back into the arms of the fireman. A lurch, and both fell out on the track. On rushed the heavy train with throttle open. Soon it entered the yards at great speed, jumped the switches and collided with an outgoing passenger train. Sounds of rending steel and splintering wood filled the air. Roaring, hissing steam drowned the cries of the injured. Over track and wreckage spread a turgid mass of strong-smelling molasses.

Before the work of rescue was half completed the air was swarming with millions of buzzing insects. Doctors, nurses, railway workers, policemen and ambulance drivers were stung into insensibility and death. To complete the awful drama some well-intentioned persons bravely started smudge fires, hoping to smoke away the bees. Now fire was added and the flames licked through the seething, treacly mass, converting it into a holocaust such as had not been witnessed since the days of the Great War. Five hundred persons lost their lives through accident, fire and stings. Thirty or forty casualties, at the most, would have been the total if it had not been for the bees.

THE NATION WAS AWAKE NOW. Complete destruction of this new pest was demanded in all the great newspapers. Expense could not be spared in such an emergency. There must be no half-hearted measures, for the very life of the country was being strangled by the creation of a madman.

Volunteers were organized all over the country. They were equipped with extension ladders and strong sacks, which they put over the suspended nest, drew tight the running string, and transferred the whole thing to a woven wire burner, where it was sprayed with gasoline and burnt. At first they seemed to make some headway, but a fine spell of weather and millions of emerging young queens gave the bees fresh impetus and the newly started nests could not be found so easily as the large old ones.

The national capital proved an especially happy hunting ground for the bees. The public buildings provided thousands of nooks and corners where the nests were not discovered until they were as large as barrels. Sometimes the weight would break them down. If they fell in a street, there were sure to be many deaths before traffic could be diverted, and men protected to the last degree destroyed the insects with flaming sprays and poison gas. At last, things became so bad that the seat of government was moved to a town in Arizona which had not yet been invaded by bees.

Many new industries sprang into being, for anything advertised to combat the pests found a ready sale. Traps of every size, shape and description were sold; many of them more ingenious to look at than practical in use. Poison baits were sold and used by the ton, many harmless animals and not a few children fell victims to its use.

In spite of everything the pests went on increasing in numbers until the country seemed on the verge of bankruptcy. When farm mortgages, considered so safe, fell due, it was not worthwhile foreclosing them, for the land was useless. The new insects did not pollinate the fruit, but they destroyed the insects that did. Farm produce rose to unheard-of prices. Passenger traffic was reduced to a minimum, for nobody traveled who could possibly avoid it. Excursions and pleasure trips seemed to be a thing of the past. Even free insurance against stings did not stimulate travel, for no one seemed keen on being stung, however big the compensation to their heirs!

When fruit reached a certain price, large syndicates bought up fertile stretches for almost nothing and screened them in at enormous cost. In these enclosures the most intensive culture known was practiced with very profitable results. Not alone were there gardeners, but numerous guards patrolled the high framework with shotguns charged with salt ready to shoot any bee that should find its way in. Common bees had to be introduced from great distances for pollination purposes.

SILAS DONAGHY GIBBERED and raved in the state asylum; when he saw anyone stung he was convulsed with mirth. From morning to night he played tricks on the attendants, doctors and other patients. They never could tell when he might have a bee concealed about his clothing or wrapped in his handkerchief. It was most disturbing to the officials to get suddenly chased by a man who held sudden death in his hand. They put him in a padded cell, but it did not disturb him in the least. When his food was brought, he imitated the buzzing of a bee so skillfully that the attendant dropped the food and ran, followed by Silas' unearthly shrieks of merriment. At times he appeared quite sane and would skillfully catch and kill every bee that accidentally got let in. When he got stung himself, which was very rarely, he would wince with the pain and fall to his knees and grope about half blinded for support while the poison coursed through his veins. Getting to his feet again, he would stagger about with the tears of agony running down his cheeks, the while laughing at himself and cursing his weakness. Those who saw him marveled, for most people collapsed in a writhing heap and mercifully became unconscious.

In his sane moments he begged for his beloved microscope and experimental equipment. At last, to humor him and incidentally save themselves unlimited trouble, they gave him a little hut in the grounds where he could do as he liked so long as he did not annoy anyone. The first thing he did was to tear off all the screen wire and let the bees have free access to his living and sleeping rooms. He even let them share his meals and they sat in rows on the edge of his plate. It wasn't long before there was a nest right above his bed; it remained there undisturbed, for no one went near his little abode. The official bee swatters kept clear of Silas, for they had their dignity to uphold and Silas made fun of their bee-tight costumes and elaborate equipment. He could kill more bees in a day, if he wanted to, than they could in a week.

The Government was still busy working out methods to control the plague. One that seemed to promise some success was the introduction of a large fly belonging to the hawk-like family that prey on honey bees, catching them on the wing and tearing them asunder to feed on the sweet juices within. These flies were bred in great numbers and distributed over the country. Spiders and bee-eating birds were also extensively tried out.

With the first cold days of autumn the nation breathed more freely, for the Borneo bees were even more sensitive to cold than the ordinary hive bees. So great was the relief that all the activities of summer began to take place in the winter. People went visiting and the railways ran excursions. Such is the spirit of the people that they quickly forget their troubles and trust that the past will bury its past. But the entomologists of the country knew and trembled at the thought of spring when the fine weather would entice from their wintering places thousands and millions of queens that would quickly construct nests and raise broods that would far exceed anything that had yet gone before. A bounty of ten cents a queen was offered and thousands of people collected the dormant insects from their hiding places. Special instructors visited all the schools, telling of the dangers that awaited them if the queens were not destroyed now.

The fine weather came and with it the queens came out of their hiding places in countless millions. Those gathered were as a drop in the bucket, compared to those left undisturbed. For a few short weeks things got steadily worse and worse. All the devices of the previous year were used and a lot of new ones. Single screen doors were no longer of any use. Double doors were better, but the most reliable system proved to be a cold passage kept at a very low temperature. In this passage the insects became chilled and could be swept up and destroyed.

Every day now seemed closer to the time when things would end. A heat wave came along and the overstrained public services collapsed. The dead lay in the streets. The frantic telephone calls went unanswered. Even the water pipes were choked with the dead insects, and the water tainted with the acrid poison that also filled the air.

Those who had the means and were able fled to other parts where the breakdown had not yet occurred. The military forces of the country were fully organized for relief purposes and those who remained were rescued from the cities of the dead.

The State Lunatic Asylum collapsed with all the rest of society and patients wandered out and were soon stung to death.

SILAS WAS UNDECIDED what to do at first. Then he thought it would be a good plan to put the screen wire back on his shack. The bees objected to the hammering, so he waited until night and did it then. He was rather disappointed at having to destroy the nest inside, but it could not be helped. Several visits to the storeroom of the asylum yielded all the food he needed. For a few days he remained in solitude, then he packed his beloved microscope, put on a light bee veil and started home over the deserted roads. He was careful not to annoy the insects in any way. He never batted at them or made quick, jerky movements, and he avoided going near their nests. He took it very easy so that he would not perspire, for bees hate the smell of sweat.

Sad sights met his gaze as he trudged along. The whitened bones of cows and horses and smaller animals littered the fields, for the insects picked their victims clean, requiring as they did a partly animal diet like ordinary wasps. A disabled truck stood by the roadside and sitting in the driver's seat was a grim skeleton. Further on a cheap touring car lay on its side and four skeletons, two large and two small, told the sad tale of a family wiped out in a few minutes. These sights did not seem to affect Silas at all; he was more interested in the nests that hung from every tree and telegraph pole and from the gables and eaves of houses and barns. Once he was overtaken by an armored and screened military ambulance. He refused their aid and they hurried on, the wheels crushing a bee at every turn. A crushed bee is smelled by the other bees and they are immediately on the warpath, so Silas had to leave the road and take to the fields.

When he reached home he found his wife

alone in the well-screened house. She had been ostracized by all the neighbors long before they had left, and only for Silas' letters of instruction, she could not have carried on singlehanded. Somehow she had expected Silas. He entered by the cellar steps and slipped through so dexterously that only seven bees got in with him. They flew to a window, where he quickly killed them, for Mrs. Donaghy, strange to say, had never been stung. He took off his outer clothing and found five more. Disposing of these, he went upstairs and carried his microscope to the study, where he carefully unpacked it and put a glass cover over it. He fussed about the study in an absentminded way until Mrs. Donaghy called him to supper. Sitting down, he looked at the place where little Silas used to sit.

"Where's the boy?" he questioned. "You know I like him to be on time to his meals."

A pained look came over the poor lady's face.

"Silas, you know he's gone."

"Gone where? What do you mean?"

She looked up, flushing, and for the first time in her married life spoke with heat: "Dead, you know he's dead; stung to death by one of your accursed bees."

Silas collapsed on the table. Covering his face with his hands, great sobs wracked his body. "My God, my God, what have I done?" he moaned.

Presently he was in his study again, looking at everything with a new light in his eyes. He was alert and methodical now, and there was a set appearance about his jaw that had not been there for a long, long while.

Taking the plug out of the keyhole, he waited till a bee came in and, dexterously catching it by the wings, brought it to his study. His tired eyes were bright now and he appeared to be looking at something he had never seen before. Frequently he came to the living-room to ask his wife questions about what had happened in the last year or so. He seemed appalled, but a glance from any window verified all she said.

That night he visited a deep bee cellar constructed underground where he used to winter some of his colonies. He found that it had been used as an ice house while he had been away. Seeing an old hive in the corner, he went over

and lifted the lid. To his utter astonishment a faint buzz greeted him that was quite different from the high note of the all-pervading pest outside. Here was the remnant of a colony of honey bees that had been forgotten. How could they have survived all this time? He didn't know, unless it was the ice making a continuous winter for two years. Shouldering the hive, he carried it out and placed it in a little screened chicken yard where Mrs. Donaghy had endeavored to raise a few vegetables. Next morning the survivors were buzzing about getting their bearings, though there wasn't much fear of their straying very far in the little enclosure,

FOR THE NEXT WEEK Silas hardly slept or took time to eat. If he wasn't at the microscope he was in the small yard where the last honey bees in North America flew about and licked up the honey given them. Little they knew that the fate of a continent depended on them.

At last he produced a drone that seemed to fill the requirements. It must be able to outfly the drones of the vicious half-breeds all around. It must be able to produce grandsons, for by the laws of parthenogenesis a drone cannot have sons that would also be swift and amorous. It must produce daughters and granddaughters resembling honey bees and incapable of surviving the winter alone.

Most scientists would have waited to test out these qualities before scattering the new product broadcast. Silas, however, was always impetuous, as the sale of his first Borneo queens had shown him to be. He realized now that the situation might be better but could not be worse.

Setting to work in his little enclosure, he bred drones in large numbers and liberated them. If only he had some way of distributing them quickly! Balloons and hydrogen? Alas, he had neither. He wandered about, thinking hard. There in the basement stood the little lighting plant with its neat row of batteries and a large jar of acid in the corner. Ha! There was hydrogen, either by electrolysis or, more quickly still, with strips of zinc or nails and the acid. Paper bags would do for the balloons.

In a day or so he was sending the drones off

on the wind by the dozen together, hoping that they would seek out the young queens wherever they went and father a new race of harmless bees that would die out entirely in the winter.

In a month he noticed young queens without the familiar red tuft on their tails. Capturing a few, he put them in his enclosure and fed them carefully, even opening a precious tin of meat to help them along; but they did not respond and some died. They were incapable of living alone. However, those put into nests flourished and outdid their vicious half-sister. It was a treat to see the new drones on the wing rushing about in their wild search for virgin queens. The workers of the new breed had barbed stings and died on using them. It was not very painful either.

Every day now Silas was in his garden getting things to rights, planting and harvesting. He smiled now at the millions of bees, for they were all different from the old race that was quickly dying off.

He often wondered if there was anyone else alive. Making a trip to the deserted village, he was rummaging around looking for canned goods when he was astonished to hear a telephone ring. It was a long-distance call searching for anyone alive.

"The bees have played themselves out," he was told. "The breed did not hold true. Nature righted herself automatically."

Silas went home smiling. He knew that he had started and ended the awful plague.

👽 👽 👽

"The Bees from Borneo" first appeared in the February 1931 issue of Amazing Stories, accompanied by an illustration by Leo Morey. SF novelist Brian Stableford wrote, "Newspaper reportage reflected anxieties about hive power in stories of 'killer bees' that became popular in the early 1970s, reflected in such novels as Arthur Herzog's The Swarm (1974)—anticipated in Will H. Gray's 'The Bees from Borneo' (1934)." Canadian author Gray was an authority on bees and beekeeping, and published several scholarly articles on the subject. He penned only two other SF tales, which also appeared in Amazing Stories.

THE WORM

BY DAVID H. KELLER

THE MILLER PATTED HIS DOG ON THE HEAD, AS HE WHISPERED, "WE ARE GOING TO STAY HERE. OUR FOLKS, YOUR ANCESTORS AND MINE, HAVE BEEN HERE FOR NEARLY TWO HUNDRED YEARS,** and queer it would be to leave now because of fear."

The gristmill stood, a solid stone structure, in an isolated Vermont valley. Years ago every day had been a busy one for the mill and the miller, but now only the mill wheel was busy. There was no grist for the mill and no one lived in the valley. Blackberries and hazel grew where once the pastures had been green. The hand of time had passed over the farms and the only folk left were sleeping in the churchyard. A family of squirrels nested in the pulpit, while on the tombstones silent snails left their cryptic messages in silvery streaks. Thompson's Valley was being handed back to nature. Only the old bachelor miller,

John Staples, remained. He was too proud and too stubborn to do anything else.

The mill was his home, even as it had served all of his family for a home during the last two hundred years. The first Staples had built it to stay, and it was still as strong as on the day it was finished. There was a basement for the machinery of the mill, the first floor was the place of grinding and storage, and the upper two floors served as the Staples homestead. The building was warm in winter and cool in summer. Times past it had sheltered a dozen Stapleses at a time; now it provided a home for John Staples and his dog.

He lived there with his books and his memories. He had no friends and desired no associates. Once a year he went to the nearest town and bought supplies of all kinds, paying for them in gold. It was supposed that he was wealthy. Rumor credited him with being a miser. He attended to his own business, asked the world to do the same, and on a winter's evening laughed silently over Burton and Rabelais, while his dog chased rabbits in his heated sleep upon the hearth.

The winter of 1935 was beginning to threaten the valley, but with an abundance of food and wood in the mill, the recluse looked forward to a comfortable period of desuetude. No matter how cold the weather, he was warm and contented. With the inherent ability of his family, he had been able to convert the waterpower into electricity. When the wheel was frozen, he used the electricity stored in his storage batteries. Every day he puttered around among the machinery, which it was his pride to keep in perfect order. He assured the dog that if business ever did come to the mill, he would be ready for it.

It was on Christmas Day of that winter that he first heard the noise. Going down to the basement to see that nothing had been injured by the bitter freeze of the night before, his attention was attracted, even while descending the stone steps, by a peculiar grinding noise that seemed to come from out of the ground. His ancestors, building for permanency, had not only put in solid foundations, but had paved the entire basement with slate flagstones three feet wide and as many inches thick. Between these the dust of two centuries had gathered and hardened.

Once his feet were on this pavement, Staples found that he could not only hear the noise, but he could also feel the vibrations that accompanied it through the flagstones. Even through his heavy leather boots he could feel the rhythmic pulsations. Pulling off his mittens, he stooped over and put his fingertips on the stone. To his surprise it was warm in spite of the fact that the temperature had been below zero the night before. The vibration was more distinct to his fingertips than it had been to his feet. Puzzled, he threw himself on the slate stone and put his ear to the warm surface.

The sound he now heard made him think of the grinding of the millstones when he was a boy and the farmers had brought corn to be ground into meal. There had been no cornmeal ground in the mill for fifty years, yet here was the sound of stone scraping slowly and regularly on stone. He could not understand it. In fact it was some time before he tried to explain it. With the habit born of years of solitary thinking, he first collected all the available facts about this noise. He knew that during the long winter evenings he would have time enough to do his thinking.

Going to his sitting room, he secured a walking stick of ash and went back to the cellar. Holding the handle of the cane lightly, he placed the other end on a hundred different spots on the floor, and each time he held it long enough to determine the presence or absence of vibration. To his surprise he found that while it varied in strength, it was present all over the cellar with the exception of the four corners. The maximum intensity was about in the center.

That evening he concentrated on the problem before him. He had been told by his grandfather that the mill was built on solid rock. As a young man he had helped clean out a well near the mill and recalled that, instead of being dug out of gravel or dirt, it had the appearance of being drilled out of solid granite. There was no difficulty in believing that the earth under the mill was also solid rock. There was no reason for thinking otherwise. Evidently some of these strata of stone had become loose and were slipping and twisting under the mill. The simplest explanation was the most reasonable: it was simply a geological phenomenon. The behavior of the dog, however, was not so easily explained. He had refused to go with his master into the cellar, and now, instead of sleeping in comfort before the fire, he was in an attitude of strained expectancy. He did not bark, or even whine, but crept silently to his master's chair, looking at him anxiously.

THE NEXT MORNING the noise was louder. Staples heard it in his bed, and at first he thought that some bold adventurer had come into the forest and was sawing down a tree. That was what it sounded like, only softer and longer in its rhythm. Buzzzzzz—Buzzzzzzzz-Buzzzzzzzzz. The dog, distinctly unhappy, jumped up on the bed and crawled uneasily so he could nuzzle the man's hand.

Through the four legs of the bed, Staples could feel the same vibration that had come to him through the handle of his cane the day before. That made him think. The vibration was now powerful enough to be appreciated, not through a walking stick, but through the walls of the building. The noise could be heard as well on the third floor as in the cellar.

He tried to fancy what it sounded like—not what it was—but what it was like. The first idea had been that it resembled a saw going through oak; then came the thought of bees swarming, only these were large bees and millions of them; but finally all he could think of was the grinding of stones in a gristmill, the upper stone against the lower; and now the sound was Grrrrrrrrr—Grrrrrrrrr instead of Bzzzzzzzzz or Hummmmmmm.

That morning he took longer than usual to shave and was more methodical than was his wont in preparing breakfast for himself and the dog. It seemed as though he knew that sometime he would have to go down into the cellar but wanted to postpone it as long as he could. In fact, he finally put on his coat and beaver hat and mittens and walked outdoors before he went to the basement. Followed by the dog, who seemed happy for the first time in hours, he walked out on the frozen ground and made a circle around the building he called his home. Without knowing it, he was trying to get away from the noise, to go somewhere he could walk without feeling that peculiar tingling.

Finally he went into the mill and started down the steps to the cellar. The dog hesitated on the top step, went down two steps and then jumped back to the top step, where he started to whine. Staples went steadily down the steps, but the dog's behavior did not add to his peace of mind. The noise was much louder than it was the day before, and he did not need a cane to detect the vibration—the whole building was shaking. He sat down on the third step from the bottom and

thought the problem over before he ventured out on the floor. He was especially interested in an empty barrel that was dancing around the middle of the floor.

The power of the millwheel was transferred through a simple series of shafts, cogs, and leather belting to the grinding elements on the first floor. All this machinery for transmitting power was in the basement. The actual grinding had been done on the first floor. The weight of all this machinery, as well as of the heavy millstones on the first floor, was carried entirely by the flooring of the basement. The ceiling of the first floor was built on long pine beams that stretched across the entire building and were sunk into the stone walls at either side.

Staples started to walk around on the slate flagstones when he observed something that made him decide to stay on the steps. The floor was beginning to sink in the middle; not much, but enough to cause some of the shafts to separate from the ceiling. The ceiling seemed to sag. He saw that light objects like the empty barrel were congregating at the middle of the cellar. There was not much light but he was easily able to see that the floor was no longer level; that it was becoming saucer-shaped. The grinding noise grew louder. The steps he sat on were of solid masonry, stoutly connected with and a part of the wall. These shared in the general vibration. The whole building began to sing like a cello.

One day he had been to the city and heard an orchestra play. He had been interested in the large violins, especially the one that was so large the player had to stay on his feet to play it. The feeling of the stone step under him reminded him of the notes of this violin the few times it had been played by itself. He sat there. Suddenly he started, realizing that in a few more minutes he would be asleep. He was not frightened but in some dim way he knew he must not go to sleep—not here. Whistling, he ran up the steps to get his electric torch. With that in his hand, he went back to the steps. Aided by the steady light, he saw that several large cracks had appeared in the floor and that some of the stones, broken loose from their fellows, were moving slowly in a drunken, meaningless way. He looked at his watch. It was only a little after nine.

And then the noise stopped.

No more noise! No more vibration! Just a broken floor and every bit of the machinery of the mill disabled and twisted. In the middle of the floor was a hole where one of the pavement stones had dropped through. Staples carefully walked across and threw the light down this hole. Then he lay down and carefully put himself in such a position that he could look down the hole. He began to sweat. There did not seem to be any bottom!

Back on the solid steps, he tried to give that hole its proper value. He could not understand it, but he did not need the whining of the dog to tell him what to do. That hole must be closed as soon as possible.

LIKE A FLASH, the method of doing so came to him. On the floor above he had cement. There were hundreds of grain sacks. Water was plentiful in the millrace. All that day he worked, carefully closing the hole with a great stopper of bags and wire. Then he placed timbers above and finally covered it all with cement, rich cement. Night came and he still worked. Morning came and still he staggered down the steps, each time with a bag of crushed stone or cement on his shoulder, or with two buckets of water in his hands. At noon the next day the floor was no longer concave but convex. On top of the hole was four feet of timbers, bags and concrete. Then and only then did he go and make some coffee. He drank it, cup after cup, and slept.

The dog stayed on the bed at his feet.

When the man woke, the sun was streaming in through the windows. It was a new day. Though the fire had long since died out, the room was warm. Such days in Vermont were called weather breeders. Staples listened. There was no sound except the ticking of his clock. Not realizing what he was doing, he knelt by the bed, thanked God for His mercies, jumped into bed again and slept for another twenty-four hours. This time he awoke and listened. There was no noise. He was sure that by this time the cement had hardened. This morning he stayed awake and shared a gargantuan meal with the dog. Then it

seemed the proper thing to go to the basement. There was no doubt that the machinery was a wreck, but the hole was closed. Satisfied that the trouble was over, he took his gun and dog and went hunting.

When he returned, he did not have to enter the mill to know that the grinding had begun again. Even before he started down the steps, he recognized too well the vibration and the sound. This time it was a melody of notes, a harmony of discords, and he realized that the thing, which before had cut through solid rock, was now wearing its way through a cement in which were bags, timbers and pieces of iron. Each of these gave a different tone. Together they all wailed over their dissolution.

Staples saw, even with first glance, that it would not be long before his cement "cork" would be destroyed. What was there to do next? All that day when hunting, his mind had been dimly working on that problem. Now he had the answer. He could not cork the hole, so he would fill it with water. The walls of the mill were solid, but he could blast a hole through them and turn the millrace into the cellar. The race, fed by the river, took only a part of what it could take, if its level were rapidly lowered. Whatever it was that was breaking down the floor of the mill could be drowned. If it was alive, it could be killed. If it was fire, it could be quenched. There was no use to wait until the hole was again opened. The best plan was to have everything ready. He went back to his kitchen and cooked a meal of ham and eggs. He ate all he could. He boiled a pot of coffee. Then he started to work. The wall reached three feet down below the surface. A charge of powder, heavy enough to break through, would wreck the whole building, so he began to peck at the wall, like a bird pecking at a nut. First a period of drilling and then a little powder and a muffled explosion. A few buckets of loosened rock. Then some more drilling and another explosion. At last he knew that only a few inches of rock lay between the water and the cellar.

All this time there had been a symphony of noises, a disharmony of sounds. The constant grinding came from the floor, interrupted with the sound of sledge or crowbar, dull explosion of powder, and crashing of rock fragments on the floor. Staples worked without stop save to drink coffee. The dog stood on the upper steps.

Then, without warning, the whole floor caved in. Staples jumped to the steps. These held. On the first day there had been a hole a few feet wide. Now the opening occupied nearly the entire area of the floor. Staples, nauseated, looked down to the bottom. There, about twenty feet below him, a mass of rocks and timbers churned in a peculiar way, but all gradually disappeared in a second hole, fifteen feet wide. Even as he looked they all disappeared in this median hole.

The opening he had been breaking in the wall was directly across from the steps. There was a charge of powder but no way of going across to light the fuse. Still, there was no time to lose and he had to think fast. Running to the floor above he picked up his rifle and went to the bottom of the steps. He was able to throw the beam from his searchlight directly into the hole in the wall. Then he shot—once—twice, and the third time the explosion told him he had succeeded.

The water started to run into the cellar. Not fast at first but more rapidly as the mud and weeds were cleared out. Finally an eight-inch stream flowed steadily into the bottomless hole. Staples sat on the bottom steps. Soon he had the satisfaction of seeing the water fill the larger hole and then cover the floor, what there was left of it. In another hour he had to leave the lower steps. He went out to the millrace and saw that there was still enough water to fill a hundred such holes. A deep sense of satisfaction filled his weary mind.

And again, after eating, he sought sleep.

When he awoke, he heard the rain angrily tapping at the windows with multi-fingers. The dog was on the woven rug by the side of the bed. He was still restless and seemed pleased to have his master awake. Staples dressed more warmly than usual and spent an extra half hour making pancakes to eat with honey. Sausages and coffee helped assuage his hunger. Then, with rubber boots and a heavy raincoat, he went out into the valley. The very first thing that he noticed was the millrace. It was practically empty. The little stream of water at the bottom was pouring into the hole he had blasted into the stone wall hours before. The race had contained eight feet of water. Now barely six inches remained, and the dread came to the man that the hole in the cellar was not only emptying the race but was also draining the little river that for thousands of years had flowed through the valley. It had never gone dry. He hastened over to the dam and his worst fears were realized. Instead of a river, there was simply a streak of mud with cakes of dirty ice, all being washed by the torrent of rain. With relief he thought of this rain. Millions of tons of snow would melt and fill the river. Ultimately the hole would fill and the water would rise again in the millrace. Still he was uneasy. What if the hole had no bottom?

When he looked into the basement he was little reassured. The water was still going down, though slowly. It was rising in the basement and this meant that it was now running in faster than it was running down.

Leaving his coat and boots on the first floor, he ran up the stone steps to the second floor, built a fire in the living room and started to smoke—and think. The machinery of the mill was in ruins; of course, it could be fixed, but as there was no more need of it, the best thing was to leave it alone. He had gold saved by his ancestors. He did not know how much, but he could live on it. Restlessly he reviewed the past week, and, unable to rest, hunted for occupation. The idea of the gold stayed in his mind and the final result was that he again put on his boots and coat and carried the entire treasure to a little dry cave in the woods about a half mile from the mill. Then he came back and started to cook his dinner. He went past the cellar door three times without looking down.

Just as he and the dog had finished eating, he heard a noise. It was a different one this time, more like a saw going through wood, but the rhythm was the same: Hrrrrrr—Hrrrrrr. He started to go to the cellar but this time he took his rifle, and though the dog followed, he howled dismally with his tail between his legs, shivering.

As soon as Staples reached the first floor, he felt the vibration. Not only could he feel the vibration, he could see it. It seemed that the center of the floor was being pushed up. Flashlight in hand, he opened the cellar door. There was no water there now—in fact there was no cellar left! In front of him was a black wall on which the light played in undulating waves. It was a wall and it was moving. He touched it with the end of his rifle. It was hard and yet there was a give to it. Feeling the rock, he could feel it move. Was it alive? Could there be a living rock? He could not see around it but he felt that the bulk of the thing filled the entire cellar and was pressing against the ceiling. That was it! The thing was boring through the first floor. It had destroyed and filled the cellar! It had swallowed the river! Now it was working at the first floor. If this continued, the mill was doomed. Staples knew that it was a thing alive and *he had to stop it!*

He was thankful that all of the steps in the mill were of stone, fastened and built into the wall. Even though the floor did fall in, he could still go to the upper rooms. He realized that from now on the fight had to be waged from the top floors. Going up the steps, he saw that a small hole had been cut through the oak flooring. Even as he watched, this grew larger. Trying to remain calm, realizing that only by doing so could he retain his sanity, he sat down in a chair and timed the rate of enlargement. But there was no need of using a watch: the hole grew larger— and larger and larger—and now he began to see the dark hole that had sucked the river dry. Now it was three feet in diameter—now four feet—now six. It was working smoothly now—it was not only grinding—*but it was eating.*

Staples began to laugh. He wanted to see what it would do when the big stone grinders slipped silently down into that maw. That would be a rare sight. All well enough to swallow a few pavement stones, but when it came to a twenty-ton grinder, that would be a different kind of a pill. "I hope you choke!" The walls hurled back the echo of his shouts and frightened him into silence. Then the floor began to tilt and the chairs to slide toward the opening. Staples sprang toward the steps.

"Not yet!" he shrieked. "Not today, Elenora! Some other day, but not today!" And then from the safety of the steps, he witnessed the final destruction of the floor and all in it. The stones slipped down, the partitions, the beams, and then, as though satisfied with the work and the food, the Thing dropped down, down, down, and left Staples dizzy on the steps looking into a hole, dark, deep, coldly bottomless, surrounded by the walls of the mill, and below them a circular hole cut out of the solid rock. On one side a little stream of water came through the blasted wall and fell, a tiny waterfall, below. Staples could not hear it splash at the bottom.

Nauseated and vomiting, he crept up the steps to the second floor, where the howling dog was waiting for him. On the floor he lay, sweating and shivering in dumb misery. It took hours for him to change from a frightened animal to a cerebrating god, but ultimately he accomplished even this, cooked some more food, warmed himself and slept.

AND WHILE HE DREAMED, the dog kept sleepless watch at his feet. He awoke the next morning. It was still raining, and Staples knew that the snow was melting on the hills and soon would change the little valley river into a torrent. He wondered whether it was all a dream, but one look at the dog showed him the reality of the last week. He went to the second floor again and cooked breakfast. After he had eaten, he slowly went down the steps. That is, he started to go, but halted at the sight of the hole. The steps had held and ended on a wide stone platform. From there another flight of steps went down to what had once been the cellar. Those two flights of steps clinging to the walls had the solid stone mill on one side, but on the inside they faced a chasm, circular in outline and seemingly bottomless; but the man knew there was a bottom, and from that pit the Thing had come—and would come again.

That was the horror of it. He was so certain that it would come again. Unless he was able to stop it. How could he? Could he destroy a Thing that was able to bore a thirty-foot hole through solid rock, swallow a river and digest grinding stones like so many pills? One thing he was sure of—he could accomplish nothing without knowing more about it. To know more, he had to watch. He determined to cut a hole through the floor. Then he could see the Thing when it came up. He cursed himself for his confidence, but he was sure it would come.

It did. He was on the floor looking into the hole he had sawed through the plank, and he saw it come; but first he heard it. It was a sound full of slithering slidings, wrathful rasping of rock against rock—but, no! That could not be, for this Thing was alive. Could this be rock and move and grind and eat and drink? Then he saw it come into the cellar and finally to the level of the first floor, and then he saw its head and face.

The face looked at the man, and Staples was glad that the hole in the floor was as small as it was. There was a central mouth filling half the space; fully fifteen feet in diameter was that mouth, and the sides were ashen gray and quivering. There were no teeth.

That increased the horror: a mouth without teeth, without any visible means of mastication, and yet Staples shivered as he thought of what had gone into that mouth, down into that mouth, deep into the recesses of that mouth and disappeared. The circular lip seemed made of scales of steel, and they were washed clean with the water from the race.

On either side of the gigantic mouth was an eye, lidless, browless, pitiless. They were slightly withdrawn into the head so the Thing could bore into rock without injuring them. Staples tried to estimate their size: all he could do was to avoid their baleful gaze. Then, even as he watched, the mouth closed and the head began a semicircular movement, so many degrees to the right, so many degrees to the left and up—and up—and finally the top touched the bottom of the plank Staples was on, and then Hrrrrrr—Hrrrrrr and the man knew that it was starting

upon the destruction of the second floor. He could not see now as he had been able to see before, but he had an idea that after grinding a while the Thing opened its mouth and swallowed the debris. He looked around the room. Here was where he did his cooking and washing and here was his winter supply of stove wood. A thought came to him.

Working frantically, he pushed the center burner to the middle of the room right over the hole he had cut in the floor. Then he built a fire in it, starting it with a liberal supply of coal oil. He soon had the stove red hot. Opening the door, he again filled the stove with oak, and then ran for the steps. He was just in time. The floor, cut through, disappeared into the Thing's maw and with it the red-hot stove. Staples yelled in his glee, "A hot pill for you this time, a HOT PILL!"

If the pill did anything, it simply increased the desire of the Thing to destroy, for it kept on till it had bored a hole in this floor equal in size to the holes in the floors below it. Staples saw his food, his furniture, the ancestral relics disappear into the same opening that had consumed the machinery and mill supplies.

On the upper floor the dog howled.

The man slowly went up to the top floor and joined the dog, who had ceased to howl and had begun a low whine. There was a stove on this floor, but there was no food. That did not make any difference to Staples: for some reason he was not hungry anymore; it did not seem to make any difference—nothing seemed to matter or make any difference anymore. Still he had his gun and over fifty cartridges, and he knew that nothing could withstand that.

He lit the lamp and paced the floor in a cold, careless mood. One thing he had determined. He said it over and over to himself.

"This is my home. It has been the home of my family for two hundred years. No devil or beast or worm can make me leave it."

He said it again and again. He felt that if he said it often enough, he would believe it, and if he could only believe it, he might make the Worm believe it. He knew now that it was a Worm, just like the night crawlers he had used so often for bait, only much larger. Yes, that was it. A Worm like a night crawler, only much larger, in fact, very much larger. That made him laugh—to think how much larger this Worm was than the ones he had used for fishing. All through the night he walked the floor and burned the lamp and said, "This is my home. No Worm can make me leave it!" Several times he went down the steps, just a few of them, and shouted the message into the pit as though he wanted the Worm to hear and understand, "This is my home! NO WORM CAN MAKE ME LEAVE IT!"

Morning came. He mounted the ladder that led to the trap door in the roof and opened it. The rain beat in. Still, that might be a place of refuge. Crying, he took his Burton and his Rabelais and wrapped them in his raincoat and put them out on the roof, under a box. He took the small pictures of his father and mother and put them with the books. Then in loving kindness he carried the dog up and wrapped him in a woolen blanket. He sat down and waited, and as he did so he recited poetry—anything that came to him, all mixed up, "Come into the garden where there was a man who was so wondrous wise, he jumped into a bramble bush and you're a better man than I am and no one will work for money and the King of Love my Shepherd is"—and on—and then....

He heard the sliding and the slithering rasping and he knew that the Worm had come again. He waited till the Hrrrrr—Hrrrrr told that the wooden floor he was on was being attacked and then he went up the ladder. It was his idea to wait till the Thing had made a large opening, large enough so the eyes could be seen, and then use the fifty bullets—where they would do the most good. So, on the roof, beside the dog, he waited.

He did not have to wait long. First appeared a little hole and then it grew wider and wider till finally the entire floor and the furniture had dropped into the mouth, and the whole opening, thirty feet wide and more than that, was filled with the head, the closed mouth of which came within a few feet of the roof. By the aid of the light from the trap door, Staples could see the eye on the left side. It made a beautiful bull's eye, a magnificent target for his rifle, and he was only a few feet away. He could not miss. Determined to make the most of his last chance to drive his enemy away, he decided to drop down on the creature, walk over to the eye and put the end of the rifle against the eye before he fired. If the first shot worked well, he could retire to the roof and use the other cartridges. He knew that there was some danger—but it was his last hope. After all, he knew that when it came to brains he was a man and this Thing was only a Worm. He walked over the head. Surely no sensation could go through such massive scales. He even jumped up and down. Meantime the eye kept looking up at the roof. If it saw the man, it made no signs, gave no evidence. Staples pretended to pull the trigger and then made a running jump for the trap door. It was easy. He did it again, and again. Then he sat on the edge of the door and thought.

He suddenly saw what it all meant. Two hundred years before, his ancestors had started grinding at the mill. For over a hundred and fifty years the mill had been run continuously, often day and night. The vibrations had been transmitted downward through the solid rock. Hundreds of feet below, the Worm had heard them and felt them and thought it was another Worm. It had started to bore in the direction of the noise. It had taken two hundred years to do it, but it had finished the task, it had found the place where its mate should be. For two hundred years it had slowly worked its way through the primitive rock. Why should it worry over a mill and the things within it? Staples saw then that the mill had been but a slight incident in its life. It was probable that it had not even known it was there—the water, the gristmill stones, the red-hot stove, had meant nothing—they had been taken as a part of a day's work. There was only one thing that the Worm was really interested in, but one idea that had reached its consciousness and remained there through two centuries, and that was to find its mate. The eye looked upward.

Staples, at the end, lost courage and decided to fire from a sitting position in the trap door. Taking careful aim, he pulled the trigger. Then he looked carefully to see what damage had resulted. There was none. Either the bullet had gone into the eye and the opening had closed or else it had glanced off. He fired again and again.

Then the mouth opened—wide—wider—until there was nothing under Staples save a yawning void of darkness.

The Worm belched a cloud of black, nauseating vapor. The man, enveloped in the cloud, lost consciousness and fell.

The Mouth closed on him.

On the roof the dog howled.

👽 👽 👽

The Lovecraftian story "The Worm" first appeared in the March 1929 issue of Amazing Stories, *along with an uncredited illustration.*

The inventive American author and psychiatrist Dr. David Henry Keller (1880–1966) was one of the most popular and influential writers during the early years of pulp science fiction and fantasy. Keller concentrated on human emotions in his stories and ocassionally wrote under various pseudonyms, including Monk Smith, Amy Worth, Jacobus Hubelaire, Cecilia Henry and Henry Cecil. Keller was also an early scholar of H.P. Lovecraft. His notable and frequently-reprinted story "The Thing in the Cellar" is a worthy tale of horror.

THE WATERS OF DEATH

BY ÉMILE ERCKMANN & ALEXANDRE CHATRIAN

THE MINERAL WATERS OF SPINBRONN, IN HUNDSRUCK, A FEW LEAGUES FROM PIRMESANS, FORMERLY ENJOYED AN EXCELLENT REPUTATION, FOR SPINBRONN was the rendezvous of all the gouty and rheumatic members of the German aristocracy. The wild nature of the surrounding country did not deter the visitors, for they were lodged in charming villas at the foot of the mountain. They bathed in the cascade which fell in large sheets of foam from the summit of the rocks, and drank two or three pints of the water every day. Dr. Daniel Haselnoss, who prescribed for the sick and those who thought they were, received his patients in a large wig, brown coat, and ruffles, and was rapidly making his fortune.

Today, however, Spinbronn is no longer a favorite watering-place. The fashionable visitors have disappeared; Dr. Haselnoss has given up his practice; and the town is only inhabited by a few poor, miserable woodcutters. All this is the result of a succession of strange and unprecedented catastrophes, which Councillor Bremen, of Pirmesans, recounted to me the other evening.

"You know, Mr. Fritz," he said, "that the source of the Spinbronn flows from a sort of cavern about five feet high, and from ten to fifteen feet across; the water, which has a temperature of 67 degrees centigrade, is salt. The front of the cavern is half hidden by moss, ivy, and low shrubs, and it is impossible to find out the depth of it, because of the thermal exhalations which prevent any entrance.

"In spite of that, it had been remarked for a century that the birds of the locality, hawks, thrushes, and turtle-doves, were engulfed in full flight, and no one knew of what mysterious influence it was the result. During the season of 1801, for some unexplained reason, the source became more abundant, and the visitors one evening, taking their constitutional promenade on the lawns at the foot of the rocks, saw a human skeleton descend from the cascade.

"You can imagine the general alarm, Mr. Fritz. It was naturally supposed that a murder had been committed at Spinbronn some years before, and that the victim had been thrown into the source. But the skeleton, which was blanched as white as snow, only weighed twelve pounds; and Dr. Haselnoss concluded that, in all probability, it had been in the sand more than three centuries to have arrived at that state of desiccation.

"Plausible as his reasoning was, it did not prevent many visitors leaving that same day, horrified to have drunk the waters. The really gouty and rheumatic ones, however, stayed on, and consoled themselves with the doctor's version. But the following days the cavern disgorged all that it contained of detritus; and a veritable ossuary descended the mountain—skeletons of animals of all sorts, quadrupeds, birds, reptiles. In fact, all the most horrible things that could be imagined.

"Then Haselnoss wrote and published a pamphlet to prove that all these bones were relics of the antediluvian world, that they were fossil skeletons, accumulated there in a sort of funnel during the universal Deluge, that is to say, four thousand years before Christ; and, consequently, could only be regarded as stones, and not as anything repulsive.

"But his work had barely reassured the gouty ones, when one fine morning the corpse of a fox, and then of a hawk, with all its plumage, fell from the cascade. Impossible to maintain that these had existed before the Deluge, and the exodus became general.

"'How horrible!' cried the ladies. 'That is where the so-called virtue of mineral waters springs from. Better die of rheumatism than continue such a remedy.'

"At the end of a week the only visitor left was a stout Englishman, Commodore Sir Thomas Hawerbrook, who lived on a grand scale, as most Englishmen do. He was tall and very stout, and of a florid complexion. His hands were literally knotted with gout, and he would have drunk no matter what if he thought it would cure him. He laughed loudly at the desertion of the sufferers, installed himself in the best of the villas, and announced his intention of spending the winter at Spinbronn."

Here Councillor Bremen leisurely took a large pinch of snuff to refresh his memory, and with the tips of his fingers shook off the tiny particles which fell on his delicate lace jabot. Then he went on:

"Five or six years before the revolution of 1789, a young doctor of Pirmesans, called Christian Weber, went to St. Domingo to seek his fortune. He had been very successful, and was about to retire, when the revolt of the negroes occurred. Happily, he escaped the massacre, and was able to save part of his fortune. He travelled for a time in South America, and about the period of which I speak, returned to Pirmesans, and bought the house and what remained of the practice of Dr. Haselnoss.

"Dr. Christian Weber brought with him an old negress called Agatha. She always enveloped her head in a sort of turban of the most startling colors; and wore rings in her ears which reached to her shoulders. Altogether she was such a singular-looking creature, that the mountaineers came from miles around just to look at her.

"The doctor himself was a tall, thin man, invariably dressed in a blue swallow-tailed coat and leather breeches. He talked very little, his laugh was dry and nervous, and his habits most eccentric. During his wanderings he had collected a number of insects of almost every species, and seemed to be much more interested in them than in his patients. In his daily rambles among the mountains he often found butterflies to add to his collection, and these he brought home pinned to the lining of his hat.

"Dr. Weber, Mr. Fritz, was my cousin and my guardian, and directly he returned to Germany he took me from school, and settled me with him at Spinbronn. Agatha was a great friend of mine, though at first she frightened me, but she was a good creature, knew how to make the most delicious sweets, and could sing the most charming songs.

"Sir Thomas and Dr. Weber were on friendly terms, and spent long hours together talking of subjects beyond my comprehension—of transmission of fluids, and mysterious things which they had observed in their travels. Another mystery to me was the singular influence which the doctor appeared to have over the negress, for though she was generally particularly lively, ready to be amused at the slightest thing, yet she trembled like a leaf if she encountered her master's eyes fixed upon her.

"I have told you that birds, and even large animals, were engulfed in the cavern. After the disappearance of the visitors, some of the old inhabitants remembered that about fifty years before a young girl, Loisa Muller, who lived with her grandmother in a cottage near the source, had suddenly disappeared. She had gone out one morning to gather herbs, and was never seen or heard of again, but her apron had been found a few days later near the mouth of the cavern. From that it was evident to all that the skeleton about which Dr. Haselnoss had written so eloquently was that of the poor girl, who had, no doubt, been drawn into the cavern by the mysterious influence which almost daily acted upon more feeble creatures. What that influence was nobody could tell. The superstitious mountaineers believed that the devil inhabited the cavern, and terror spread throughout the district.

"One afternoon, in the month of July, my cousin was occupied in classifying his insects and re-arranging them in their cases. He had found some curious ones the night before, at which he was highly delighted. I was helping by making a needle red-hot in the flame of a candle.

"Sir Thomas, lying back in a chair near the window and smoking a big cigar, was regarding us with a dreamy air. The commodore was very fond of me. He often took me driving with him, and used to like to hear me chatter in English. When the doctor had labelled all his butterflies, he opened the box of larger insects.

"'I caught a magnificent horn-beetle yesterday,' he said, 'the *lucanus cervus* of the Hartz oaks. It is a rare kind.'

"As he spoke I gave him the hot needle, which he passed through the insect preparatory to fixing it on the cork. Sir Thomas, who had taken no notice till then, rose and came to the table on which the case of specimens stood. He looked at the spider of Guyana, and an expression of horror passed over his rubicund features.

"'There,' he said, 'is the most hideous work of the Creator. I tremble only to look at it.'

"And, sure enough, a sudden pallor spread over his face.

"'Bah!' said my guardian, 'all that is childish nonsense. You heard your nurse scream at a spider, you were frightened, and the impression has remained. But if you regard the creature with a strong microscope, you would be astonished at the delicacy of its organs, at their admirable arrangement, and even at their beauty.'

"'It disgusts me,' said the commodore, brusquely. *'Pouff!'*

"And he walked away.

"'I don't know why,' he continued, 'but a spider always freezes my blood.'

"Dr. Weber burst out laughing, but I felt the same as Sir Thomas, and sympathized with him.

"'Yes, cousin, take away that horrid creature,' I cried. 'It is frightful, and spoils all the others.'

"'Little stupid,' said he, while his eyes flashed, 'nobody compels you to look at them. If you are not pleased you can go.'

"Evidently he was angry, and Sir Thomas, who was standing by the window regarding the mountains, turned suddenly round, and took me by the hand.

"'Your guardian loves his spiders, Frantz,' he said, kindly. 'We prefer the trees and the grass. Come with me for a drive.'

"'Yes, go,' returned the doctor, 'and be back to dinner at six.' Then, raising his voice, 'No offense, Sir Thomas,' he said.

"Sir Thomas turned and laughed, and we went out to the carriage.

"The commodore decided to drive himself, and sent back his servant. He placed me on the seat beside him, and we started for Rothalps. While the carriage slowly mounted the sandy hill, I was quiet and sad. Sir Thomas, too, was grave, but my silence seemed to strike him.

"'You don't like the spiders, Frantz; neither do I. But, thank Heaven! there are no dangerous ones in this country. The spider which your cousin has in his box is found in the swampy forests of Guyana, which is always full of hot vapors and burning exhalations, for it needs a high temperature to support its existence. Its immense web, or rather its net, would surround an ordinary thicket, and birds are caught in it, the same as flies in our spiders' webs. But do not think any more about it; let us drink a glass of Burgundy.'

"As he spoke he lifted the cover of the seat, and, taking out a flask of wine, poured me out a full leathern goblet.

"I felt better when I had drunk it, and we continued our way. The carriage was drawn by a little Ardennes pony, which climbed the steep incline as lightly and actively as a goat. The air was full of the murmur of myriads of insects. At our right was the forest of Rothalps. At our left was the cascade of Spinbronn; and the higher we mounted, the bluer became the silver sheets of water foaming in the distance, and the more musical the sound as the water passed over the rocks.

"Both Sir Thomas and I were captivated by the spectacle, and, lost in a reverie, allowed the pony to go on as he would. Soon we were within a hundred paces of the cavern of Spinbronn. The shrubs around the entrance were remarkably green. The water, as it flowed from the cavern, passed over the top of the rock, which was slightly hollowed, and there formed a small lake, from which it again burst forth and descended into the valley below. This lake was shallow, the bottom of it composed of sand and black pebbles, and, although covered with a slight vapor, the water was clear and limpid as crystal.

"The pony stopped to breathe. Sir Thomas got out and walked about for a few seconds.

"'How calm it is,' he said.

"Then, after a minute's silence, he continued: 'Frantz, if you were not here, I should have a bathe in that lake.'

"'Well, why not?' I answered. 'I will take a walk the while. There are numbers of strawberries to be found a little way up that mountain. I can go and get some, and be back in an hour.'

"'Capital idea, Frantz. Dr. Weber pretends that I drink too much Burgundy; we must counteract that with mineral water. This little lake looks inviting.'

"Then he fastened the pony to the trunk of a tree, and waved his hand in adieu. Sitting down on the moss, he commenced to take off his boots, and, as I walked away, he called after me:

"'In an hour, Frantz.'

"They were his last words.

"An hour after, I returned. The pony, the carriage, and Sir Thomas's clothes were all that I could see. The sun was going down and the shadows were lengthening. Not a sound of bird or of insect, and a silence as of death filled the solitude. This silence frightened me. I climbed on to the rock above the cavern, and looked right and left. There was nobody to be seen. I called; no one responded. The sound of my voice repeated by the echoes filled me with terror. Night was coming on. All of a sudden I remembered the disappearance of Loisa Muller, and I hurried down to the front of the cavern. There I stopped in affright, and glancing towards the entrance, I saw two red, motionless points.

"A second later I distinguished some dark moving object farther back in the cavern, farther perhaps than human eye had ever before penetrated; for fear had sharpened my sight, and given all my senses an acuteness of perception which I had never before experienced.

"During the next minute I distinctly heard the chirp, chirp of a grasshopper, and the bark of a dog in the distant village. Then my heart, which had been frozen with terror, commenced to beat furiously, and I heard nothing more. With a wild cry I fled, leaving pony and carriage.

"In less than twenty minutes, bounding over rocks and shrubs, I reached my cousin's door.

"'Run, run,' I cried, in a choking tone, as I burst into the room where Dr. Weber and some invited friends were waiting for us. 'Run, run; Sir Thomas is dead; Sir Thomas is in the cavern,' and I fell fainting on the floor.

"All the village turned out to search for the commodore. At ten o'clock they returned, bringing back Sir Thomas's clothes, the pony, and carriage. They had found nothing, seen nothing, and it was impossible to go ten paces into the cavern.

"During their absence Agatha and I remained in the chimney-corner; I, still trembling with fear, she, with wide open eyes, going from time to time to the window, from which we could see the torches passing to and fro on the mountain, and hear the searchers shout to one another in the still night air.

"At her master's approach Agatha began to tremble. The doctor entered brusquely, pale, with set lips. He was followed by about twenty woodcutters, shaking out the last remnants of their nearly extinguished torches.

"He had barely entered before, with flashing eyes, he glanced round the room, as if in search of something. His eyes fell on the negress, and without a word being exchanged between them the poor woman began to cry.

"'No, no, I will not,' she shrieked.

"'But I will,' returned the doctor, in a hard tone.

"The negress shook from head to foot, as though seized by some invisible power. The doctor pointed to a seat, and she sat down as rigid as a corpse.

"The woodcutters, good, simple people, full of pious sentiments, crossed themselves, and I, who had never yet heard of the hypnotic force, began to tremble, thinking Agatha was dead.

"Dr. Weber approached the negress, and passed his hands over her forehead.

"'Are you ready?' he said.

"'Yes, sir.'

"'Sir Thomas Hawerbrook.'

"At these words she shivered again.

"'Do you see him?'

"'Yes, yes,' she answered, in a gasping voice, 'I see him.'

"'Where is he?'

"'Up there, in the depths of the cavern—dead!'

"'Dead!' said the doctor; 'how?'

"'The spider! oh, the spider!'

"'Calm yourself,' said the doctor, who was very pale. 'Tell us clearly.'

"The spider holds him by the throat—in the depths of the cavern—under the rock—enveloped in its web—*Ah!*'

"Dr. Weber glanced round on the people, who, bending forward, with eyes starting out of their heads, listened in horror.

"Then he continued: 'You see him?'

"'I see him.'

"'And the spider. Is it a big one?'

"'O Master, never, never, have I seen such a big one. Neither on the banks of the Mocaris, nor in the swamps of Konanama. It is as large as my body.'

"There was a long silence. Everybody waited with livid face and hair on end. Only the doctor kept calm. Passing his hand two or three times over the woman's forehead, he recommenced his questions. Agatha described how Sir Thomas's death happened.

"'He was bathing in the lake of the source. The spider saw his bare back from behind. It had been fasting for a long time, and was hungry. Then it saw Sir Thomas's arm on the water. All of a sudden it rushed out, put its claws round the commodore's neck. He cried out, *Mon Dieu, Mon Dieu.*" The spider stung him and went back, and Sir Thomas fell into the water and died. Then the spider returned, spun its web round

him, and swam slowly, gently back to the extremity of the cavern; drawing Sir Thomas after it by the thread attached to its own body.'

"I was still sitting in the chimney corner, overwhelmed with fright. The doctor turned to me.

"'Is it true, Frantz, that the commodore was going to bathe?'

"'Yes, cousin.'

"'At what time?'

"'At four o'clock.'

"'At four o'clock? It was very hot then, was it not?'

"'Yes; oh, yes.'

"'That's it. The monster was not afraid to come out then.'

"He spoke a few unintelligible words, and turned to the peasants.

"'My friends,' he cried, 'that is where the mass of *débris* and those skeletons come from. It is the spider which has frightened away your visitors, and ruined you all. It is there hidden in its web, entrapping its prey into the depths of the cavern. Who can say the number of its victims?'

"He rushed impetuously from the house, and all the woodcutters hurried after him.

"'Bring fagots, bring fagots!' he cried.

"Ten minutes later two immense carts, laden with fagots, slowly mounted the hill; a long file of woodcutters followed, with hatchets on their shoulders. My guardian and I walked in front, holding the horses by the bridle; while the moon lent a vague, melancholy light to the funereal procession.

"At the entrance of the cavern the *cortége* stopped. The torches were lighted and the crowd advanced. The limpid water flowed over the sand, reflecting the blue light of the resinous torches, the rays of which illuminated the tops of the dark, overhanging pines on the rocks above us.

"'It is here you must unload,' said the doctor. 'We must block up the entrance of the cavern.'

"It was not without a feeling of dread that they commenced to execute his order. The fagots fell from the tops of the carts, and the men piled them up before the opening, placing some stakes against them to prevent their being carried away by the water. Towards midnight the opening was literally closed by the fagots. The hissing water below them flowed right and left over the moss, but those on the top were perfectly dry.

"Then Dr. Weber took a lighted torch, and

himself set fire to the pile. The flames spread from twig to twig, and rose towards the sky, preceded by dense clouds of smoke. It was a wild, strange sight, and the woods lighted by the crackling flames had a weird effect. Thick volumes of smoke proceeded from the cavern, while the men standing round, gloomy and motionless, waited with their eyes fixed on the opening. As for me, though I trembled from head to foot, I could not withdraw my gaze.

"We waited quite a quarter of an hour, and Dr. Weber began to be impatient, when a black object, with long, crooked claws, suddenly appeared in the shadow, and then threw itself forward towards the opening. One of the men, fearing that it would leap over the fire, threw his hatchet, and aimed at the creature so well that, for an instant, the blood which flowed from its wound half-quenched the fire, but soon the flame revived, and the horrible insect was consumed.

"Evidently driven by the heat, the spider had taken refuge in its den. Then, suffocated by the smoke, it had returned to the charge, and rushed into the middle of the flames. The body of the horrible creature was as large as a man's, reddish violet in color, and most repulsive in appearance.

"That, Mr. Fritz, is the strange event which destroyed the reputation of Spinbronn. I can swear to the exactitude of my story, but it would be impossible for me to give you an explanation. Nevertheless, admitting that the high temperature of certain thermal springs furnishes the same conditions of existence as the burning climate of Africa and South America, it is not unreasonable to suppose that insects, subject to its influence, can attain an enormous development.

"Whatever may have been the cause, my guardian decided that it would be useless to attempt to resuscitate the waters of Spinbronn; so he sold his house, and returned to America with his negress and his collection."

"The Waters of Death" is a translation of the French story "L'Araignée Crabe," which appeared in Les Contes Fantastiques *(1860). This translation, along with the illustrations by Paul Hardy, was first published in the January 1899 issue of* The Strand Magazine *as "The Spider of Guyana."*

The popular writing team of French authors Émile Erckmann (1822–1899) and Alexandre Chatrian (1826–1890) produced numerous stories, novels and plays. The famed English ghost story writer M. R. James praised the duo's supernatural tales, which include "The Wild Huntsman" (1871) and "The Man-Wolf" (1876).

HOW WEIRD IS THAT?

IN THIS INCIPIENT INSTALLMENT OF HOW WEIRD IS THAT?, LET US FIRST reiterate the topic: Insidious Insects. No, not the band. (Yes, there is a band.)

Insidious. Gradually, subtly harmful. Treacherous. Crafty. Oh yes, we will soon see just how well those words fit this class of creatures.

We won't spend time on mosquitos, the vectors for diseases that sicken and kill vast numbers of people. These are the front-line shock troops, and everybody knows their story. We will focus instead on sneaky guerilla attacks and agents of misfortune.

Indeed, the word "bug" itself has come to mean a hidden problem that is messing up the works. Many have heard that the first use of the term "bug in the system" was a moth that got stuck in a relay in an early computer, but this is not quite so. The term "bug" was already commonplace for hidden defects in 1947, so that the computer scientists who found the moth found it amusing to actually discover a real bug causing a problem. They taped the moth onto their notes, and that notebook is now in the Smithsonian Institution; among the many thousands of moth specimens found there, it might be the only one that influenced the English language. No report on whether it also influenced the WingDings fonts.

But the story is not all fun and laughs. It turns dark in a hurry.

Picture yourself by the bedside of a mortally ill relative, in the middle of a 17th- or 18th-century night, the room dimly lit by a few tapers. The ill one sleeps, and you have only yourself for company. But no, something else is near. A sound starts, like a clock ticking, but it pauses: six ticks, a pause; eight ticks, a pause. All night long, ticks, pause, ticks, pause. Readers in 2020 might no longer have a memory of this, but if you were that bedside companion of centuries ago, you would fully understand that the end was near. For the deathwatch beetle, it was well known, only ticked for that reason. Would it bring death there in the dark, or might one be granted a glimpse of dawn? No further hope could remain.

Of course, the deathwatch beetle's ticking was mostly audible in silent rooms, and so the association was spurious. Indeed, the death that should be watched for is the beetle's own: adults cannot eat, and die shortly after laying the eggs for the next generation of oakwood-munching larvae. And those larvae are hunted by the steely blue beetle, who lays her own eggs at the door, and whose hungry children ramble the halls of the deathwatch's galleries, devouring inhabitants.

We will see these patterns recur in many of the tales to be recounted here. Insects, going about their natural activities, of course, attacking each other in scoundrelly ways, and giving people the creeps, or worse. Coincidentally or not, those seem to be good survival strategies.

Let us begin with insects in our lives. In our

homes, on our skin, under our skin, in our stomachs, inside our heads.

...chewing, chewing quietly, while you read, while you sleep, incessant chewing....

There's actually a bug with "insidious" right in its name. The insidious flower bug: *Orius insidiosus.* This small, handsomely colored true bug eats a lot of crop pests, but it is not entirely a friend, as it sometimes swarms like gnats and delivers bunches of painful bites on humans, who cannot reasonably be mistaken for aphids. But this bug is not subtle in its attentions either; such behavior is hardly insidious. Let's look deeper.

Deeper, under the surface. Quietly chewing away at all times, but seldom detected, are insects trying to gradually gnaw civilization apart. Termites and carpenter ants devour structural wood at shocking rates, and swarm in the thousands at mating time, yet many people would have to admit they have not even seen one. Silverfish and book lice are eating our very knowledge, hiding snugly between the pages. Beetle and moth larvae are chewing clothes, carpets, furniture and flour.

We found a carpenter ant queen on our house the other day, which means that hordes of them are chewing away nearby, possibly in the dozens of ash trees that have been killed in recent years by the emerald ash tree borer, a small invasive beetle that has devastated tens of millions of trees in the eastern half of the United States, so far. That follows the devastation of other tree species by invasive gypsy moths and elm bark beetles spreading the fungus that causes Dutch Elm Disease. These insects stow away on ships like anarchists' time bombs, and also find new welcoming habitats on their home continents as climates change in their favor. Usually the trees in these insects' native ranges are resistant to their attacks, and only dying trees are commonly infested. But when trees that have not faced them before are suddenly swarmed, they rapidly die in staggering numbers. The adults arrive silently, the larvae chew surreptitiously, and soon the forest will please only the woodpeckers.

...chewing, chewing somewhere in the dark, unobserved, undisturbed....

Some infestations can be relatively benign,

but still sneaky and shocking. Honeybee hives are frequently found inside the walls of homes, and must be extracted with care, all the more so now that preserving the bees has become urgent, with populations in such severe decline. Hives of multiple stories have been found, built by hundreds of thousands of bees over periods of decades, with the four-limbed residents completely unaware. Quietly building, and building, and building while they slept.

Yellowjackets often nest hidden away, in the ground, or in rotting stumps. They are easily riled, and may pour out and swarm on somebody so inconsiderate as to mow their lawn.

Deeper still, under a different surface, lurk the toe-biter bugs. These are a kind of giant water bug ("giant" meaning two inches long, but it's big bug in a small pond) that will interrupt your pleasant cooling dip by stabbing you with a sharp beak and sucking your blood. Should you shun the waters as a result, it may fly after you and find you under a porch light one otherwise sublime summer evening.

Pick a part of the body that you would like to think is safe. Now get rid of that notion by reading further. Insects are universally rude house guests.

Bedbugs slip into your bed at night and quietly kiss you, but this is not the tryst of your dreams. These bloodsuckers are hidden away by the time the target of their attention notices the bites, and those red marks ain't lipstick. If one hopes for a clean breakup, they won't go easily, able to live without food for over a year, and to resist many ejection efforts.

Three kinds of lice enjoy your snug and hairy parts. Head lice, body lice and pubic or crab lice have divvied up your body like robbers with stolen loot. They grab a ride on a hair or your clothes, occasionally dropping in on the skin café for a refreshing drink of blood, or to lay a few eggs, then hanging out again. Perhaps some will find themselves neighbors to louse flies that live the same lifestyle—mostly on birds, but occasionally on unfortunate pigeon keepers.

If you run outside to avoid these little pals, their cousins are waiting to spoil your picnic. Kissing bugs wait in the cracks of your deck or picnic table, then quietly bite and suck, as these lovers too want your blood. If they are feeling generous, they might poop in the wound, thus sharing the parasite that causes Chagas disease, deadly especially to children and pets.

In childhood, my ear canals were especially attractive to gnats for some reason, and my mother frequently had to remove them with baby oil to end the painful incursion. Had I known what else could have been going on in there, I might have considered myself lucky. Cockroaches, well known for hiding in large numbers right under our noses, are not picky eaters. Less well known is that they sometimes will hide *inside* noses, or ears, and occasionally get stuck in there. German cockroaches in particular like the smell of earwax, and when they find a nice warm cozy café serving up the good stuff, they will tuck in a bib. Often, though, the waking, itching host sticks a finger in there and crushes the roach, flooding the ear with infectious and fungal goo. Unusual dining by roaches often occurs where they are found in large numbers, or in confined spaces. Sailors on long journeys sometimes must wear gloves to protect their fingernails and cuticles, as well as earplugs, but there is little to be done about eyelids and other targets.

At least the belief that earwigs infest ears is a myth. They are one of only a few orders of insects that won't pester you.

...chewing, chewing away, not far from

where you sit, mindlessly chewing....

In tropical and subtropical regions, various kinds of flies look for alarming nurseries in which to lay eggs. Despite their charming names, the botfly, blowfly and screwfly are difficult to read about without revulsion. These are typically more of a problem for livestock and herd animals, but they do inflict horrors on people as well. Their favored sites include wounds, eyes, and fur that is giving off attractive fecal odors. Eggs are laid in the location, larvae hatch and then chew their way in, and set up shop. The penetrated area is likely to get infected. Larvae may swim through the vitreous of the eye and even penetrate the optic nerve, wreaking havoc with sight. In other cases, the victim can see the growing larva wiggling under the skin. They can be difficult to safely remove, because if they come apart or die in the process, infections and worse are certain. Besides the depredations of the larva itself, these flies carry many dangerous diseases, such as dysentery, tuberculosis, sleeping sickness, river blindness and leishmaniasis.

Insects themselves do not escape these intimate attentions. Perhaps the most insidious are those that creep up on, and live among and inside, insects. The crypt-keeper wasp co-opts a gall wasp's protective home, killing it and using its head to block the door until the newly-grown crypt-keepers are ready to pull it free and fly. There is a *Dinocampus* wasp that inserts an egg and a virus into ladybugs; when ready, the larva departs the ladybug and the virus attacks its nervous system, so that it twitches a dance of the dead to deter attacks on the pupa now nestled in a cocoon underneath the ladybug. Various wasps make a precision sting to paralyze a cockroach, spider or other critter, providing a helpless living larder to its ravenous brood to eat from the inside out.

And there's a fly whose larva causes an ant to leave the nest, so that when it enters the ant's head and cuts it off like launching a lifeboat from a sinking ship, the head will fall to the ground instead of being cleaned up by the ants inside the colony.

Eaten alive, mind-controlled to suicide, beheaded so that larvae can live in one's head—

if any horror writer ever asks where they can get some ideas, they have not explored real nature thoroughly enough. It's like Dante missed an exquisitely horrifying circle of Hell. Think of what Breughel would have painted if he had only looked down.

Another diabolical insect is the ant lion, or more specifically, the immature ant lion (the adults are pretty chill). The larvae are mostly mandible, and they dig a pit in the sand and bury themselves at the bottom. Ants and other critters, out getting their daily steps in, walk or slide into the pit, to be seized by the ant lion, quickly rendering (or rending) their cardio program moot. Even more diabolical is the female chalcid wasp, which purposefully invites itself to the ant lion luncheon, but lays an egg on the larva, so the dining tables are turned.

...chewing, chewing quietly, while you read, while you sleep, incessant chewing....

Various wasps, spiders and even caterpillars mimic the chemistry of ants in order to infiltrate their colonies. And there's a parasitic wasp that finds its caterpillar host by first finding the ant colony that the caterpillar preys upon. When it finds one, it delivers an aggression signal to the ants so that they attack each other and leave the wasp to its business. On the other hand, some caterpillars, fearing an attack by such a wasp, will manipulate ants into serving as their bodyguards by secreting a drug that turns them into aggressive defenders of their kindly neighborhood drug lord.

Such specialized life cycles are theoretically vulnerable to extinction if any link is ever made difficult or impossible. But these behaviors have existed for millions of years; as elaborate as some of them are, they appear to be a robust survival strategy.

Insects inhabit every nook and cranny of this planet. To underscore that there is a war against the insidious every moment of every day and night, over $5 billion is spent annually in the U.S. on insecticides to combat harmful and nuisance insects. Some comfort perhaps, until one considers who is really winning that war. When I escaped suburbia to a rural place to live, I was surprised to learn that 130 million insects per acre were going to be living there with me. Many of these are ants, but the vast majority are springtails, which we never notice or think about. Do not think of angering them; they are very small, but they can afford a few million casualties to take you down.

Who doesn't enjoy a home-cooked meal of delicious ingredients? Expect the insects to seat themselves with you. In fact, the food you buy is legally allowed to contain significant quantities of bug parts, specified in detail by the Food and Drug Administration, so this is really only a secret to those who prefer not to know. Examples include up to 60 mites per 100 grams of frozen broccoli, or 75 in 100 grams of mushrooms; one maggot per 100 grams of tomato paste; four larvae or ten whole insects per 500 grams of berries (you can induce these to wiggle out into view by submerging the berries in water for a while). Wash it down with orange juice and its accompanying one maggot per 250 milliliters. For a snack, how about three ounces of fig cookies and 13 insect heads? None of this accounts for bugs, beetles, weevils and moths that arrive after you place the food into your pantry. If you are like me, talking about food makes you peckish—go ahead and rush to the kitchen now that your appetite is whetted. *Black Infinity* will be here when you get back.

...chewing, chewing quietly, just down the street, or under your feet....

We often think of insects as noisy. Chirping, and buzzing, and trilling—we wouldn't recognize a summer day without these sounds, and there is no experience like the night chorus in a woods filled with katydids and tree crickets. But beneath this din, insects are also secretly communicating with each other by nearly silent vibration. Insects such as carrion beetles and leaf hoppers have systems of vibrating the air or a blade of grass to speak to other insects. Scientists have only begun working out what these sly messages might mean. If these codes can be cracked, perhaps they can be used to repel insects from tasty crops. And, oh yeah, to gain early warning of the insect insurrection.

Other creatures insidiously sneak up on the insects. There are parasitic worms that force crickets to jump in a lake and drown, in order to complete the worm's reproductive cycle. Then there is the flatworm that forces an ant to crawl up a blade of grass, there to wait until it is incidentally eaten by a grazing beast, which will host the worm's larvae. Who's insidious now, eh? In an earlier column we talked about other such examples—there are hundreds of the most astonishing life cycles that are based on manipulating insects.

If we expanded our attention to the insects' close relatives, we could talk about recluse and trap door spiders, or scorpions hiding in your boots, or mites and chiggers that nest and poop in your skin, but they deserve their own full attention some other day, when your nightmares have faded and you need a reminder.

Examining the facts, one must come to terms with the truth: insects are in, on, and all around you at all times, many of them waiting for their chance to take what they need from you. If it's consolation: this has always been the case, every day that you lived your normal life. They will lurk, bite and steal, but they probably won't kill you. Not quickly, anyway.

♥ ♥ ♥

Illustration on page 169 by Allen Koszowksi.

SHIPWRECKED

SYMBIOTIC

TWO NEW DRABBLES BY VONNIE WINSLOW CRIST

THE LAST THING TORBJORN RECALLED BEFORE OPENING HIS EYES IN A strange medical bay, was his vessel plummeting toward Delphi-Seven's surface.

Spotting a nurse, Torbjorn tried to ask about his crew, but a breathing mask muffled his words. When the white-clad individual turned to face him, he raised his hands.

The nurse clicked mandibles and shook her head. She reached for Torbjorn with clawed arms, but stopped short of touching him.

As her complex eyes studied Torbjorn's face, he heard, *We help you*, in his mind.

My crew? Ship? he thought.

Gone, replied the insectoid. *Now, you nest with us.*

"HOW CAN WE DIGEST GALANTHUS VEGETABLES?" INQUIRED STIG AS he ate stir-fry. "They're nothing like Earth plants."

"Gut-flies," replied Denni.

"What!"

"Gut-flies lay eggs on veld-flea mouthparts. When the fleas bite a human, gut-fly eggs transfer to us," explained Denni. "They hatch. The larva migrate to our stomach, release a protective enzyme, and mature. Then, we expel them. The larva become adults. The cycle resumes."

"How does that help us?" asked Stig feeling nauseous.

Denni yawned. "Gut-fly enzyme alters our body chemistry."

"When we leave Galanthus, does it return to normal?"

"Nope," answered Denni. "The relationship is symbiotic and permanent."

"Shipwrecked" and "Symbiotic debut here. Vonnie Winslow Crist, SFWA, HWA, is author of The Enchanted Dagger, Owl Light, The Greener Forest, Murder on Marawa Prime, *and other award-winning books. Her fiction is included in* Amazing Stories, Cast of Wonders, Lost Signals of the Terran Republic, Defending the Future: Dogs of War, Best Speculative Indie Fiction: 2018, Outposts of Beyond, *and elsewhere. A cloverhand who has found so many four-leafed clovers that she keeps them in jars, Vonnie strives to celebrate the power of myth in her writing. Visit her at* <u>vonniewinslowcrist.com</u>

PLANET OF DREAD
Murray Leinster

MORAN, NATURALLY, DID NOT MEAN TO HELP IN THE CARRYING OUT OF THE PLANS WHICH WOULD MEAN HIS DESTRUCTION ONE WAY OR ANOTHER. THE PLANS WERE THRASHED OUT VERY PAINSTAKINGLY, IN FORMAL CONFERENCE ON the space-yacht *Nadine*, with Moran present and allowed to take part in the discussion. From the viewpoint of the *Nadine*'s ship's company, it was simply necessary to get rid of Moran. In their predicament he might have come to the same conclusion; but he was not at all enthusiastic about their decision. He would die of it.

The *Nadine* was out of overdrive and all the uncountable suns of the galaxy shone steadily, remotely, as infinitesimal specks of light of every color of the rainbow. Two hours since, the sun of this solar system had been a vast glaring disk off to port, with streamers and prominences erupting about its edges. Now it lay astern, and Moran could see the planet that had been chosen for his marooning. It was a cloudy world.

There were some dim markings near one lighted limb, but nowhere else. There was an ice cap in view. The rest was—clouds.

The ice cap, by its existence and circular shape, proved that the planet rotated at a not unreasonable rate. The fact that it was water-ice told much. A water-ice ice cap said that there were no poisonous gases in the planet's atmosphere. Sulfur dioxide or chlorine, for example, would not allow the formation of water-ice. It would have to be sulphuric-acid or hydrochloric-acid ice. But the ice cap was simple snow. Its size, too, told about temperature-distribution on the planet. A large cap would have meant a large area with arctic and sub-arctic temperatures, with small temperate and tropical climate-belts. A small one like this meant wide tropical and sub-tropical zones. The fact was verified by the thick, dense cloud-masses which covered most of the surface—all the surface, in fact, outside the ice cap. But since there were ice caps there would be temperate regions. In short, the ice cap proved that a man could endure the air and temperature conditions he would find.

Moran observed these things from the control room of the *Nadine*, then approaching the world on planetary drive. He was to be left here, with no reason ever to expect rescue. Two of the *Nadine*'s four-man crew watched out the same ports as the planet seemed to approach. Burleigh said encouragingly, "It doesn't look too bad, Moran!"

Moran disagreed, but he did not answer. He cocked an ear instead. He heard something. It was a thin, wabbling, keening whine. No natural radiation sounds like that. Moran nodded toward the all-band speaker.

"Do you hear what I do?" he asked sardonically.

Burleigh listened. A distinctly artificial signal came out of the speaker. It wasn't a voice-signal. It wasn't an identification beacon, such as are placed on certain worlds for the convenience of interstellar skippers who need to check their courses on extremely long runs. This was something else.

Burleigh said, "Hm ... Call the others, Harper."

Harper, prudently with him in the control room, put his head into the passage leading away. He called. But Moran observed with grudging respect that he didn't give him a chance to do anything drastic. These people on the *Nadine* were capable. They'd managed to recapture the *Nadine* from him, but they were matter-of-fact about it. They didn't seem to resent what he'd tried to do, or that he'd brought them an indefinite distance in an indefinite direction from their last landing-point, and they had still to re-locate themselves.

THEY'D BEEN ON CORYUS THREE and they'd gotten departure clearance from its spaceport. With clearance-papers in order, they could land unquestioned at any other spaceport and take off again—provided the other spaceport was one they had clearance for. Without rigid control of space travel, any criminal anywhere could escape the consequences of any crime simply by buying a ticket to another world. Moran couldn't have bought a ticket, but he'd tried to get off the planet Coryus on the *Nadine*. The trouble was that the *Nadine* had clearance papers covering five persons aboard—four men and a girl, Carol. Moran made six. Wherever the yacht landed, such a disparity between its documents and its crew would spark an investigation. A lengthy, incredibly minute investigation. Moran, at least, would be picked out as a fugitive from Coryus Three. The others were fugitives too, from some unnamed world Moran did not know. They might be sent back where they came from. In effect, with six people on board instead of five, the *Nadine* could not land anywhere for supplies. With five on board, as her papers declared, she could. And Moran was the extra man whose presence would rouse spaceport officials' suspicion of the rest. So he had to be dumped.

He couldn't blame them. He'd made another difficulty, too. Blaster in hand, he'd made the *Nadine* take off from Coryus III with a trip-tape picked at random for guidance. But the trip-tape had been computed for another starting-point, and when the yacht came out of overdrive it was because the drive had been dismantled in the engine-room. So the ship's location was in doubt. It could have travelled at almost any speed in practically any direction for a length of time that was at least indefinite. A liner could relocate itself without trouble. It had elaborate observational equipment and tri-di star-charts. But smaller craft had to depend on the Galactic Directory. The process would be to find a planet and check its climate and relationship to other planets, and its flora and fauna against descriptions in the Directory. That was the way to find out where one was, when one's position became doubtful. The *Nadine* needed to make a planet-fall for this.

The rest of the ship's company came into the control room. Burleigh waved his hand at the speaker.

"Listen!"

They heard it. All of them. It was a trilling, whining sound among the innumerable random noises to be heard in supposedly empty space.

"That's a marker," Carol announced. "I saw a costume-story tape once that had that sound in it. It marked a first-landing spot on some planet or other, so the people could find that spot again. It was supposed to be a long time ago, though."

"It's weak," observed Burleigh. "We'll try answering it."

Moran stirred, and he knew that every one of the others was conscious of the movement. But they didn't watch him suspiciously. They were alert by long habit. Burleigh said they'd been Underground people, fighting the government of their native world, and they'd gotten away to make it seem the revolt had collapsed. They'd go back later when they weren't expected, and start it up again. Moran considered the story probable. Only people accustomed to desperate actions would have remained so calm when Moran had used desperate measures against them.

Burleigh picked up the transmitter-microphone.

"Calling ground," he said briskly. "Calling ground! We pick up your signal. Please reply."

He repeated the call, over and over and over. There was no answer. Cracklings and hissings came out of the speaker as before, and the thin and reedy wabbling whine continued. The *Nadine* went on toward the enlarging cloudy mass ahead.

Burleigh said, "Well?"

"I think," said Carol, "that we should land. People have been here. If they left a beacon, they may have left an identification of the planet. Then we'd know where we are and how to get to Loris."

Burleigh nodded. The *Nadine* had cleared for Loris. That was where it should make its next landing. The little yacht went on. All five of its proper company watched as the planet's surface enlarged. The ice cap went out of sight around the bulge of the globe, but no markings appeared. There were cloud-banks everywhere, probably low down in the atmosphere. The darker vague areas previously seen might have been highlands.

"I think," said Carol, to Moran, "that if it's too tropical where this signal's coming from, we'll take you somewhere near enough to the ice cap to have an endurable climate. I've been figuring on food, too. That will depend on where we are from Loris because we have to keep enough for ourselves. But we can spare some. We'll give you the emergency kit, anyhow."

THE EMERGENCY KIT contained antiseptics, seeds, and a weapon or two, with elaborate advice to castaways. If somebody were wrecked on an even possibly habitable planet, the especially developed seed-strains would provide food in a minimum of time. It was not an encouraging thought, though, and Moran grimaced.

She hadn't said anything about being sorry that he had to be marooned. Maybe she was, but rebels learn to be practical or they don't live long. Moran wondered, momentarily, what sort of world they came from and why they had revolted, and what sort of setback to the revolt had sent the five off in what they considered a strategic retreat but their government would think defeat. Moran's own situation was perfectly clear.

He'd killed a man on Coryus III. His victim would not be mourned by anybody, and somebody formerly in very great danger would now be safe, which was the reason for what Moran had done. But the dead man had been very important, and the fact that Moran had forced him to fight and killed him in fair combat made no difference. Moran had needed to get off-planet, and fast. But space-travel regulations are especially designed to prevent such escapes.

He'd made a pretty good try, at that. One of the controls on space-traffic required a ship on landing to deposit its fuel-block in the space-port's vaults. The fuel-block was not returned until clearance for departure had been granted. But Moran had waylaid the messenger carrying the *Nadine*'s fuel-block back to that space-yacht. He'd knocked the messenger cold and presented himself at the yacht with the fuel. He was admitted. He put the block in the engine's gate. He duly took the plastic receipt-token the engine only then released, and he drew a blaster. He'd locked two of the *Nadine*'s crew in the engine room, rushed to the control room without encountering the others, dogged the door shut, and threaded in the first trip-tape to come to hand. He punched the take-off button and only seconds later the overdrive. Then the yacht—and Moran —was away. But his present companions got the drive dismantled two days later and once the yacht was out of overdrive they efficiently gave him his choice of surrendering or else. He surrendered, stipulating that he wouldn't be landed back on Coryus; he still clung to hope of avoiding return—which was almost certain anyhow. Because nobody would want to go back to a planet from which they'd carried away a criminal, even though they'd done it unwillingly. Investigation of such a matter might last for months.

Now the space-yacht moved toward a vast mass of fleecy whiteness without any visible features. Harper stayed with the direction-finder. From time to time he gave readings requiring minute changes of course. The wabbling, whining signal was louder now. It became louder than all the rest of the space-noises together.

THE YACHT TOUCHED ATMOSPHERE and Burleigh said, "Watch our height, Carol."

She stood by the echometer. Sixty miles. Fifty. Thirty. A correction of course. Fifteen miles to surface below. Ten. Five. At twenty-five thousand feet there were clouds, which would be particles of ice so small that they floated even so high. Then clear air, then lower clouds, and lower ones still. It was not until six thousand feet above the surface that the planet-wide cloud-level seemed to begin. From there on down it was pure opacity. Anything could exist in that dense, almost palpable grayness. There could be jagged peaks.

The *Nadine* went down and down. At fifteen hundred feet above the unseen surface, the clouds ended. Below, there was only haze. One could see the ground, at least, but there was no horizon. There was only an end to visibility. The yacht descended as if in the center of a sphere in which one could see clearly nearby, less clearly at a little distance, and not at all beyond a quarter-mile or so.

There was a shaded, shadowless twilight under the cloud-bank. The ground looked like no ground ever seen before by anyone. Off to the right a rivulet ran between improbable-seeming banks. There were a few very small hills of most unlikely appearance. It was the ground, the matter on which one would walk, which was strangest. It had color, but the color was not green. Much of it was a pallid, dirty-yellowish white. But there were patches of blue, and curious veinings of black, and here and there were other colors, all of them unlike the normal color of vegetation on a planet with a sol-type sun.

Harper spoke from the direction-finder: "The signal's coming from that mound, yonder."

There was a hillock of elongated shape directly in line with the *Nadine*'s course in descent. Except for the patches of color, it was the only considerable landmark within the half-mile circle in which anything could be seen at all.

The *Nadine* checked her downward motion. Interplanetary drive is rugged and sure, but it does not respond to fine adjustment. Burleigh used rockets, issuing great bellowings of flame, to make actual contact. The yacht hovered, and as the rocket flames diminished slowly she sat down with practically no impact at all. But around her there was a monstrous tumult of smoke and steam. When the rockets went off, she lay in a burned-out hollow some three or four feet deep with a bottom of solid stone. The walls of the hollow were black and scorched. It seemed that at some places they quivered persistently.

There was silence in the control room save for the whining noise which now was almost deafening. Harper snapped off the switch. Then there was true silence. The space-yacht had come to rest possibly a hundred yards from the mound which was the source of the space signal. That mound shared the peculiarity of the ground as far as they could see through the haze. It was not vegetation in any ordinary sense. Certainly it was no mineral surface! The landing-rockets had burned away three or four feet of it, and the edge of the burned area smoked noisesomely, and somehow it looked as if it would reek. And there were places where it stirred.

Burleigh blinked and stared. Then he reached up and flicked on the outside microphones. Instantly there was bedlam. If the landscape was strange, here, the sounds that came from it were unbelievable.

There were grunting noises. There were clickings, uncountable clickings that made a background for all the rest. There were discordant howls and honkings. From time to time something unknown made a cry that sounded very much like a small boy trailing a stick against a picket fence, only much louder. Something hooted, maintaining the noise for an impossibly long time. And persistently, sounding as if they came from far away, there were booming noises, unspeakably deep-bass, made by something alive. And something shrieked in lunatic fashion and something else still moaned from time to time with the volume of a steam-whistle....

"This sounds and looks like a nice place to live," said Moran with fine irony.

Burleigh did not answer. He turned down the outside sound.

"What's that stuff there, the ground?" he demanded. "We burned it away in landing. I've seen something like it somewhere, but never taking the place of grass!"

"That," said Moran as if brightly, "that's what I'm to make a garden in. Of evenings I'll stroll among my thrifty plantings and listen to the delightful sounds of nature."

Burleigh scowled. Harper flicked off the direction-finder.

"The signal still comes from that hillock yonder," he said with finality.

Moran said bitingly: "That ain't no hillock, that's my home!"

Then, instantly he'd said it, he recognized that it could be true. The mound was not a fold in the ground. It was not an up-cropping of the ash-covered stone on which the *Nadine* rested. The enigmatic, dirty-yellow-dirty-red-dirty-blue-and-dirty-black ground cover hid something. It blurred the shape it covered, very much as enormous cobwebs made solid and opaque would have done. But when one looked carefully at the mound, there was a landing-fin sticking

up toward the leaden skies. It was attached to a large cylindrical object of which the fore part was crushed in. The other landing-fins could be traced.

"It's a ship," said Moran curtly. "It crash-landed and its crew set up a signal to call for help. None came, or they'd have turned the beacon off. Maybe they got the lifeboats to work and got away. Maybe they lived as I'm expected to live until they died as I'm expected to die."

Burleigh said angrily: "You'd do what we are doing if you were in our shoes!"

"Sure," said Moran, "but a man can gripe, can't he?"

"You won't have to live here," said Burleigh. "We'll take you somewhere up by the ice cap. As Carol said, we'll give you everything we can spare. And meanwhile we'll take a look at that wreck yonder. There might be an indication in it of what solar system this is. There could be something in it of use to you, too. You'd better come along when we explore."

"Aye, aye, sir," said Moran with irony. "Very kind of you, sir. You'll go armed, sir?"

Burleigh growled: "Naturally!"

"Then since I can't be trusted with a weapon," said Moran, "I suggest that I take a torch. We may have to burn through that loathesome stuff to get in the ship."

"Right," growled Burleigh again. "Brawn and Carol, you'll keep ship. The rest of us wear suits. We don't know what that stuff is outside."

MORAN SILENTLY WENT to the spacesuit rack and began to get into a suit. Modern spacesuits weren't like the ancient crudities with bulging metal casings and enormous globular helmets. Non-stretch fabrics took the place of metal, and constant-volume joints were really practical nowadays. A man could move about in a late-model spacesuit almost as easily as in ship-clothing. The others of the landing party donned their special garments with the brisk absence of fumbling that these people displayed in every action.

"If there's a lifeboat left," said Carol suddenly, "Moran might be able to do something with it."

"Ah, yes!" said Moran. "It's very likely that the ship hit hard enough to kill everybody aboard, but not smash the boats!"

"Somebody survived the crash," said Burleigh, "because they set up a beacon. I wouldn't count on a boat, Moran."

"I don't!" snapped Moran.

He flipped the fastener of his suit. He felt all the openings catch. He saw the others complete their equipment. They took arms. So far they had seen no moving thing outside, but arms were simple sanity on an unknown world. Moran, though, would not be permitted a weapon. He picked up a torch. They filed into the airlock. The inner door closed. The outer door opened. It was not necessary to check the air specifically. The suits would take care of that. Anyhow the ice cap said there were no water-soluble gases in the atmosphere, and a gas can't be an active poison if it can't dissolve.

They filed out of the airlock. They stood on ash-covered stone, only slightly eroded by the processes which made life possible on this planet. They looked dubiously at the scorched, indefinite substance which had been ground before the *Nadine* landed. Moran moved scornfully forward. He kicked at the burnt stuff. His foot went through the char. The hole exposed a cheesy mass of soft matter which seemed riddled with small holes.

Something black came squirming frantically out of one of the openings. It was eight or ten inches long. It had a head, a thorax, and an abdomen. It had wing-cases. It had six legs. It toppled down to the stone on which the *Nadine* rested. Agitatedly, it spread its wing-covers and flew away, droning loudly. The four men heard the sound above even the monstrous cacophony of cries and boomings and grunts and squeaks which seemed to fill the air.

"What the devil—"

Moran kicked again. More holes. More openings. More small tunnels in the cheese-like, curd-like stuff. More black things squirming to view in obvious panic. They popped out everywhere. It was suddenly apparent that the top of the soil, here, was a thick and blanket-like sheet over the whitish stuff. The black creatures lived and thrived in tunnels under it.

Carol's voice came over the helmet-phones.

"They're—bugs!" she said incredulously. "They're beetles! They're twenty times the size of the beetles we humans have been carrying around the galaxy, but that's what they are!"

Moran grunted. Distastefully, he saw his predicament made worse. He knew what had happened here. He could begin to guess at other things to be discovered. It had not been practical for men to move onto new planets and subsist upon the flora and fauna they found there. On some new planets life had never gotten started. On such worlds a highly complex operation was necessary before humanity could move in. A complete ecological complex had to be built up; microbes to break down the rock for soil, bacteria to fix nitrogen to make the soil fertile; plants to grow in the new-made dirt, insects to fertilize the plants so they would multiply, and animals and birds to carry the seeds planet-wide. On most planets, to be sure, there were local, aboriginal plants and animals. But still, terrestrial creatures had to be introduced if a colony was to feed itself. Alien plants did not supply satisfactory food. So an elaborate adaptation job had to be done on every planet before native and terrestrial living things settled down together. It wasn't impossible that the scuttling things were truly beetles, grown large and monstrous under the conditions of a new planet. And the ground....

"This ground stuff," said Moran distastefully, "is yeast or some sort of toadstool growth. This is a seedling world. It didn't have any life on it, so somebody dumped germs and spores and bugs to make it ready for plants and animals eventually. But nobody's come back to finish up the job."

Burleigh grunted a somehow surprised assent. But it wasn't surprising; not wholly so. Once one mentioned yeasts and toadstools and fungi generally, the weird landscape became less than incredible. But it remained actively unpleasant to think of being marooned on it.

"Suppose we go look at the ship?" said Moran unpleasantly. "Maybe you can find out where you are, and I can find out what's ahead of me."

He climbed up on the unscorched surface.

It was elastic. The parchment-like top skin yielded. It was like walking on a mass of springs.

"We'd better spread out," added Moran, "or else we'll break through that skin and be floundering in this mess."

"I'm giving the orders, Moran!" said Burleigh shortly. "But what you say does make sense."

He and the others joined Moran on the yielding surface. Their footing was uncertain, as on a trampoline. They staggered. They moved toward the hillock which was a covered-over wrecked ship.

The ground was not as level as it appeared from the *Nadine*'s control-room. There were undulations. But they could not see more than a quarter-mile in any direction. Beyond that was mist. But Burleigh, at one end of the uneven line of advancing men, suddenly halted and stood staring down at something he had not seen before. The others halted.

Something moved. It came out from behind a very minor spire of whitish stuff that looked like a dirty sheet stretched over a tall stone. The thing that appeared was very peculiar indeed. It was a—worm. But it was a foot thick and ten feet long, and it had a group of stumpy legs at its fore end—where there were eyes hidden behind bristling hair-like growths—and another set of feet at its tail end. It progressed sedately by reaching forward with its fore-part, securing a foothold, and then arching its middle portion like a cat arching its back, to bring its hind part forward. Then it reached forward again. It was of a dark olive color from one end to the other. Its manner of walking was insane but somehow sedate.

Moran heard muffled noises in his helmet-phone as the others tried to speak. Carol's voice came anxiously:

"What's the matter? What do you see?"

Moran said with savage precision, "We're looking at an inchworm, grown up like the beetles only more so. It's not an inchworm any longer. It's a yard-worm." Then he said harshly to the men with him, "It's not a hunting creature on worlds where it's smaller. It's not likely to have turned deadly here. Come on!"

He went forward over the singularly bouncy ground. The others followed. It was to be noted that Hallet the engineer, avoided the huge harmless creature more widely than most.

They reached the mound which was the ship. Moran unlimbered his torch. He said sardonically, "This ship won't do anybody any good. It's old-style. That thick belt around its middle was dropped a hundred years ago, and more." There was an abrupt thickening of the cylindrical hull at the middle. There was an equally abrupt thinning, again, toward the landing-fins. The sharpness of the change was blurred over by the revolting ground-stuff growing everywhere. "We're going to find that this wreck has been here a century at least!"

Without orders, he turned on the torch. A four-foot flame of pure blue-white leaped out. He touched its tip to the fungoid soil. Steam leaped up. He used the flame like a gigantic scalpel, cutting a square a yard deep in the whitish stuff, and then cutting it across and across to destroy it. Thick fumes arose, and quiverings and shakings began. Black creatures in their labyrinths of tunnels began to panic. Off to the right the blanket-like surface ripped and they poured out. They scuttled crazily here and there. Some took to wing. By instinct the other men—the armed ones—moved back from the smoke. They wore space-helmets but they felt that there should be an intolerable smell.

Moran slashed and slashed angrily with the big flame, cutting a way to the metal hull that had fallen here before his grandfather was born. Sometimes the flame cut across things that writhed, and he was sickened. But above all he raged because he was to be marooned here. He could not altogether blame the others. They couldn't land at any colonized world with him on board without his being detected as an extra member of the crew. *His* fate would then be sealed. But they, also, would be investigated. Official queries would go across this whole sector of the galaxy, naming five persons of such-and-such description and such-and-such fingerprints, voyaging in a space-yacht of such-and-such size and registration. The world they came from would claim them as fugitives. They would be returned to it. They'd be executed.

Then Carol's voice came in his helmet-phone. She cried out, "Look out! It's coming! Kill it! Kill it—"

He heard blast-rifles firing. He heard Burleigh pant commands. He was on his way out of the hollow he'd carved when he heard Harper cry out horribly.

He got clear of the newly burned-away stuff. There was still much smoke and steam. But he saw Harper. More, he saw the thing that had Harper.

It occurred to him instantly that if Harper died, there would not be too many people on the *Nadine*. They need not maroon him. In fact, they wouldn't dare.

A ship that came in to port with two few on board would be investigated as thoroughly as one that had too many. Perhaps more thoroughly. So if Harper were killed, Moran would be needed to take his place. He'd go on from here in the *Nadine*, necessarily accepted as a member of her crew.

Then he rushed, the flame-torch making a roaring sound.

II

THEY WENT BACK to the *Nadine* for weapons more adequate for encountering the local fauna when it was over. Blast-rifles were not effective against such creatures as these. Torches were contact weapons but they killed. Blast-rifles did not. And Harper needed to pull himself together again, too. Also, neither Moran nor any of the others wanted to go back to the still un-entered wreck while the skinny, somehow disgusting legs of the thing still kicked spasmodically—quite separate—on the whitish ground-stuff. Moran had disliked such creatures in miniature form on other worlds. Enlarged like this....

IT SEEMED INSANE that such creatures, even in miniature, should painstakingly be brought across light-years of space to the new worlds men settled on. But it had been found to be necessary. The ecological system in which human beings belonged had turned out to be infinitely complicated. It had turned out, in fact, to be the ecological system of Earth, and unless all parts of the complex were present, the total was subtly or glaringly wrong. So mankind distastefully ferried pests as well as useful creatures to its new worlds as they were made ready for settlement. Mosquitos throve on the inhabited globes of the Rim Stars. Roaches twitched nervous antennae on the settled planets of the Coal-sack. Dogs on Antares had fleas, and scratched their bites, and humanity spread through the galaxy with an attendant train of insects and annoyances. If they left their pests behind, the total system of checks and balances which make life practical would get lopsided. It would not maintain itself. The vagaries that could result were admirably illustrated in and on the landscape outside the *Nadine*. Something had been left out of the seeding of this planet. The element—which might be a bacterium or a virus or almost anything at all—the element that kept creatures at the size called "normal" was either missing or inoperable here. The results were not desirable.

HARPER DRANK THIRSTILY. Carol had watched from the control room. She was still pale. She looked strangely at Moran.

"You're sure it didn't get through your suit?" Burleigh asked insistently of Harper.

Moran said sourly, "The creatures have changed size. There's no proof they've changed anything else. Beetles live in tunnels they make in fungus growths. The beetles and the tunnels are larger, but that's all. Inchworms travel as they always did. They move yards instead of inches, but that's all. Centipedes—"

"It was—" said Carol unsteadily. "It was thirty feet long!"

"Centipedes," repeated Moran, "catch prey with their legs. They always did. Some of them trail poison from their feet. We can play a blow-torch over Harper's suit and any poison will be burned away. You can't burn a space-suit!"

"We certainly can't leave Moran here!" said Burleigh uneasily.

"He kept Harper from being killed!" said Carol. "Your blast-rifles weren't any good. The—creatures are hard to kill."

"Very hard to kill," agreed Moran. "But I'm

not supposed to kill them. I'm supposed to live with them! I wonder how we can make them understand they're not supposed to kill me either?"

"I'll admit," said Burleigh, "that if you'd let Harper get killed, we'd have been forced to let you take his identity and not be marooned, to avoid questions at the spaceport on Loris. Not many men would have done what you did."

"Oh, I'm a hero," said Moran. "Noble Moran, that's me! What the hell would you want me to do? I didn't think! I won't do it again. I promise!"

The last statement was almost true. Moran felt a squeamish horror at the memory of what he'd been through over by the wrecked ship. He'd come running out of the excavation he'd made. He had for weapon a four-foot blue-white flame, and there was a monstrous creature running directly toward him, with Harper lifted off the ground and clutched in two gigantic, spidery legs. It was no less than thirty feet long, but it was a centipede. It travelled swiftly on grisly, skinny, pipe-thin legs. It loomed over Moran as he reached the surface and he automatically thrust the flame at it. The result was shocking. But the nervous systems of insects are primitive. It is questionable that they feel pain. It is certain that separated parts of them act as if they had independent life. Legs—horrible things—sheared off in the flame of the torch, but the grisly furry thing rushed on until Moran slashed across its body with the blue-white fire. Then it collapsed. But Harper was still held firmly and half the monster struggled mindlessly to run on while another part was dead. Moran fought it almost hysterically, slicing off legs and wanting to be sick when their stumps continued to move as if purposefully, and the legs themselves kicked and writhed rhythmically. But he bored in and cut at the body and ultimately dragged Harper clear.

Afterward, sickened, he completed cutting it to bits with the torch. But each part continued nauseatingly to move. He went back with the others to the *Nadine*. The blast-rifles had been almost completely without effect upon the creature because of its insensitive nervous system.

"I think," said Burleigh, "that it is only fair for us to lift from here and find a better part of this world to land Moran in."

"Why not another planet?" asked Carol.

"It could take weeks," said Burleigh harassedly. "We left Coryus three days ago. We ought to land on Loris before too long. There'd be questions asked if we turned up weeks late! We can't afford that! The spaceport police would suspect us of all sorts of things. They might decide to check back on us where we came from. We can't take the time to hunt another planet!"

"Then your best bet," said Moran caustically, "is to find out where we are. You may be so far from Loris that you can't make port without raising questions anyhow. But you might be almost on course. I don't know! But let's see if that wreck can tell us. I'll go by myself if you like."

He went into the airlock, where his suit and the others had been sprayed with a corrosive solution while the outside air was pumped out and new air from inside the yacht admitted. He got into the suit. Harper joined him.

"I'm going with you," he said shortly. "Two will be safer than one—both with torches."

"Too, too true!" said Moran sardonically.

He bundled the other suits out of the airlock and into the ship. He checked his torch. He closed the inner lock door and started the pump. Harper said, "I'm not going to try to thank you—"

"Because," Moran snapped, "you wouldn't have been on this planet to be in danger if I hadn't tried to capture the yacht. I know it!"

"That wasn't what I meant to say!" protested Harper.

Moran snarled at him. The lock-pump stopped and the ready-for exit light glowed. They pushed open the outer door and emerged. Again there was the discordant, almost intolerable din. It made no sense. The cries and calls and stridulations they now knew to be those of insects had no significance. The unseen huge creatures made them without purpose. Insects do not challenge each other like birds or make mating-calls like animals. They make noises because it is their nature. The noises have no meaning. The two men started toward the wreck to which Moran had partly burned a passageway. There were clickings from underfoot all around them. Moran said abruptly, "Those clicks come from the beetles in their tunnels underfoot. They're practically a foot long. How big do you suppose bugs grow here—and why?"

Harper did not answer. He carried a flame-torch like the one Moran had used before. They went unsteadily over the elastic, yielding stuff underfoot. Harper halted, to look behind. Carol's voice came in the helmet-phones.

"We're watching out for you. We'll try to warn you if—anything shows up."

"Better watch me!" snapped Moran. "If I should kill Harper after all, you might have to pass me for him presently!"

He heard a small, inarticulate sound, as if Carol protested. Then he heard an angry shrill whine. He'd turned aside from the direct line to the wreck. Something black, the size of a fair-sized dog, faced him belligerently. Multiple lensed eyes, five inches across, seemed to regard him in a peculiarly daunting fashion. The creature had a narrow, unearthly, triangular face, with mandibles that worked from side to side instead of up and down like an animal's jaws. The head was utterly unlike any animal such as breed and raise their young and will fight for them. There was a small thorax, from which six spiny, glistening legs sprang. There was a bulbous abdomen.

"This," said Moran coldly, "is an ant. I've stepped on them for no reason, and killed them. I've probably killed many times as many without knowing it. But this could kill me."

The almost yard-long enormity standing two and a half feet high, was in the act of carrying away a section of one of the legs of the giant centipede Moran had killed earlier. It still moved. The leg was many times the size of the ant. Moran moved toward it. It made a louder buzzing sound, threatening him.

Moran cut it apart with a slashing sweep of the flame that a finger-touch sent leaping from his torch. The thing presumably died, but it continued to writhe senselessly.

"I killed this one," said Moran savagely, "because I remembered something from my childhood. When one ant finds something to eat and can't carry it all away, it brings back its friends to get the rest. The big thing I killed would be such an item. How'd you like to have a horde of these things about us? Come on!"

Through his helmet-phone he heard Harper breathing harshly. He led the way once more toward the wreck.

BLACK BEETLES SWARMED about when he entered the cut in the mould-yeast soil. They popped out of tunnels as if in astonishment that what had been subterranean passages suddenly opened to the air. Harper stepped on one, and

it did not crush. It struggled frantically and he almost fell. He gasped. Two of the creatures crawled swiftly up the legs of Moran's suit, and he knocked them savagely away. He found himself grinding his teeth in invincible revulsion.

They reached the end of the cut he'd made in the fungus-stuff. Metal showed past burned-away soil. Moran growled, "You keep watch. I'll finish the cut."

The flame leaped out. Dense clouds of smoke and steam poured out and up. With the intolerably bright light of the torch overwhelming the perpetual grayness under the clouds and playing upon curling vapors, the two space-suited men looked like figures in some sort of inferno.

Carol's voice came anxiously into Moran's helmet-phone. "Are you all right?"

"So far, both of us," said Moran sourly. "I've just uncovered the crack of an airlock door."

He swept the flame around again. A mass of undercut fungus toppled toward him. He burned it and went on. He swept the flame more widely. There was carbonized matter from the previously burned stuff on the metal, but he cleared all the metal.

Carol's voice again: "There's something flying.... It's huge! It's a wasp! It's—monstrous!"

Moran growled, "Harper, we're in a sort of trench. If it hovers, you'll burn it as it comes down. Cut through its waist. It won't crawl toward us along the trench. It'd have to back toward us to use its sting."

He burned and burned, white light glaring upon a mass of steam and smoke which curled upward and looked as if lightning-flashes played within it.

Carol's voice: "It—went on past.... It was as big as a cow!"

Moran wrenched at the port-door. It partly revolved. He pulled. It fell outward. The wreck was not standing upright on its fins. It lay on its side. The lock inside the toppled-out port was choked with a horrible mass of thread-like fungi. Moran swept the flame in. The fungus shriveled and was not. He opened the inner lock-door. There was pure blackness within. He held the torch for light.

For an instant everything was confusion, because the wreck was lying on its side instead of standing in a normal position. Then he saw a sheet of metal, propped up to be seen instantly by anyone entering the wrecked space-vessel.

Letters burned into the metal gave a date a century and a half old. Straggly torch-writing said baldly:

This ship the Malabar crashed here on Tethys II a week ago. We cannot repair. We are going on to Candida III in the boats. We are carrying what bessendium we can with us. We resign salvage rights in this ship to its finders, but we have more bessendium with us. We will give that to our rescuers.

Jos. White, Captain

Moran made a peculiar, sardonic sound like a bark.

"Calling the *Nadine*!" he said in mirthless amusement. "This planet is Tethys Two. Do you read me? Tethys II! Look it up!"

A pause. Then Carol's voice, relieved: "Tethys is in the Directory! That's good!" There was the sound of murmurings in the control-room behind her. "Yes!... Oh—wonderful! It's not far off the course we should have followed! We won't be suspiciously late at Loris! Wonderful!"

"I share your joy," said Moran sarcastically. "More information! The ship's name was the *Malabar*. She carried bessendium among her cargo. Her crew went on to Candida III a hundred and fifty years ago, leaving a promise to pay in more bessendium whoever should rescue them. *More* bessendium! Which suggests that some bessendium was left behind."

Silence. The bald memorandum left behind the vanished crew was, of course, pure tragedy. A ship's lifeboat could travel four light-years, or possibly even six. But there were limits. A cast-away crew had left this world on a desperate journey to another in the hope that life there would be tolerable. If they arrived, they waited for some other ship to cross the illimitable emptiness and discover either the beacon here or one they'd set up on the other world. The likelihood was small, at best. It had worked out zero. If the lifeboats made Candida III, their crews stayed there because they could go no farther. They'd died there, because if they'd been found this ship would have been visited and its cargo salvaged.

Moran went inside. He climbed through the compartments of the toppled craft, using his torch for light. He found where the cargo-hold had been opened from the living part of the ship. He saw the cargo. There were small, obviously heavy boxes in one part of the hold. Some had been broken open. He found scraps of purple bessendium ore dropped while being carried to the lifeboats. A century and a half ago it had not seemed worth while to pick them up, though bessendium was the most precious material in the galaxy. It couldn't be synthesized. It had to be made by some natural process not yet understood, but involving long-continued pressures of megatons to the square inch with temperatures in the millions of degrees. It was purple. It was crystalline. Fractions of it in blocks of other metals made the fuel-blocks that carried liners winging through the void. But here were pounds of it dropped carelessly....

Moran gathered a double handful. He slipped it in a pocket of his space-suit. He went clambering back to the lock.

He heard the roaring of a flame-torch. He found Harper playing it squeamishly on the wriggling fragments of another yard-long ant. It had explored the trench burned out of the fungus soil and down to the rock. Harper'd killed it as it neared him.

"That's three of them I've killed," said Harper in a dogged voice. "There seem to be more."

"Did you hear my news?" asked Moran sardonically.

"Yes," said Harper. "How'll we get back to the *Nadine*?"

"Oh, we'll fight our way through," said Moran, as sardonically as before. "We'll practice splendid heroism, giving battle to ants who think we're other ants trying to rob them of some fragments of an over-sized dead centipede. A splendid cause to fight for, Harper!"

He felt an almost overpowering sense of irony. The quantity of bessendium he'd seen was riches incalculable. The mere handful of crystals in his pocket would make any man wealthy if he could get to a settled planet and sell them. And there was much, much more back in the cargo-hold of the wreck. He'd seen it.

But his own situation was unchanged. Bessendium could be hidden somehow—perhaps between the inner and outer hulls of the *Nadine*. But it was not possible to land the *Nadine* at any spaceport with an extra man aboard her. In a sense, Moran might be one of the richest men in the galaxy in his salvagers' right to the treasure in the wrecked *Malabar*'s hold. But he could not use that treasure to buy his way to a landing on a colonized world.

Carol's voice; she was frightened. "Something's coming! It's—terribly big! It's coming out of the mist!"

Moran pushed past Harper in the trench that ended at the wreck's lock-door. He moved on until he could see over the edge of that trench as it shallowed. Now there were not less than forty of the giant ants about the remnants of the monstrous centipede Moran had killed. They moved about in great agitation. There was squabbling. Angry, whining stridulations filled the air beneath the louder and more gruesome sounds from farther-away places. It appeared that scouts and foragers from two different ant cities had come upon the treasure of dead—if twitching—meat of Moran's providing. They differed about where the noisome booty should be taken. Some ants pulled angrily against each other, whining shrilly. He saw individual ants running frantically away in two different directions. They would be couriers, carrying news of what amounted to a frontier incident in the city-state civilization of the ants.

Then Moran saw the giant thing of which Carol spoke. It was truly huge, and it had a gross, rounded body, and a ridiculously small thorax, and its head was tiny and utterly mild in expression. It walked with an enormous, dainty deliberation, placing small spiked feet at the end of fifteen-foot legs very delicately in place as it moved. Its eyes were multiple and huge, and its forelegs, though used so deftly for walking, had a horrifying set of murderous, needle-sharp saw-teeth along their edges.

It looked at the squabbling ants with its gigantic eyes that somehow appeared like dark glasses worn by a monstrosity. It moved primly, precisely toward them. Two small black creatures tugged at a hairy section of a giant centipede's leg. The great pale-green creature—a mantis; a praying mantis twenty feet tall in its giraffe-like walking position—the great creature loomed over them, looking down as through sunglasses. A foreleg moved like lightning. An ant weighing nearly as much as a man stridulated shrilly, terribly, as it was borne aloft. The mantis closed its arm-like forelegs upon it, holding it as if piously and benignly contemplating it. Then it ate it, very much as a man might eat an apple, without regard to the convulsive writhing of its victim.

It moved on toward the denser fracas among the ants. Suddenly it raised its ghastly saw-toothed forelegs in an extraordinary gesture. It was the mantis' spectral attitude, which seemed a pose of holding out its arms in benediction. But its eyes remained blind-seeming and enigmatic—again like dark glasses.

Then it struck. Daintily, it dined upon an ant. Upon another. Upon another and another and another.

From one direction parties of agitated and hurrying black objects appeared at the edge of the mist. They were ants of a special caste—warrior-ants with huge mandibles designed for fighting in defense of their city and its social system, and its claim to fragments of dead centipedes. From another direction other parties of no less truculent warriors moved with the swiftness and celerity of a striking task force. All the air was filled with the deep-bass notes of something huge, booming beyond visibility, and the noises as of sticks trailed against picket fences, and hootings which were produced by the rubbing of serrated leg-joints against chitinous diaphragms. But now a new tumult arose.

From forty disputatious *formicidae*, whining angrily at each other over the stinking remains of the monster Moran had killed, the number of ants involved in the quarrel became hundreds. But more and more arrived. The special caste of warriors bred for fighting was not numerous enough to take care of the provocative behavior of foreign foragers. There was a general mobilization in both unseen ant-city states. They became nations in arms. Their populations rushed to the scene of conflict. The burrows and dormitories and eating-chambers of the underground nations were swept clean of occupants. Only the nurseries retained a skeleton staff of nurses—the nurseries and the excavated palace occupied by the ant-queen and her staff of servants and administrators. All the resources of two populous ant-nations were flung into the fray.

From a space of a hundred yards or less, containing mere dozens of belligerent squabblers, the dirty-white ground of the fungus-plain became occupied by hundreds of snapping, biting combatants. They covered—they fought over—the half of an acre. There were contending battalions fighting as masses in the center, while wings of fighting creatures to right and left were less solidly arranged. But reinforcements poured out of the mist from two directions, and momently the situation changed. Presently the battle covered an acre. Groups of fresh fighters arriving from the city to the right uttered shrill stridulations and charged upon the flank of their enemies. Simultaneously, reinforcements from the city to the left flung themselves into the fighting-line near the center.

Formations broke up. The battle disintegrated into an indefinite number of lesser combats; troops or regiments fighting together often moved ahead with an appearance of invincibility, but suddenly they broke and broke again until there was only a complete confusion of unorganized single combats in which the fighters rolled over and over, struggling ferociously with mandible and claw to destroy each other. Presently the battle raged over five acres. Ten. Thousands upon thousands of black, glistening, stinking creatures tore at each other in murderous ferocity. Whining, squealing battle cries arose and almost drowned out the deeper notes of larger but invisible creatures off in the mist.

Moran and Harper got back to the *Nadine* by a wide detour past warriors preoccupied with each other just before the battle reached its most savage stage. In that stage, the space-yacht was included in the battleground. Fights went on about its landing-fins. Horrifying duels could be followed by scrapings and bumpings against its hull. From the yacht's ports the fighting ants looked like infuriated machines, engaged in each other's destruction. One might see a warrior of unidentified allegiance with its own abdomen ripped open, furiously rending an enemy without regard to its own mortal wound. There were those who had literally been torn in half, so that only head and thorax remained, but they fought on no less valiantly than the rest.

At the edges of the fighting such cripples were more numerous. Ants with antenna shorn off or broken, with legs missing, utterly doomed —they sometimes wandered forlornly beyond the fighting, the battle seemingly forgotten. But even such dazed and incapacitated casualties came upon each other. If they smelled alike, they ignored each other. Every ant-city has its particular smell which its inhabitants share. Possession of the national odor is at once a certificate of citizenship in peacetime and a uniform in war. When such victims of the battle came upon enemy walking wounded, they fought.

And the giant praying mantis remained placidly and invulnerably still. It plucked single fighters from the battle and dined upon them while they struggled, and plucked other fighters, and consumed them. It ignored the battle and the high purpose and self-sacrificing patriotism of the ants. Immune to them and disregarded by them, it fed on them while the battle raged.

Presently the gray light overhead turned faintly pink, and became a deeper tint and then crimson. In time there was darkness. The noise of battle ended. The sounds of the day diminished and ceased, and other monstrous outcries took their place.

There were bellowings in the blackness without the *Nadine*. There were chirpings become baritone, and senseless uproars which might be unbelievable modifications of once-shrill and once-tranquil night-sounds of other worlds. And there came a peculiar, steady, unrhythmic pattering sound. It seemed like something falling upon the blanket-like upper surface of the soil.

Moran opened the airlock door and thrust out a torch to see. Its intolerably bright glare showed the battlefield abandoned. Most of the dead and wounded had been carried away. Which, of course, was not solicitude for the wounded or reverence for the dead heroes. Dead ants, like dead centipedes, were booty of the only kind the creatures of this world could know. The dead were meat. The wounded were dead before they were carried away.

Moran peered out, with Carol looking affrightedly over his shoulder. The air seemed to shine slightly in the glare of the torch. The pattering sound was abruptly explained. Large, slow, widely-separated raindrops fell heavily and steadily from the cloud-banks overhead. Moran could see them strike. Each spot of wetness glistened briefly. Then the rain-drop was absorbed by the ground.

But there were other noises than the ceaseless tumult on the ground. There were sounds in the air; the beating of enormous wings. Moran looked up, squinting against the light. There were things moving about the black sky. Gigantic things.

Something moved, too, across the diminishingly lighted surface about the yacht. There were glitterings. Shining armor. Multifaceted eyes. A gigantic, horny, spiked object crawled toward the torch-glare, fascinated by it. Something else dived insanely. It splashed upon the flexible white surface twenty yards away, and struggled upward and took crazily off again. It careened blindly.

It hit the yacht, a quarter-ton of night-flying beetle. The air seemed filled with flying things. There were moths with twenty-foot wings and eyes which glowed like rubies in the torch's light. There were beetles of all sizes from tiny six-inch things to monsters in whom Moran did not believe even when he saw them. All were drawn by the light which should not exist under the cloud-bank. They droned and fluttered and performed lunatic evolutions, coming always closer to the flame.

Moran cut off the torch and closed the lock-door from the inside.

"We don't load bessendium tonight," he said with some grimness. "To have no light, with what crawls about in the darkness, would be suicide. But to use lights would be worse. If you people are going to salvage the stuff in that wreck, you'll have to wait for daylight. At least then you can see what's coming after you."

They went into the yacht proper. There was no longer any question about the planet's air. If insects which were descendants of terrestrial forms could breathe it, so could men. When the first insect-eggs were brought here, the air had to be fit for them if they were to survive. It would not have changed.

Burleigh sat in the control-room with a double handful of purple crystals before him.

"This," he said when Moran and Carol re-entered, "this is bessendium past question. I've been thinking what it means."

"Money," said Moran drily. "You'll all be rich. You'll probably retire from politics."

"That wasn't exactly what I had in mind," said Burleigh distastefully. "You've gotten us into the devil of a mess, Moran!"

"For which," said Moran with ironic politeness, "there is a perfect solution. You kill me, either directly or by leaving me marooned here."

Burleigh scowled. "We have to land at spaceports for supplies. We can't hope to hide you, it's required that landed ships be sterilized against infections from off-planet. We can't pass you as a normal passenger. You're not on the ship's papers and they're alteration-proof. Nobody's ever been able to change a ship's papers and not be caught! We could land and tell the truth, that you hijacked the ship and we finally overpowered you. But there are reasons against that."

"Naturally!" agreed Moran. "I'd be killed anyhow and you'd be subject to intensive investigation. And you're fugitives as much as I am."

"Just so," admitted Burleigh.

Moran shrugged.

"Which leaves just one answer. You maroon me and go on your way."

Burleigh said painfully, "There's this bessendium. If there's more—especially if there's more—we can leave you here with part of it. When we get far enough away, we charter a ship to come

and get you. It'll be arranged. Somebody will be listed as of that ship's company, but he'll slip away from the spaceport and not be on board at all. Then you're picked up and landed using his name."

"If," said Moran ironically, "I am alive when the ship gets here. If I'm not, the crew of the chartered ship will be in trouble, short one man on return to port. You'll have trouble getting anybody to run that risk!"

"We're trying to work out a way to save you!" insisted Burleigh angrily. "Harper would have been killed but for you. And—this bessendium will finance the underground work that will presently make a success of our revolution. We're grateful! We're trying to help you!"

"So you maroon me," said Moran. Then he said, "But you've skipped the real problem! If anything goes wrong, Carol's in it! There's no way to do anything without risk for her! That's the problem! I could kill all you characters, land somewhere on a colonized planet exactly as you landed here, and be gone from the yacht on foot before anybody could find me! But I have a slight aversion to getting a girl killed or killing her just for my own convenience. It's settled. I stay here. You can try to arrange the other business if you like. But it's a bad gamble."

Carol was very pale. Burleigh stood up.

"You said that, I didn't. But I don't think we should leave you here. Up near the ice cap should be infinitely better for you. We'll load the rest of the bessendium tomorrow, find you a place, leave you a beacon, and go."

He went out. Carol turned a white face to Moran.

"Is that—is that the real trouble? Do you really—"

Moran looked at her stonily.

"I like to make heroic gestures," he told her. "Actually, Burleigh's a very noble sort of character himself. He proposes to leave me with treasure that he could take. Even more remarkably, he proposes to divide up what you take, instead of applying it all to further his political ideals. Most men like him would take it all for the revolution!"

"But—but—"

Carol's expression was pure misery. Moran

walked deliberately across the control room. He glanced out of a port. A face looked in. It filled the transparent opening. It was unthinkable. It was furry. There were glistening chitinous areas. There was a proboscis like an elephant's trunk, curled horribly. The eyes were multiple and mad.

It looked in, drawn and hypnotized by the light shining out on this nightmare world from the control-room ports.

Moran touched the button that closed the shutters.

III

WHEN MORNING CAME, its arrival was the exact reversal of the coming of night. In the beginning there was darkness, and in the darkness there was horror.

The creatures of the night untiringly filled the air with sound, and the sounds were discordant and gruesome and revolting. The creatures of this planet were gigantic. They should have adopted new customs appropriate to the dignity of their increased size. But they hadn't. The manners and customs of insects are immutable. They feed upon specific prey—spiders are an exception, but they are not insects at all—and they lay their eggs in specific fashion in specific places, and they behave according to instincts which are so detailed as to leave them no choice at all in their actions. They move blindly about, reacting like automata of infinite complexity which are capable of nothing not built into them from the beginning. Centuries and millennia do not change them. Travel across star-clusters leaves them with exactly the capacities for reaction that their remotest ancestors had, before men lifted off ancient Earth's green surface.

The first sign of dawn was deep, deep, deepest red in the cloud-bank no more than fifteen hundred feet overhead. The red became brighter, and presently was as brilliant as dried blood. Again presently it was crimson over all the half-mile circle that human eyes could penetrate. Later still—but briefly—it was pink. Then the sky became gray. From that color it did not change again.

Moran joined Burleigh in a survey of the landscape from the control-room. The battlefield was empty now. Of the thousands upon thousands of stinking combatants who'd rent and torn each other the evening before, there remained hardly a trace. Here and there, to be sure, a severed saw-toothed leg remained. There were perhaps as many as four relatively intact corpses not yet salvaged. But something was being done about them.

There were tiny, brightly-banded beetles hardly a foot long which labored industriously over such frayed objects. They worked agitatedly in the yeasty stuff which on this world took the place of soil. They excavated, beneath the bodies of the dead ants, hollows into which those carcasses could descend. They pushed the yeasty, curdy stuff up and around the sides of those to-be-desired objects. The dead warriors sank little by little toward oblivion as the process went on. The up-thrust, dug-out material collapsed upon them as they descended. In a very little while they would be buried where no larger carrion-eater would discover them, and then the brightly-colored sexton beetles would begin a banquet to last until only fragments of chitinous armor remained.

BUT MORAN AND BURLEIGH, in the *Nadine*'s control room, could hardly note such details.

"You saw the cargo," said Burleigh, frowning. "How's it packed? The bessendium, I mean."

"It's in small boxes too heavy to be handled easily," said Moran. "Anyhow the *Malabar*'s crew broke some of them open to load the stuff on their lifeboats."

"The lifeboats are all gone?"

"Naturally," said Moran. "At a guess they'd have used all of them even if they didn't need them for the crew. They could carry extra food and weapons and such."

"How much bessendium is left?"

"Probably twenty boxes unopened," said Moran. "I can't guess at the weight, but it's a lot. They opened six boxes." He paused. "I have a suggestion."

"What?"

"When you've supplied yourselves," said Moran, "leave some spaceport somewhere with papers saying you're going to hunt for minerals on some plausible planet. You can get such a clearance. Then you can return with bessendium coming out of the *Nadine*'s waste-pipes and people will be surprised but not suspicious. You'll file for mineral rights, and cash your cargo. Everybody will get busy trying to grab off the mineral rights for themselves. You can clear out and let them try to find the bessendium lode. You'll be allowed to go, all right, and you can settle down somewhere rich and highly respected."

"Hmmm," said Burleigh. Then he said uncomfortably, "One wonders about the original owners of the stuff."

"After a hundred and fifty years," said Moran, "who'd you divide with? The insurance company that paid for the lost ship? The heirs of the crew? How'd you find them?" Then he added amusedly, "Only revolutionists and enemies of governments would be honest enough to worry about that!"

Brawn came into the control room. He said broodingly that breakfast was ready. Moran had never heard him speak in a normally cheerful voice. When he went out, Moran said, "I don't suppose he'll be so gloomy when he's rich!"

"His family was wiped out," said Burleigh curtly, "by the government we were fighting. The girl he was going to marry, too."

"Then I take back what I said," said Moran ruefully.

They went down to breakfast. Carol served it. She did not look well. Her eyes seemed to show that she'd been crying. But she treated Moran exactly like anyone else. Harper was very quiet, too. He took very seriously the fact that Moran had saved his life at the risk of his own the day before. Brawn breakfasted in a subdued, moody fashion. Only Hallet seemed to have reacted to the discovery of a salvageable shipment of bessendium that should make everybody rich —everybody but Moran, who was ultimately responsible for the find.

"Burleigh," said Hallet expansively, "says the stuff you brought back from the wreck is worth fifty thousand credits, at least. What's the whole shipment worth?"

"I've no idea," said Moran. "It would certainly pay for a fleet of space-liners, and I'd give all of it for a ticket on one of them."

"But how much is there in bulk?" insisted Hallet.

"I saw that half a dozen boxes had been broken open and emptied for the lifeboat voyagers," Moran told him. "I didn't count the balance, but there were several times as many untouched. If they're all full of the same stuff, you can guess almost any sum you please."

"Millions, eh?" said Hallet. His eyes glistened. "Billions? Plenty for everybody?"

"There's never plenty for more than one," said Moran mildly. "That's the way we seem to be made."

Burleigh said suddenly, "I'm worried about getting the stuff aboard. We can't afford to lose anybody, and if we have to fight the creatures here and every time we kill one its carcass draws others."

Moran took a piece of bread. He said, "I've been thinking about survival tactics for myself as a castaway. I think a torch is the answer. In any emergency on the yeast surface, I can burn a hole and drop down in it. The monsters are stupid. In most cases they'll go away because they stop seeing me. In the others, they'll come to the hole and I'll burn them. It won't be pleasant, but it may be practical."

Burleigh considered it.

"It may be," he admitted. "It may be."

Hallet said, "I want to see that work before I trust the idea."

"Somebody has to try it," agreed Moran. "Anyhow, my life's going to depend on it."

Carol left the room. Moran looked after her as the door closed.

"She doesn't like the idea of our leaving you behind," said Burleigh. "None of us do."

"I'm touched."

"We'll try to get a ship to come for you, quickly," said Burleigh.

"I'm sure you will," said Moran politely.

But he was not confident. The laws governing space-travel were very strict indeed, and enforced with all the rigor possible. On their enforcement, indeed, depended the law and order of the planets. Criminals had to know that they could not escape to space whenever matters got too hot for them aground. For a spaceman to trifle with interstellar-traffic laws meant at the least that they were grounded for life. But the probabilities were much worse than that. It was most likely that Burleigh or any of the others would be reported to spaceport police instantly they attempted to charter a ship for any kind of illegal activity. Moran made a mental note to warn Burleigh about it.

By now, though, he was aware of a very deep irritation at the idea of being killed, whether by monsters on this planet or men sent to pick him up for due process of law. When he made the grand gesture of seizing the *Nadine*, he'd known nothing about the people on board, and he hadn't really expected to succeed. His real hope was to be killed without preliminary scientific questioning. Modern techniques of interrogation were not torture, but they stripped away all concealments of motive and to a great degree revealed anybody who'd helped one. Moran had killed a man in a fair fight the other man did not want to engage in. If he were caught on Coryus or returned to it, his motivation could be read from his mind. And if that was done the killing—and the sacrifice of his own future and life—would have been useless. But he'd been prepared to be killed. Even now he'd prefer to die here on Tethys than in the strictly painless manner of executions on Coryus. But he was now deeply resistant to the idea of dying at all. There was Carol....

He thrust such thoughts aside.

MORNING WAS WELL BEGUN when they prepared to transfer the wreck's treasure to the *Nadine*. Moran went first. At fifteen-foot intervals he burned holes in the curd-like, elastic ground-cover. Some of the holes went down only four feet to the stone beneath it. Some went down six. But a man who jumped down one of them would be safe against attack except from directly overhead, which was an unlikely direction for attack by an insect. Carol had seen a wasp fly past the day before. She said it was as big as a cow. A sting from such a monster would instantly be fatal. But no wasp would have the intelligence to use its sting on something it had not seized. A man should be safe in such a foxhole. If a creature did try to investigate the opening, a torch could come into play. It was the most practical possible way for a man to defend himself on this world.

Moran made more than a dozen such holes of refuge in the line between the *Nadine* and the wreck. Carol watched with passionate solicitude from a control-room port as he progressed. He entered the wreck through the lock-doors he'd uncovered. Harper followed doggedly, not less than two foxholes behind. Carol's voice reassured them, the while, that within the half-mile circle of visibility no monster walked or flew.

Inside the wreck, Moran placed emergency lanterns to light the dark interior. He placed them along the particularly inconvenient passageways of a ship lying on its side instead of standing upright. He was at work breaking open a box of bessendium when Harper joined him. Harper said heavily, "I've brought a bag. It was a pillow. Carol took the foam out."

"We'll fill it," said Moran. "Not too full. The stuff's heavy."

Harper watched while Moran poured purple crystals into it from his cupped hands.

"There you are," said Moran. "Take it away."

"Look!" said Harper. "I owe you plenty—"

"Then pay me," said Moran, exasperatedly, "by shutting up! By making Burleigh damned careful about who he tries to hire to come after me! And by getting this cargo-shifting business in operation! The *Nadine*'s almost due on Loris. You don't want to have the spaceport police get suspicions. Get moving!"

Harper clambered over the side of doorways. He disappeared. Moran was alone in the ship. He explored. He found that the crew that had abandoned the *Malabar* had been guilty of a singular oversight for a crew abandoning ship. But, of course, they'd been distracted not only by their predicament but by the decision to carry part of the ship's precious cargo with them, so they could make it a profitable enterprise to rescue them. They hadn't taken the trouble to follow all the rules laid down for a crew taking to the boats.

Moran made good their omission. He was back in the cargo-hold when Brawn arrived. Burleigh came next. Then Harper again. Hallet came last of the four men of the yacht. They did not make a continuous chain of men moving back and forth between the two ships. Three men came, and loaded up, and went back. Then three men came again, one by one. There could never be a moment when a single refuge-hole in the soil could be needed by two men at the same time.

Within the first hour of work at transferring treasure, the bolt-holes came into use. Carol called anxiously that a gigantic beetle neared the ship and would apparently pass between it and the yacht. At the time, Brawn and Harper were moving from the *Malabar* toward the *Nadine*, and Hallet was about to leave the wreck's lock.

He watched with wide eyes. The beetle was truly a monster, the size of a hippopotamus as pictured in the culture-books about early human history. Its jaws, pronged like antlers, projected two yards before its huge, faceted eyes. It seemed to drag itself effortfully over the elastic surface of the ground. It passed a place where red, foliated fungus grew in a fantastic absence of pattern on the surface of the ground. It went through a streak of dusty-blue mould, which it stirred into a cloud of spores as it passed. It crawled on and on. Harper popped down into the nearest bolt-hole, his torch held ready. Brawn stood beside another refuge, sixty feet away.

Carol's voice came to their helmet-phones, anxious and exact. Hallet, in the lock-door, heard her tell Harper that the beetle would pass very close to him and to stay still. It moved on and on. It would be very close indeed. Carol gasped in horror.

The monster passed partly over the hole in which Harper crouched. One of its clawed feet slipped down into the opening. But the beetle went on, unaware of Harper. It crawled toward the encircling mist upon some errand of its own. It was mindless. It was like a complex and highly decorated piece of machinery which did what it was wound up to do, and nothing else.

Harper came out of the bolt-hole when Carol, her voice shaky with relief, told him it was safe. He went doggedly on to the *Nadine*, carrying his bag of purple crystals. Brawn followed, moodily.

HALLET, WITH A SINGULARLY exultant look upon his face, ventured out of the airlock and moved across the fungoid world. He carried a king's ransom to be added to the riches already transferred to the yacht.

Moving the bessendium was a tedious task. One plastic box in the cargo-hold held a quantity of crystals that three men took two trips each to carry. In mid-morning the bag in Hallet's hand seemed to slip just when Moran completed filling it. It toppled and spilled half its contents on the cargo-hold floor, which had been a sidewall. He began painstakingly to gather up the precious stuff and get it back in the bag. The others went on to the *Nadine*. Hallet turned off his helmet-phone and gestured to Moran to remove his helmet. Moran, his eyebrows raised, obeyed the suggestion.

"How anxious," asked Hallet abruptly, gathering up the dropped crystals, "how anxious are you to be left behind here?"

"I'm not anxious at all," said Moran.

"Would you like to make a deal to go along when the *Nadine* lifts?—*If* there's a way to get past the spaceport police?"

"Probably," said Moran. "Certainly! But there's no way to do it."

"There is," said Hallet. "I know it. Is it a deal?"

"What is the deal?"

"You do as I say," said Hallet significantly. "Just as I say! Then...."

The lock-door opened, some distance away. Hallet stood up and said in a commanding tone, "Keep your mouth shut. I'll tell you what to do and when."

He put on his helmet and turned on the phone once more. He went toward the lock-door. Moran heard him exchange words with Harper and Brawn, back with empty bags to fill with crystals worth many times the price of diamonds. But diamonds were made in half-ton lots, nowadays.

Moran filled their bags. He was frowning. As Harper was about to follow Brawn, Moran almost duplicated Hallet's gestures to have him remove his helmet.

"I want Burleigh to come next trip," he told Harper, "and make some excuse to stay behind a moment and talk to me without the helmet-phones picking up everything I say to him. Understand?"

Harper nodded. But Burleigh did not come on the next trip. It was not until near midday that he came to carry a load of treasure to the yacht.

When he did come, though, he took off his helmet and turned off the phone without the need of a suggestion.

"I've been arranging storage for this stuff," he said. "I've opened plates between the hulls to dump it in. I've told Carol, too, that we've got to do a perfect job of cleaning up. There must be no stray crystals on the floor."

"Better search the bunks, too," said Moran drily, "so nobody will put aside a particularly pretty crystal to gloat over. Listen!"

He told Burleigh exactly what Hallet had said and what he'd answered. Burleigh looked acutely unhappy.

"Hallet isn't dedicated like the rest of us were," he said distressedly. "We brought him along partly out of fear that if he were captured he'd break down and reveal what he knows of the Underground we led, and much of which we had to leave behind. But I'll be able to finance a real revolt, now!"

Moran regarded him with irony. Burleigh was a capable man and a conscientious one. It would be very easy to trust him, and it is all-important to an Underground that its leaders be trusted. But it is also important that they be capable of flint-like hardness on occasion. To Moran, it seemed that Burleigh had not quite the adamantine resolution required for leadership in a conspiracy which was to become a successful revolt. He was—and to Moran it seemed regrettable—capable of the virtue of charity.

"I've told you," he said evenly. "Maybe you'll think it's a scheme on my part to get Hallet dumped and myself elected to take his identity. But what happens from now on is your business. Beginning this moment, I'm taking care of my own skin. I've gotten reconciled to the idea of dying, but I'd hate for it not to do anybody any good."

"Carol," said Burleigh unhappily, "is much distressed."

"That's very kind," said Moran sarcastically.

"Now take your bag of stuff and get going."

Burleigh obeyed. Moran went back to the business of breaking open the strong plastic boxes of bessendium so their contents could be carried in forty-pound lots to the *Nadine*.

Thinking of Carol, he did not like the way things seemed to be going. Since the discovery of the bessendium, Hallet had been developing ideas. They did not look as if they meant good fortune for Moran without corresponding bad fortune for the others. Obviously, Moran couldn't be hidden on the *Nadine* during the spaceport sterilization of the ship which prevented plagues from being carried from world to world. Hallet could have no reason to promise such a thing. Before landing here, he'd urged that Moran simply be dumped out the airlock. This proposal to save his life....

Moran considered the situation grimly while the business of ferrying treasure to the yacht went on almost monotonously. It had stopped once during the forenoon while a giant beetle went by. Later, it stopped again because a gigantic flying thing hovered overhead. Carol did not know what it was, but its bulging abdomen ended in an organ which appeared to be a sting. It was plainly hunting. There was no point in fighting it. Presently it went away, and just before it disappeared in the circular wall of mist it dived headlong to the ground. A little later it rose slowly into the air, carrying something almost as large as itself. It went away into the mist.

Again, once a green-and-yellow caterpillar marched past upon some mysterious enterprise. It was covered with incredibly long fur, and it moved with an undulating motion of all its segments, one after another. It seemed well over ten yards in length, and its body appeared impossibly massive. But a large part of the bulk would be the two-foot-long or longer hairs which stuck out stiffly in all directions. It, too, went away.

But continually and constantly there was a bedlam of noises. From underneath the yielding skin of the yeast-ground, there came clickings. Sometimes there were quiverings of the surface as if it were alive, but they would be the activities of ten and twelve-inch beetles who lived in subterranean tunnels in it. There were those preposterous noises like someone rattling a stick along a picket fence—only deafening—and there were baritone chirpings and deep bass boomings from somewhere far away. Moran guessed that the last might be frogs, but if so they were vastly larger than men.

SHORTLY AFTER WHAT WAS probably midday, Moran brushed off his hands. The bessendium part of the cargo of the wrecked *Malabar* had been salvaged. It was hidden between the twin hulls of the yacht. Moran had, quite privately, attended to a matter the wreck's long-dead crew should have done when they left it. Now, in theory, the *Nadine* should lift off and take Moran to some hastily scouted spot not too far from the ice cap. It should leave him there with what food could be spared, and the kit of seeds that might feed him after it was gone, and weapons that might but probably wouldn't enable him to defend himself, and with a radio-beacon to try to have hope in. Then—that would be that.

"Calling," said Moran sardonically into his helmet-phone. "Everything's cleaned up here. What next?"

"*You can come along*," said Hallet's voice from the ship. It was shivery. It was gleeful. "*Just in time for lunch!*"

Moran went along the disoriented passages of the *Malabar* to the lock. He turned off the beacon that had tried uselessly during six human generations to call for help for men now long dead. He went out the lock and closed it behind him. It was not likely that this planet would ever become a home for men. If there were some strangeness in its constitution that made the descendants of insects placed upon it grow to be giants, humans would not want to settle on it. And there were plenty of much more suitable worlds. So the wrecked spaceship would lie here, under deeper and ever deeper accumulations of the noisome stuff that passed for soil. Perhaps millennia from now, the sturdy, resistant metal of the hull would finally rust through, and then —nothing. No man in all time to come would ever see the *Malabar* again.

Shrugging, he went toward the *Nadine*. He walked through bedlam. He could see a quarter-mile in one direction, and a quarter-mile in another. He could not see more than a little distance upward. The *Nadine* had landed upon a world with tens of millions of square miles of surface, and nobody had moved more than a hundred yards from its landing-place, and now it would leave and all wonders and all horrors outside this one quarter of a square mile would remain unknown....

He went to the airlock and shed his suit. He opened the inner door. Hallet waited for him.

"Everybody's at lunch," he said. "We'll join them."

Moran eyed him sharply. Hallet grinned widely.

"We're going to take off to find a place for you as soon as we've eaten," he said.

There was mockery in the tone. It occurred abruptly to Moran that Hallet was the kind of person who might, to be sure, plan complete disloyalty to his companions for his own benefit. But he might also enjoy betrayal for its own sake. He might, for example, find it amusing to make a man under sentence of death or marooning believe that he would escape, so Hallet could have the purely malicious pleasure of disappointing him. He might look for Moran to break when he learned that he was to die here after all.

Moran clamped his lips tightly. Carol would be better off if that was the answer. He went toward the yacht's mess-room. Hallet followed close behind. Moran pushed the door aside and entered. Burleigh and Harper and Brawn looked at him, Carol raised her eyes. They glistened with tears.

Hallet said gleefully, "Here goes!"

Standing behind Moran, he thrust a hand-blaster past Moran's body and pulled the trigger. He held the trigger down for continuous fire as he traversed the weapon to wipe out everybody but Moran and himself.

IV

MORAN RESPONDED INSTANTLY. His hands flew to Hallet's throat, blind fury making him unaware of any thought but a frantic lust to kill. It was very strange that Moran somehow noticed Hallet's hand insanely pulling the trigger of the blast-pistol over and over and over without result. He remembered it later. Perhaps he shared Hallet's blank disbelief that one could pull the trigger of a blaster and have nothing at all happen in consequence. But nothing did happen, and suddenly he dropped the weapon and clawed desperately at Moran's fingers about his throat. But that was too late.

There was singularly little disturbance at the luncheon-table. The whole event was climax and anticlimax together. Hallet's intention was so appallingly murderous and his action so shockingly futile that the four who were to have been his victims tended to stare blankly while Moran throttled him.

Burleigh seemed to recover first. He tried to pull Moran's hands loose from Hallet's throat. Lacking success he called to the others. "Harper! Brawn! Help me!"

It took all three of them to release Hallet. Then Moran stood panting, shaking, his eyes like flames.

"He—he—" panted Moran. "He was going to kill Carol!"

"I know," said Burleigh, distressedly. "He was going to kill all of us. You gave me an inkling, so while he was packing bessendium between the hulls, and had his spacesuit hanging in the airlock, I doctored the blaster in the spacesuit pocket." He looked down at Hallet. "Is he still alive?"

Brawn bent over Hallet. He nodded.

"Put him in the airlock for the time being," said Burleigh. "And lock it. When he comes to, we'll decide what to do."

Harper and Brawn took Hallet by the arms and hauled him along the passageway. The inner door of the lock clanged shut on him.

"We'll give him a hearing, of course," said Burleigh conscientiously. "But we should survey the situation first."

To Moran the situation required no survey, but he viewed it from a violently personal viewpoint which would neither require or allow discussion. He knew what he meant to do about Hallet. He said harshly, "Go ahead. When you're through I'll tell you what will be done."

He went away. To the control room. There he paced up and down, trying to beat back the fury which rose afresh at intervals of less than minutes. He did not think of his own situation, just then. There are more important things than survival.

He struggled for coolness, with the action before him known. He didn't glance out the ports at the half-mile circle in which vision was possible. Beyond the mist there might be anything; an ocean, swarming metropoli of giant insects, a mountain-range. Nobody on the *Nadine* had explored. But Moran did not think of such matters now. Hallet had tried to murder Carol, and Moran meant to take action, and there were matters which might result from it. The matter the crew of the *Malabar* had forgotten to attend to—

He searched for paper and a pen. He found both in a drawer for the yacht's handwritten log. He wrote. He placed a small object in the drawer. He had barely closed it when Carol was at the control room door. She said in a small voice, "They want to talk to you."

He held up the paper.

"Read this later. Not now," he said curtly. He opened and closed the drawer again, this time putting the paper in it. "I want you to read this after the Hallet business is settled. I'm afraid that I'm not going to look well in your eyes."

She swallowed and did not speak. He went to where the others sat in official council. Burleigh said heavily:

"We've come to a decision. We shall call Hallet and hear what he has to say, but we had to consider various courses of action and decide which were possible and which were not."

Moran nodded grimly. He had made his own decision. It was not too much unlike the one that, carried out, had made him seize the *Nadine* for escape from Coryus. But he'd listen. Harper looked doggedly resolved. Brawn seemed moody as usual.

"I'm listening," said Moran.

"Hallet," said Burleigh regretfully, "intended to murder all of us and with your help take the *Nadine* to some place where he could hope to land without spaceport inspection."

Moran observed, "He didn't discuss that part of his plans. He only asked if I'd make a deal to escape being marooned."

"Yes," said Burleigh, nodding. "I'm sure—"

"My own idea," said Moran, "when I tried to seize the *Nadine*, was to try to reach one of several newly-settled planets where things aren't too well organized. I'd memos of some such planets. I hoped to get to ground somewhere in a wilderness on one of them and work my way on foot to a new settlement. There I'd explain that I'd been hunting or prospecting or something of the sort. On a settled planet that would be impossible. On a brand-new one people are less fussy and I might have been accepted quite casually."

"Hallet may have had some such idea in his mind," agreed Burleigh. "With a few bessendium crystals to show, he would seem a successful prospector. He'd be envied but not suspected. To be sure!"

"But," said Moran drily, "he'd be best off alone. So if he had that sort of idea, he intended to murder me too."

Burleigh nodded. "Undoubtedly. But to come to our decision. We can keep him on board under watch—as we did you—and leave you here. This has disadvantages. We owe you much. There would be risk of his taking someone unawares and fighting for his life. Even if all went as we wished, and we landed and dispersed, he could inform the spaceport officials anonymously of what had happened, leading to investigation and the ruin of any plans for the future revival of our underground. Also, it would destroy any hope for your rescue."

Moran smiled wryly. He hadn't much hope of that, if he were marooned.

"We could leave him here," said Burleigh unhappily, "with you taking his identity for purposes of landing. But I do not think it would be wise to send a ship after him. He would be resentful. If rescued, he would do everything possible to spoil all our future lives, and we are fugitives."

"Ah, yes!" said Moran, still more wryly amused.

"I am afraid," said Burleigh reluctantly, "that we can only offer him his choice of being marooned or going out the airlock. I cannot think of any other alternative."

"I can," said Moran. "I'm going to kill him."

Burleigh blinked. Harper looked up sharply.

"We fight," said Moran grimly. "Armed exactly alike. He can try to kill me. I'll give him the same chance I have. But I'll kill him. They used to call it a duel, and they came to consider it a very immoral business. But that's beside the point. I won't agree to marooning him here. That's murder. I won't agree to throwing him out the airlock. That's murder, too. But I have the right to kill him if it's in a fair fight. That's justice! You can bring him in and let him decide if he wants to be marooned or fight me. I think he's just raging enough to want to do all the damage he can, now that his plans have gone sour."

Burleigh fidgeted. He looked at Harper. Harper nodded grudgingly. He looked at Brawn. Brawn nodded moodily.

Burleigh said fretfully, "Very well ... Harper, you and Brawn bring him here. We'll see what he says. Be careful!"

Harper and Brawn went down the passageway. Moran saw them take out the blasters they'd worn since he took over the ship. They were ready. They unlocked and opened the inner airlock door.

There was silence. Harper looked shocked. He went in the airlock while Brawn stared, for once startled out of moodiness.

Harper came out. "He's gone," he said in a flat voice. "Out the airlock."

All the rest went instantly to look. The airlock was empty. By the most natural and inevitable of oversights, when Hallet was put in it for a temporary cell, no one had thought of locking the outer door. There was no point in it. It only led out to the nightmare world. And out there Hallet would be in monstrous danger. He'd have no food. At most his only weapon would be the torch Moran had carried to the *Malabar* and brought back again. He could have no hope of any kind. He could feel only despair unthinkable and horror undiluted.

There was a buzzing sound in the airlock. A spacesuit hung there. The helmet-phone was turned on. Hallet's voice came out, flat and metallic and desperate and filled with hate:

"What're you going to do now? You'd better think of a bargain to offer me! You can't lift off!

I took the fuel-block so Moran couldn't afford to kill me after the rest of you were dead. You can't lift off the ground! Now give me a guarantee I can believe in or you stay here with me!"

Harper bolted for the engine-room. He came back, his face ashen. "He's right. It's gone. He took it."

Moran stirred. Burleigh wrung his hands. Moran reached down the spacesuit from whose helmet the voice came tinnily. He began to put it on. Carol opened her lips to speak, and he covered the microphone with his palm.

"I'm going to go out and kill him," said Moran very quietly. "Somebody else had better come along just in case. But you can't make a bargain with him. He can't believe in any promise, because *he* wouldn't keep any."

Harper went away again. He came back, struggling into a spacesuit. Brawn moved quickly. Burleigh suddenly stirred and went for a suit.

"We want torches," said Moran evenly, "for our own safety, and blasters because they'll drop Hallet. Carol, you monitor what goes on. When we need to come back, you can use the direction-finder and talk us back to the yacht."

"But—but—"

"What are you going to do?" rasped the voice shrilly. "You've got to make a bargain! I've got the fuel-block! You can't lift off without the fuel-block! You've got to make a deal."

THE OTHER MEN CAME BACK. With the microphone still muffled by his hand, Moran said sharply, "He has to keep talking until we answer, but he won't know we're on his trail until we do. We keep quiet when we get the helmets on. Understand?" Then he said evenly to Carol. "Look at that paper I showed you if—if anything happens. Don't forget! Ready?"

Carol's hands were clenched. She was terribly pale. She tried to speak, and could not. Moran, with the microphone still covered by the palm of his hand, repeated urgently, "Remember, no talking! He'll pick up anything we say. Use gestures. Let's go!"

He swung out of the airlock. The others followed. The one certain thing about the direction

Hallet would have taken was that it must be away from the wreck. And he'd have been in a panic to get out of sight from the yacht.

Moran saw his starting-point at once. Landing, the *Nadine* had used rockets for easing to ground because it is not possible to make delicate adjustments of interplanetary drive. A take-off, yes. But to land even at a spaceport one uses rockets to cushion what otherwise might be a sharp impact. The *Nadine*'s rockets had burned away the yeasty soil when she came to ground. There was a burnt-away depression down to bedrock in the stuff all around her. But Hallet had broken the scorched, crusty edge of the hollow as he climbed up to the blanket-like surface-skin.

Moran led the way after him. He moved with confidence. The springy, sickeningly uncertain stuff underfoot was basically white-that-had-been-soiled. Between the *Nadine*'s landing-spot and the now-gutted wreck, it happened that only that one color showed. But, scattered at random in other places, there were patches of red mould and blue mould and black dusty rust and greenish surface-fungi. Twenty yards from the depression in which the *Nadine* lay, Hallet's footprints were clearly marked in a patch of orange-yellow ground-cover which gave off impalpable yellow spores when touched. Moran gestured for attention and pointed out the trail. He gestured again for the others to spread out.

Hallet's voice came again. He'd left the *Nadine*'s lock because he could make no bargain for his life while in the hands of his companions. He could only bargain for his life if they could not find him or the precious fuel-block without which the *Nadine* must remain here forever. But from the beginning he knew such terror that he could not contrive, himself, a bargain that could possibly be made.

He chattered agitatedly, not yet sure that his escape had been discovered. At times he seemed almost hysterical. Moran and the others could hear him pant, sometimes, as a fancied movement aroused his panic. Once they heard the noise of his torch as he burned a safety-hole in the ground. But he did not use it. He hastened on. He talked desperately. Sometimes he boasted, and sometimes he tried cunningly to be reasonable. But he hadn't been prepared for the absolute failure of what should have been the simplest and surest form of multiple murder. Now in a last-ditch stand, he hysterically abused them for taking so long to realize that they had to make a deal.

HIS FOUR PURSUERS went grimly over the elastic surface of this world upon his trail. The *Nadine* faded into the mist. Off to the right a clump of toadstools grew. They were taller than any of the men, and their pulpy stalks were more than a foot thick. Hallet's trail in the colored surface-moulds went on. The giant toadstools were left behind. The trail led straight toward an enormous object the height of a three-storey house. When first glimpsed through the mist, it looked artificial. But as they drew near they saw that it was a cabbage; gigantic, with leaves impossibly huge and thick. There was a spike in its middle on which grew cruciform faded flowers four feet across.

Then Hallet screamed. They heard it in their helmet-phones. He screamed again. Then for a space he was silent, gasping, and then he uttered shrieks of pure horror. But they were cries of horror, not of pain.

Moran found himself running, which was probably ridiculous. The others hastened after him. And suddenly the mistiness ahead took on a new appearance. The ground fell away. It became evident that the *Nadine* had landed upon a plateau with levels below it and very possibly mountains rising above. But here the slightly rolling plateau fell sheer away. There was a place where the yeasty soil—but here it was tinted with a purplish overcast of foliate fungus—where the soil had given way. Something had fallen, here.

It would have been Hallet. He'd gone too close to a precipice, moving agitatedly in search of a hiding-place in which to conceal himself until the people of the *Nadine* made a deal he could no longer believe in.

His cries still came over the helmet-phones. Moran went grimly to look. He found himself gazing down into a cross-valley perhaps two hundred feet deep. At the bottom there was the incredible, green growing things. But they were not trees. They were some flabby weed with thick reddish stalks and enormous pinnate leaves. It grew here to the height of oaks. But Hallet had not dropped so far.

From anchorages on bare rock, great glistening cables reached downward to other anchorages on the valley floor. The cables crossed each other with highly artificial precision at a central point. They formed the foundation for a web of geometrically accurate design and unthinkable size. Cross-cables of sticky stuff went round and round the center of the enormous snare, following a logarithmic spiral with absolute exactitude. It was a spider's web whose cables stretched hundreds of feet; whose bird-limed ropes would trap and hold even the monster insects of this world. And Hallet was caught in it.

HE'D TUMBLED FROM the cliff-edge as fungoid soil gave way under him. He'd bounced against a sloping, fungus-covered rocky wall and with fragments of curdy stuff about him had been flung out and into the snare. He was caught as firmly as any of the other creatures on which the snare's owner fed.

His shrieks of horror began when he realized his situation. He struggled, setting up insane vibrations in the fabric of the web. He shrieked again, trying to break the bonds of cordage that clung the more horribly as he struggled to break free. And the struggling was most unwise.

"We want to cut the cables with torches," said Moran sharply. "If we can make the web drop we'll be all right. Web-spiders don't hunt on the ground. Go ahead! Make it fast!"

Burleigh and the others hastened to what looked like a nearly practicable place by which to descend. Moran moved swiftly to where one cable of the web was made fast at the top. It was simple sanity to break down the web—by degrees, of course—to get at Hallet. But Hallet did not cooperate. He writhed and struggled and shrieked.

His outcry, of course, counted for nothing in the satanic cacophony that filled the air. All the monsters of all the planet seemed to make discordant noises. Hallet could add nothing. But his struggles in the web had meaning to the owner of the trap.

They sent tiny tremblings down the web-cables. And this was the fine mathematical creation of what was quaintly called a "garden spider" on other worlds. *Epeira fasciata.* She was not in it. She sat sluggishly in a sheltered place, remote from her snare. But a line, a cord, a signal-cable went from the center of the web to the spider's retreat. She waited with implacable patience, one foreleg—sheathed in ragged and somehow revolting fur—resting delicately upon the line. Hallet's frantic struggles shook the web. Faintly, to be sure, but distinctively. The vibrations were wholly unlike the violent, thrashing struggles of a heavy beetle or a giant cricket. They were equally unlike those flirtatious, seductive pluckings of a web-cable which would mean that an amorous male of her own species sought the grisly creature's affection.

Hallet made the web quiver as small prey would shake it. The spider would have responded instantly to bigger game, if only to secure it before the vast snare was damaged by frenzied plungings. Still, though there was no haste, the giant rose and in leisurely fashion traversed the long cable to the web's center. Moran saw it.

"Hallet!" he barked into his helmet-phone, "Hallet! Hold still! Don't move!"

He raced desperately along the edge of the cliff, risking a fall more immediately fatal than Hallet's. It was idiotic to make such an attempt at rescue. It was sheer folly. But there are instincts one has to obey against all reason. Moran did not think of the fuel-block. Typically, Hallet did.

"*I've got the fuel-block,*" he gasped between screams. "*If you don't help me—*"

But then the main cable nearest him moved in a manner not the result of his own struggles. It was the enormous weight of the owner of the web, moving leisurely on her own snare, which made the web shake now. And Hallet lost even the coherence of hysteria and simply shrieked.

MORAN CAME TO A PLACE where a main anchor-cable reached bed-rock. It ran under yeasty groundcover to an anchorage. He thrust his torch deep, feeling for the cable. It seared through.

The web jerked wildly as one of its principal supports parted. The giant spider turned aside to investigate the event. Such a thing should happen only when one of the most enormous of possible victims became entangled.

Moran went racing for another cable-anchorage. But when he found where the strong line fastened, it was simply and starkly impossible to climb down to it. He swore and looked desperately for Burleigh and Brawn and Harper. They were far away, hurrying to descend but not yet where they could bring the web toppling down by cutting other cables.

The yellow-banded monster came to the cut end of the line. It swung down. It climbed up again. Hallet shrieked and kicked.

The spider moved toward him. Of all nightmarish creatures on this nightmare of a planet, a giant spider with a body eight feet long and legs to span as many yards was most revolting. Its abdomen was obscenely swollen. As it moved, its spinnerets paid out newly-formed cord behind it. Its eyes were monstrous and murderously intent. The ghastly, needle-sharp mandibles beside its mouth seemed to move lustfully with a life of their own. And it was somehow ten times more horrible because of its beastly fur. Tufts of black hairiness, half-yards in length, streamed out as its legs moved.

There was another cable still. Moran made for it. He reached it where it stretched down like a slanting tight-rope. He jerked out his torch to sever it—and saw that to cut it would be to drop the spider almost upon Hallet. It would seize him then because of his writhings. But not to cut it—

He tried his blaster. He fired again and again. The blaster-bolts hurt. The spider reacted with fury. The blaster would have killed a man at this distance, though it would have been ignored by a chitin-armored beetle. But against the spider the bolts were like bites. They made small wounds, but not serious ones. The spider made a bubbling sound which was more daunting than any cry would have been. It flung its legs about, fumbling for the thing that it believed attacked it. It continued the bubbling sounds. Its mandibles clashed and gnashed against each other. They were small noises in the din which was the norm on this mad world, but they were more horrible than any other sounds Moran had ever heard.

The spider suddenly began to move purposefully toward the spot where Hallet jerked insanely and shrieked in heart-rending horror.

Moran found himself attempting the impossible. He knew it was impossible. The blast-pistol hurt but did not injure the giant because the range was too long. So—it was totally unjustifiable—he found himself slung below the downward-slanting cable and sliding down its slope. He was going to where the range would be short enough for his blast-pistol to be effective. He slid to a cross-cable, and avoided it and went on.

Burleigh and Brawn and Harper were tiny figures, very far away. Moran hung by one hand and used his free hand to fire the blaster once more. It hurt more seriously, now. The spider made bubbling noises of infinite ferocity. And it moved with incredible agility toward the one object it could imagine as meaning attack.

It reached Hallet. It seized him.

Moran's blast-pistol could not kill it. It had to be killed. Now! He drew out his torch and pressed the continuous-flame stud. Raging, he threw it at the spider.

It spun in the air, a strange blue-white pinwheel in the gray light of this planet's day. It cut through a cable that might have deflected it. It reached the spider, now reared high and pulling Hallet from the sticky stuff that had captured him.

The spinning torch hit. The flame burned deep. The torch actually sank into the spider's body.

And there was a titanic flame and an incredible blast and Moran knew nothing.

A LONG TIME LATER he knew that he ached. He became aware that he hurt. Still later he realized that Burleigh and Brawn and Harper stood around him. He'd splashed in some enormous thickness of the yeasty soil, grown and fallen from the cliff-edge, and it was not solid enough to break his bones. Harper, doubtless, had been most resolute in digging down to him and pulling him out.

He sat up, and growled at innumerable unpleasant sensations.

"That," he said painfully, "was a very bad business."

"It's all bad business," said Burleigh in a flat and somehow exhausted tone. "The fuel-block burned. There's nothing left of it or Hallet or the spider."

Moran moved an arm. A leg. The other arm and leg. He got unsteadily to his feet.

"It was bessendium and uranium," added Burleigh hopelessly. "And the uranium burned. It wasn't an atomic explosion, it just burned like sodium or potassium would do. But it burned fast! The torch-flame must have reached it."

He added absurdly, "Hallet died instantly, of course. Which is better fortune than we are likely to have."

"Oh, that...." said Moran. "We're all right. I said I was going to kill him. I wasn't trying to at the moment, but I did. By accident." He paused, and said dizzily; "I think he should feel obliged to me. I was distinctly charitable to him!"

Harper said grimly, "But we can't lift off. We're all marooned here now."

Moran took an experimental step. He hurt, but he was sound.

"Nonsense!" he said. "The crew of the *Malabar* went off without taking the fuel-block from the wreck's engines. It's in a drawer in the *Nadine's* control room with a note to Carol that I asked her to read should something happen to me. We may have to machine it a little to make it fit the *Nadine's* engines. But we're all right!"

Carol's voice came over his helmet-phone. It was shaky and desperately glad. "You're—all right? Quite all right? Please hurry back."

"We're on the way," said Moran.

He was pleased with Carol's reaction. He also realized that now there would be the right number of people on the *Nadine;* they would take off from this world and arrive reasonably near due-time at Loris without arousing the curiosity of spaceport officials.

He looked about him. The way the others had come down was a perfectly good way to climb up again. On the surface, above, their trail would be clear on the multicolored surface rusts. There were four men together, all with blast-pistols and three with torches. They should be safe.

Moran talked cheerfully, climbing to the plateau on which the *Nadine* had landed, trudging with the others across a world on which it was impossible to see more than a quarter-mile in any direction. But the way was plain. Beyond the mist Carol waited.

"Planet of Dread" first appeared in the May 1962 issue of Fantastic Stories of Imagination, *with illustrations by Dan Adkins.*

During an incredibly prolific career spanning sixty years, American author and inventor William Fitzgerald Jenkins (1896–1975) published over 1500 short stories and articles (mostly as Leinster, but sometimes as Will F. Jenkins) in publications ranging from such leading pulps as Amazing Stories, Black Mask, *and* Argosy, *to mainstream magazines such as* Collier's, Esquire, *and* The Saturday Evening Post; *as well as hundreds of scripts for radio, television and movie productions. Despite his undoubtedly busy writing schedule, Jenkins took time out to help invent the front-projection process frequently used in the creation of cinematic special effects prior to the age of CGI.*

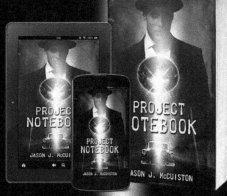

MANY MONUMENTAL STRUCTURES HAVE RISEN ON EARTH--THE PYRAMIDS, THE GREAT WALL OF CHINA, THE MOUNT RUSHMORE STONE FACES...BUT NONE OF THESE EARTHLY WONDERS CAN COMPARE WITH THE GREAT STONE FACE OF SPACE, CARVED OUT OF HALF A WORLD! GIGANTIC, FANTASTIC, MYSTERIOUS...WHAT ANSWER IS THERE TO THE RIDDLE OF...

the SPACE LORELEI

203

A BONANZA! YAYYYY!

TRAP DOOR!

HELP! AAAAA!

IT'S A TRAP! WE'RE SLIDING DOWN INSIDE THE ASTEROID!

DEEP UNDERGROUND IN A GLOOMY CAVERN...

A HUGE SPIDER WEB!

GIANT SPIDER! NO-NO! AAAA!

SO THAT'S THE HORRIBLE ANSWER TO THE STONE FACE! THE MONSTER LOOKS INTELLIGENT AND EVIL! A RACE OF GIANT SPIDERS BUILT THE STONE FACE AS A LURE--FOR FOOD!

ONE BY ONE THE SPACEMEN ARE ENTWINED IN TH STICKY STRANDS...

IT...IT'S WRAPPING US UP FOR A LEISURELY MEAL LATER! UGH!

CURSE THAT STONE FACE! CURSE IT TO THE END OF TIME! IT LED US TO DEATH!

JARK HUDSON HAS BEEN LEFT, TO THE LAST, AND...

GOT MY KNIFE OUT...MAYBE I CAN HACK MY WAY FREE!

COMING FOR ME NOW! ONE MORE STRAND...

JUST IN TIME! THANK THE STARS!

RAY-GUN BLASTS ARE NO GOOD AGAINST IT! GOT TO RUN!

HUDSON ESCAPES THE MONSTER IN A NARROW PASSAGEWAY...

TUNNELS ALL OVER! IT SEEMS THIS WHOLE ASTEROID IS HONEYCOMBED! IS IT JUST A BIG NEST OF THE GIANT SPIDERS?

THEN... HOLY COMETS! A **CITY!** MAYBE I CAN GET HELP!

AND ANOTHER RIDDLE! HELLO! ANYBODY HERE? NOT A SOUND IT'S A DEAD CITY OF SOME VANISHED CIVILIZATION! JUST MY LUCK!

THESE STATUES SHOW THE PEOPLE WERE HUMAN! WAIT...THAT STATUE IS ODD...SOMEHOW IT SEEMS TO BE BECKONING ME ON!

THIS IS LEADING TO SOMETHING--BUT WHAT?

A TOMB...A GIANT TOMB!

THE PEOPLE, ALL PERFECTLY PRESERVED--WHY? AND WHY ONLY WOMEN? NOT A SINGLE MAN HERE! WHAT IN THE NAME OF SATURN IS THIS ALL ABOUT?

A FINAL STATUE-- THIS LEVER--AND NOW A BLAST OF COMPRESSED AIR SWEEPING THROUGH THE PLACE! WHAT NEXT?

MOST STARTLING OF ALL-- THE WOMEN...COMING ALIVE! THEY WERE IN SUSPENDED ANIMATION, NOT DEAD! SLEEPING BEAUTIES, WAKING UP!

UH-OHH!

BY MENTAL TELEPATHY THE EARTH-MAN COMMUNICATES WITH THE INCREDIBLE ASTEROID WOMEN--

A MAN! AT LAST WE ARE RESCUED FROM OUR AGE-LONG SLEEP! WE KNEW THAT SOME DAY OUR STONE FACE WOULD SAVE US!

YOU BUILT THE STONE FACE, NOT THE MONSTERS!

YES! HARKEN, O MAN! AN AGE AGO, OUR MEN DIED OFF IN A TERRIBLE PLAGUE THAT STRUCK ONLY MALES! FACED WITH RACIAL EXTINCTION, WE SURVIVING WOMEN CONSTRUCTED THE GIANT STONE FACE-- TO LURE MEN OF THE FUTURE HERE! IT WAS OUR ONLY HOPE TO SAVE OUR CIVILIZATION FROM COMPLETE OBLIVION!

5

THE END

"The Space Lorelei" captures the flavor of several cheesy male-fantasy SF movies of the 1950s that began with the first of such films, the frequently-copied *Cat-Women of the Moon*, which premiered on September 3, 1953: the male crew of a spaceship land on a world (or an asteroid, in the case of this comics story) populated entirely by beautiful, Amazonian women who fall head over heels for these extremely average men; and, relevant to this issue's theme, the crew always manage to have a run-in with a big ugly spider or two. "The Space Lorelei" originally appeared in the November 1952 issue (#6) of *Fantastic Worlds*, published by Standard Comics, and predates *Cat-Women* by about a year. Pulp SF author Otto Binder scripted the tale. Pencils and inks are by George Roussos.

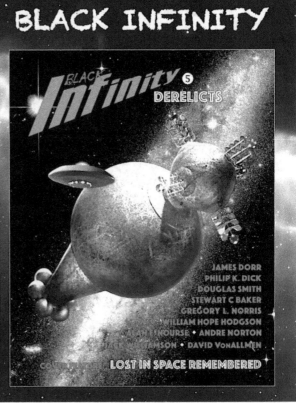

CPSIA information can be obtained
at www.ICGtesting.com
Printed in the USA
LVHW061501281120
672907LV00045B/1587